East Pittsburgh Downlow

Dave Newman

j.new books

j.new books

This is a work of fiction. Names, characters, places, and incidents are a product of the author's imagination. Locales and public names are sometimes used for atmospheric purposes. Any resemblance to actual people, living or dead, or to businesses, companies, events, institutions, or locales is completely coincidental.

East Pittsburgh Downlow © 2019 by Dave Newman

All rights reserved. Printed in the United States of America. No part of this publication may be reproduced, distributed or transmitted in any form or by any means, including photocopying, recording, or other electronic or mechanical methods, without the prior written permission of the publisher, except in the case of brief quotations embodied in critical reviews and certain other noncommercial uses permitted by copyright law. For permission requests, write to the publisher, addressed "Attention: Permissions Coordinator," J New Books 105 110 Dreamville, Jinhae Gu, Changwon-si 51701 Republic of Korea or email permissions@jnewbooks

Cover Design by Liana Moisescu

ISBN 978-1-7339388-2-2

Jakiela!!!!

"Writing a book is a horrible, exhausting struggle, like a long bout with some painful illness. One would never undertake such a thing if one were not driven on by some demon whom one can neither resist nor understand."

-George Orwell

"My mother would say to me, 'Look for the helpers. You will always find people who are helping.' To this day, especially in times of disaster, I remember my mother's words, and I am aways comforted by realizing that there are still so many helpers, so many caring people in this world."

-Mister Rogers

fuck
the whole muthafucking thing
all i want now is my woman back
so my soul can sing

-Etheridge Knight

Prologue: Handcuffs, Mills, Matriarchy, Pizza

A woman stands next to a police car, a towel filled with ice pressed to her eye. I sit in my car at the stop light. This is Turtle Creek, Pennsylvania, a mill town without a mill, without a mill for decades, located just east of Pittsburgh, in a valley divided by a river no wider than a house. It's Friday night. Drunks drive. Cops chase. People sometimes fight.

The cop's cruiser sits in the alleyway between an old dilapidated bar and ShellyPie, the pizzeria located on the first floor of an old VFW. I am so starved for pizza I could've tasted the grease through the phone when I placed my order. I flip my turn signal to be safe. The cop walks to another cop then back to the woman. Red and blue lights flash like punches flying from a boxer wearing flags for gloves.

Back in 1960, a bunch of high school buddies recorded "5 O'Clock World," a song about not being owned by your job, in a studio down the road from here. A hundred years before that, George Westinghouse proudly said, "The work we do is honorable and will change the world," before cutting the ribbon on a manufacturing plant that would help bring electricity to America.

    The woman takes the ice from her eye and speaks with her hands.

    The cop appears very patient, nodding, shuffling his cop feet.

    The woman appears pissed off.

    The woman's shirt is ripped down the middle so she uses her free hand to hold the fabric together to keep her tits from falling out.

    I don't judge, especially when I'm hungry.

    The amount of pepperoni on a ShellyPie is like the stars in the sky on a clear night.

    I have been writing all day and forgot to eat.

    I jogged nine miles.

    I read eighty pages in a Russian novel.

    I feel like I should have ordered a medium or maybe a large. I feel like I should have ordered the garlic knots and the wedding soup.

    The light turns green and I take a left and loop around the dilapidated bar, which was also a rooming house before being condemned, and pull into the back parking lot.

    Another cop talks to a different woman in a business suit.

    She is much older than the woman packing ice and a ripped blouse.

    Her hands are cuffed but in front.

    The cop appears to be laughing.

    The woman appears to be laughing.

    I should probably go home.

    Once you meet my mother, you'll appreciate the handcuffs.

    She is a woman who knows how to avoid arrest.

PART ONE

Old Wrestlers Write Poems

I'm at my desk, an ancient chunk of metal and fake wood, trying to muster the juice to write a lecture on George Orwell that a bunch of students with full-time jobs will both understand and give a shit about, when Berryman stops in the hallway outside my door and says he wants to wrestle on the back lawn. Berryman wears funky yellow sneakers made of suede and a fancy green track suit, like a weird cross between a middle-aged Italian woman from a gangster film set in the Bronx and a young hip-hop dude who can't tell the difference between his pointer finger and a pistol.

"Not now, Berryman," I say. "I have papers to correct."

Berryman says, "I think you're scared," and stands in my office doorway.

"Nope," I say.

Berryman says, "One period. We'll keep time on my watch."

"You're kidding yourself," I say.

No offense to Berryman but he's as pin-able as an old athlete can be. I know this because I have pinned him multiple times on the back lawn behind the cafeteria at the community college here in Western Pennsylvania where we both teach. The previous match lasted sixty seconds, long enough for Berryman to lose all his breath and flop like a fish while I drove his back into the grass. "Don't make me shoot legs," I said, clamping down on Berryman's neck. Under the thought of more humiliation he quietly said, "I'm pinned," and quit flailing. I stood and pulled Berryman up. A few students, packing lunches, drinking energy drinks, cheered for my victory and I bowed. Berryman dismissed them with a wave.

Berryman is a short man of moderate girth with a master's degree in writing from Yale. He wrestled in high school, 138 pounds, but he approaches two hundred these days, easily, solid in the chest and arms but bulging and sloppy around the middle, no longer a wrestler, barely fit for exercise. He published a book of poems before he finished graduate school. The book won a couple of prizes, got reviewed in The New Yorker, and brought him as much acclaim as a book of poems can. He stayed on at Yale post-masters and taught creative writing for a couple years. I believe it was during this time he started smoking pot and eating cheesesticks, though the pot may have happened earlier. After Yale he spent a year on fellowship in Rome, writing and eating fancy chocolate. He traveled to Spain. He traveled to Romania. In Romania he met a woman who worked in an orphanage. He fell in love with her, both her beauty and compassion. He loved the orphanage. He loved the country. The woman loved Berryman and his poetry then she fell out of love with Berryman and his poetry. Then she fell in love with a Romanian oil tycoon and quit her job at the orphanage, leaving the orphans for a small castle with a maid and a butler. I guess Berryman saw this injustice and responded. Something in his soul fluttered and made him believe he should be working with disadvantaged students, the poetry orphans of America. I read about him in Poet & Writers magazine, like he was a celebrity, the next Claudia Rankin or Sharon Olds or Gerald Stern or whoever could be considered famous and a poet, only better because he was kind-hearted and socially conscious. Poets & Writers never mentioned Berryman's love of cheesesticks. I refuse to stop bringing it up.

Berryman will be thirty soon and he feels it and thinks thirty is some kind of monument, a year closer to death.

I'm getting close to forty and I could give a shit.

I am jealous of Berryman's literary success, of which I have none.

Maybe that's why I pin him so viciously in our matches.

I wrestled through college, 138 pounds my senior year, starving myself, running relentlessly, but I barely weigh one-sixty now, fifteen years after my last official match. I have an undergraduate degree in writing from the University of Pittsburgh, the branch campus in Johnstown, where I was coached by Lawrence Riggins, the only collegiate wrestler to ever win six national titles as a heavyweight and who went on to play professional football with the Pittsburgh Steelers.

I did not play professional football.

Upon graduation I found a job working for a landscaping company, cracking roots with an axe and spreading mulch. By September, when they started to cut our hours, I was brown as tree bark and exhausted. When the weather turned cold and the yards turned to snow and the one-hundred-and-six resumes I sent out all stayed unanswered, I started smoking Marlboro lights while jogging laps at the high school stadium to ward off the fear I felt about my future and the regret I felt for attending college on a half-assed wrestling scholarship and a pile of student loans. It's not easy to smoke and jog simultaneously, especially in sub-freezing temperatures, but I deserved it and took it seriously. This went deep into winter. I signed up at a job center and started collecting food stamps, something I never imagined college graduates doing. The price of cigarettes, even years ago, annulled my addiction, but I kept running, the laps around the track saving me from the laps around my mind. I read Russian novels, sounding out the names in my lonely apartment. Alexei Ivanovich. Bazarov. Kirsnov. Having found myself unemployed and seemingly unemployable, I took a course in welding at the community college, this community college, gained credentials, and worked on bridges for the next eleven years.

I am a professor by employment, a welder by trade, and a writer by vocation.

It's the kind of humble statement that reeks of arrogance, I know.

Now Berryman leans deeper into my office, his face and chest coming towards me, a pushup in my doorframe, and says, "Coward," smiling though, having fun.

"You're embarrassing yourself, Berryman," I say. "Go write a poem that doesn't make any sense. You're almost famous."

"My poems make sense," he says. "Don't you think?" He pauses, introspective, vulnerable. "Why are you always saying my poems don't make sense?"

"You write like a turtle, Berryman, that's why," I say.

"What?" he says. "What's that mean?"

"Look it up in one of your poems," I say.

Berryman loves me because I was raised poor by a single mother who abandoned my father, her criminal husband, who later died from booze and car lust. Berryman's dad worked for Goldman Sachs Financial as a lawyer and they lived in a gated community in New Jersey where he attended a private high school and lettered in three sports while taking courses on John Donne and the metaphysical poets.

All my poverty makes him jealous.

"Give me one more re-match, please," Berryman says. "You caught me off guard last time. I thought I could use my size against you."

I say, "You did use your size against me. It was much harder for me to throw you around than if you'd been smaller." I pick up a pen and a magic marker and dance them around my desk like wrestlers until the skinny blue Bic pins the fat Sharpie. I say, "I would have pinned a smaller Berryman in twenty seconds, tops. You would have cried like a bitch when your skinny bones bounced on the ground."

Berryman says, "You're just being mean."

"You think I'm being mean because you're not getting your way."

"You always make it sound like I'm pouting. I miss the competition. I played sports nonstop when I was growing up. Do you know how many people played competitive sports when I was getting my MFA?"

"Zero," I say.

"That's right," Berryman says. "None."

I say, "If you promise, in writing, to never publish a nonsensical poem again, I will grant you a re-match, and I will allow you to start in the position of your choosing."

Berryman says, "Poetry is my life."

"That's your problem," I say.

"You can't make a man chose between his calling and an un-refereed wrestling match with a colleague for fun."

"Serious artists make choices like that every day."

"Quit busting my nuts," Berryman says. "I need the exercise."

I say, "That's the truth."

Berryman should take a walk while he thinks of writing his next obscure poem about what could be the Syrian conflict or how he once made a black lady feel bad because he was white. A couple miles would clean those poems right out. Dance aerobics would work too. Berryman could afford a personal trainer. His parents would pay for it, I think. I've seen his apartment in Lawrenceville, a hipster neighborhood in Pittsburgh, and it's not the apartment a man teaching at a community college could afford. Skylights on his bathroom ceiling open to the sky. It was three bedrooms. Outside the apartment a sign said: luxury living.

Berryman says, "I've never heard you say a mean word to anyone, not your students, not any of our colleagues, not even the security guard who everyone agrees is a total dick. But I can never tell if you're joking with me or if you really hate me."

"You're the best, Berryman," I say. "I mean it."

"Half the campus calls me Berryman now," he says.

"Wait," I say. "That's not your real name?"

He says, "You want to work out at the gym?"

"Nope," I say.

Berryman sits down like a student in one of the plastic chairs facing my desk. He frumps. He looks around my office. He no longer comments on its sparseness and lack of décor. He is no longer confused that I don't have a membership to LA Fitness.

I jog five miles at least four times a week.

I write western novels under the name Montana Jones.

I love jogging.

I would like to not write western novels at all under any name and have been resisting the impulse, which is good for my spirit but less so for my bank account.

More on that later but it too makes Berryman jealous. He googled me when he first came to campus and sometimes I do interviews under my real name, Sellick Hart, which also sounds vaguely fake, which is what happens when your teenage mom who loves TV and hates her husband decides to name you after a man with a mustache on a bad detective show but can't remember how the man spells his last name. Berryman cornered me when he started and said, "Writing western novels is a noble pursuit. I bet Louis L'Amour made more people happy than T.S. Elliot," and I said, "You should write a western novel," and he said, "I've never read one," and I said, "That's the truth."

Berryman teaches here because he wants to enlighten young people.

The government sent him on some program, an Americorps-type thing. They pay him a little, the community college pays him a little, his parents kick in an apartment and a car payment, and we get a famous poet walking the halls of a four-building college where you can major in plumbing and furnace repair.

I am here because it is better than welding bridges.

PART TWO

Welder Reads Books

W**hile I worked on bridges**, and when jobs stalled out around Pittsburgh, I traveled the country, following the money, usually getting on in a river city, Toledo, Ohio or somewhere near the Mississippi River. I stayed in dive motels and cooked off a hotplate, living thin as a dime. If you make your money with a torch while straddling steel and staring down at water and boats, a line of asphalt and cars in between, you must get paid. Get paid then get gone. I took all the overtime they offered and saved as much as possible and waited until the gigs slowed and they only wanted locals then I headed home to Pittsburgh, usually on a train because I hated busses and never brought my car. Sometimes I didn't own a car. For fun, if time allowed fun, I watched Sunday matinees at artsy theaters, smuggling in my own candy. If I drank, and I seldom drank when I gigged outside of Pittsburgh, I hit happy hour and sucked down whatever watery draft was cheapest, spoke only when spoken to, and usually left early to shop for paperbacks at whatever used bookstore I found.

And I found all the bookstores, used and new, every city every time, first day off and last day before leaving, a stack of books to help me carry on. I stuck with the Russians, I read junky mysteries, I scanned the poetry sections and bought the books the students sold back. Being covered in rust and old paint chips in a strange city is a secular purgatory, a place you pray yourself out of with long hours and fine seams. For ten, twelve, fourteen hours a day, I put my eyeballs into the wind while suspended over strange rivers on sunny days that turned my vision to bright splotches and blurry twinkles. By evening my head throbbed, my eyes sometimes watered, and my concentration wilted, but not my desire to read. I propped up with a book in the dark, in the almost-dark behind thin curtains, under a lamp, under a light bulb, in the bathroom with a flashlight, whatever it took to see the words with blurry eyes.

I have survived on reading as much as food.

I've gone three days without eating.

I've never gone a day without a book.

MY LIBRARY COACH

My dreams of literature, whatever they may be, I inherited from my high school librarian, Miss Dee Ann Marsh, who we were allowed to call Miss Dee, a woman with a long gray ponytail and a quiver in her voice. She demanded I read Louis L'Amour because her grandfather had read Louis L'Amour to all his grandchildren. She pushed for Hemingway because he was Hemingway. She handed me Faulkner because all of us come from some county and Western Pennsylvania was not so different than Faulkner's imagined homeland of Yoknapatawpha. Our poor were poor. Our illiterates looked at books like strange fish. "Don't be proud," she said. "Read at your level and rise up." I said, "I don't understand Faulkner," and tried to go back to Louis L'Amour, and she said, "Oh you do too understand Faulkner," and took my Louis L'Amour paperback and chucked it under the counter and made me read Flannery O'Connor, the story of the loudmouth grandma who finally gets shot by the roadside murderer who believes language to be as cruel, or crueler, than bullets. I loved it.

During college, when I could escape for a weekend, I returned to

Miss Dee's library and humble-bragged all the books I'd been reading, Camus and Sartre, de Beauvoir and Jean Genet, anything French because France sounded smart, every writer went there, they all drank in cafes and bars and wanted to meet James Joyce. I wanted to sound smart. Working-class kids always do. "Look at you," Miss Dee would say, "I remember when you used to read Louis L'Amour."

Did I say she was lovely?

She was but like a nun.

You could feel the righteousness come off her like perfume and her oversized tweed blazer revealed less than a nun's tunic. She quietly hummed gospel songs while she shelved books, never singing the words because we were a public school and to sing the words would have violated someone's rights. She believed in respect. Her library was a shrine to that. She said I could be a writer because I was a serious reader and writers were basically serious readers with extra time and more paper. When all I wanted to do was shoot the single leg, I believed her and decided I could be two things at once, an artist and an athlete, a kid who trusted and engaged both his mind and body, even as my coach said, "That book's not an ass, pumpkin, take your head out of it."

WESTERN NOVELS ARE ROMANCE NOVELS FOR MEN

I never lost the glow of Miss Dee, not even on the bridges, but the desire to write dimmed considerably against the exhaustion of most days and my reading navigated towards books involving dead bodies and the men who killed them and the women who inspired murder.

"Don't be proud," Miss Dee had said. "Read at your level and rise up."

Or go down.

She never mentioned that.

I figured I'd be reading Spanish novels in Spanish by the time I was thirty but instead I learned to love Jim Thompson and James Cain and Agatha Christie, masters of the shoot-'em-up, the drifter, and the who-done-it.

Around this time I met a woman who wrote romance novels and made her living at it.

We were sort of a couple, sort of not.

I'd gotten herpes from a wrestling mat or an infected wrestler during my senior year of college, three people on our team did, mine was on my arm, my teammates blistered up on their neck and back, respectively. Even though the doctor explained the whole process and how we weren't contagious unless there was an outbreak and another person could only be exposed and infected by direct contact, in my case by touching my blistered arm, and even though I never had another breakout and still haven't all these years later, I was buggy about having herpes and it made me feel dirty. Herpes was what you got from getting laid in a truckstop restroom. I was immobilized with fear that I'd give it to someone else, especially a woman I cared about, and so I got weird romantically, meaning I didn't have much romance in my life.

This was one of those times, romance but not.

I turned twenty-six that summer and Deborah, not Deb or Debbie, Deborah, was twenty-five and drove a big-ass truck and had recently purchased a dive-bombed apartment building in Wilkinsburg, a struggling neighborhood in Pittsburgh, which she planned to remodel and rent out. She made her money—for the truck and the apartment building and everything else—from writing romance novels. "The sun set like a wilting rose over the vase of my heart," was the opening line to one of her books. Deborah wrote the opposite of how she lived. She lived rough. She kissed rough, holding my head between her hands, though we seldom kissed more than a smooch when sober and stretching out in the same bed made us both nervous.

I didn't believe her, that someone could make a living by writing anything, least of all romance novels, even though my mom read and loved them. In the corner of our bathroom, when I was growing up, stood a basket with a stack of paperbacks, their covers showing muscular men with flowing hair clutching big-boobed women who looked desperate for love and adventure and maybe a sexy little slap.

Deborah said, "Here, that's me," one night back at her apartment.

I looked at the book, the author photo.

I said, "You wrote this?"

"You don't think I'm smart enough to write a book?"

"Of course I do," I said, thinking a monkey with a wet pussy could write a romance novel. "You used your real name," I said.

"Why wouldn't I?" she said.

I said, "You're touchy."

She said, "Everyone scoffs at romance novels. I'm sick of it."

I said, "There's a woman with her dress falling off on the cover. Her tits are so big she makes a Barbie doll look proportional."

"Yeah," Deborah said, "but she's falling into the arms of a guy with super-big muscles," like this somehow made the writing more legitimate.

"I can see that," I said.

She said, "How much money have you made off your writing?"

I started to count on my fingers then said, "Zero dollars and zero-zero cents," meaning neither of the two stories I'd published paid anything. One appeared online and the formatting was a mess and I felt embarrassed at how the story looked, let alone read. The other was a semifinalist for the Jane Bowles Prize, meaning it was neither an honorable mention, nor a finalist, but appeared in the same issue as the winners, albeit buried in the middle next to a story they'd accidentally omitted from the previous issue. I liked to think some kid at the University of Delaware, who published the journal, liked the story, though I never heard that, and the acceptance letter was completely impersonal, so the audience I imagined reaching, one student, probably didn't exist. No money. No love.

"Exactly," Deborah said. "I'm a professional."

"That makes me the amateur."

"Do you want a drink?" she said.

"Yes," I said. "Need one."

Deborah and I continued to see each other for months. We were good friends, two writers who barely knew any writers, so we pretended it might be something like love. On weekends, when I wasn't working, we drank a lot of vodka mixed with various juices because it seemed healthier. We never had sex. We kissed a lot, sometimes passing out mid-kiss then waking to start again. Deborah had gotten divorced the previous summer after three months of marriage. She caught her husband, who'd been her high school boyfriend, banging a stripper in his truck, which was really Deborah's truck, she'd made all the payments, so she instantly reclaimed her vehicle and dropped papers on her man then sold the truck and used the money as a down payment on her fixer-upper apartment complex. Then she wrote another novel and bought a better truck, one with a hitch to tow a trailer. At some point during these desperate times she found Jesus without reading the Bible or going to church and decided she would become celibate until she married again, which she never planned to do. Drunk, I could kiss her tits but nothing below the waist. She was free with the handjobs so I was fine with it, the kissing and boozing and sometimes drunken touching, relieved even, keeping my herpes shame to myself while learning how to make money off writing books. Once I asked her why handjobs never appeared in her books, why intimacy was always smoky rough coitus with relentless eye contact. She said, "Handjobs aren't romantic," and scrunched up her face like everyone knew that handjobs weren't romantic, though that's all we did, drunken tugging. I nodded her off, like sure, absolutely, completely obvious, but I felt bad and a little ashamed and maybe clownish but not enough to decline the next drunken jerkjob

Deborah wrote every day. She finished another romance novel while we pretended to date. She'd been writing two books a year for almost four years.

I couldn't stop with the questions.

"Who reads these?" I said.

"Mostly old ladies."

"Where do they buy them?"

"They join a book club and a new paperback arrives in the mail every week."

"Are they all set in olden times on strange islands?"

Deborah said, "Most of them but the publisher wants to reach younger women too. They're starting an imprint called Pink Dress. Once I finish the series I'm working on now, I get to write a book for Pink Dress."

I said, "What's the difference?"

"Pink Dress books are contemporary."

"Contemporary women don't like to get slapped around by muscle dudes."

"It's all fantasy, you dumbass."

Deborah was a fantasy. Dudes who watched home remodeling shows would have loved to bang her because she looked hot in a tool belt without trying to look hot, while being insulted by the notion of hotness. "Don't look at my ass," she said every time she climbed a ladder.

I said, "So Pink Dress books are set on modern islands and the chicks wear bikinis instead of long flowing dresses with their bosoms popping out?"

"No," she said. "Pink Dress books are supposed to be stories about working women who end up finding romance. There are all kinds of rules."

"They give you rules?" I said.

"Of course they give you rules," she said. "You really don't know anything about professional writing, do you?"

"Nothing," I said. "I know more about professional wrestling."

I dropped an elbow on her, so we fell deeper into the couch.

The couch was a thing from Goodwill she'd bought for twenty bucks and reupholstered. It looked like a tweed coat from a Norman Rockwell photo.

"Off me, you lug," she said.

She was tiny but wore shit-kicking boots.

I moved before she could respond.

I hated when she kicked.

She said, "They gave me three-page plot outlines I needed to follow for my first couple books until I proved myself."

"Now you just get rules?"

"Yes."

"Like what?"

"Like all the books have to be set in New York or Los Angeles. This is for the Pink Dress imprint, what I'm talking about. All the food has to be fancy and the wines fine, even if the main character is just learning about food and wine. The main character has to have an interest in shopping for something, diamonds or shoes or whatever. The rules are basic. Fancy purse, love, shoes, fears about snacking. It's just stuff other women can relate to."

"What about the men?"

"They read westerns."

"No one reads westerns anymore."

"Old men do," she said. "Millions of old men."

"No kidding," I said, finishing my drink, thinking of Louis L'Amour.

I pictured millions of old men and the paperbacks they read and it was like building a city in my mind, a fortress of paper bricks, rows of mass-market skyscrapers where the craftsmen get paid for their contributions to the buildings.

"Uh oh," she said. "Someone looks like he's thinking about selling his soul."

I poured another drink, a vodka kiwi.

I said, "It's hard being on bridges."

I said, "I tried to grow a beard one winter and the sparks from the welding gun burned away chunks of the hair."

I said, "It's so bright up in the sky."

I said, "I'm scared of falling."

I stopped but I didn't need to.

Deborah said, "Let me see what I can do."

I toasted her with my vodka kiwi.

The next day she contacted her editor who contacted an editor who contacted another editor in the department that published what they called adventure books, all action stuff geared towards men of a certain age, old guys who hated TV because of the profanity. The editor was a woman. All the editors —romance, mysteries, Pink Dress, westerns, crossword puzzles – were women. One of their husbands owned the company, I think. It was all secretive. The woman editor sent me an outline and a contract. Five grand upon completion plus royalties. No longer than two-hundred pages in manuscript. Next book due within six months. The company owned everything, story, title, film rights, world rights, even my characters' names. Terrible deal, absolutely horrible. I immediately signed the contract. I sat down at Deborah's computer with a bottle of vodka, a bowl of ice, and a six-pack of pineapple juice. I poured a drink and typed, "He didn't think of himself as a real cowboy, but his father owned the Bullet Hole Ranch out west in Wyoming," and finished the novel three days later, still drunk, my main character riding south to Mexico on a palomino with the woman he'd always loved.

"Not bad," the editor said.

"Thanks," I said, meaning the check, not the compliment.

"The least you can do is have the balls to use your own name," Deborah said.

"Montana Jones," I said. "It's my nom de fucking plume."

PART THREE

My Short But Not Illustrious Academic Career

Five years ago I started teaching here, Westmoreland County Community College, as a part-time lecturer. It was a fluke. The president of the college, Michelle Bronse, Dr. Bronse, read an article in the local paper about my western books and life as a welder and how I'd trained in the community college boilermaker program years before. I said some nice things about the college, nicer things than I said about Pitt-Johnstown where I'd dumped all my student loan money and earned my useless English degree. It flattered the president. It made her feel like the work she'd been doing for years, trying to educate and train kids from working-class backgrounds, mattered, like she'd made a difference, which the community college had.

She contacted me through my publisher and invited me out for a talk and a reading with a question-and-answer session to follow.

My editor, oddly exasperated that I'd gotten attention, said, "What the fuck kind of college invites out a pissy dime-store western novelist?"

"A community college," I said, "that trains welders."

My editor said, "They don't invite romance novelists out to college, that's for fucking sure," and chugged her diet soda right into the phone so the conversation sounded like a drowning swimmer. My editor was a feminist, "a loud feminist," she said. Occasionally, she referred to herself as a "a mighty cock crusher." Any success I had reinforced her notion that America was a patriarchal cesspool where only men could thrive. She was cruel and self-centered and rich and I paid her absolutely no attention. I was honored to be invited back to the community college that enabled me to make a living and appeared to care that I wrote books, no matter how silly.

I showed up at the college for my reading with a stack of books to sell but those in attendance numbered exactly six, including the president and the head of the English department, a middle-aged woman with blond hair who ate her fingernails and never made eye contact. No one seemed surprised by the poor attendance. The janitor stood in the back of the auditorium with his mop and listened intently. I skipped the reading segment of my visit out of embarrassment and fear my voice would crack in front of so few listeners but I talked about loving books and the importance of learning a trade and my dream of one day writing a real novel or story collection. The president stood and applauded, her eyes dewy with tears. She tried to buy all my books but I pretended they weren't for sale, that I'd lugged them here specifically to give away, and made her take a stack, which she insisted I sign. She hugged me twice. I hugged her back. I'd never considered what a thankless job being a community college president could be, as if thanklessness didn't kiss us all.

The janitor yelled from the back of the room, "You ever write any mysteries?" and I yelled back, "Not yet."

The president whispered, "You're an inspiration."

A week later her secretary called and asked if I would take a call from Dr. Bronse.

I said, "Is that a thing?"

The secretary said, "Is what a thing?"

"Calling someone to ask if they can take a call?"

"Dr. Bronse knows how busy you are."

I said, "I'd be honored to take the call."

I assumed the call would happen another day or week but sixty seconds later the phone rang and it was Dr. Bronse, sounding kind and generous, apologizing for bothering me.

"Thanks again for having me out," I said. "That janitor was great."

She said, "Would you be interested in teaching a class for us?"

"Like a welding class?"

"Like a writing class."

I paused, scared, imagining a classroom, student-eyes shining back. I pictured the eyes red, like lasers, and ready to fire.

She said, "We'd provide you a syllabus, of course."

I said, "I've never taught a class before."

She said, "I read all your western novels. They were wonderful."

"Thank you," I said. Then, almost on accident, I said, "I wrote them for money."

"Everyone does everything for money. That's nothing to be ashamed of."

"But no one admits that."

She said, "You mentioned the desire to write other books."

I said, again falling into honesty, "I've written three I like. I wrote five. Two I had to throw off bridges because they were so bad."

She said, "Think about teaching. If you want to teach a welding class until you're comfortable, I could arrange it, but I think our writing students would adore you."

I said, "What about the department head, the woman chewing her fingernails off? Is she okay with you offering me a class?"

"She is," Dr. Bronse said. "She suggested it. She's taking some time off. She's nervous and doesn't know why."

"I'll think about it and call you back."

"Think about it and come see me," she said.

So I did.

I showed up at Dr. Bronse's office in my best dress pants and a button-up shirt and clean boots, afraid she wouldn't recognize me, afraid there'd be an interview where I'd be asked to answer questions about pedagogy and other words I was confused by even after looking them up. I was afraid there'd be a complex grammar quiz and I'd flunk it.

She saw me in her doorway and said, "You in?"

I said, "I'm in."

She stood at her desk and, again, applauded.

I taught a class.

I worked around town so I could make the class on time and not worry about canceling.

I loved it, instantly.

I knew nothing but realized from the students' attentive eyes and/or indifferent faces that they knew less and their ignorance comforted me. It was easy to be successful when most everyone in attendance neither recognized success nor failure. They either loved books or were required to take the class. I respected both choices and focused on whoever listened and did their work. Basically, we talked about the best way to tell stories.

The head of the English department died the next semester, she fell off a bridge and broke her neck when she landed on a railroad track, though everyone privately called it a suicide, and they promoted the next oldest person in the department to chair and they allowed me to teach that person's classes. I teach them still and the president assures me the job is mine, full-time with benefits, outside the tenure stream but still permanent, and I believe her.

PART FOUR

Berryman Has Friends

Berryman catches me in the hallway on my way to class. He wears a purple sweatsuit, three white stripes going up the sleeves, and some fancy hightop sneaks.

"Hey," he says, "I have some buddies coming in from New Jersey in a couple weeks. You want to show us around Pittsburgh?"

"Ah, come on," I say.

THE COMMUNITY COLLEGE WORKSHOP

Today, my students workshop their stories. They turn their desks in a circle so everyone can see everyone else. A podium stands off in the corner but I never use it. I seldom walk around the classroom. To teach from the standing position still makes me uncomfortable, more uncomfortable than walking the high deck on a bridge, so I sit at the old wooden table in the front of the room where I can see the whole class and the chorus of students lingering in the hall. It's late March, unseasonably hot. Most of the college offers central air but these old rooms on the backside of campus heat up like boxes of fire. We all sweat. People fan their faces with tablets and folders. I chug ice water from a sports bottle. Tabs on soda cans pop.

The first student reads her story. It's okay. The writing just bumbles along because the student hasn't read many books yet. The verbs she uses bounce between *was* and *has* and *is*. The whole narrative happens in the narrator's head, which is common for young writers. Lots of student stories start with someone in a bathtub, relaxing, then thinking out the narrative. They need that place, the bathtub, to allow their character to think and explain. This story tells the story of a cat adoption while the narrator pets a cat. I say some nice things and offer a few gentle criticisms. The class does the same.

The next story starts on a bus. The narrator thinks the whole story while she rides the bus to see her grandma in the hospital.

The next student reads her story.

Her voice quivers.

The story does not.

From the first sentence—which reads: It embarrassed me that my dad was a plumber—I know it's going to be great. The rest of the story builds and turns on that detail, following the plumber through his life and showing what it means to work with pipes and water when the world assumes you only work with toilets and shit but then sometimes not finding jobs with pipes and water and having to work with toilets and shit, then coming back to the plumber because we never leave our jobs, we never escape what we do to make a living, ever.

Community college students understand that.

Writers mostly do not.

MORE STORIES, MORE WORKSHOP

I fan my face with a notebook while I follow along, making notes on the plumber story as she reads. A drop of my sweat hits the page and forms a tiny puddle before soaking into the paper.

The student's name is Megan. Megan waits tables at Harry's Bar in Greensburg. Her grandmother owns the bar. Her grandmother's name is Harriet but the regulars call her Harry. Harry brings free popcorn to the tables and offers to drive drunks home even though her family took her license years ago. She will charm you with what she forgets and double-charm you with what she remembers. I hang at Harry's Bar more than I should, which is probably still not enough. Three nights a week. Four. Five at the most. Sometimes I go there and correct papers or write on my novel or watch a game and eat a sandwich. I don't always drink alcohol but sometimes I drink as much alcohol as I can pour into my body. During the last Olympics I spent more time at Harry's Bar than I did at home, watching sprinters lean into finishing lines and pole-vaulters soar and Gabby Douglas plant landing after landing on the mats and the uneven bars and the horse. It was a good couple weeks, America and beer and sports. In theory I shouldn't drink at Harry's Bar because Megan is my student but she was my bartender before I was her professor so I feel that takes precedent, life over career, friendship over academics, feeling over intellect, and who gives a shit anyway. I wish she'd marry me.

Megan's story is about an old woman who runs a bar and her relationship with her son, the plumber who wants out of plumbing, and his relationship with his daughter, the narrator, a waitress. The woman who runs the bar decides to give the bar away one piece at a time. She misses her husband and she's ready to meet him in Heaven. She sends one drunk home with a stool. She sends another home with a basket of chicken fingers. Lots of people get mugs. The bar is not very busy so this goes on for months. The son tries to stop it. He wants to inherit the bar and run the bar and stop waking up at four in the morning to rush to some customer's house where their basement is flooded with shit. The narrator negotiates both sides. She understands the desire to walk into heaven after having been cleansed of your worldly possessions and she understands the desire to abandon a job where you spend your days, at worst, in other people's bathrooms and, at best, standing under pipes and waiting for a leak. But the bar keeps disappearing. The tables go. The bottles go. The last drops of beer from the tap. Even the popcorn machine. Then it's empty. The bar, as bars are known, is no more. The bar has become a room. The old woman fills with joy. In slippers and her robe, she slowly dances on the few squares of carpet that have not been pulled from the concrete floor. The son sits by the front door on a chair he brought from his apartment. His daughter waits outside. The old woman keeps pain pills at home, what she calls her quiet stash, in case God does not take her soon enough. The plumber accepts his lack of inheritance. He knows about the quiet stash and has replaced the pills with aspirin. He loves his mother more than he hates his job. The daughter who narrates the story moves home to be with her dad and to have a cheap place to stay while she looks for a new job. The story ends at a diner. No one talks. Everyone eats sandwiches and French fries and drinks Cokes. The father goes to the bathroom and stands for a long time in front of a mirror but looking down to notice the details of the sink.

In the classroom we sit quietly.

Megan feels like the silence comments negatively on her story. It does not. The students seldom speak without being prompted, including Megan, the best writer in the class. Megan shifts in her chair. She writes on her own pages, imagined notes, something to do to feel natural until the class gathers enough courage to properly praise. Megan will be thirty soon, the end of the semester. She takes this class as an elective. She wants to be a nurse or an X-Ray tech or something in the medical field, she doesn't know, anything that pays well and provides security, a profession where you can't get laid off when the job is done, a profession running opposite of plumbing and her dad who works construction and hustles from job to job, one site to the next, sometimes going out of state to lay pipe and stop leaks.

Megan goes to college, like so many of these students, to not be.

Being itself is almost unimaginable.

She wants to not be a bartender.

To not be a bartender or a plumber is the dream.

Megan's long brown hair mostly goes up in a ponytail but sometimes falls down her back and sometimes she wears a baseball hat and all her clothes fit tight enough to make you not want to breathe. Her boobs are not big but they are nice and almost always exposed because people love boobs and Megan is proud of her boobs and she works for tips and a button-up shirt is seldom tippable. Right now, vulnerable, waiting for praise or for her work to be derided, she unconsciously tugs at the v-neck in her t-shirt, covering her cleavage.

At the beginning of the semester Megan told me, "All I want to do is read." It was the best thing a student had said, ever, and I felt something like Dr. Bronse must have felt reading about my western novels in the *Tribune Review*. Sometimes Megan and I sit in the bar afterhours and eat popcorn and talk about books. We both grew up on Stephen King and somehow graduated to Hunter Thompson and Tom Wolfe then to Joan

Didion and James Baldwin with nothing more than a library card and a subscription to *Rolling Stone* magazine between us. When Megan heard that I was going to teach full time at the community college, she grabbed me by the face and kissed me full on the mouth and said, "You're my hero," then she signed up for English Writing and Creativity. I have known her for six or seven or eight years now, from before I taught. I know I could love her and maybe already do. Or, more honestly, I love her and do not know what to do with that love. Nothing, probably. I am a romantic wimp. With mat herpes.

I say, "What's everyone think about this story?"

No one says anything.

They all look down.

A few tiny flaws mark the story, shifts in tense, a missing detail or two, but the rest feels truthful and ironclad. We, the students and me both, are embarrassed to have to comment on something so good, something we know about the world but have never seen on the page before.

One guy looks up and pulls the hood of his sweatshirt down so we can see his face then takes his earphones out and he says, with complete sincerity, "That story was fucking great."

THE NEXT STORY

The next story is very good. Pretty good, at least. It's also a grandma story. Working-class kids, raised by two working parents, love their grandmas. Told from the third person, the story bounces from character to character, each one passing details forward about the grandma's condition, how she wants to commit suicide so she can be in heaven with her son who has recently died of cancer. The pain of losing a child, an adult child, fills the pages. The student, who is nineteen or twenty, writes years beyond her age. She knows details of careers she couldn't have possibly worked. She knows wallpaper prints and knickknacks in the house from years before she was alive. So much is happening and holding together until the narrative reaches the grandmother who, instead of revealing the real truth, the truth of self, walks into the barn and says, "Honey, I'm coming home," then blows her head off with a pistol. Kablewy! The bullet goes into one ear and out the other, blood and brains forming a temporary skidmark in the air before falling down on grandma's dress. It's graphic and gross and unnecessary but, in defense of the student, probably essential in an early draft and probably a lot of fun to write. It's movie stuff, death and glory, when a light lunch and a can of Pepsi would do.

But at least it's something we can discuss in class and learn from.

I say, "Well, comments. Anyone."

Up until the gunshot, this was the best story we've had in weeks, save Megan's story, which is the best story we've had ever, which should be published, which should be the basis for some indie film starring Casey Affleck and Helen Mirren and some pop singer who wants to change her reputation and gain grit by acting in a roughed-up movie.

"I'm digging the old lady," someone says.

"Me too," I say. "The old lady's a great character. Her desire to be with her son, that she's missing him, sets the whole narrative in motion."

The student looks at me like I'm speaking French.

I may be.

I still struggle with the language of workshop. As an undergraduate, I took a lot of poetry courses and most of them were taught by the same guy, an old white dude who only looked at poems through the prism of form. We counted syllables. We counted stresses. Occasionally, we discussed content but only in its relationship to form which, to me as an adult and a teacher, seems to be reversed, that form should be discussed in terms of how it delivers content. I mean, form is a bucket. What material that bucket is made from and how it's shaped and what size it is are only important details once we know what goes inside, water or paint or gasoline. I use that metaphor in class and the students nod like they understand but somewhere in my brain I hear my poetry teacher, a man who never published a book and who treated college like an extension of high school, of junior high even, where certain things were not discussed, meaning content, meaning the world, meaning the world was rude, the world was gross, it was sex and money and shame, and my poetry teacher rings a bell in my ear until my hearing opens like a scared flower and he says, "One must elevate the diction to have higher thoughts."

Maybe that's why I liked my welding classes.

The language served the course, the career.

It was useful.

Either way, whether I sound like a welder teaching a college class or a man unwantingly educated on the significance of iambic pentameter to the oral tradition, I try to be clear and useful in my comments. I try not to dominate the workshop because the students do better when I follow, when I ask questions about their comments, about where their ideas come from, which is usually from Stephen King books and Quentin Tarantino films and, sadly, video games.

I don't want to elevate the diction.

I want to be a blowtorch.

Megan says, "First, I really love this. My only questions is, and I get that this is a story about suicide, why does the grandmother kill herself?"

Did I say I love Megan?

Her intelligence is only matched by her kindness.

I want to respond, to echo.

But I keep waiting.

What I want to say next is, "Does a character this close to death need to die?" meaning: she doesn't need to die. Her grief is already there. Every move she makes links us to the loss of her adult son. No need for the pistol. You can have a pistol or a machine gun in literature but they should appear proportionally to your own life. Represent the world you exist in, not the one you see on TV. Not all of us are robbers. Not all of us are cops with fancy mirrored sunglasses. Some of us have been around gun owners our whole lives but never touched a bullet.

Brandon, who comes to class stoned and mean and who sometimes drinks malt liquor by his car in the parking lot and who is not a kid but a young man, says, "I fucking loved it when she blew her brains out." He makes a motion like he's pulling a truck horn, fist clenched, arm up, elbow swinging. He says, "Get to that faster."

This is not the comment I hoped for.

Brandon is seldom the student I hope for.

His forehead grows a huge pimple like a pumpkin I'd like to pop with my fist, not that I can see much of his face, his hair long and greasy but somehow bald on top. All he talks about are comic books and sci-fi novels, which the right person could make charming but which Brandon makes sound like imminent doom, like he personally fingers the button to all our deaths. He once said, "Science fiction is intelligent fiction because the worlds are imagined," the undercurrent being that what I taught was not intelligent, so I said, "Every world is imagined," because it was true and because I dislike sci-fi novels and I usually dislike adults who love sci-fi novels. Brandon is at least thirty, maybe older. He has not returned to college to find a new way to make a living or to enlighten himself. He attends college habitually, a class or two a year, mostly to bully his professors and talk about his own artistic merits between shifts at the grocery store where he manages the produce section. On the first day of class he said, "I'm writing a fantasy trilogy based on a British TV show no one in America knows about," then, before I could respond, he asked, "Can we smoke?" I said, "Here? In the classroom?" He said, "Yeah." I said, "No, you cannot smoke in the classroom." After class I asked around and everyone, all my colleagues and the janitors and the women in the cafeteria, knew Brandon and disliked him and found him disruptive but harmless, except maybe not harmless, maybe a serial killer, maybe a guy who skins people in his basement and eats their lungs, except not, except maybe.

Right now Brandon says, "More killing. I mean it. The grandmother could easily take out the family before she takes out herself."

I do what I always do when Brandon mentions killing: I look at his hand and verify it is not a pistol then I look at his backpack and make sure it is not a bomb.

Welding would be a good job for Brandon.

Welders would tell him to shut the fuck up.

Brandon says, "I see you looking at me, Mr. Professor. I can talk about violence. Marquis De Sade. What about that? He was violent. I know my shit. Tell me to stop."

I have not read more than twenty pages of the Marquis De Sade but I can throw down.

I say, "I'm willing to bet you can't name one book by Marquis De Sade," but I say it calm, almost joking, having fun.

Brandon says, "I can."

I say, "Okay."

"Right now?"

"Sure, if you want."

He says, "I saw the movie."

"Me too," I say, which is true and I own a couple De Sade books but the prose is as purple as an eggplant. Twenty pages and I'm bored and a little grossed out.

Brandon says, "I read that one book about buttfucking."

The class makes a collective sound for: gross.

Megan says, "How old are you?"

I say, "Brandon, why don't you take a cigarette break while the rest of us talk about the excellent parts of this story where brains are not getting blown out."

Brandon says, "It won't affect my grade if I leave for a cigarette?"

I say, "It may actually help your grade."

He says, "Cool," and walks out, leaving his backpack but fishing a hard pack of Marlboro Lights from his front shirt pocket.

Megan looks at me and tries not to laugh.

I nod at her, two people locked in an attic but planning our escape.

Hours from now, at two o'clock, when the bar is closing, I'll make sure I tip her fifty percent. She'll give me more free drinks than she should.

Right now Brandon closes the door behind him.

Someone else in the class says, "That dude scares me."

"Let's not be afraid," I say. "Let's talk about the good stuff in this story."

The girl who wrote the story, who is barely five feet tall and sometimes wears her waitress uniform to class because she is often coming from or going to her shift, says, "I didn't know how to end it. That's why I did the stupid thing with the gun."

BRANDON'S NOVEL

Near the beginning of the semester Brandon asked me to read his newest and greatest novel, a mystery. I stood there, bugged-eyed and shocked, thinking of excuses. The hallway near my office bustled with students strolling to class. Brandon stepped uncomfortably close.

"Personal space," I said, and stepped back.

Brandon stepped closer.

I stepped back.

"Don't do that again," I said. "It's not necessary for us to be that close."

He said, "I stopped by at office hours yesterday."

"I didn't have office hours yesterday but nice try."

"Maybe it was the day before."

I did not want to read a novel written by a student who I disliked, who the entire campus disliked, a space intruder whose artistic intellect consistently rolled in at low tide with the garbage shows and dead fish books, but I also hate feeling neglectful. I remember being young and desperate for writerly attention so I mumbled about being extremely busy this semester and stuttered about tutoring a woman from the basketball team who really showed some promise as a writer then I stuck a finger in my ear and twisted it around like my brain needed to be cleaned or at least prodded. The community college doesn't have a basketball team.

Eventually Brandon pushed aside his greasy bangs and said, "You get paid to read my novels. My tuition pays your salary."

"Actually," I said, "I get paid to teach writing. It's on the syllabus. What I want to read from students outside of class is my choice. Your tuition pays for the soda machine by the cafeteria. I'm pretty sure it doesn't go directly to my salary."

He said, "Look, it's a page long."

I said, "What?" and brightened. "What's a page long? Your list of complaints?"

He said, "My novel. It's one page. All my novels are one page. I call them compressions. My compressions are sarcastic compressions of genre fiction."

"Like you write one-page science fiction novels?"

"No. I do not consider science fiction a type of genre fiction. I consider science fiction the future of literature. Genre fiction includes mysteries, police procedurals, and romance novels, to name but a few. Sniper books."

I said, "So you have a one-page mystery novel you'd like me to read?"

He sighed and shook his head at my idiocy and said, "I have a satiric compression based on the detective genre, also known as noir, that I expect you to read."

"Sure," I said. "I can read a page, no problem."

Brandon pulled out the page.

I took it.

It was less than a page, more like a couple of big paragraphs.

I said, "I'll get this back to you by our next class."

He said, "You'll get it back to me now?" in a question, not aggressive but still demanding, still kicking at the door of my job.

"No," I said, "I'm not going to read while you wait, even if this thing is a page long. I'm not McDonalds and this isn't fast food."

"Until we meet again," Brandon said, and started to walk away before turning around to ask, "You do know what satire is?"

"I think I can figure it out," I said, and stepped into my office and locked the door.

I looked at the page.

This was a while ago but it's still worth sharing.

Brandon's novel, in its entirety, without criticism, is as follows:

DETECTIVE DICKWAD AND THE HOLLYWOOD CAPER

My name is Detective Dickwad. I hate the cops. Cops hate me. My fees are negotiable and I drink too much. I once shot a man in the anus for all the wrong reasons.

It's pretty hard to tell the good from the bad here in the City of Angels. Hookers, movie stars, debutantes, Matt Damon—they all look the fucking same. I'm tracking them all. When I catch them, I'm going to find out what the fuck's up with the missing jewels. I'm going to find out what's up with the murdered teenaged girls. I'm going to find out what's up with the dude in the basement who keeps pretending his penis is a vagina and singing Culture Club songs. I'm going to smoke a cigarette, flick it to the wind, and find out why the fuck Morgan Freeman acts in so many bad thrillers with Ashley Judd. Ashley Judd can't act but is related to Wynona Judd. I'm gonna find out why Wynona Judd is fat as fuck and sings horrible country songs with her sick mom who has hepatitis C from (I'm assuming) sharing dirty needles with those Jesus-loving retards in Nashville who write all those songs about God and big asses and burned-out Chevy trucks. I'm about to kill those fuckers when

I solve this shit.

Take last week: I had to sit on Nic Cage's face. I saw him on the cover of *People* magazine. I knew he was a suspect. I sat on that half-bald head, put my gun to his temple, and said, "Goddamn it, why do you suck in so many movies?" I slapped Nic Cage a good one, really cuffed him with my pistola, then asked, "Why are you trying to be an action star when it's so obvious that you're a pansy?" I kept the questions coming. I asked him, "Why do you think an Elvis impression is appropriate in every movie you do?" Nic cage said, "I don't know," but maybe that was just the sound of my bullet going through the other side of his head.

As for the Judds and Morgan Freeman, I'm on to you people.

—An American Compression by Brandon Holmes

I have a copy of the story in my desk drawer, the main one where I keep my paperclips and pens. The original I returned to Brandon but I see the copy every time I need a pen and it reminds me to be safe. I read Brandon's name and I remember there are other, better students. I see the title and I understand my luck, that Brandon's half-page novel could have been longer than a half-page, that it could have been a real novel with hundreds of pages. Did I say it reminds me to be safe? I know bad writing is usually bad writing but I also know the story could be a fantasy or a metaphor or a plan of action written in code and I could be either Morgan Freeman or, possibly, Ashley Judd or her sister or her mom, the Hep C junkie.

I hope I'm not Nic Cage.

No one wants to be Nic Cage.

PART FIVE

Berryman, Trying To Be My Friend

Berryman says, "What if I did something nice for you? Could we hang out then?"

I say, "We're hanging out now."

"This is just talk between classes. A student mentioned that you drink at Harry's Bar. Maybe you could take me there? I'd love to have a beer with you."

"Berryman," I say, "I am a professional and you have insulted me. That is a slanderous rumor. I hereby challenge you to a wrestling match on the back lawn."

"Seriously?" Berryman says. "You'll wrestle me?"

"Absolutely," I say. "You can't be talking to students about where I drink. That's bullshit. I think you know as much. You're selling me out."

"I just overheard something."

"I just overheard something, he says," I say, impersonating Berryman but whiny.

We go to the back lawn, a square of brown grass and mud with a little green where the sun cracks through. I take Berryman to the green so I don't muddy his track suit.

"You ready?" I say.

Berryman assumes a box stance.

No one of any skill assumes the box stance.

I go sugarfoot, right leg out.

Berryman comes aggressive and I shoot the fireman and get between both legs and under his crotch and feel the velour of his track suit on my cheek and lift his fat body higher than necessary and plant him hard on the ground so he is certain about the order of things. This is not New Jersey or Yale. You are, exclusively, what you are in the field behind the building where students learn to be plumbers. Reality is less subjective in Western Pennsylvania at the community college level. Metaphor means shit.

"I can't breathe," Berryman says, on his back, scared but still breathing.

Down the River

Dr. Bronse stops by my office. She stops by everyone's office, popping in, saying hi. She brings balloons. She brings flowers. She brings books she thinks you should read, usually self-helpie stuff and left-leaning political books, though sometimes novels. She hugs, more than I like but I'm not a hugger, so it's probably an appropriate amount of hugging. On your birthday she'll bring a cupcake with one lit candle and she'll turn the lights down and she'll sing "Happy Birthday" and hers is not a singing voice but the kindness carries the song. She asks questions about things that can be improved, academic and practical, class size and number of spaces in the parking lot, and she writes answers on a small pink tablet. She pretends to be a Luddite but I see her tapping on her office computer and talking on her cell phone so she knows people don't speak in-person anymore. She knows humans are turning to robots, rewiring their brains with technology to become technology, but she ignores it and pretends we want to see her and she's right, we do want to see her. Her interactions restore what technology tries to erase.

She says, "Are you interested in a kayak trip?"

"I don't know," I say. "Maybe?"

"You'd be good on the river," she says.

"Is this for a class?"

"Student activities. They got a grant to promote nature learning. They all hate nature. None of them can swim. No one will admit to writing the grant. I'd take the students myself but I'm in Virginia at a conference that week."

Dr. Bronse is maybe sixty with completely gray hair falling past her shoulders which she wears out or pulls back in a ponytail, sometimes both within minutes if her thoughts require some twisting. She looks thin in the conservative suits she wears around campus, like today's blue-jacketed thing, but in shorts and a tanktop, walking around the gym or the nature trail in the evening, her arms and legs are muscular and filled with energy. On her walks, which she calls her jaunts, an old tennis visor comes down low so her eyes are barely visible, Clark Kent's glasses to hide her inner Superman. She walks fast, arms pumping, earphones in. Once or twice a year she runs 10K races for charity. I see her training on Route 70, a highway much too busy for joggers, and she acts oblivious to the cars whipping by, to danger. For weeks afterwards she says, "My old knees," but she walks fine and starts running again in a couple months.

Now she says, "I'd hate to see the money go to waste."

"Sure," I say, pausing. "I'd love to kayak," and I would. I like nature but I've been too busy to stand with the trees and listen to rivers for most of my life. Maybe this trip will be a new invitation to become one with the woods. I'll buy a tent and cuddle foxes and write poems and be the new Mary Oliver. I'll find the river's true name and return every year on a pilgrimage. My soul will become a leaf. The wind will lift it.

Dr. Bronse says, "You look serious."

"I'm thinking about nature."

"Not much time for it?"

"Hardly at all."

"Me neither, not since I was a little girl."

"Kayaking will be fun," I say.

"Fantastic," she says and makes a mark on her pink notebook. "Get the Americorps guy to go with you. He seems like the kayak type."

"Berryman?" I say.

She laughs and says, "Oh, stop that. People will think that's his real name."

"Isn't it?"

"You're bad."

But Dr. Bronse understands.

She grew up in Wilmerding, another mill town without mills, the constant stream of trains slowed to a few coal cars passing through each week. She graduated valedictorian of her high school and went to Harvard because that's what valedictorians did and she hated Harvard where all her classmates had attended private high schools or prep schools and not public schools and certainly not public schools in towns named by George Westinghouse where the teachers all worked summer jobs because the pay was so bad. "Never again," she told me one night after a reception and two glasses of red wine. "I crushed Harvard before Harvard could crush me, 4.0 across the board. I learned to row and became captain of the team, just to spite the girls in my dorm that had been rowing their whole lives." She said, "We'll show Harvard, won't we?" and she turned and looked into my eyes but I think she was talking to herself.

DEATH AND THE ADJUNCTS

Berryman shares an office with three adjuncts. They are never around. I see them sometimes, streaks of sweaters and thrift-store dresses rushing from their classrooms to correct papers in their cars while eating fast food and bags of pretzels. They drive off to teach part-time at other colleges and universities, worrying about gas, worrying about traffic, worrying about time. They are broke. They are as broke as Walmart employees except the adjuncts all have Masters degrees and PhDs and student loans. Everyone believes the adjuncts should be paid more but no one actually pays them, not the universities nor the private colleges nor the for-profit schools nor my community college, so the adjuncts open their hearts like gas cans and fill their chests with hope, the only fuel they can afford.

I would be an adjunct, were it not for Dr. Bronse, except I would not.

If I were an adjunct, I'd quit and go back to welding.

I'd write more westerns.

To adjunct is, essentially, to accept an earlier death for love of career and students. Dedication, as a word, understates their cause. They live on credit cards or cannot pay their bills or maybe live off a supportive spouse and feel ashamed because they contribute so little financially to their household. Then, with great enthusiasm, they stand up and teach frustrated kids building their first lives and desperate adults coming back to school with new dreams and goals and hopes for a second career. Then our adjuncts sit down to correct hundreds of papers. Then they get paid and weep. Then they do it again, maybe somewhere else, another school that likes them even less. A woman adjuncts at Duquesne University for twenty-five years, teaching classes in French and Medieval Literature, but completely lacks a pension and proper healthcare. She can't retire. At eighty-three years old she has a heart attack on campus. The university denies culpability. The priests say some mean things about her teaching style. A twenty-something English instructor for the University of Pittsburgh sleeps in his car in the faculty parking lot because he can't afford rent. Eventually, the university police catch him then force him out. His contract is not renewed. He moves into a tent by the river with a bunch of homeless people and picks up three online courses with the University of Phoenix which he teaches from the Carnegie Library. He does this for so many years, his story becomes a non-story.

I make way less money teaching college full-time than I did welding and I make four times as much money as the average adjunct teacher.

So, for me, never.

The top of a bridge would barely be far enough away from that kind of job.

PART SIX

Rig's Million Dollar Voice

Berryman says, "You want to wrestle?"

I look up from a larger stack of papers on my desk. It's like my uncorrected papers have humped each other and started a family of other uncorrected papers.

Berryman says, "Just kidding. I've officially retired."

I say, "You'll ask again."

"Probably."

"Your desire to lose is outstanding."

"I really think I can beat you."

"Probably not."

"I'm twice your size."

The phone on my desk, an ancient tank with a roto-dial, rings and I answer.

"No shit," the voice says, "you really are teaching college."

"I really do," I say, joking, confused, almost recognizing the voice but not.

"You know who this is?"

"I think so, sort of."

"I think so, sort of," he says. "This is Rig, man."

"Lawrence?" I say.

"Who else," he says, and laughs.

The people rattle behind him like they're all drunk or on stage somewhere, singing off-key.

Berryman says, "Is that your mom?"

I give Berryman a look and spin away with the phone so I face the wall and obliterate his fat face from the landscape of my office.

Rig is Lawrence Riggins, former all-pro guard for the Pittsburgh Steelers, former national collegiate wrestling champion, former WPIAL state wrestling champion even though his high school didn't have a wrestling team and he signed up for states as an independent, something no kid had ever done. During college I wrestled at the same school that Rig had wrestled at years before, a tiny Pitt branch campus in Johnstown, an old mill town known mostly for being twice destroyed by floods. Rig is legend there. They have a day for him in Johnstown.

Because you probably don't know anything about Johnstown or wrestling, let alone Lawrence Riggins, who used to act as a volunteer coach at UPJ, who used to toss me around practice like an old sock for fun, allow me to explain his immense popularity amongst those of us who know his life and accomplishments: Lawrence Riggins, as a junior heavyweight wrestler for a nobody school, a kid raised by an alcoholic father and a disappeared mother, beat Kurt Angle who went on to become an Olympic champion so famous that companies begged with millions of dollars for him to endorse their products, which Kurt Angle did before becoming a pro wrestler for the WWE, where he flew from top ropes and got bopped in the head with steel chairs and ended up a rockstar on t-shirts I still see little kids wearing.

Here's the millionaire superstar Kurt Angle.

But here's Lawrence, pinning the millionaire's shoulders to the mat.

JAIL TIME

"It's good to hear from you, Rig," I say. "How'd you know I was teaching here?"

Rig says, "We can discuss that when you come and pick me up at the Allegheny County Jail," and the music in the background sounds less like music and more like cops and criminals trying to get along. He says, "You still there?"

"Still here," I say. "You need bail?" I say, hoping he doesn't, knowing he's been a mess for years and has stepped on and over friends for money and favors.

"Nope, I'm out," he says. "I just need a ride home."

"I'll be there," I say.

"Good man," he says. "Rig has always appreciated that about you."

I hang up the phone.

Berryman says, "You have a friend in jail?"

"Sort of," I say. "He's more like a mentor. You want to come for a ride?"

"Hell yeah," Berryman says, glowing. "I can't believe you have a mentor who is in jail." He pauses then says, "Have you ever been in jail? I'm not judging."

"Stop it, Berryman," I say. "I'm the opposite of jail."

He says, "How do you know this guy?"

"You know who Kurt Angle is?"

"The greatest shoot wrestler of all time?"

"That's Dan Gable," I say, "but close."

Berryman says, "I know who Kurt Angle is. Everyone does. I used to watch him fake-wrestle on TV every week once he turned pro. I've You-Tubed all his college matches."

"Well, my friend who was in jail beat his ass back in college."

"Like in a fight?"

"No, like on the mat."

Our Exit

I've taught my classes for the day but Berryman needs to stop by the secretaries' glass booth and make plans to cancel his evening class. He looks ashamed to be canceling. The secretaries smile and nod. They don't care who cancels so long as they are not hassled by confused students. The light in their booth is unnatural and bright. Berryman finishes and continually waves as he steps backwards from the booth in his Berryman way. His parents must be terrifically polite.

We walk past students, most too timid to say hello to one professor, let alone two, rushing across campus. We pass a soda machine and I stop and unload some bills and silver change because what we are about to do requires caffeine, lots of it.

I say, "Berryman, you have any money?"

Berryman hands over some ones.

I buy two more bottles of Coke Zero, four total.

Berryman says, "Chemicals," and takes a couple bottles.

We go back to rushing.

I hadn't been on a college campus in years until I was invited to visit here and read from my western novels but I remember my undergraduate university as clunky and old and decrepit in places, like decrepit was a style, a stance, a calling to thought. Now everything looks modern and clean, not space-aged but close, something I never notice when I'm strolling to class or walking with students who need an adult voice, these huge windows allowing sunlight to pour in, a couple computer labs filled with new computers and students wrapped in headphones, a bookstore that sells more sweatshirts than books, more mugs than notebooks.

We pass a gazebo on the front lawn where students hang and smoke. So many students smoke. The stress of being at a community college, of needing a career as much or more than you need an education, requires nicotine in enormous quantities no matter how expensive and deadly. The parking lots are huge and remarkably free of cigarette butts.

Berryman says, "I really like it here."

"Everyone smokes," I say.

"Yeah, that's bad," he says.

"Necessary," I say. "That's different."

We walk faster.

"Can you drive?" I say. "Your car is bigger than mine and we'll have to take Rig back to Johnstown. Big guys require big cars."

Berryman says, "You drive a truck, a truck with the benchseat thing in the back."

"I know. That's too big for what we need to do."

I stop at Berryman's car, a Ford something with an ample backseat.

He takes out his keys and sighs.

FOLLOW THE RIVER

Berryman, driving his thoughtful Ford, says in his thoughtful Berryman voice, "Should I take the Turnpike to Pittsburgh?"

"Should I hit you?" I say. "The Turnpike charges a buck per two miles now."

I point to a backroad then another and another so we pass barns and fields and stretches of pine trees and more barns and farms of dark brown dirt waiting to sprout corn and hay and beans. Eventually, the rural turns urban or what was urban, small cities once packed with families who depended on steel mills and industry, both long gone, so the entire east end of Pittsburgh is populated with those who couldn't afford to leave and the few oldies who loved their homes too much to go. It's dismal and the opposite of that too. You've never seen beauty until you've seen a place that was but still is to the people who stayed.

Pittsburgh isn't New York. We built it.

I read that on the t-shirt of an old guy buying a newspaper.

The t-shirt was probably made in China.

History holds value but to be practical for most people's lives, it needs to be monetized. Here was a steel mill. It's dead now. Give us twenty-five dollars and we'll take you on the tour. Look at the work our dads burned through and the brick houses our mothers raised us in. Please deposit additional dollar bills to hear us weep.

Berryman says, "Where the fuck are we?"

"The Electric Valley," I say.

"I don't know where that is," Berryman says, "but that's the best name ever."

"It's pretty great," I say. "We're going to turn onto Electric Avenue soon."

Berryman says, "God, this whole place is so fucking gritty."

We pass the Hollywood Showbar and pick up Route 30 right by Vincent's Pizza, the best pizza around, where a medium pie will stuff two fat guys easily, eights slices glorious with bubbly crust and pepperoni grease. I switch lanes. I weave back. Every light flips red and stops us until we catch the Parkway, the fastest route into the city, but it's packed, rush hour going both ways, so we hop and dip around and through neighborhoods, the edge of Squirrel Hill, the tip of Greenfield, over the bridge into Oakland with students from four universities bouncing through crosswalks without looking up, little ballcap wearers and short-skirt skippers borrowing money to study with adjunct teachers who can't make a living.

Then Berryman realizes where we are and says, "This is too crowded."

I point and Berryman steers and we circle back and dip under the Parkway overpass and ride Second Avenue along the river until we reach the jail.

A huge building of red brick and concrete and impenetrable glass stacked to the sky, the jail overlooks a walking trail and the Monongahela River where barges still move coal. Yachters come out all weekend in the summer to float on the Mon and be obnoxious and, beyond that, the Southside where City Books stood and where Jack's Bar still stands, a beautiful dive-y drinking establishment open every day of the year and made for me and you.

There, on a concrete bench, beneath a jagged pyramid of gray bricks and a sign identifying the jail for what and where it is, sits Lawrence Riggins, who stands and moves towards Berryman's car, a car he's never seen before but somehow knows.

Lawrence Riggins wears jeans and a white tank top.

He looks exactly like Lawrence Riggins if Lawrence Riggins had eaten himself. Rig's arms and chest are still huge and solid but the gut is enormous, a globe the size of a flooded city. His head is shaved. His face is not. He looks like Shel Silverstein, the famous children's author who also wrote dirty country songs, if Shel Silverstein would have given up songwriting and kiddie lit to slam weights in a gym and drink dark beer between massive bites of steak.

I climb from the car.

Berryman says, "Should I get out?"

"Hush, Berryman," I say. "This man is my friend."

"I thought he was your mentor."

"I just said: hush."

I step on the sidewalk and walk toward the jail.

Rig says, "Lawrence Riggins is sure as shit happy to see you, you skinny little bastard. You look like you could wrestle 154. I eat fish sandwiches bigger than you."

I say, "Nothing could be finer than to see a man walk from prison with his sense of humor still intact."

"Prison?" Rig says. "That's a fucking jail, dumbass," and he lifts me in a bear hug meant to love and crush my bones.

I give him a big kiss on his shiny black forehead.

He puts me down and pulls me to his side like a pet. We turn toward the car and Berryman leans against the driver's-side door, assuming what would be a tough guy stance for a man with an MFA in poetry from Yale.

Rig says, "You got a driver? You a fancy fucker now," and he laughs.

Turtle Creek and Points East

We do not drive to Johnstown where Rig lives and where his father lives and where his wife and children lived until two weeks ago when his wife decided to move to Miami to be closer to her family, which devastated Rig completely.

"To see your wife scared of you when all you did is slap around the refrigerator a little bit, it's a very sad realization. Was I pissed? Yeah, I was pissed. But we leaking money like a sieve, how can I not be pissed. My wife comes from money. She don't work. She has a MBA she never used. She thinks the man should provide. Maybe the man should provide. I'd provide if I could. I like being the provider. I am the provider. But Rig needs better work. Rig ain't an athlete anymore. His executive status is gone. I'm throwing boxes for UPS at night and managing the stockroom of a grocery store during the day and, frankly, fucking up both. Understand?"

"I think so," I say.

"You don't," Rig says, "but that's okay. You too polite to understand. I know you come from a single mom and I was always impressed you turned out so well. My dad is an alcoholic but he was around. Still around. I see what that means as I get older. It's important to be there, even if you a fuck-up. I hope to do better by my own kids. Your mom done right by you."

To be less polite, assuming I am supposed to be less polite, I say, "You played pro football. You were an all-pro for a couple years. That's millions of dollars."

"Right," Rig says, laughing. "You would think so."

We share the backseat, the hump between us. I keep meaning to introduce Berryman, to explain that he is not actually my chauffeur, but Rig talks so much and with such force, and about such important things, any interruption would be a squeak, a flashing headlight against his river of darkness. Berryman has the rearview mirror on us, listening intensely, maybe excited but maybe scared. Maybe confused. Berryman knows rich people who tumble down then get help and somehow stand up and still stay rich. Berryman's sister is a drug addict and she floats in and out of rehab but she also sometimes lives in Paris and sometimes works in the fashion industry doing fashion-industry stuff, taking photographs, being photographed. Very few people I know or have ever known are rich. The few people that I know who were rich fucked up when they had money and lost it forever, a steady trickle of cash that floated them back to the class they came from or lower. Those of us without serious money are not prepared for serious money. The lucky few who climb or fall up see it as a vacation and understand the inevitable return flight from the fancy hotel and gourmet food to the home with the busted water heater and off-brand boxes of cereal.

Luxury does not last.

Misery does.

To believe otherwise would make us traitors against all we see and know.

Right now we drive towards Turtle Creek, another tumbledown neighborhood east of Pittsburgh and west of the Allegheny Mountains that makes the news for its heroin problem and lack of jobs instead of its ability to survive economic depression and seasonal floods and still exist. For years, for decades, Turtle Creek was a Westinghouse town, same as Wilmerding and Wall, a place that took its namesake's ideas about electricity and motion and turned those into products the world could use. Now Turtle Creek has a good pizza place and a couple huge stone churches with rotting wooden windows and a high school, Woodland Hills, that somehow manages to grow the occasional pro football player. The town is filled with hundreds of citizens doing their best, same as better areas, same as worse.

Berryman says, "Am I still going the right direction?"

"Doing great," Rig says, and reaches up and pats Berryman's shoulder. "You know this place at all?"

"I'm from Jersey," Berryman says.

"I'm sorry to hear that," Rig says, and laughs.

Houses nearly leaning against other houses pass by like clouds, like rows of sky, so the ones collapsing look like country decorations next to the ones with new flowers filling up planters and fresh-cut grass dusted across their front walks. It is, like so much of Western Pennsylvania, both a neighborhood on a mountain and a neighborhood in the shadow of a mountain, hills and valleys, green and concrete, the basketball court beneath the dirt trail that cuts through the trees and leads to either a shopping mall or the old man who lives in the shack and hopes you trespass because he loves to pump his shotgun and point the barrel.

Berryman says, "Is Johnstown near here?"

Rig says, "You really are from Jersey."

We pass the WolvArena, a new stadium where the high school teams play football and soccer and where the cheerleaders build human pyramids their relatives can applaud while slugging hot chocolate and remembering their own athletic glory. We stop at the lights by the Rite Aid, the closest thing there is to a grocery market, save the Dollar Store that jacks up toilet paper prices and gouges for potato chips.

Across the road sits the police station.

Across the intersection sits the old Turtle Creek High School, which is now Woodland Hills Academy, an alternative school, I think. I'm not sure if alternative means kids who hate school and lash out and punch each other or if alternative means super-smart kids who walk all over their peers' grades and need to be challenged. It's all so confusing, how and where kids end up. Maybe the alternative school is private or a charter school, which may be different words for the same thing. I read articles in the newspaper and forget what I read because I'm single and too confused by romance to make a baby. I'd be a nervous parent anyway, wondering what the best education for my family was and how to afford it. My children would sit quietly at the bus stop, weeping. Dad did the wrong thing again. Dad never knows what to do.

Forget that.

Pay no attention to my imagined family.

I'll be your tour guide from here on out.

Beyond that sits the Post Office, one of the oldest in the country, which houses art from the 1930s, government-funded art designed to give people work. A wood relief of Indians and pilgrims signing a treaty or having just signed a treaty or just not slaughtering each other hangs above the checkout counter. Years ago I did repair work on the Westinghouse Bridge up the road so I would spend my downtime eating and walking and sometimes drinking in the towns of the Electric Valley, an alley of industry cut through the earth then abandoned. When my job stabilized, I moved up the hill.

Time blurs everything, history and my memory, and what remains are old buildings of solid brick and rotten lumber, the Greek Festival at Olympia Hall in the summer, the Hollywood Show Bar year round, churches abandoned and churches hanging on with old air conditioners in their windows, closed factories and factories renovated into coffee shops and fitness centers, people taking busses up the hill to their jobs at Walmart and Little Caesar's Pizza. I used to eat at a Chinese restaurant inside a two-story house in Chalfant. No sign out front. No advertisements. The owners cooked with vegetables grown in their own backyard. They barely spoke English but I'd drink a Coors Light and smile at the woman while she gathered up my almond chicken. Beyond all this sits the atom smasher, which used to smash atoms, something I still don't understand. We were considered great for it, smashing atoms, it was a revolution in energy or bombs or both or maybe a unique way to power washers and dryers and color TVs. The atom smasher was industry then history, a tool then a monument, an epic story old men passed around bars and still do. Their wives explained it to their children around the dinner table and their children bragged about it to their friends. But the atom smasher may have been taken down and dragged away while we were busy working other jobs. It may be condos up there now.

Rig says, "Rig appreciates you and your driver coming out to get me."

"It's great to meet you," Berryman says, assuming the role of driver.

"Berryman used to wrestle," I say. "I told him you pinned Kurt Angle."

Rig reaches for Berryman and touches his cheek gently then rubs like he's petting a cat and says, "Your skin too soft for wrestling."

Berryman, embarrassed, says, "It was rougher when I was young."

Rig says, "Rig likes you, Berryman. You a good driver and you was a wrestler. Wrestling is a spiritual occupation for those of us who treat it as such. Zeus wrestled. Did you know that? I'da beat his ass anywhere—Greece, Heaven, Johnstown. You alright, Berryman."

"Thanks," Berryman says.

Rig says, "All the bad shit that happened to Rig happened when I wasn't wrestling. Ain't no one gets rich on wrestling. Make a living maybe, but never rich. You do it because you love it. Rig loved it. Rig loves it still. He'd love to be on the mat again." Rig looks out the window. He says, "Sellick loved it, little skinny bastard, but no one loved it like Rig. Ain't that right, Sellick? Rig loved it the most?"

"You were the best," I say, an undeniable truth.

Rig says, "Rig knows what he's talking about."

Years ago, after lightning and thundering his way out of pro football, when Rig would come around UPJ and help the wrestling coach, he used to speak of himself in the third person as a joke, when he wanted to brag about his successes or make light of one of his transgressions, when he wanted to speak of the athlete in the newspaper who was only a fraction of the real person in the world. Can you believe Rig beat Kurt Angle and now Kurt Angle is a millionaire? Or: can you believe Rig had a multi-million-dollar contract from the Pittsburgh Steelers, his very own hometown team? Or: can you believe Rig still tossing young heavyweights around?

Now he flops between first and third person and I'm not sure why or if he's conscious of his flopping. It makes him sound a little crazy or damaged, which is probably unavoidable, considering the years he spent on mats and football fields, but I keep hoping the third-person talk is a tick, an embarrassed joke, a way to cover the awkwardness of being in jail and having an old friend pull you out by the sleeve.

"What's in Pitcairn?" I say.

"Ain't nothing in Pitcairn now," Rig says. "Used to be mill town."

"I mean, why are we taking you there? I know Pitcairn."

"Work, what else," Rig says. "I got to see a guy about a job."

Around And Not Around Rig

I want to ask Rig what he did to get arrested but I can't ask, not because he wouldn't answer but because he would. He moves and speaks like a man whose mom cracked out and whose father stayed and struggled and still drinks his liver into a death sentence. His entryway to success has always been: look at where I've been, look at the wreck I stepped from. But that only works for so many years, for so many mistakes, for so many successes, then it reverses and cuts more than it heals. Your childhood will get you a pass into adulthood. Your arrest record will not lead you safely into old age. Rig is indifferent to those facts or oblivious. No one told him to be less honest. No one told him the world is not a mirror, the world is not a window you pose in front of, the world is not a loudspeaker to shout through.

No one told him to save some of himself for himself.

No one told him to shut the fuck up.

No one tells him to shut the fuck up.

I love to be around Rig when I'm not around him.

I love to be around Rig when I am around him.

Then I am around him and I don't want to be around him.

Then I am around him and his endless talking makes me want to sew my ears shut with a needle and thread to block his endless barrage of story, of success and failure.

Then I leave.

Then I worry I should be around him, that he needs a friend to talk to.

Then I remember he will talk to anyone.

Then I am fine and go back to focusing on my own troubles and joys.

When he was still with the Steelers, Rig dipped into rehab one winter after the season ended. His quest for sobriety made a couple lines in the sports section. Back then, before the internet became a monster, reporters would still allow athletes and celebrities to have personal lives. No arrest, no story. The next season started and the narrative was the same as the previous season, how Lawrence Riggins, a wrestler with no college football experience, had been voted all-pro and was now becoming the best player in the league at his position. The season ended. Rig went to the pro bowl. The pro bowl ended. Rig checked back into rehab.

Rig checked out of rehab.
Rig checked into rehab.
Rig checked out of rehab.
Into rehab.
Out of rehab.
Rig checked out of football.
Rig checked into punching strangers who wanted to know why he quit football.
Rig disappeared as much as a man of his size and profile can disappear.
A few guys from the wrestling team passed word around like gossip, concerned but showy, a subtle dig in every line. You hear about Rig? He drank thirty-seven vodkas at The Shore Bar on the Southside. Johnny Picollo saw it all. You hear about Rig? Jamal Jackson saw Rig at McDonalds at midnight, eating 15 double cheeseburgers. DeShaun Watson tried to hire Rig to work for his waste removal company and fucking Rig showed up with a $1500 Rimowa suitcase and wanted to live in his house. Rig wanted to borrow a hundred bucks. Rig wanted to borrow ten grand. Rig wanted. Rig needed. What a wrestler that Rig was but we all worry about the dude. So sad. Tragic. Then: what a recovery. Amazing. He paid back the five grand he owed. He showed up at my kid's wrestling match. Lucky to know him. Great dude. The greatest.
Everyone knew Rig drank too much and sometimes binged on drugs so the information became overwhelming. "Keep me in the loop," I told one guy then quit answering his calls.
I quit commenting on the group texts.
Then I started deleting before reading.
My jobs and finances and family required all of my emotional energy.
But people still reached out with gossip and concern.

Backwards Motorcycle

This is a truth.
I heard it from the gossip-and-concern gang then I heard it from Rig. During one stint in rehab Rig became frustrated or bored or the de-

sire to drink overrode the desire not to drink so he walked out again and got on his motorcycle and drove to a bar and ordered a beer and a whiskey. He did that all night, same order, beer and whiskey. He drank until he couldn't drink anymore then he did some blow with a stranger who recognized Rig as a Steeler and wanted to be his friend, the friend of a professional athlete, the most famous friend you can have in a city that is not New York or Hollywood, so the new friend kept offering blow and Rig kept doing blow so he could drink more because it was always about drinking, even success as an athlete was about drinking, about earning a drink, about winning championships and making money so you could justify waking up one morning and taking a break from all that greatness to get smashed. Rig drank until the bar closed, thanked his new drug buddy for the coke, then hopped on his motorcycle with intent to check himself back into rehab, mistake made, thirst quenched, start again, renew, get the greatness back.

But the motorcycle almost drove itself as he moved through the streets of Pittsburgh and he'd never really ridden around the city, not this late at night, not with so little traffic, not with so many green lights, not with the bike steering the man and so effortlessly.

Rehab could wait.

It was one of life's constants: the sun, the moon, a counselor telling you not to drink. Rig kept great health insurance and rehab loved health insurance, and what was an hour with the moon out and the engine set to roar.

He drove downtown and crossed over one bridge to the North Shore and took another bridge back to downtown, yellow metal to yellow metal, and took another bridge, more yellow metal, over the same river, the Allegheny, and ended up in Millville, which was a couple main streets, one coming and one going.

He knew Millvale.

He ate at Pamela's Diner sometimes when he wanted to be alone. He'd go late in the morning and order an omelet and the pancakes. The pancakes were not fluffy like the pancakes his dad made when Rig was growing up but more like crepes, only not that skinny, just huge circles, crispy around the edges, yellow hill of butter melting in the middle of the top cake. He'd douse them in maple syrup and pour syrup over his sausage too.

Now he turned around and headed to Troy Hill which is where rich women lived, he thought, he couldn't remember, maybe he'd heard that on the news, maybe it was rich families, so he passed through then circled back and grabbed the 31st Street Bridge and ended up in the Strip, which made Rig hungry. Rig was always hungry. Beer made Rig hungry. Being sober made Rig hungry. Blowing through a street lined up to sell food made Rig starved. He could feel the food behind the glass and wooden storefronts, Peppi's with their steak sandwiches on the cloud buns, the shitty pizza place that was really pretty decent after a couple beers, all those Italian stores with their buckets of parmesan cheese and little stands selling meatball sandwiches and hot sausage sandwiches. Other stands, away from the Italian stores, sold street Chinese food. He passed the little taco place, an empty metal cart at this hour, and the other Chinese place with the better eggrolls, and he remembered how the Chinese woman running the stand kept them hot on a grill but not burned. Rig realized he was driving the wrong way on a one-way street, but so what, and how late, and he kept on. He passed a butcher shop, sticks of meat hanging on ropes in the window. Could you sell meat like that, meat not in a refrigerator? He guessed you could. He guessed he'd bought some during one of his benders. He finally swerved onto a side street by Klavon's Ice Cream where he once ate three Mallow Cup sundaes with the same spoon and wanted to order a fourth but it was becoming an attraction, big man on a little stool.

He downshifted to third then up to fifth gear and revved the throttle until he made Bloomfield, an old neighborhood where the Italians and the Poles still lived, all aging now, all fat and getting toothless, but very few black folk, not that it mattered, he was Rig, pro athlete. People only worried about black people when they were poor and by worried Rig meant terrorized. Fucking white people. He hated them but they were okay. Fine. Even sweet. Lots of good ones. Always sold the best drugs. Helpful as hell. But scared. Always scared. Middle class—he hoped to never end up there. Down or up. Preferably up. Way up. That's why he liked money: no one fucked with you.

He cruised through Shadyside.

Shadyside was a shitshow of purse shops and fancy clothing stores.

He throttled on to Oakland with all its universities but the students were sleeping and the bike revved and swerved without command and Rig allowed the engine to steer him. He cranked the throttle then took his hands off the handlebars. He saw the Cathedral of Learning, a tower of dirty brown bricks and steps and steeple, like a church stacked on top of a church on top of twenty churches. Kids learned in there. They took classes. Rig was proud to have gotten his degree all those years ago, first in his family to graduate college, first in his family to play professional football. First in his family to make a million dollars.

How many families can say that?

He stopped for a second and considered his options, first being rehab, second being the Cathedral steps and his motorcycle, rubber on concrete, which seemed a more manageable choice than a counselor asking, "Why do you drink?" He held the clutch and backed his bike to the edge of the concrete, rear tire in the grass. He revved the engine. When life refuses to be challenging, you invent your own challenges. He stepped through the gears until the bike was in neutral. He took his helmet off and put it on backwards so he could only see darkness. It was not a comfortable feeling, blackness in your eyes, the engine in your ears, egging you on.

He took the helmet off and put it back on so he could see through the visor.

The Cathedral, churches stacked on churches.

Who the fuck thought that was a good idea?

He took his helmet off and put it back on, visor in the back, blindness up front.

You live to be great.

You have to live to be great.

And fuck it so he hit the throttle and popped the bike in gear and shifted again so his wheel popped off the ground as he raced forward and he leaned back and pretty soon the steps were underneath him, bouncing him skyward, bouncing him towards the landing by the main door, a place to park and reflect, to consider the accomplishment of racing blind on two wheels. No one had ever driven a motorcycle without sight up the steps of a college building and succeeded.

Then he wasn't bouncing, he was flying, backwards or sideways or tumbling, the bike hit something, some beam or bench or ashtray made of stone, and Rig released the handlebars and gained more air and passed over the top railing of the Cathedral, one flight up, arms out, gravity gone, how he'd always wanted to feel, weightless, then back down to earth, to the fountain beneath the steps, water everywhere, blood in the water, Rig's blood, most of it from his broken wrist where the bone pushed through, not that he noticed, exactly, it was a feeling, one of completion.

He did a hard thing: backwards helmet, concrete steps, still alive.

He woke up in an ambulance then again in the ICU with a tube up his nose.

That made the news.

That made all the papers.

The Good People of Pitcairn

We cruise along the main street, Broadway Boulevard, which leads to the Tri Boro Expressway, the state highway that knifes through all the rust of old industry and follows the creeks that flow into the Monongahela River. We slow and look for parking. Cars block the street, waiting in line at the two-pump gas station. A tow truck flashes its lights, trying to leave the wrecking yard. The second-hand store is closed, gate up. Tenants linger on the front stoops of apartments that open onto the sidewalk. One woman has a collection of potted ferns outside her front door. Berryman crosses lanes and pulls up at the curb, facing the wrong direction, though half the cars face the wrong direction. He pops his Ford into park. The sidewalk jumps with people, kids in strollers, old men talking. Bar doors swing open and closed. Signs advertising beer specials hang in the windows. Half a block down and around the bend on the right, the community center advertises an old Disney film, *Finding Nemo,* playing for free. A few families linger outside waiting for the doors to open and the show to start.

Rig climbs out and I follow through the same door so we both end up on the sidewalk. He adjusts his tanktop so it covers his gut and makes his chest look even huger, the pecs hanging out the side like engines to power his arms.

Berryman rolls down his window and says, "Should I just wait here?"

and looks like a man who wants to answer his own question.

Rig says, "You keep that car running."

I look at Rig and hope this is not a robbery, that he is not Clyde and I am not Bonnie and we are not about to treat a bar like a bank and make off with the loot.

Rig looks around and says, "This town got class."

"A lot of people out tonight," I say.

"That free movie for kids down the street there," Rig says, "that would have made a big deal to a kid like me."

I nod yeah, me too, but I'm lying.

My mom made sure I saw movies.

She made sure I heard music and went to museums.

She hated the PTA. She hated mothers who thought staying home with your kid was a career. She hated volunteer moms. She laughed at fathers who coached baseball with any sort of seriousness. She once threatened to punch another mother who complained about not having enough time to get her nails done. Joanie dismissed it all but she dragged me anywhere she thought I could learn from, where she thought we could learn, cultural places, Shakespeare plays, concerts in the park, craft shows, flea markets with men selling their woodwork, not because she cared about culture but because she knew it was collateral, that you could buy status with it.

They couldn't fuck you over if you knew their shit.

So we learned their shit.

Somewhere in there I fell in love with all of it.

STILL OUTSIDE THE BAR

I ask Rig if he feels okay. He puts his hands on his waist and turns like he needs to crack something then makes a full circle with his upper body.

I say, "You look nervous."

"Nah," Rig says. "I'm tight, that's all. I hate sleeping standing up in jail." He says, "This won't take long," but he doesn't move.

A guy in an electric wheelchair, with no lower legs, rolls after a woman in a tanktop, her boobs bubbling out, her ass hanging from her yellow cotton shorts. She must be twenty-five. He must be fifty. His head is wrapped tight in a blue scarf and his stumps are stuffed in tight white stockings which stick out like pillows from his cutoff jeans. He looks pissed, using his right hand to steer a joystick and move through the crowd.

"You took my fucking money," he says, still rolling. "I paid ten dollars to see those titties. Get the fuck back here."

Suddenly she turns and says, "You saw these titties. You see them now, Francis. Look, titties," and she bends over a little and shakes her chest. "See them, Francis? Titties. Great big mounds of joy. And what the fuck kind of pussy name is Francis, Francis?"

"For ten bucks, you should pull them out," he says, calmer, more business-like. "I thought you was gonna pull you tubetop down."

"For ten bucks?" she says.

"Francis was my grandpa's name. He fought in World War II."

Francis turns his billyclub eyes into pools of brown.

The woman shakes her head and sighs.

She says, "Okay." She bends at the waist, still taller than the wheelchair. She says, "Here's you some titties, Francis whose grandpa fought in World War II," and she pulls down her tanktop so her beautiful brown tits fall out, one then the other as she stretches and lowers the green fabric of her shirt, her nipples somewhere between soft and hard, her hands holding them in place, captured titties, perfect titties, then the titties disappear just as quickly, one then the other, as she loads them back into her top. She stands straight and adjusts everything with a jiggle and says, "Tell your grandpa I appreciate his service."

Francis says, "My grandpa is dead."

"Thank him anyway," she says and turns and walks off, past a middle-aged woman leading her old mother into the local pharmacy, the middle-aged woman somehow holding the door and her mother by the elbow and her mother's cane in her other hand, as the mother focuses and tries to step up with her weak legs.

Rig says, "We arrived just in time."

Inside Shadowland

I'll admit it: Shadowland is a great name for a bar. Out in Hollywood or in New York, rich and seedy types would wear bowler hats and gingham dresses and gather here to discuss plans—movie-making, real estate, sports franchises—just to hear their own bluster.

Here in Pitcairn the bar is barely filled, an empty train car with a row of red vinyl stools along a kicked-up wooden bar, another row of tables against the wall. It's not a dive, just old, the last breath of class. The bar ends with two bathrooms and double metal swinging doors that open into what could be a kitchen or a graveyard. Things are clean. No spilled beer, no peanut shells, no piss smell wafting from the corner. The light is mostly big screen TVs, three of them crammed behind the bar and two others hanging from the ceiling near the tables. The few decorations are black-and-white photos of steam trains nailed to the walls in frames made from old model railroad tracks. The walls are dark wood. The floor is dark wood and scuffed.

Two guys sit in the far corner of the bar like this place is their office, like they are about to interview new employees. Both guys are white, one skinny and young and dressed in a Cleveland Cavaliers basketball jersey, the other older and large and dressed in construction clothes, jeans and flannel and paint-splattered boots. I can smell drugs, metaphorically, like this place is an alley away from a crack deal. I've done drugs. I like drugs. I understand the emotional grace of having to get fucked-up, that retreat. But everything around drugs snaps my heart to attention.

Rig says, "Get you a drink at the bar, a beer or something," and he nudges me with his shoulder in case I don't understand.

But I understand and instantly move sideways.

He walks straight to the white guys.

I pull out a stool and sit.

The bartender puts down the TV remote and walks toward me.

I check her.

I check the door.

I check the tinted front window.

I check the fire exit.

I check my feet to make sure they've not run away.

I have worked relentlessly my whole life to stay out of both debt and trouble and it was only luck, meaning a newspaper article about my western novels and a generous community college president, that allows me to live the way I do, which I love, being a professor is the greatest, I love teaching, I love writing, I love reading, I love students, I love napping, I love summers off, I love helping my mom with my extra time, I love lunch with my Nona. I have an office, I have a computer in my office, I love the campus library, I love the campus bookstore, I have a kind boss who went to an Ivy League school and hated it and I love her, I love that she runs 10Ks for charity, that she hired me because I had a trade and a degree, all of it, thank you, I am lucky and blessed and rewarded. But if a cop walks through the door of The Shadowland Lounge in five seconds or five minutes or however long we are going to be here, I will turn and point at Rig and his white buddies and say: that's them, officer, there're the dudes you want.

I am in it to win, same as every honest person, no matter how small the trophy.

The bartender says, "Please don't say water."

"Water with lemon?"

"You're kidding?"

"I am," I say.

She looks fifty, maybe forty, somewhere between, great face, beautiful smile, a black woman with curves and shoulder-length straight hair, light brown, almost blonde, sort of fake looking but good fake. She's dressed in nice business clothes, black skirt, white shirt, black sweater, low high heels, like she came from another job as a sales rep or a store manager, or maybe she owns this place and wants to combat the drug dealers with a nice professional look.

She says, "Place your order. Please make it alcoholic."

I say, "Can I get a Yuengling?"

She says, "Bucket of Yuenglings on sale for Happy Hour."

"Bucket of Yuenglings," I say. "Thanks."

The TVs play louder than Rig and his new friends speak so I quit trying to listen to things I don't want to hear anyway. The bartender brings me four green bottles of beer in a bucket packed with ice, all the tops already popped.

She says, "You want a tab?"

"I'll pay as I go," I say, and pull out my wallet.

"Eight bucks," she says.

"Two bucks a beer?" I say. "That's a good deal."

She says, "They don't call it sad and ugly hour," and laughs.

I hand her a ten from my wallet and say, "Keep it, thanks."

"You been in here before?"

"Just passing through."

"You a cop?"

"Not at all."

"You know if I ask you if you a cop, you have to answer honestly if you a cop."

"Still not a cop," I say.

"You look like a cop. You're skinny and fast looking. You vote Republican?"

"Never in my life. Raised by a single mom who loved Jimmy Carter and had a crush on Bill Clinton. Hung an Obama sign in my front window. Support the assassination of Donald Trump but would deny having ever said that. I'm a card-carrying member of the United Steelworker's Union. Boilermaker by heart."

"You a steelworker?"

"Welder."

"Welder?"

"I was for years."

She says, "Why'd you quit? That's a good job."

"I got a job teaching college."

"They teach welding at college?"

"They do but I teach writing."

She looks at me big-eyed like I could be lying.

"It's the truth," I say.

She says, "How'd you jump that spot in line?"

"It's sort of confusing."

"I'm open to explanations."

I say, "I wrote western novels while I was welding. Before that, I actually went to college for writing. My degree is in English. But I couldn't get a job with an English degree so I went back to the community college and learned how to weld and got certified and went to work on bridges. Then the cowboy books. Then teaching."

"A writer of western novels, no shit? You ever see that *Deadwood* on HBO?"

"Only every single episode," I say.

"Those cowboys know how to cuss," she says.

"Al Swearengen," I say, meaning the bartender on the show, a mean bastard with a poet's mouth and a boot knife and a disdain for authority.

She says, "Al to the motherfucking Swearengen, oh!"

We both throw up are arms and wave it out and laugh.

I pull a beer from the ice.

She says, "I'll be back to talk to you, cowboy writer, after I see if your buckethead friend and the looney twosome need some drinks." She walks toward Rig and the others and she says in their direction, "Please none y'all be water drinkers. I'm not walking down the bar for that, gentlemen. Understand?"

THE MYSTERIES OF RUSSIA

The bartender loves mystery novels. She pulls one from behind the bar, a Tony Hillerman, some Indian feathers and a pick-up truck on the cover.

"I've always meant to read him," I say.

"He's good. He's a white dude but it's mostly Indian shit. I always meant to go out west and never had the time. He makes me feel like I been there."

"Russia," I say.

"Russia what?"

I say, "You want to go out west. I always wanted to visit Russia. I read a lot of Russian novels when I was younger and got serious about reading. It was just a farce at first. I thought people would think I was smart if I read the Russians but then I started loving what I was reading. Now I'd love to go to Russia."

"Russia sounds cold," she says. "You see that documentary about how they used to make all their Olympic athletes take steroids? They didn't even tell them they were steroids," and she goes into a Russian accent and says, "Yah, here's your breakfast vitamins, open vide," and she stops to laugh at herself. She says, "That was a bad place. They even gave the girl athletes steroids. Little fifteen-year-old girls be having beards and stuff, losing their periods. Why would you want to go to Russia? Putin is a motherfucker. That dude don't read. He kills people. Is it still a bad place? It has to be. It's hard to turn a battleship around."

"It is still a bad place," I say, and imagine Vladimir Putin, president again, president always, shirtless, on a horse, off a horse, still shirtless, holding a machine gun, and how their journalists randomly get murdered for trying to write the truth, which was maybe my point to begin with, what I love about Russia, writers telling the truth in the face of imminent death, how Isaac Babel, a gentle and bespectacled Jewish journalist, risked his life to ride with the Russian Cavalry when they were fighting the Poles, and how he changed that experience into lines like, "The orange sun is rolling across the sky like a severed head," and, "Her sponge cakes had the aroma of crucifixion." When I think of Russia, I mean the country inside the man and not the man inside the country. When the secret police came for Babel, to arrest him on trumped-up charges, knowing he was going to be tortured and forced to confess, he turned to his wife and said, "They did not let me finish," meaning the stories and plays and screenplays on his desk. Babel was Jewish and Russian and a writer and a man but not in any order or with any consistency, just a constellation of moving stars, shining whatever was needed, whenever it was needed, a writer here, a Jew there, a Russian on the front lines of a war, then death snuffed out his entire universe because he thought and believed and tried to tell the truth.

That's the country I'd like to visit: Isaac Babel's heart.

The bartender says, "You just drifted off to a bad place. I seen it in your eyes. I didn't mean to criticize your Russia. I love Florida and it's the worst place in America. I had a cousin pulled over by a cop down there and the cop tazed him for no good reason. Black cop, too. His white partner standing by, laughing."

"Black police showing off for the white cop," I say.

She leans back and smiles and says, "You one of those white boys listen to Ice Cube and wear your ballcap with a straight brim?"

"I'm one of those white men approaching middle-aged who listen to NWA while they jog laps around the high school track at night so they can sleep better."

"I'll take it," she says. "Now you drink your beer for a while. I'll leave you alone. Then you buy some more beer. Buy a lot of beer."

"Thanks for the conversation," I say. "I'm going to finally read a Tony

Hillerman novel because of you."

"You come back soon," she says, "and I'll give you this one I'm about to finish."

"I'll do that," I say, and she walks off and I immediately try to hear Rig and his cronies over the TV and I do but it's mostly fake laughter.

BUCKETHEAD

Rig walks up behind me and says, "We done."

I'm on my last Yuengling, half a bottle left, staring at ESPN on a TV screen the size of a mattress hanging above the bar. The bartender thought she was bothering me by talking about books, that she was messing with my drinking, so she walked back to her stool and novel and ironic glass of lemon water, but I wish she would look up from her mystery novel and talk to me some more about reading before I have to leave.

Rig says, "Nevermind. I have to piss first."

"You do that," I say.

The bartender is a statue of beauty, curves on a stool, with her eyes pacing words across the page, probably dreaming about South Dakota or North Dakota or wherever the hell Tony Hillerman novels are set. I could talk books for hours, the way some people gamble, the way some people lift weights until their muscles roll like boulders.

I am also scared to be here.

Drugs.

Cronies.

Rig comes back from the bathroom.

He takes my bottle.

He checks to see how full then chugs the remainder.

"We in a hurry now?" I say.

"Not really," Rig says, "but yes."

I wave to get the bartender's attention.

She looks up and says, "You need a bucket?"

I say, "Thanks for talking and the book recommendation."

She says, "Come back again and buy some more beers. I'll have this Tony Hillerman novel waiting for you."

"I will," I say, and mean it.

Rig says, "Thank you, ma'am."

She says, "You bet, buckethead," and goes back to her book.

Rig and I step into the street.

Rig says, "She called me buckethead."

I say, "She meant it as a compliment."

Rig says, "The fuck she did," but sad, not angry.

Berryman, reclined in the front seat to be invisible but with the window still down to eavesdrop, pops up and says, "I thought you two were lost in there."

"Not yet," Rig says. "We gonna be one more minute. Stay right there."

Before Berryman can respond, Rig takes me by the hand like I'm his girlfriend at a carnival and leads me half a block up the street like we're walking to the Ferris wheel.

Then we duck into the alley.

The alley is dark, all the streetlights but one busted to black. A rusted-out yellow car, matching the dirty yellow bricks of the building and looking like it has not moved in a decade, sits near a dumpster. Garbage cans line up like clumsy soldiers. Rig walks with purpose. I stand and wait. The alley is too small for another car so a cop would have to be on foot and I'm white and Rig is black and I'm in good shape and Rig is not so I think I could run and not get caught while they fired a taser into Rig, which is such a terrible thought on such an uncomfortable day, a good deed gone south, Rig following his addictions like a map, me constantly worried about me, wanting to preserve my life as it is now. He reaches for a garbage can, the lid rattling like a cymbal as he removes it. Without warning my throat clinches and I cough. Rig reaches inside the can, adjusts something, and pulls out a backpack. He drops the lid to the busted-up asphalt with a clang and turns and starts walking back to me.

"I don't want to get arrested," I say, almost in a whisper.

Rig says, "No one is getting arrested, least of all you and Rig," and he walks past me and touches my back so I know to follow.

In the car Berryman says, "You didn't have a backpack before," and he sounds like a man talking to a shooter who's firing slow-moving bullets, like he can convince the shooter to stop or the bullets to fire themselves back into the gun. He says, "You didn't have a backpack when we picked you up and you didn't have a backpack when you came out of the bar and now you have a backpack. That's a new backpack. From that alley."

Rig and I buckle up.

Berryman says, "No one saw you. You can put the backpack back wherever it came from. Just walk it out of my car and back around the corner." He says, "Please."

Rig adjusts his seatbelt and gets comfortable.

Berryman says, "Please. I'm asking nicely."

"How else would you ask?" Rig says, gruff, very gruff.

"Calm down, Berryman," I say. "And drive."

Berryman says, "I am calm," and his voice warbles like his mouth might tip over.

"Good," I say, "then drive."

Berryman puts the car in drive and turns the steering wheel.

I turn and look for cars.

I say, "It's clear."

Berryman looks at me in the rearview and says, "He didn't have a backpack before. That's all I'm saying."

Then Rig says to me, "Please tell your driver to shut the fuck up."

I don't say anything and Berryman pulls away.

Sally Forth, Berryman

We pull—unarrested—into the parking lot of the community college. The excitement in the alleyway and the ride back to campus calmed me in an unnatural way, making me exhausted instead of antsy. Berryman breathes like his lungs are out of jail after months of inhaling concrete and metal bars. Rig neither speaks nor moves. He looks like Buddha. Or: he looks like a very large but exhausted man. Berryman reaches for the glove compartment and pulls out a small container of wipes. The sound of his hand popping the plastic lid ripples through the car.

I say, "Berryman, why do you have baby wipes in your glove compartment?"

Berryman, pulling out a wipe, says, "They're not baby wipes, they're for greasy skin. I get oily during the day or when I'm nervous."

Rig says, "Sorry I made you nervous," and sounds sincere.

Berryman says, "It was me, not you."

Rig says, "Please."

Berryman starts to wipe his nose then goes around his mouth and chin.

"Keep those pimples away," I say.

Berryman says, "I have habits."

He finishes with his oily skin and puts the wipes back in the glovebox.

I lean the side of my head against the window.

I know Berryman thinks he has completed some magical task and earned the crown and is now free to roam the hinterlands of poetry but I'm tired and I have to prep for tomorrow and I'm sick of Rig, as much as I love him, as much as I want him to be safe and to succeed. I pull my face from the window and turn back to the car with decisions rattling my mind. Rig clutches the backpack to his chest like it's his child, a thing to be nurtured. I'm assuming the backpack holds more drugs than I've ever done or even seen.

Berryman kills the engine and turns to us, elbow coming between the front seats.

He says, "Everyone okay?"

Rig says, "I apologize for lashing out back there, Mr. Berryman."

"I panicked," Berryman says. "It's on me."

Rig says, "I shouldn't use language like that. You were doing me a solid."

"Berryman," I say. "I still have to prep for tomorrow. Can you deliver my good friend Lawrence Riggins back to his home in Johnstown? Thank you, I appreciate it. You'll love Johnstown. It's got a lot of grit. You two'll be pals."

Berryman says, "It's dark out."

Rig doesn't say anything.

He breathes deep and slides down in the seat.

I wait.

Berryman looks at me, his eyes little ballbats swinging for my fence.

Rig's eyes are closed.

He rasps out his breaths.

I say, "Rig, can I suggest you put that backpack in the trunk? Then maybe you move up front and grab a couple winks while Berryman ferries you home."

I say, "Berryman, you're a soldier."

I say, "Rig, call me. I don't want to get arrested but I want to help. We can figure that out, I bet. Never forget that you beat Kurt Angle and played right guard for the Pittsburgh Steelers and that you're a great man with an unbelievable work ethic. And a little bit of an asshole. And a madman. But good hearted. I'm glad you called."

I say, "Berryman, you're a good driver."

I say, "I will see you both soon."

Rig opens his eyes and says, "Rig feels bad about this."

Berryman says, "I'm going to be honest and just say I'm scared. I'm not from Pennsylvania and I've never driven anywhere with more than a six pack and maybe two joints and that was in high school."

The parking lot is empty save for a motorcycle and a Dodge Charger colored like a bumblebee and the yellow-white moon reaching down with its cratered face.

I say, "Gentleman, I will leave it to you both to work out the details."

Outside, the cool air whips my face.

I double check for lingering students.

Then I unbutton my shirt and breathe in as much of the campus as I can fit in my nose.

Onward, Bookstore

Instead of heading home to prep, I drive to Monroeville and hit one of the few remaining Barnes and Noble bookstores in the area. I am in the mood to see that the stories I love and participate in barely exist in the marketplace. Confirming the world is both small and wrong often provides hope and, if not hope, motivation. I park and bolt inside. I ask one of the clerks what's selling in the New Literature section.

She says, "This," and cradles the book like it's a baby.

It's a novel about Iran, escaping Iran, something.

Iran must be in vogue.

My crazy student Brandon thinks so with his crazy one-page novel.

I skim the description on the back but it's vague and not well-written, not as perfect as the woman on the cover in a headscarf. I don't doubt this woman's plight, the character nor the atmosphere she was pulled from, but Americans have always been horrible about recognizing their own problems and deficiencies, how the needy somehow look needier abroad when they wear different clothes and have different skins. For more than sixty years, Americans have treated their own poor in literature the way they treat them in the street and in the rough neighborhoods: they avoid them, they step over them, they step on them and blame them for being in the way.

But this woman from Iran, well.

The blurb on the back cover reads, "Epic!"

It's six hundred pages long.

I open the book and read the first sentence in each paragraph.

The first three pages describe a mountain or a desert or a mountain in the desert, I can't tell. I flip back the pages and read more closely. A lot of rocks and sand are being described in a way that is meant to convey both beauty and harshness.

I turn the book back over.

Another reviewer describes the book as, "A wonder!"

The sales clerk, who is really a kid, a long-haired twenty-something woman in business-y clothes and sensible shoes, who probably doesn't realize she will be in poverty once her student loans come due and her parents ask her to please move out, stands by as I skim, waiting, excited, either genuinely enthusiastic about the novel or genuinely enthusiastic about a job that allows her to look at other novels and books of poems and plays and biographies of rock stars and stock them on shelves and sell them to the few people left in America who buy books.

"Looks good," I say.

"Right," she says. "I know."

I hand her the novel and say, "I'm looking for a book that deals with work or not being able to find work or just not having any money. Do you have anything like that? A novel?"

She considers my request and says, "That's going to take some thinking."

PART SEVEN

Class Is Class

I don't prep so I am unprepared for class.
On the syllabus it says we will be comparing and contrasting an Isaac Babel story with a piece of contemporary fiction. I'd said contemporary fiction because I hadn't decided what would be a good piece because the class had yet to enroll and I like to tailor the material to my students because sometimes I have lots of restaurant workers and sometimes students who work in retail sales and sometimes stay-at-home moms. It's important to show them that their lives can be material. It's not all hobbits and superheroes and terrorists, it's not all mobsters and cowboys and puppies, it's not all zombies.

But then Rig, but then jail, but then Pitcairn, but then distraction.

Last night, too tired to think, I decided to prep for class this morning over breakfast and coffee. This morning I slept in then jogged five miles.

Now I stand near the podium with a piece of chalk in my hand.

East Pittsburgh Downlow

"Did everyone read the Babel story?" I say.

They mostly nod yes.

"Okay," I say. "Keep it in your head for next class. I'll bring a handout of a contemporary story that we can compare and contrast it with. I really want to talk about the images in the Babel story and how the language is not necessarily what we would expect from soldiers. Maybe it will get us to think about the images and language we use in our own stories and how the lives we lead here in Western Pennsylvania might offer something that a lot of books need. Does that sound okay?"

They mostly nod yes.

Megan, my favorite student, my bartender, my crush, is not here.

Brandon, the writer of compressions, those one-page novels, is.

He looks ready to pounce, a not unusual look for him.

I keep thinking: Rig, Berryman, alleyway, drugs.

Even after a morning run, my brain and stomach pull and stretch with nerves, overthinking and overfeeling, bickering and upsetting each other. I'd like to have more to say to this class but I don't. It's like the mat herpes: something happens then I'm unable to act on something else. Even that comparison embarrasses me.

Brandon says, "The character names in the Babel story remind me of some of the fantasy stories I've been reading."

"Interesting," I say. "Save that for next week."

Discussion of a fantasy story would make my ears fall off.

I put the chalk back in the tray.

The class is a small puddle of faces.

I could stop teaching and send them home early. I usually teach for the full period and I've never called off but talking about Western Pennsylvania and what it can offer literature—especially our language, which always filters through jobs—makes me think of Barnes and Noble and the young sales clerk offering me the novel about Iran with such enthusiasm then going blank when I asked for a book dealing with working-class American lives. It's something I think about often, maybe because I'm trying to publish a novel about working-class people, maybe because I took out so many loans to go to college then had to learn a trade, maybe because my writing teacher in college scoffed at poems or stories not enamored with trees and birds, or maybe I think about it as one of

{81}

our country's great problems of the last fifty years, America's inability to recognize Americans who do the hardest jobs, the heaviest lifting, who spend the longest amount of time on their feet for the littlest amount of pay. After college I was headed to Walmart, maybe in the stockroom, maybe the deli counter, maybe as a cashier, scanning and bagging and being complained upon, until I decided to get a trade.

So why the fuck are there no novels about Walmart?

Why are there no novels set in McDonalds?

The places where most Americans work are the places least likely to appear in American novels. The last book I read about coal miners was set in Chile. The last novel I read about a concrete factory was set in Russia and published in 1925, though a concrete factory that sits on bedrock twenty miles from my office has been operating for more than a century and is run by the same family.

Why?

Because successful writers come from successful families?

Yes.

Because successful families operate away from the lives of people who do the worst paid and least rewarding work?

Yes.

Even the most solidly middle-class person, one with a pension or a 401K, one with a manageable mortgage and a paid-off car, one not drowning in student loan debt, knows the people above them, the bosses and company presidents and CEOs, could build a better robot or find a cheaper person and replace them, so they protect what they have. Whether by instinct or intellect, people actively block the class beneath them from rising up. Help those people? At the expense of your own life and family and geography?

Fuck that.

It's easier to look away—miles, countries, cultures.

The more distant the life, the easier to care, the more distant the life, the harder to be of service, the harder to be of service, the less service required, the less service required, the easier to care, the easier to talk, the easier to write books about people under boot, for should they rise up and revolt, they are miles, countries, and cultures away. The revolution must happen on the other side of the world, not the other side of town.

I say something like this to my students.

I try not to sound dismal.

I say, "Class cuts across all lines, gender and race and sexual orientation."

They mostly nod yes.

I nod yes back at them.

I say, "Am I making any sense?"

They mostly nod yes.

Then I instantly feel embarrassed to teach something as intimate as class, to monologue, to explicitly present my opinion, when for years I've encouraged discussion and dissent.

Brandon says, "That's why science fiction is so important."

I don't know what he means so I say, "Talk about that."

He says, "I'd rather write about it."

"Okay," I say. "Anyone have any questions?"

They mostly nod no.

I say, "Sorry I talked so much. We'll pick up next class with the Babel and whatever handout I dig up. Keep thinking about the language you use."

They gather up their papers and pick up their backpacks and scoot their chairs and rise and stretch and check their phones then head for the door, most of their heads down, looking away, but some nodding so long, see you soon. A few students wave or actually speak their goodbyes. I wave and speak back.

One kid says, "Pretty good class, prof."

"Thanks," I say.

I wait for Brandon to stick around, to bully me about whatever novel he's been reading, but he leaves the room, already fishing for a cigarette, his nicotine addiction greater than his desire to break fantasy novels over my head.

The rest of the class finally clears save for one girl who never speaks and seldom turns in her assignments, a white chick who sits in the back of the room and plays with her phone. Right now she appears more shy-looking than her usual bored and disgusted. She stands with her hands in her denim pockets, eyes averted, book-weighted backpack like a hunch across her shoulders. Perhaps, finally, I said something that resonated with her. It's funny the way intellect suddenly appears in kids who never knew they were smart. Perhaps, finally, she realized she belongs here, in college. Perhaps she has a story she wants to tell and never felt like she could tell it and now she does because she understands she has the language, that the language is around all of us, here in the bottom corner of Western Pennsylvania.

Or maybe she just wants to know her grade.

Maybe she wants to complain.

Maybe she wants to see if she can turn in late work because they all ask if they can turn in late work even though everyone knows I accept assignments whenever they turn them in because college is not their life—their jobs are, their families are—and I want them to do well so I grade easy and accept past-due assignments.

Maybe she needs a dollar for the soda machine.

She lingers so I linger, fake smiling, trying to make her comfortable.

"Do you have a question?" I say.

She steps to the side of my face in a way that makes me think she is going to bite my neck or kiss my neck or snot on my shoulder, who knows, but instead she whispers into my ear, "Were you talking about the niggers?"

She steps back but not much, still close enough to kiss, bite, or snot.

I have an overwhelming desire to punch her.

Then I have an overwhelming desire to hug her.

Or I could run.

I am a great runner.

Then I take a breath, a huge breath, a breath meant to gather enough wind to blow her from my personal space, and exhale.

Suddenly nervous she says, "That's what I heard."

"What?" I say.

She says, "That's what I heard when you were talking."

"That's not what you heard," I say.

"How do you know what I heard?" she says, less nervous, more aggressive.

I say, "I was talking about people who hold terrible jobs and how we don't know anything about them because we never see them in books or on TV or in films. Because we never see them, we can't help them. We don't recognize their problems. That's what I was saying. I was talking about all kinds of people. I was talking about most people because most people have bad jobs. I thought that was understood. Jobs diminish us all and they shouldn't."

She chews her thumbnail and thinks.

She says, "I took a class at Pitt, down in the city, and I had a white teacher tell me to check my white privilege, and a bunch of black students were like: uh huh, check it."

I stand here, flexing my brain, reaching for the right words.

None come.

"I'm sorry you had a bad experience down at Pitt," I say.

She says, "I'm a waitress at Denny's in fucking North Versailles, and some white bitch with a PhD is telling me to check my privilege? Fuck her."

I say, "All I was talking about were people with terrible jobs. All colors. All everything. You work a terrible job. Lots of white people work terrible jobs. Black people work terrible jobs. Almost all the cashiers at the Walmart in North Versailles are black women. All the cashiers at the McDonalds in Monroeville are black. I'll buy a filet o' fish from anyone. I wish they all got paid better. When I was a welder and worked in Pittsburgh, half the guys were black. When I worked in Missouri, half the guys were black and half the guys were Mexicans. When I worked up in Erie, all the welders were white and we drank at a bar where all the bartenders were white chicks. Most people work bad jobs and they don't appear in books so they're invisible to the rest of America. That's all I'm saying. That's all I was trying to say." Then, trying to be generous, I say, "I apologize if it sounded like something else."

She shrugs and steps away from me and, not in a whisper, says, "I thought you were talking about niggers."

"Be fucking nicer," I say.

I say, "Please."

I say, "At least try."

ALLERGIES

I don't see Berryman on campus. I check his office. I check the parking lot for his mid-sized Ford. I assume he is traumatized, possibly home with his parents in the great state of New Jersey, or not traumatized and still in the great city of Johnstown, begging to be wrestled to the ground by a former national champion who is twice his size.

My phone rings twice but neither call is Rig.

I teach my next class then retreat back to my office.

Last week I dreamed Dr. Bronse, president of this place, talked to me about a kayak trip then later in the week I realized she may have stopped by my office and talked to me about taking students on a kayak trip.

Then I forgot both dream and reality.

Then I remembered it happened, the trip planning.

I wrote it down so I wouldn't forget.

Now, on a post-it note pushed under my keyboard, I see the words: kayak trip.

I write a newer, stickier post-it note and press it to the edge of my computer screen, reminding myself to get the details about the trip. I could use a kayak adventure. I bet Berryman could too. I know the students could, especially since it's paid for, especially since they never have time for adventure, for nature. Most have never been in the mountains to hike or ride a bike or walk around, let alone kayak. Their jobs and classes do not allow escape, the time for or the money to. So they pick from the garden of Walmart. Maybe they swim in a public pool during the summer. They breathe deep between car rides to responsibility.

This time of year the rivers at Ohiopyle roll over the rocks with the winter melt rising the water and the summer heat still in the distance so an oar and a rubber boat feel like a time machine you paddle into another era or a clock stopped exactly where you want it stopped. Trees hang down from the sides of the mountains. Rocks the size of small houses frame the river and have stood there for thousands of years. The sun feels closer and hotter and the water cools whatever it touches. The air is more breathable.

I visited Ohiopyle when I was sixteen on a high school field trip to see Fallingwater, the house Frank Lloyd Wright built over a waterfall for the Kauffman family. The Kauffmans owned all the fancy department stores in and around Pittsburgh and wanted a weekend house, a place to retreat to, something to replace the decrepit cabins on their hundred acres of land, and because they were the Kauffmans, Pittsburgh cultural barons who knew artists and opera singers, world travelers and politicians, designers and great thinkers, they knew Wright, former genius architect who'd gradually gone out of style over the years. When they wanted to hire Wright, he was in his sixties. For a decade he'd consistently hired himself out to commercial projects he thought were beneath him. He'd married too often and fathered too many kids he wasn't interested in raising and he loved his mistress more seriously than he loved his wife. He was a mess. So he took the job. Arguments ensued. The Kauffmans knew what they wanted. Wright knew what they needed. Walls were built and torn down. Plans were followed and not. The foundation was reinforced with extra steel or it wasn't, no one could say, not Wright or the Kauffmans or the engineer. None of it mattered. Wright poured concrete and stacked stone and layered wood so it looks like Falling Water was born and not built, its place in nature no different than the flowers and trees and water it surrounds and embraces.

Or, as one of my classmates put it, "Holy shit."

A city kid from Bloomfield who knew how to ride a crosstown bus not long after I started walking, I imagined myself living at Fallingwater, not the house itself but one of the cabins back in town or in a tent or under a tree, in the midst of beauty, nature, in the calm, no one flicking cigarettes or hustling to a job, no horns, no old women sweeping their porches, no sewer drains overflowing with nasty rainwater. Or I'd stay in the city but at least come back to the Allegheny Mountains to hike and picnic and foliage, whatever the fuck that meant, foliage, or to stretch out shirtless on a warm rock in the summer and read mystery novels and hear the quiet spin of the wheel in my head and watch the leaves turn to red and orange then brown and fall like rusted spaceships finally traveling back to earth. My life, always a hustle, would be consumed by peace and harmony, by the ability to reside within nature.

I saw it, I thought it, I believed it.

Then I went back to the city.

I wanted to be a writer.

I attended school every day.

I worked part-time bussing tables for Del's, an Italian restaurant.

The woman who owned Del's said to me, literally, "You are a piece of shit."

Then she went back to her wine and shouted at other people.

I kept bussing.

I ate the food off plates that customers didn't eat.

I wrestled and ran track.

I needed to apply to colleges.

I applied to colleges.

I worked part-time, asking for more hours.

The woman who owned Del's said, "Who are you?"

I walked home after my shift, smelling of garlic and bleach.

I lingered.

I watched.

I learned to love the women sweeping their stoops. Fat Polish and Italian ladies with corn straw brooms they bought from fund-raisers at their churches swept and chased the dirt away like the priests and pastors and communion chased away their sins. It was holy work, cleaning. I knew it because I did it myself. I picked up dirty dishes at Del's and scraped them in the trash or into my holy mouth. I washed napkins and tablecloths. Crumbs disappeared under the suction of the vacuum as I roamed around the restaurant after closing. At home I scrubbed our old vinyl kitchen floor and emptied my mom's ashtray. I threw away her booze bottles. I sprayed the tile in the shower with bleach and dug in with a sponge. The world was a mess. Then it wasn't. I could do that. Anyone could. All you needed was a broom and a rag and the desire to make something clean.

So I didn't return to Ohiopyle and the Allegheny Mountains and Fallingwater for more than fifteen years, not until this job found me and offered me summers off and a long winter break and blew the sparks from my welding torch cold. Beauty is only beauty when you have time for the vision. Truly. The rest is intentional blindness and pushing away the feeling of being cheated. I could have easily lived my entire adult life stomping concrete and eating McDonalds, grateful to grab a nap after nine hours on the job, grateful to have a holiday off or to work the holiday and get paid double-time.

We need so little, it's an embarrassment.

I'm trying to accept more, to refuse less.

I love to have the time to sit under trees.

Now I put my head down on my desk, thinking of water, of waterfalls, of a wealthy family befriending an old architect no one cared about anymore. I do not think about Rig and alleys and drugs, I do not think about jail. I say water in my head so it loops around my brain, though I keep hearing Rig and alleys and drugs and jail and poor young white women saying nigger, saying nigger more than once, and I try not to cry and I am not a crier and tears come anyway, enough that I could blame it on my allergies should anyone appear and ask why I'm red-eyed.

NAP

With my face down I sleep so deeply I feel like I'm falling through my desk then the floor then the dirt underneath the building then the earth then I'm floating in space, free from gravity, and only wake up when someone knocks on my open door.

It's been seven minutes.

I instantly realize I'm drooling.

At least I'm not crying.

I wipe the drool on my sleeve then wipe my sleeve on my pants.

Brandon stands there, greasy haired, almost smiling.

A cluster of pimples circles his mouth.

"What's up?" I say.

He says, "Were you sleeping?"

He wears a green hooded sweatshirt, unzipped, the hood pulled up from the back then down over his forehead so his eyebrows are hidden and his eyes look to be a piece of the hood and not his face, like a young adult dressed as an alien or an alien lost in Western Pennsylvania and dressed as a community college student.

"No," I say. "I wasn't sleeping. It's my allergies."

"It looked like you were sleeping."

"Nope."

"I want to talk to you about class."

"Okay."

He says, "Not really about class."

"Are you going on the kayak trip?" I say.

"The what?" he says.

"The kayaking trip. I thought I dreamed it but Dr. Bronse really told me about the trip. It's through student services. It's free. They got a grant to pay for everything. You should go. I think it will be fun. You look like you could use some sunlight."

"I don't do outdoors."

"Sunlight creates vitamin D. Vitamin D really helps out with our moods. I think it's good for skin too. And it makes healthy bones. I get miserable then I get in the sun and feel better."

"My mood is fine."

"I'm going to be one of the chaperones. I'm not sure if I'm supposed to be recruiting people or not. I'd love to see you on the river."

"I haven't been camping since I was like three."

"It might do you some good."

He says, "But then again it might not."

"Okay," I say. "Let me know if you change your mind."

He pulls his backpack from his shoulder and I wait for a gun to appear because Brandon gives off the energy of fear and disgust which usually leads to hate which usually leads to violence. I know there's no gun but still. I wish I wasn't so afraid all the time.

He pulls out a single sheet of paper.

"Late work?" I say.

"It's a compression," he says.

"One of your mini-novels?"

"Yeah."

"Great. Just leave it on my desk."

"Can you get it back to me by the end of today?"

"No," I say. "I can't."

"I'll stop back," he says, not saying when, probably later today.

READING A COMPRESSION UNDER SURVEILLANCE

I read Brandon's one-page novel in a couple breaths, even though I don't want to read it at all. The entire text takes ninety seconds, two minutes tops. I read it again. I read it a third time. He must have left my class, smoked a cigarette, and typed this up in the library, an outrageous combination of action film and cultural insensitivity filtered through a distorted version of what I said in my last lecture. I feel like I may recognize the film *Midnight Express* in here somewhere, though that was set in Turkey and this is set in Iran. I read it again, looking for something, some code to break. The words feel like spinning a heavy metal album backwards, long drawn-out syllables that mean less than the actual song. I read it again as satire. It's all creepy but maybe I'm too sensitive. My reading is crowded by the white chick who said racist things only a few hours ago. Brandon's compression starts, "Deserts suck. The raging storm of Aldo." I don't know what that means but it sounds bad. Aldo sounds awfully close to Adolph.

Did I say I'm too sensitive?

I scare easily and tend to judge the judgmental.

I also get nervous.

The things that make me nervous are too many to mention, an endless array of worries like I was born on an arc and loaded with fears that marched on two-by-two so they couple multiply.

I pretend not to be nervous and put the compression in the top drawer.

Brandon stops by fifteen minutes later.

He says, "Can I get my compression back with comments now?"

"I haven't had the chance to read it yet."

"I thought I saw you reading it."

I say, "Do you have cameras in here?"

"I waited in the hall."

"Check with me after our next class."

"Seriously?"

"Is that somehow unrealistic?"

He shakes his head like it's a bomb he's trying to unscrew so it falls off his shoulders and explodes in my office.

He says, "You love to ignore the fact that I pay tuition."

"Paying tuition doesn't make me your man-servant."

"I get that you feel like you're better than everyone else," he says, disgusted.

"I don't," I say.

"We'll see about that," he says.

"I hope not," I say.

"We'll see."

"How am I acting like I'm better than everyone?"

"All the books you talk about," he says, like it's the definitive answer.

I say, "I teach writing and literature. Talking about books is what I'm supposed to do. Would you rather have a teacher who doesn't talk about books? That'd be a math class."

He says, "I'd rather have a teacher who doesn't talk about the books you talk about."

"What books should I be talking about?"

"Science fiction, mystery."

"I like mysteries," I say, which is true, then I say, "I like some sci-fi," which is not true, "but I don't think you need a college course to understand either. I don't see the value in teaching the bestseller list or a book that's just been made into a movie."

Brandon says, "That's pretty much the bullshit answer I'd expect from a professor."

"If you're constantly going to judge people," I say, "you really need to learn to call bullshit on yourself," accidentally letting some honesty spill into our space.

He says, "I call bullshit on myself by calling bullshit on you."

I stand and come around my desk and I politely show him the door by placing my hand gently on his shoulder. When I am near Brandon, he grows smaller, less a wall of disgust, more a ball of embarrassment and fear. Maybe he knows I wrestled in college. Maybe he saw me wrestle Berryman. Maybe he does not realize my wrestling skills, unlike many other wrestlers' skills, do not translate to fighting. I've never punched anyone. There are people I would have liked to have punched and I am not against punching but whatever connects my fists to my desire broke a long time before I had the chance to use it.

Basically, I'm a pussy.

Even as a kid, third and fourth grade, fighting just off school property, I danced around and ducked and hoped to land a headlock and squeeze until my opponent lost his desire to pummel my eyes black and yellow and make me look like a bitch.

Now I approach middle-age, punchless.

Brandon stands in the hallway.

Maybe he feels my punchlessness and it makes him large.

He steps towards me then back.

I don't budge.

He says, "So."

I wait for him to walk.

He says, "You're not as smart as you think you are."

I say, "I bet you say that to all your professors," and close my office door.

THE IRAN COMPRESSION, CHARLIE BROWN

I sit down and read the compression again and think maybe I shouldn't teach anymore, maybe I should weld, maybe I should stick with steel beams and rivets. There are variables to welding but they can be managed. The variables to teaching are endless, each student their own collapsing bridge in need of repair or replacement.

Here is Brandon's compression, his mini-novel, in its entirety:

IRAN, IRAN

Deserts suck. The raging storm of Aldo. The Iranian prison was bad. One cave wall was painted. One cave wall was dust. The guards wore green camo in the desert sun, so I knew they'd not been properly trained. Training is essential, as is wearing the correct color of camo. The guards were mostly children, ages eighteen to twenty-five. They used to fling each other in the nuts, then laugh hysterically at the other person's pain. These men were Muslims.

Their nut-flinging was another custom outside my belief system. In America, a Christian country, we nut-fling in junior high. In American prisons, we neck-stab and trade cigarettes. Does this sound humorous? I hope I'm not implying my life in Tehran was anything less than a bottle of sand poured down my throat while my eyes were doused with mustard gas. Deserts do suck. The raging storm of Aldo.

No one spoke English in the Iranian prison, so I was getting raped a lot. You think you'd adjust, but it's pretty much like that Ice Cube song where no one gets Vaseline. After a year, I whittled my own dick into a sword and killed two prison guards by fucking them in the butts, their painful deaths a reward for my painful life in captivity. "An eye for an eye," is a line from all the major spiritual texts, both Christian and Muslim. With much effort and bloody feet, I made it to the prison's roof where I rescued myself with a helicopter I built from the bones of a teacher that had been sentenced to death by the Ayatollah for encouraging women to read. Those Ayatollahs are some crazy motherfuckers when it comes to teaching young women to read. I mean, they'll smash your head in with a rock and leave your helicopter bones on the roof to be re-assembled by foreign trash. They all know deserts suck. Aldo?

Perhaps you've heard of me because I'm famous now, the backpacker with a six-inch sword for a pecker and the sour taste of Iranian porridge in my throat.

When I got back to America, the President invited me to the White House. We ate turtle soup and I got a merit badge. A merit badge is a big deal. They give them to Boy Scouts and other deserving folk. Ray Bradbury deserves a merit badge, but the powers that be refuse to acknowledge that science fiction is the only true American literature. I digress. I danced a jig because I was so proud in my American way for receiving my American award for escaping an Iranian jail. Americans tend to be lazy and eat too much Burger King and not travel abroad or even read outside the cannon. Long live HP Lovecraft! Being fat and couch-bound and semi-illiterate makes it hard to end up in an Iranian jail, let alone escaping. But I did it! Yay me! Yay my pecker-sword!

Later, after the ceremony, the President, tipsy on single malt bourbon, said, "Son, we should clone you."

I said, "Sir, you already have."

He thought I meant Americans, but I meant Iranians. Their deadliness is my own. My deadliness is theirs. See how our hearts pump sand.

Sometimes I think about Iran and the people I met while backpacking in the desert and in prison. I'm sad that they didn't like me, especially those guards with their nut-flinging, but also the dogs I ate while in captivity. I mean, I'm an American. I have a merit badge. Even Ray Bradbury doesn't have a merit badge. I'm an American. I have a garden. It's autumn, and the pumpkins I grow are huge. Ask Charlie Brown, not Aldo. Desert sands still rage in the desert winds. Aldo. Nuts. Always nuts.

THE END

WHY WRITERS WRITE

Brandon writes for the same reason all writers write: to have a voice. Because he believes his voice is denigrated, because people treat science fiction as unintelligent, or maybe because he loves science fiction more than anything else in the world, more than money or family or music or God, he feels like he should turn other voices, voices that are not science fiction or interested in science fiction or voices that would mock science fiction, into horrible jokes.

He needs his voice to be the loudest.

He needs his voice to be the most powerful.

Now tell that to a young man at a community college who spends his nights in the produce section of a grocery store, stocking lettuce and mushrooms, and lives at home with his mom because he can't afford anything else, and tell it to this young man in a kind and thoughtful way even though the young man is the opposite of kind and thoughtful.

I'm asking you to do it.

Because I probably can't.

WRONG DEMOCRACY

Basically, I'm a progressive government and I believe in democracy and someone—I'm not sure who—said I should invade a small country on the other side of the globe because their leader is a cruel and tyrannical dictator who tortures his own people. I go with it. I make the place safe. I provide a good economy and lots of freedom to speak and act. Everyone loves me as a progressive government, except sort of not because my food is smelly and I sound funny and look weird and know very little of their history. The people listen to me for a while then grow sick of me and call for an election. Now the people vote in a new leader and he hates me as a progressive government, even though I've basically handed him the country he leads.

Now I need to insert a new leader, one who looks and acts like me.

Only I don't insert a new leader.

I allow the leader I empowered who hates me to stay.

He slanders me a lot.

The other people in the country realize the new leader is not so great but he talks a lot and they dislike speaking and they've never felt comfortable speaking what they think anyway.

This is life teaching writing at a community college.

WHAT I COULD SAY, A LITERARY INSIGHT

With writing, the act, each writer is equal. The page does not judge. What you say matters more than what any other writer has to say. Speak out. The freedom is absolute.

But publishing is different.

When I talk to students about publishing, I try to be honest about the difficult and complex realities of getting a book out there. My students don't have money and want to understand how their time can be monetized, how they can justify not having a second job, how writing a book might eventually hold some practical value, meaning cash. I talk about how books get picked for publication and why certain people from a certain class value certain stories and styles more than others and what stories the market pays the most for.

What Brandon is talking about, I think, is reception, how what a writer has published is received. He assumes science fiction is devalued because it is not critically acclaimed in *The New York Times* like a Johnathan Frazen novel or a Roxanne Gay essay collection but he does not realize or acknowledge or understand that science fiction is received with readers and readers mean money and movie deals, which mean more money and TV deals, which mean even more money and viewers, which are like readers but lazier but which still provide the science fiction writer with an endless stream of attention and cash.

You've won, I should tell Brandon.

You've stomped a mudhole in our stupid literary hearts.

PART EIGHT

My Mom

My mom waits outside the door. Her voice gives her away but I still peek through the curtain. She turns and looks at something on the street while smoking a Marlboro Light. Last month, after thirty-five years of smoking unfiltered Camels, she switched brands to get healthy. Such is the logic of my highly intelligent and highly opinionated mother, a woman who once explained to her doctor that having seven drinks on Saturday is as healthy as the recommended one drink per night because those seven drinks were daily drinks that had been properly accumulated. Your body, she explained, doesn't care when it gets its seven drinks, just as long as those seven drinks arrive. The doctor asked, "So, in theory, you could have three hundred and sixty-five drinks on New Year's Day and not have to worry about drinking the rest of the year?" and my mom answered, "Of course not. Three hundred and sixty-five drinks would kill me."

Now she knocks again.

It's Saturday.

I am terrifically hungover.

I tiptoe away from the window.

"I hear you in there," she says.

I turn and walk to the door.

"It's a mouse," I say.

"Bullshit," she says. "Open up."

"I can't," I say.

I lean on the door with my back. I could fall over. I could sleep standing up, like Rig in jail. Hangover, I say to my hangover, what's wrong with you? Megan, my bartender, my student, my secret love, another woman I'm afraid to give mat-herpes to, locked the doors at Harry's Bar after last call and the five of us still inside drank until morning. It must have been magical because I can barely feel my tongue and my eyes are burning slits.

"Let me in," my mom says.

"I'm dying," I say.

"You're not dying. You're hungover."

I slide down the door.

The floor is cool and dry.

"I am too dying," I say.

"I want to buy you some lunch."

"Really?"

"Yes, really," she says. "I'm your mother."

I crawl away from the door and say, "It's unlocked."

I stretch out on my back. My hangover is a matchstick lighting my organs on fire. I need a shower and a fan and a cool nonalcoholic drink.

But I cannot move from the floor.

My dehydrated brain launches missiles against the backs of my eyeballs.

The door opens.

I turn to my side so I can see.

Smoke appears like a theatrical curtain then my mother walks through the smoke. She wears her black business suit, the one she pulls on when upper management forces her to fire someone at the office. Her heels are ridiculously high for a woman past fifty. Her hair is too blonde. When we go out together, men my age (or younger) buy her drinks. She adores this attention. She is beautiful and works at being beautiful and she deserves it. She is fun. Men of all ages enjoy fun, especially the kind my mom manufactures. She would tell you as much. She would tell you she is the genius of a good time. Not long ago she told one of her cranky female friends, "Menopause is for losers, lighten the hell up."

I say, "Why are you working on a Saturday?"

She says, "Why are you crawling around on the floor in your underwear?"

"I'm not crawling around in my underwear," I say.

Then I stand up and run as casually as possible for the bathroom and puke.

Preparation

"I think the puking helped," I say, newly showered and shiny.

"That's good to know," my mom says.

I take an energy drink from the refrigerator.

She says, "Are those sugar-free? Give me one."

Lunch

We eat at Fat Head's in Pittsburgh, on the South Side, one glass storefront on a street filled with glass storefronts, most of them bars, a few good dives remaining though much of the street has become gentrified and boring, purse shops and organic soap stores, mega-gyms where firm bodies run on treadmills, dress shops for skinny women, men's clothing stores for men who want to dress like they live in New York and make million-dollar deals. Tom's Diner is gone and the Pittsburgh Steak Company is dying and the new restaurants are places where people take pictures of their small-plate food before they eat, before they take their tiny bites of artisanal cuisine. A new vegetarian place pops up every week and disappears before the month ends. Fancy cupcake shops come and go. On the other side of town a bakery named Toast, where a slice of toast cost five dollars, finally closed its doors forever. An art gallery opened in its place.

Fat Head's is the opposite of that.

No trends, steady evolution.

Twenty years ago Fat Heads Head's served sandwiches the size of your head, hence the name, and poured beer from twenty or so countries, Mexico and China and Belgium, plus all the big American beers. Now, decades later, Fat Head's serves sandwiches the size of your head and wings and cheesesticks and all the bar food you can drop in a fryer but they also pour beer from all the good microbreweries around the country and all the local ones too, Full Pint in North Versailles and East End on the edge of Homewood and North Country located an hour outside the city in Slippery Rock where you can buy a beer named Bucco Blonde after the local baseball team. At Fat Head's you can still drink a Heineken or a Red Stripe. They won't snicker if you order a Bud Light. Their logo is a happy glutton, usually wearing sunglasses, always smiling.

Today, I skip the beer and get a big Mountain Dew.

For food I order the Cuban which, if it were authentic, would feed half of Cuba, a monster sandwich of pulled pork, ham, Swiss cheese, pickles, and a hot sauce to burn up whatever impurities need sweated from my system after a night of boozing.

I ask for the honey mustard on the side, mostly to dunk my chips in. I love their homemade chips.

My mom, whose name is Joanie, who I have been calling Joanie since I was thirteen when she said, "Quit calling me mom, it makes me sound old," orders a coffee and a fruit salad. She adds sweetener to the coffee. Joanie is extremely healthy in that she almost never eats and what she does eat is made from low-calorie and low-fat chemicals. Her other food groups include tobacco and mangos. And booze. Once a week she cooks meatballs in sauce served over pasta in a red sauce or meatballs in brown gravy served over mashed potatoes, which we sometimes eat together while watching TV or which she eats alone while watching TV. Joanie loves HBO, all the cop and gangster stuff, and if things get too intense, she breaks out the ice cream.

"I wish this was a mango," she says about her melon cup.

"I figured as much."

"A girl could live on mango."

"You've proved that. You want a bite of my Cuban?"

"Yes," she says. "But no. What do they call that thing again?"
"The Bay of Pigs."
"A sandwich named after what was almost the end of the world."
"That's the missile crisis."
"Is the Bay of Pigs when Castro took over?"
"Yes, and it really tastes great," I say, lifting it to my mouth with two hands.

The waitress goes to fill Joanie's mug with coffee and Joanie blocks the opening of her mug by using her hand like a lid.

"It's a delicate balance," Joanie says.

The waitress nods.

Joanie says, "Too sweet, too dark, just right. You understand."

"I do," the waitress says.

She must be nineteen, beautiful, with a beehive hairdo and cat glasses like she's confused about the decade. One of her arms is a sleeve of tattoos. A rockabilly chick on the UFO of cool. She walks to the next table, skinny as a coke habit. She swings back and looks at my Dew.

I drink the rest of my soda and say, "I'll have another, thanks."

She takes my glass and walks off.

Joanie says, "Look at the butt on her. She should pray to never get old. I had a knife ass when I was that age too."

I say, "Why are you in your black dress?"

Joanie says, "I have to fire someone."

"Have to or did?"

"Have to. I was supposed to fire him this morning for missing so much work but he didn't bother to come in. He was supposed to cover the weekend. Maybe I'll leave him a message. I could text the little dickhead. That'd be modern."

I eat some of my chips, extra-salting them first, then dunking each one in the side cup of honey mustard. This is how I eat: dip bite dip bite. I have to ask for more honey mustard. Honey mustard might be my favorite food.

Joanie says, "Are you trying to die?"

"Because I got drunk last night?"

"Because you're eating a pig farm."

I shrug.

I eat the farm.

She says, "I think I'm morally opposed to a sandwich that size but it looks so delicious. A small pile of meat falls off every time you pick it up."

"I know," I say, mouth filled. "But then I pick up the small pile of meat and eat that too," and I show her how.

She says, "I'm going to eat eighty-five meatballs on my splurge day."

Joanie has a rationale for lunch, for bringing us together, because she always brings a narrative to restaurants, especially when it's her turn to pay. Did she fight another younger woman outside a pizza shop for unknown reasons, possibly over a sexy man? We're beyond that. Big stories roll away from my mom like boulders so she can make room on the mountain of her life for more stories made of hard things that fall. Just watch. She knows why she's here but not how to explain why she shows up when she shows up. The story or stories move slowly through her head and heart and, even though she's my mother, through her sex and romantic life too, until they fall out on the table like a coffee spill that never spreads or rolls over the edge into anyone's lap, a hot mess to be easily wiped up—"and anyway, I got arrested but they didn't press charges," and other less criminal versions of similar stories. My mom will fight a young bitch who looks at a man she is interested in. So be it. My mother is active and sometimes aggressive but seldom dangerous.

This is the way my mom works: something new in her life, a surprise visit to me, her son; a gesture of kindness; a few random insults; a few random compliments; big news that is in fact small news revealed in a dramatic fashion; she picks up the tab.

Then I give her a hug.

Then we stumble apart to build and start again.

Now she sighs and says, "Can I smoke in here?"

I say, "There's a small child sleeping in a car seat," and I gesture with my head to a table across the room. "Of course you can't smoke in here."

"I used to smoke when you were small."

"That's why my lungs hate you."

"I want to run a marathon," she says. "Maybe not a marathon. A marathon is the big one, right? That would crush me. You have to be a tri-athlete or something to do those. I think I want to run a 5K, a 10K, one of those reasonable ones, maybe for breast cancer or some cause, hunger or the local museum or a decrepit high school. When I was growing up, girls couldn't be athletic. We had outfits we wore in gym class and we all pretended to have our periods anyway."

All the ham has slid from my sandwich so I pick it up and eat it separately until my ham pile is a greasy spot on the glass plate. There is never enough ham even when there is enough ham. There is never enough pork, never enough sausage, never enough pig. Even if I would have ordered an extra side of bacon with my sandwich, it would still be ten strips short of perfection. A pile of bacon requires another additional pile of bacon. So many religions hate the pig because pig tastes like God. They resent the beauty of God's cloven foot.

Joanie says, "Can you hear me over that sandwich?"

"I can."

"How do you stay so skinny? You still look like a wrestler."

"It's your good genes," I say. "And I jog twenty-five miles a week, minimum."

She says, "That's exactly what I'm talking about. Can I have just the smallest of bites of that monstrosity? Just a little piece from the side you haven't chewed up."

I take my knife and cut her a quarter and use my knife to lift it to her plate.

"You're a darling," she says.

I say, "Is that what this about? You want to run a race because you were born in 1961 and girls didn't run races then?"

"I was born in 1962," she says.

She delicately bites the sandwich, the deliciousness of it turning her eyes to happy glossy planets. She pushes her fruit bowl away and drinks very slowly and consciously from my Mountain Dew, a strawful, maybe two.

"Good?" I say.

She takes a final bite and chews and says with her mouth full, "I could eat like this every day and just become a fatty and be happy at every meal."

"You should," I say. "You've earned it."

She says, "I've earned a kick in the ass," and waves me off.

She goes into her purse for a Marlboro Light even though it clearly says No Smoking everywhere and I have warned her.

She says, "Don't look at me that way. I'm letting my cigarette breathe a little before I take it outside and allow it to return my appetite to normal."

"Thank you," I say.

She says, "I have a new boyfriend. He's your age, almost. He's a little younger. You're a little older. He's handsome and it's only going to be as serious as I allow it to be." She places the unlit cigarette to her mouth. She says, "Look, he's a runner, obviously. He jogs 5Ks or one of those type things." She takes the cigarette from her mouth and holds it in the V of her fingers. She exhales like she's been smoking. She says, "Let's not make a big deal out of this."

"That's more like it," I say, neither surprised nor hurt by my mother who I have loved and not been surprised or hurt by in years, her kindness and consistency and hard work trumping whatever news she table-drops, even if she brings awkward and outrageous like summer storms that pour and recede. I do not care that she wants to date a man my age. She wants me to care about people who she dates, period. She needs to be loved from as many angles as possible. Rule number one framed as a question in my mother's heart: for if there is not drama, how can it be real? This is all I know and accept as truth.

I pick at the rest of the sandwich so I can consider my response.

She says, "Look at you, all thoughtful."

I say, "The first thing you'll need to do is get a good pair of running shoes. Then you'll need some shorts and a knee brace. You can get everything at Dick's or Dunham's or even Footlocker at the mall. You can probably get it at Gabriel Brother's for half the price. I've bought good running shoes there before. They were supposed to be seconds but I couldn't tell. Buy New Balance. They're made in America. Once you've equipped yourself, I'll watch you jog and give you a couple tips. After that you're on your own."

"That was more than I'd hoped for," she says.

"You should order one of these sandwiches," I say, "and run it off."

"How many miles would one of those be?" Joanie says.

"A million," I say.

"I'll order it," she says. Then, "But you have to eat my chips."

I nod.

She waves at the waitress, who walks over with her knife ass facing the wrong way and pulls out her pen and pad to take Joanie's second order.

Bookstores

All the bookstores on the South Side have closed. Most of them lived short lives anyway, pop-ups owned by rich kids who thought art would save their lives then decided to get an MBA or open an artisanal lawn-mower repair shop. City Books, located right on Carson Street near the 10th Street Bridge, held out for thirty years. The owner, a philosophy professor from Duquesne University, a Catholic school, the whitest college you could imagine but positioned on the edges of the Hill District, one of Pittsburgh's oldest black neighborhoods, was a crank who always implied you were stealing. If you carried a backpack, he demanded you set it down. If you carried a purse, he asked you to leave it at the counter before you headed upstairs. I suppose someone else worked there, that it would have been impossible to run a business alone, but I only ever saw the owner. He leaned or paced around the store, pushing his thinning gray hair back, pulling the shag into a ponytail then releasing the ponytail and wandering back to the cash register like it might suddenly manufacture money. His beard always needed to be trimmed and he always stared at the book in his hands like the text was slapping his nose and demanding he respond. Upstairs, he installed a coffee bar, basically a cappuccino machine, but I never saw anyone buy or drink coffee. City Books was from another era, a time when people came to bookstores for books, not anything specific but to search and find something unexpected, not thank-you cards and sunglasses, not dark chocolate bars and expensive ballpoint pens, but a travel book about Morocco or a book of poems written by a pig farmer with a PhD or a memoir written by a lesbian who didn't know she was a lesbian until after she'd married a dude because she'd grown up in Nebraska and people in Nebraska pretend not to have sex organs and struggle to find their liberal hearts and shiny vaginas.

The last time I shopped at City Books, the owner barely looked up from the shelf he stocked. He never said hello. He never accused me of stealing. Rumors around town said he was closing the shop. I believed the rumors and knew I'd miss the experience of roaming his stacks.

I walked to the second floor, taking the winding staircase, and focused on things I wanted to remember: the hardwood floors and odd-shaped shelves, the open space and huge windows, the thousands upon thousands of used books.

When I was younger, I would drink at Jack's Bar, the only bar in the city open three hundred and sixty-five days a year, then take my buzz down the block to City Books and load up on old hardbacks, two or three for twenty bucks. I bought a novel by Kalexi here when I was maybe twenty or twenty-one. Kalexi said, "Your wild self only dies when you offer it death." I loved that, the truth and the romance.

The last time I shopped at City Books, I stood upstairs and tried to remember other books I'd pulled and paid for and loved. It was hard being in there and knowing the end perched on every shelf. I paced the aisles. I stood on the stairs and thought about what a bookstore means to a young writer, especially one outside the academy, a writer who writes alone, without community, or with a community of books instead of writers. I looked down at the old rugs strewn across the floor, the nicked-up shelves scavenged from thrift stores and rich people's homes. The books appeared to be as endless as a river, the store overflowing with pages, useless college textbooks no one would ever buy and books on religion people bought all the time and the rows of F. Scott Fitzgerald books, paperbacks and hardbacks, none for collectors, all readable editions for people who couldn't afford new books or who wanted their books lived in and scarred up with notes and pencil-scratched thoughts and lines of help.

Thank you, City Books, I thought or maybe said.

Then the owner saw me and said, "You can't take that backpack up there."

I said, "I'm already up here. I'm coming back down."

He said, "You need to leave your backpack down here."

He said, "You can pick it up on the way out."

He said, "People are always trying to steal my fucking books."

Dave Newman

He said, "What's wrong with you?"

PART NINE

Sunday Student Papers

I have 109 student papers to correct today. At five pages a pop, that's 545 pages of iffy grammar and potential gunplay and lots of grandma love. Gems reside in this stack, I know, but whatever metal the shovel of my brain is made of feels weak today.

It won't dig.

It can't dig.

Sorry, great students.

I shall uncover your brilliance another day.

The sun peeks through the curtain like a creepy neighbor. It's almost noon. I have three channels on my TV. "The Price is Right" is about to begin. I hate game shows but some days I need noise, not music, not conversation. Noise. I'm on my fourth can of Mountain Dew, sugar-peaked on the caffeine cliff knowing it will end soon. I wrote on my novel for almost five hours. The narrator got in a fight with a bully. A teacher pulled them apart and the bully, having not thrown a punch, suddenly lunged and pushed my narrator into a brick wall where his head bounced like a soft melon. My main character and his aunt are at Children's Hospital, waiting on a diagnosis, either a concussion or something more serious. Who is going to pay for this? No one is sure if the kid's parents have insurance or, if they do, if he's on one of their policies. I think I could write more but then I think I've written enough. The doctors hovering around don't understand violence, fighting. They're Ivy Leaguers. They played soccer on traveling teams their dads coached. A social worker comes in and asks about filing charges, if that's a possibility, asks about anger management, if that's a problem. The kid, the main character, is confused, concussed, distraught. His aunt looks like a woman who has no money, who wears a dress from Goodwill. I stop. I write a little more. The nurse's aide, who is about to wheel the main character's stretcher to radiology, used to box when he was a teen and kept boxing into his twenties, Golden Gloves champ, six and two as a pro. He touches the kid's forehead, gently moves his hair. He tells the kid, "You did good, champ. You know how to fight."

Tomorrow, I'll finish his dialogue.

I stand.

I pace.

I sit back down.

Above my desk I have a portrait of Anna Akhmatova. It's a reproduction on a postcard of an oil painting, originally painted by her neighbor, Sergei Prushkin, a farmer who usually painted landscapes and his cows. Akhmatova commissioned the painting because she knew Prushkin needed the money to keep his farm operating but it remains the painting most resembling her, her truth and not her beauty. The clarity is startling, the way her bangs are uneven and how her eyes see past the artist and the barn where he worked and the wall where he stacked his tools. The image is more famous than any of the dozen paintings Modigliani produced of her in Italy. I have a quote thumbtacked underneath it that reads, "I go forth and seek," from one of Akhmatova's poems, but the line I most often think of is, "Why is this century worse than those others?"

I worry I write too much.

I worry I don't write enough.

I worry I don't understand the world.

I worry I understand the world too much.

From where I sit the centuries look so similar.

Fucking money, fucking death, fucking money.

Akhmatova, you write so well, thank you.

I love you, Akhmatova.

I don't smoke anymore but it still looks fun, albeit deadly, and I always think cigarettes would help with my writing, empower it, extend the streak, the number of pages.

I'm so hungry my stomach rattles like a penny dropped on a drum.

I can afford to order pizza with two toppings or even three. I have the metabolism. I have a career where a man does not have to budget for pizza. Most of my life I have budgeted for everything. Thank you, community college. I know my gifts, my luck. When I'm full of pizza, I sleep better. I could sleep all day and the fine would be manageable, maybe not even a fine.

Is it possible to feel too good?

Too rich?

How can I be rich when I owe thousands in student loans?

One of my credit cards is overstuffed, one is empty.

I live in a hovel.

"The Price Is Right" keeps playing.

The first commercial is for Papa John's Pizza.

The owner, in a red company shirt and apron, has a fat face.

I read a lot about the livable wage and companies that work against it.

Maybe that's why I feel rich: I have the time to educate myself.

I'm fucking royalty.

I am the king who demands Papa John provide his employees with health insurance and a livable wage and I shall make no mention of the price increase on a large pepperoni pie.

I hereby decree it.

My Mom, The Great

My mom calls and leaves a message, fake urgent but sweet. She called earlier, around seven, then at eight and nine and ten and eleven, even though she knows my writing schedule, the hours I value. All her messages are sad and hopeful and a little aggressive. Or a lot aggressive. I love her anyway. I love her always. I love her because. To have survived her maternal glow while still growing up was not unlike a vaccine—a prick of medicine to stave off the world.

Now, in adulthood, it's the kookiness and her resilience I admire and anticipate.

Her second-to-last message says, "Sweetie, I know how much you value your writing time, I really respect that, so I want you to know that this is important too."

Her last message says, "Love your mother and call me the fuck back."

When I started writing for money, my mom read all my westerns and praised them as only a mother could, buying them for her friends, for her neighbors, for her co-workers, leaving single copies in odd places for people to find, hoping they'd like the book then seek out and purchase others. She called libraries and demanded they order copies. Libraries ordered copies that no one ever checked out. Why hadn't Hollywood called? My novels read better than all the westerns she'd seen in the last twenty years. We needed to get to Hollywood before Clint Eastwood died. The real men were going fast and my novels would need a real man to play the lead. My mom wanted me to write western novels forever and maybe sneak in a romance novel under a female name, a raunchy one, because the real women were fading away too.

My mom doesn't quite understand my current quest to write and sell a literary novel about poor people but still she encourages it in her cynical way, saying, "That's sweet but you should write a Stephen King book too, while you're writing your literary novel, just in case. People like Stephen King books. They like to be scared. It sucks being poor. Stephen King is a millionaire."

My Mom, Still Calling

Because my mom's new shoes are hot pink Nike trainers and her new boyfriend is a young good-looking runner, she has decided to take half the day off from her office job, change clothes from a black skirt to nylon shorts in the office bathroom, and wants to meet me for a jog at three o'clock sharp to see if her knees and hips still work after a lifetime of not-jogging and wearing high-heel shoes from the Designer Shoe Warehouse.

Into my voicemail she says, "I know you hear these messages. Now be a gentleman and come help your mother be a jogger."

She says, "Don't be a cunt."

She says, "No offense."

I pull another Mountain Dew and grab some crackers and sit at my desk.

I turn off my computer.

I pull out my school work.

I read the first line of a random student paper I pluck from the pile. It says, "I fucking hate this class." I draw a smiley face next to the line then close my eyes. For years I have been able to pretend these fuck-you fuck-off go-fuck-yourself students have not existed so I can better focus on the positive, decent, talented students, the ones who express an interest in learning. Now I feel slimed by the dunces. The good students feel distant.

Have they gotten that much worse in five years?

Have I?

I hold off on the pizza.

The sugar crash hits and I nap with a book on my face.

Later, right before three o'clock, I find my shorts and pull on my New Balance sneaks.

New Balance sneakers are assembled in America, assembled which is not made in America, but those of us who love America celebrate what's left. I gave this advice to my mom and she bought the hot pink Nikes I mentioned.

She knocks on my front door then lets herself in, not trusting me to meet her at the track, though I always meet her when called upon.

"You're ready," Joanie says. "I'm surprised."

It's not her pink Nikes but the matching skin-tight jogging pants and the hoodie styled for a teenage girl. She looks like a chunk of bubblegum.

"Truly," I say, "you look ridiculous."

"Maybe," she says, tugging at her ill-colored and ill-fitting outfit. "But at least I don't have 108 student papers to correct."

"You win again," I say.

"Let's get my ass in motion," she says.

GET YOUR LAPS IN

Joanie runs one lap. One lap is one quarter mile. The pace immediately goes from a semi-sprint to a cloggish clop. Then she stops completely, not moving into a walk, and gets very puffy, like her upper body is a huge lung atop legs. I wait for her. I say encouraging things. I jog circles around the statue she's become. She gasps.

I say, "One more lap but slower."

"Go," she puffs.

"Walk," I say. "Don't stand still, you'll cramp."

She nods and slowly moves forward.

I back away then start to run.

I run three miles, twelve laps in the outside lane, pacing hard. I could run more, another three miles, five or six. I've always run. I love to run. I run away my hangovers. I run away my student papers. I used to run to erase my bills, my credit score. I still run to lessen my student loans, to pay off my credit card. I run and write novels in my head. The novels are better than when I put them on the page but so what. I keep sentences. I keep characters. I keep running for more. I run and start stories, find lines—"Eric wanted to buy a watermelon but he had six cents and a coupon for ice cream." The only time I own the brain that makes me who I am is when I put the rest of my body in motion at the fastest speed I can handle so the requirements of the world fall away or line up as song. Speed, fuckers.

Sing the praises of legs, those of us who still have them.

NOT YET

I sit in my office, door closed, sort of avoiding Brandon, sort of avoiding the world.

Someone knocks.

I stop breathing and close my eyes and wait.

I hate Brandon's voice, especially coming through wood.
Berryman says, "You in there?"
I pretend that I am not.
This happens again and again.

More Running

I stop to walk with my mom.
She says, "You're barely breathing," but furious.
I suck up and let out a big fake breath.
She says, "What's wrong with you?"
She walks her fourth lap, inside lane, almost one mile. Her make-up burns her eyes so she wipes her sweaty face with her new hoodie and stains the fabric with powder and mascara. Her hair is frizzy and lopsided, the sweat loosening the hairspray.
She says, "I don't know how you do this."
"I went to gym class," I say. "I never pretended to have my period."
Then I quit talking and start to run.
I run until my mom says, "Take me home."

Name

I have decided to call my mom by her name, Joanie, exclusively, going forward, because it feels more honest and she would otherwise be disappointed.

Boyfriend

Joanie buys a dog. I think it's a poodle. It's terribly ugly with a dirty white afro and a long snout. Is it possible to breed lions with ants? This is the result.

Days later she shows up at the community college as I'm leaving campus and stands beside my car in the parking lot. She clutches her new dog. She wants to run again and she wants me to run with her for inspiration.

"Or we can just get some pizza," she says.

"I thought you were against pizza."

"I'm thinking about giving in and getting fat. Either getting really skinny or really humongously fat. I can't decide yet. I think fat might be sexy."

"What happened to cigarettes and artificial sweeter and cottage cheese?"

"Let's run. You're right. Run with me. I need a partner in this shit."

We do this periodically, spend inordinate amounts of time with each other, then Joanie becomes disgusted that I don't share all her interests, which include cigarettes and romance novels and cable TV shows and her boyfriends, and she goes back to smoking and meeting men and watching *The Sopranos,* and I keep doing what I've been doing but with more intensity and freedom. No malice appears in this process, just a thoughtful break so we can renew and start again in a few months. Fat is bad. The rest is good.

I say, "You wouldn't believe how much work I have to do."

"One hundred and eight student papers."

"One hundred and nine."

"I acknowledge your pain," she says. "Please acknowledge mine."

Earlier, all day, I apologized to students for not correcting their one hundred and nine papers. They responded with yawns, smiles, and some open hostility indicated by slow sideways head shaking and the loud zipping of backpacks.

Basically, it was all fine and Brandon.

I have not returned his compression about butt-raping Iranian prison guards and he awaits my confirmation of his genius. He stopped by my office and said, "Nothing?" and I said, "It's been a really busy week," and he said, "Busy is the White Desert in the middle of Egypt," then bolted from my office. I was like: what, twat? At least he didn't throw an axe at my head. I read somewhere that axe throwing is popular with young people.

Joanie's dog looks at me and barks, happily.

"Why'd you get white?" I say. "You'll never keep her clean."

"I like white," she says. "It's virginal."

I say, "Please."

The dog licks Joanie on the neck with its saliva-y tongue, smearing Joanie's make-up and messing with her fake-pearl necklace.

Joanie says, "Come on, you little fucker," and shoves the dog's snout away.

It somewhat pains me to tell you that this runner that my mother is dating and desperately trying to impress is also a veterinarian.

BERRYMAN, WHERE ARE YOU?

I agree to meet my mother at the track for a few laps, which will be good for us both. The pizza I am undecided on and I make this clear. I want to be home by dark.

Joanie acknowledges my demands by saying, "You can't resist pizza," and walks off with her dog and her gym bag, heading for the community college gymnasium to use their locker rooms to change into a wad of pink.

As I pull away, Berryman steps from the building.

I toot and wave and wait.

He jogs across the campus lawn, his chubby body stiff and awkward in his fancy Nike sweat suit and high-top kicks. His shoe collection is enormous, like famous-lady size. I should invite him to jog with my mom but I'm not sure I can handle Berryman in an off-campus setting where we aren't trying to help someone who has recently been arrested. One jog could easily spill over into a routine. Pretty soon he'd consider us pals. Pretty soon he'd be sleeping on my couch. I roll down the passenger-side window. Berryman leans in.

"You're sweating," I say. "You jogged like one hundred feet."

Berryman says, "I was sweating in my office. The heat still turns on sometimes."

I say, "You're out of breath too."

"Well," he says, "that's because I'm fat."

"So how'd things go with Rig? Sorry I stuck you with him."

Berryman says, "I've wanted to talk to you about this for days."

"I'm sure," I say.

"What's that mean?" he says.

He knows what it means.

"I really appreciate it," I say, and I do, I'm sincere.

Berryman says, "We were all together, me and you and Rig, then we weren't."

"I know," I say.

"I came by your office," he says.

"I know," I say, "sorry I missed you."
Berryman says, "It's bad enough you beat my ass at wrestling."
"I know."
"Were you in your office and not answering the door?"
"Come on, Berryman" I say. "Go easy."

I don't bother to explain because I seldom explain and for years—for my whole fucking life—most of my relationships have worked like this: I see people regularly then I disappear for millions of practical reasons but also because people see each other too often and become bored with each other and less useful to each other and start to build up petty resentments. When a natural break occurs in a relationship, I accept it as a gift. I learned this from Joanie, my genius mother. Time happens in its unavoidable way then friends and acquaintances realize I have not been present and become frustrated and I pretend they're not frustrated and the relationships become as distant as planets. Then time happens in its unavoidable way and we come together and the space that seemed so awkward becomes less so then becomes normal as the cycle repeats. Good to see you. So long, old friend. Good to see you again. So long, hello.

Berryman says, "You're not sorry."

I say, "I'm a little sorry."

Berryman says, "You just..." and he can't think of what. He says, "I'm just not used to it, the way you do stuff."

I say, "I know."

Berryman says, "Whatever." He regroups and says, "I think Rig's a mess but I couldn't quite tell. He's an odd guy and it's obvious he's a proud guy. I don't know him well enough to tell what's him being odd and what's a problem. I know I'm a rube but those were drugs in that bag, correct?"

I say, "I would assume so, yeah."

"Has he always been a drug dealer?"

"He was an all-pro lineman for the Pittsburgh Steelers, so no."

"Hard times?"

"Hard times."

"You want to get a beer?" he says.

"I'd love to," I say, "but I'm going to meet my mom for a jog."

"Your mom jogs?"

"She's trying. She's in our school's locker room right now with a poodle, changing into her running clothes. I have to run home to get some shorts and my shoes."

"Could I go in and meet her?"

"While she dresses in the locker room?"

"No, obviously," he stutters. "Just like in the hallway. Or in the parking lot."

"You could. Just tell her you're my colleague, Berryman."

"Everyone calls me that now. And your buddy Rig thinks I'm your driver."

"He didn't realize you'd won the prestigious Margaret Saunders Poetry Prize and were published by Brown University Press?"

Berryman says, "Did you say your mom has a poodle?"

I say, "I did. A white one."

He says, "Hmm," and thinks about that, white poodles, my mom.

I say, "It's weird."

He says, "Last thing before you go. It looks like Rig is maybe being evicted. He made me drive by his house, which was really big, like New Jersey big. All brick too. A lot of these new houses are siding. His was like an old mansion. But he said he couldn't stay there anymore. He didn't say why. That's when I got the eviction feeling. He was really sad but sort of proud too. He really knows a lot about Johnstown. He said Andrew Carnegie caused the Johnstown Flood. I need to look that up. His wife is in Florida or something. I had no idea what to say. I mostly just listened and drove. We sat in front of his house for a while. Then he made me take him to Subway. He bought two twelve-inch seafood subs and made me eat one. He wanted to stay with his aunt so we pulled up in front of her house. He knocked and she came out after a couple minutes. She was dressed in an old housecoat and had her hair in curlers. She was ancient, like ninety years old. It looked like he woke her up and she was pissed. She shoved him around and poked him with her finger until he finally put up his hands like she was the cops and he walked away. She weighed maybe eighty pounds in her slippers. I drove him across town and back to his house. It was really dark, like the electric-turned-off dark. He thanked me and said he would have invited me inside but the place was a mess from his wife moving out. He couldn't have been more polite but he didn't use the front door. He walked around back and the lights never came on. I don't even know if it was his house. I probably shouldn't have told you this. I worry. I'm sorry. I'm really rooting for Rig. I think he's the greatest guy I've ever met."

"You're such a privileged cunt, Berryman."

"You don't think I know that?"

"Let's talk soon," I say. "We'll get a beer."

"Seriously?" Berryman says, his kid face lit up like a lamp Lawrence Riggins couldn't afford to light. "Any chance I could jog with you and your mom?"

"No chance," I say, and start to drive away.

Berryman walks with the car then pulls his head out of my window as I accelerate.

Across from campus they've cleared land to make room for a new ballfield, one with bleachers and a dugout and a homerun fence. Beyond that, cornstalks no higher than grass start to poke through the earth.

PART TEN

The Tomorrow People

I sit in my office, correcting papers. The stack is huge. When I first started as a college teacher, I collected assignments and handed them back almost immediately, not because I was good but because I was nervous. Now I am less nervous and less efficient. I see the pointlessness of efficiency in the classroom. None of my colleagues turn around papers one class to the next. The president has not suggested I correct faster. Students expect their papers to come back immediately with happy words written in the corners and great grades next to their titles but they seldom complain when it takes two or three weeks to get something back.

What's to say about any of their stories, anyway?
They're all pretty good.
The great ones I love.
The terrible ones I forgive and blow past.
All my students need to write more.
They need to read more.

They need to acknowledge that technology and intellect are almost incompatible or that technology is the result of intellect and not the inverse. On the first day of every class I say, "You can't be an artist with your face glued to a phone," and half the class moans at my perceived ignorance while the other half nods that constant communication and a steady stream of useless and negative information is intellectual and emotional death.

A student asked me recently, "How many months will it take to become a writer, like approximately?"

I said, "Give yourself one hundred and twenty months and if it still hasn't happened, give yourself another one hundred and twenty more months."

She laughed and I laughed but she knew I was serious and I knew I'd lowballed her, that twenty years to become a writer for a student from Western Pennsylvania who will have to work eight hours a day at the minimum to survive was an optimistic number, a prediction made of gold and silver and lies.

She could write for fifty years and never publish a book.

She could write for fifty years and never finish a book.

Or she could write westerns.

Or she could write romance novels.

For so many years I did not write enough because I could not imagine being a writer, because I did not know writers, because I did not know how it worked, being a writer. The end result of writing I could imagine—my name on a cover. I could not imagine the process. Writing a book was as simple as typing. But to finish a book, to find the perfect moment and match that moment with the exact words it required, stood beyond my comprehension. And should I finish a book, a stack of pages that really wasn't a book even but a book waiting to become a book, then what? What the fuck does someone in East Pittsburgh do with a finished novel about Pittsburgh? Find a blowtorch and go back to work on a bridge?

And yet, and yet.

Turgenev said, "The word tomorrow was invented for indecisive people and children," and he grew up with wealthy parents and was educated at the best schools in Russia and traveled around Europe at his leisure.

And yet.

The curse of class is inevitable but not insurmountable. To be a writer who starts on your own, or to be a writer who starts at a community college, means you will have to give up more than the writer who starts at a university or the writer who has parents who read and love books and encourage creativity over practicality. The writer starting on the undercard will have to watch less TV and take fewer naps and eat shittier food. The maps you will actually need, the ones you will use, will be the size of your thumb because you will not travel and you will not leave because travel and leaving cost money and money is the price we pay for time and time is the currency writers deal in.

Most of my students are not going to write past their last creative course because being a writer requires the dedication of a jail sentence without guards. Very few people can lock themselves down and stay there.

Very few will keep reading.

But I hope they understand answers are possible if you are willing to stretch your brain then put those thoughts and stories into writing. There can be hope within the bubble of hopelessness. I became a welder because I read and wrote and took the time to think each day, and because I became a welder I learned to survive and pay my bills, and because I could pay my bills, I learned to focus and grow. I expanded my love of books and started writing seriously. I wrote western novels and made money, and because I wrote westerns and understood the shittiness of it, the ridiculousness of heroes and villains, I believed and believe I can become a real writer, one who makes books that linger because of language and story and not violence and cliché and escape.

I think I am here, teaching, to prove that.

Motherfuck I want a book of my own.

So Sayeth Us All

The phone rings.

It's Berryman

He says, "You interested in getting lunch?"

"With you?" I say.

"Come on," he says. "Yes, with me."
I say, "I have a stack of student papers to grade."
"How many?"
"A lot."
I pick one up and read a line: Working at the car wash in wintertime was worse because my gloves froze like popsicles.
I draw a star next to it and say: this is a great opening line!
He says, "You could skim-correct them."
"I could," I say, "but I'd feel guilty."
"Next week?"
"Will I be done correcting papers?"
"Well yeah," Berryman says, "and can we get lunch?"
"You bet," I say.
He says, "You're not going to give me the nudge next week when I call?"
"I might," I say.
"Good enough," Berryman says. "I'll talk to you next week."
I hang up and pick up the next student paper.
Then I set aside my students' papers, the whole stack, and open a book, a collection of recently translated poems by Sergei Yesenin. Yesenin was a madman of Russian literature, a poet of simple words about daily living who drank too much and married too often, a romantic who once divorced his second wife to marry an American dancer who was twenty years older than him and knew eighteen words of Russian and Yesenin spoke no English. He knocked up women like a Moscow bartender pours vodka shots and he eventually married the granddaughter of Leo Tolstoy. Mayakovsky, another Russian poet of love and money, once said, "Readers now know Yesenin more from the police log than they do from his poems," which may have been true, though Yesenin kept writing poems and drinking and marrying up until his suicide in a hotel room where he stepped from a chair with a rope around his neck. The poems he left behind are direct and clear, little heart punches of romance and sweeping the floor.

The Russian people loved him.

Whom shall I call on, Yesenin wrote, who will share with me the wretched happiness of staying alive?

That's what I try to teach my students, the wretched happiness of staying alive.

That's what I try to learn every day.

The places to fall down are numerous and inevitable but there are moments to rise up within each collapse and enjoy success.

I said Yesenin committed suicide but theories exist that he was murdered, that the communists grew weary of his popularity, a personal art that exceeds the state.

But then all our suicides are murders, so sayeth all of us on our worst days.

PART ELEVEN

Harry's Bar

M**egan bartends, hustling, pouring**, snagging tips, then stopping to talk between hustles and pours and silver change and wet dollar bills. She machines the whole room in direct lines but still manages to be friendly, to stop and chat with most of the customers who usually come here a couple times a week for a drink or a sandwich. The afternoon crowd, mostly men and women from the courthouse, people concerned with sandwiches and French fries and getting back to work, drops away, and the construction crowd arrives, guys and a few women in dirty jeans and flannel shirts who sneak drafts while their wives and girlfriends and mothers and boyfriends and husbands and priests and ministers think they're plastering and painting and plumbing the world.

I sit at the bar, drinking a draft, happy to be near Megan, happy to watch someone who so obviously cares about people and taking care of them. If I taught like she served, my students would rule small companies. I dream it for myself and them.

Megan pours me another beer.

Then another.

The draft is cold enough to drink in two sips, though I try to use three because I want to make the time last. Megan drinks beer from a juice glass between her strolls through the bar, sometimes peeling a peanut for nutrition when she comes back to rest and regroup and chat.

She says, "I would do the protein diet if I could drink beer while I was on it," and she pops an unshelled peanut in her mouth followed by one in a shell to suck for salt before spitting it into the trashcan.

I say, "I don't think it works like that. Beer is like communion, not a meat."

"What do you know about dieting?"

"I'm on the everything diet."

"You're so skinny."

"I run constantly."

She says, "Every time I see you, you have a Mountain Dew in one hand and a Slim Jim, or some shitty meat stick, in the other but you never get fat."

"Slim Jims are great," I say, "but it's usually jerky, preferably extra hot. I get huge bags from Bundy's Up In Smoke House."

"There is no such place," she says, and laughs. "That's not a real name."

"There is and that's the name. I smelled it up on Route 22, past Murrysville."

"Bullshit," she says. "You always have these weird eating places. And you've never dieted in your life."

"I wrestled for years. I always dieted. I lived on canned tuna in high school then chicken breasts when I was in college."

She says, "Did you really wrestle Kurt Angle?"

"I really did not," I say. "That was my friend Lawrence Riggins. You don't listen to any of my stories, do you?"

"Eat a peanut, wiseguy," she says, and pushes me the basket of mostly shells. She says, "I listen to all your stories, you big vagina."

She flicks a shell from the bar so it flies at my head.

I bat it back so it sticks in her hair and she has to pick it out.

She says, "Look at those reflexes."

"Wrestling," I say. "It's all diet and mad skill."

"I still can't get over that you were a wrestler. All the wrestlers I knew in high school were total lunkheads. And all my professors are total pussies. I have this world history class and the professor weeps constantly. Holocaust, weep. Palestine, weep."

"He's an equal-opportunity weeper."

"He is, and a total pussy. I like him but I don't know how he functions in the world. Everything brings him to tears. I mean, I get it. Palestine should be its own state. The world is awful. But it's everywhere. That probably shouldn't be a constant epiphany. All my teachers are just such wimps. I just can't imagine a wrestler, or an athlete of any kind, ending up on whatever track one ends up on to be a professor. It just seems like if you start as a wrestler or a football player or whatever, you end up as a truck driver. To end up a professor you have to start with professor parents or whatever."

"That could be true."

"Except for you."

"Probably not just me."

She says, "Because you were raised by a single mom and wrestled and worked as an iron guy on bridges or whatever, you ended up a professor—is that it?"

"Sort of," I say. "I had an amazing librarian in high school that was really encouraging and I wrote a bunch of western novels."

Megan smiles and says, "Why won't you let me read your western novels?"

"Because they're embarrassing, even though I'm proud to have written them."

"What was your pen name?"

"Yeah, no way," I say, still keeping that private.

"Oh come on, Louis L'Amour! You have to tell!"

I finish my beer in a chug as an answer and she refills it.

She says, "I'll be back. I have to check on my more forthcoming customers." She says, "I bet your pen name was Slim Howdy."

She punches my arm as she walks by.

I turn my mug so the handle is on the right side and will be ready to be lifted by my drinking hand once I'm thirsty again. In the last month I have switched from drinking bottles to drafts in hopes of building on my paltry savings account. My plan is to reduce my alcohol spending by thirty-three percent, increase my savings by thirty-four cents on the dollar for every drink I take that is not bottled, then buy a couple extra books and make time to read them by spending less time in bars.

I may even purchase a new lamp.

I look forward to the time alone, though I sometimes become overly reflective and retreat to the company of others, if only the sounds of strangers.

Currently, on most Thursdays, I come here with sixty bucks and spend it all, a task that always feels impossible yet I conquer it easily. I get drunk. I get happy. I get friendly. Next round on me, strangers. I love the jukebox and soft pretzels dipped in cheese. I love fried cheese sticks. I love fried anything. Those costs add up. During the weekend and early parts of the week, I do better. I tuck my money and focus on sandwiches and tall glasses of cold Mountain Dew with free refills. *Free Refills* should be a logo on a shirt I'd wear.

Megan swings back with empties to refill and says, "You look serious."

"I'm making big financial plans in my head."

"Make enough for both of us."

"Stock market stuff," I say. "Big time things."

She fills one mug and slides another under the still running tap without spilling a drop, a golden river filling many oceans.

She says, "I'll sell you this bar."

"That's not saving me money," I say.

The angels of money-saving circle me and whisper in my ear to quit being such a generous douche. I need to quit swatting them away. I need to not buy drinks for strangers when I am not drinking, when I am there for the soup and crackers.

Megan takes the beers, four in two hands, and goes back to the crowd.

My lunch budget is the next cut.

No more sandwich combos, even when they sound inexpensive.

Pretzels are fine.

I could get through the day on jerky and canned soda.

I could eat peanut butter and jelly sandwiches like I'm in fourth grade.

From across the bar Megan yells, "I see you making a budget in your head."

Customers look and laugh.

"Lies," I say, loud enough so they can hear. "All lies."

Next month my savings account should appear like a thin head of foam on a large draft of debt if I manage my social spending, even though my social spending provides much of the joy in my life. Please be my friend, all of you.

Apartment? The cheapest box I could find.

Truck? Years old with tread still on the tires.

Students loans? Yes, enormous, forever.

Vacations? Never.

Fancy clothes? None.

Bag lunches and lonely dinners are the answer.

I have nowhere else to cut.

Megan completes her task and sits down on my side of the bar on the next stool.

She says, "Drinks on me tonight."

"No way," I say.

Megan reaches over the bar and grabs a white rag to wipe up while she sits.

She says, "You give but you don't know how to accept."

"I accept," I say. "I let my gram buy me lunch a while ago."

"Did you offer to pay?" she says, and stands and wipes around me and circles me with her body so it's against mine and she keeps wiping until she is back behind the bar.

"I felt you doing that sexy wiping," I say.

"That wasn't sexy wiping," she says. "Those were my tits against your back."

"That makes it sound dirty," I say.

"Never," she says, and drops the rag and covers her chest and makes an exasperated face like tits are dirty and need to be hidden by cupped hands and she'd never noticed until I pointed it out.

"I see you mocking me," I say.

"I'm flirting with you," she says. "When are you going to learn the difference?"

She moves her hands and smiles.

She says, "Don't make me juggle my tits."

I scrunch up my eyes and say, "I can't see anything."

"You're safe," she says. "I'm not juggling."

Her boobs stretch the fabric of her black v-neck t-shirt. She wears extra make-up tonight, not too much but certainly more than she needs. Tips require it, or so she believes. Some nights her face is clean and smooth and the lines around her eyes do magic and make her look younger. Always, her jeans are tight. Always, it's jeans. One time, at a poetry reading I made my class attend, she wore a skirt and a sweater. When she walked in the door, I thought she was the visiting writer. Then the visiting writer, a woman I'd never seen before, showed up in a black leather jacket and black jeans. She wore more rings than she had fingers and sported dark sunglasses in a dimly lit room, a sixty-three-year-old woman dressed like a teenage hoodlum from a greaser movie. She read in an affected voice. Her stories blew fake air. Megan's stories never blow. She lives the kind of life the visiting writer romanticized, waitressing, bartending, all the grit but with none of the suffering and broke-ass status. Megan writes truth like most of us breathe. The visiting writer dreamed grit and woke up fancy.

Now Megan wipes the far end of the bar and tosses the rag in the sink.

If she were not my bartender, my student, my sometimes drug connection, I think I would ask her to marry me. I've said that before, maybe more than once. Because she is my bartender and my student and my sometimes connection, I would marry her. I've probably said that too. I wish she would see me as the marrying kind. But I think she doesn't believe in marriage, the trap of it. Underneath my wrestling-welding veneer I am a romantic and monogamous and Megan sees it. She feels my desire for stability and connection and it makes her unsure. She hears me mutter that I'd like kids, little boy and girl wrestlers to wake up and play with, and she imagines small children ruining her perfect tits and baby puke on her favorite jeans.

I think so and hope not.

Into the Evening, Buzzed

Megan says I should sleep with my students, her regular joke. "You know the ladies like you," she says. She pushes her shoulder into me, like: come on.

How to say lovely and in love?

Kiss me, Megan, please.

I'll stay here all night.

HARRIET

Harriet, the owner, Megan's grandmother, has finished popping the popcorn, the one job she refuses to concede. The bar smells like a movie theater, like buttered heaven. When Harriet walks, she doesn't take her feet off the floor. Most nights she wears slippers. When Megan tells her that slippers are no good for her feet, Harriet wears running shoes with bulky white tube socks that she pulls up to her knees like stockings. Nona wears tube socks like that sometimes. Harriet is older than Nona and the years have worked Harriet over in worse ways.

Harriet says, "More popcorn?"

I say, "More popcorn would be great."

She says, "It's always good to see you."

I say, "It's always good to see you."

She takes my basket and starts her slow shuffle towards the popcorn machine that sits at the back of the bar by the office door.

She says, to me I think, "It's always good to see you but you drink too much," and she laughs and raises the empty basket over her head to make her point.

"It's true," Megan says. "You drink too much."

"You serve too much," I say.

So it is that another night ends in jokes and dreams.

PART TWELVE

The River Awaits Us

But, for now, Berryman waits in an empty office. I buy a Coke Zero and a Mountain Dew and cut through the cafeteria. I'm obsessed with Mountain Dew. It's the superfruit of sodas. The office Berryman shares is cinderblock and painted institutional yellow. When I knock on the open door and lean in, I see Berryman playing some card game on his laptop.

"Don't you ever correct papers?" I say.

"Already done," he says.

"Where're the adjuncts?"

"They hate me because I have this Americorps job and it's full-time. I assured them the job is temporary, which maybe helped a little."

"You want to go kayaking?"

"Me and you?"

"No, Berryman," I say, "with the school. Student services needs chaperones."

"Hell yeah," Berryman says. "I'm in."

"Alright, I'll tell the boss."

I toss him a Coke Zero.

He fumbles the can then grabs it before it hits the floor.

He reads the label, very thoughtful, like he's never seen a Coke Zero.

I say, "It's better than Diet Coke."

He says, "There're chemicals in this, worse than Diet Coke, I think."

"No," I say. "Only good chemicals in there."

He says, "I wasn't allowed sugar growing up."

"And you're fat now," I say. "My mom force-fed me sugar and Mc-Donalds."

"I wouldn't say I'm fat," he says, eyes turned down on his gut.

"I guess you wouldn't say that."

He pops the Coke Zero and says, "When is it?"

"The kayaking trip?" I say. "The boss didn't mention a date."

Berryman says, "Because I have a trip planned to go back to New Jersey and see my parents in a couple weeks."

"Always with the fucking New Jersey," I say.

MORE ON KAYAKING

The next day I see Dr. Bronse, dressed in a professional skirt and blazer but without shoes and wearing socks over her pantyhose, power-walking down the hall.

She smiles and waves but doesn't stop.

I say, "Exercising or rushing somewhere?"

She says, "We may have to cancel the kayaking trip."

"It's okay," I say. "Just let me know."

"You're the best," she says, and waves and pushes on.

The next time I see her she wears shoes and says, "Kayaking trip is back on."

PART THIRTEEN

My Hero, Gorilla Mike

Right now I'm writing my seventh consecutive unpublished literary novel.

My sixth unpublished literary novel is about the summer Mike Polarski, aka Gorilla Mike, age fourteen, lived in his parents' house by himself while they divorced and each pretended the other person would handle the parenting. Mike's dad drove truck over the road. Mike's mom cut hair and did color at the Hair Works beauty salon. Down to an apple and three slices of Wonder Bread, and realizing neither parent would be back soon, Mike woke early one morning and walked a couple miles to the construction site where they were building a strip mall, a huge L-shaped plaza with fast food restaurants to follow and line up along the edge of the parking lot.

Mike needed work because Mike needed money, because Mike needed food.

When the foreman wouldn't hire him—because he couldn't hire kids—Mike started carrying lumber, eavesdropping on the foreman then acting on his own, grabbing stacks of wood and bags of concrete. Running for tools. Carrying water. No one stopped him. At the end of the first day the crew kicked up a few bucks to pay Mike for his efforts. The next day Mike came back. They sent him for sandwiches and coffee.

They sent him for shingles and pipe. This went on. Mike worked. Mike got paid. Mike slept. Mike worked again. He rode his bike to Giant Eagle and bought groceries. June into July. The same thing.

After he'd saved some money, a stack of twenties rolled up and gum-banded then stuffed in a Band Aid box in the bathroom closet, after he'd fished in Sewickley Creek on Friday night and Saturday morning and Saturday night and Sunday morning, after he caught thirty-six trout and cleaned them and ate two cooked in a pan with butter and put the rest in the freezer, Mike gave some money to his creepy neighbor, Gonzo Billy, real name William Gongoware, to buy two cases of cheap beer. Mike invited over his pals and everyone got rotted. They drank and ate fried fish and puked in the bushes out back and rode skateboards down the carpeted gameroom stairs. Everyone slept over. Everyone woke late and went home.

Mike cleaned up.

He cooked eggs and ate eggs.

Then, on Monday, Mike walked back to the construction site and did his job and kept doing his job. By August his body had widened and thickened and browned in the sun until someone, another fourteen-year-old goof who didn't have to work construction to buy peanut butter and white bread, said, "Look at the size of Mike. Dude's a gorilla," and Mike nodded, badass, Gorilla Mike, it stuck, a walking trophy for learning to survive.

In real life, back in my neighborhood, this happened over seven months. Mike balanced school and work and fishing, sans parents, as the utilities turned off one by one. All the other kids in the neighborhood kept Mike's secret because we knew our parents would call the cops and the cops would drop Mike in the system and we knew foster kids. Foster kids were fucked.

Around Thanksgiving Mike's aunt tracked him down and forced Mike to move in. Then she forced him out. Mike slept in the woods. His aunt tracked him down and found him under a sleeping bag and said, "You can't sleep in the woods," but she didn't say where he could sleep. Mike said, "Okay," and kept sleeping in the woods. Then Mike lived with his grandpa. His grandpa said, "Okay, you're Mike," like they were strangers meeting at the bus stop. Mike said, "I'm Mike, yeah." His grandpa frowned and offered Mike the couch in the basement.

Then he lived with his mom in her new place, his mom who acted appalled then threatened to call the cops on his dad, the truckfuck who was supposed to be caring for Mike. She said, "Mike, you're my strong little man," and bought him some fancy Adidas sneaks.

A month later her boyfriend, a Pagan with a neck tattoo, finished running drugs from Florida and showed back up and wondered why some kid was living in his apartment with his old lady. Mike moved back in with his aunt, who had her own middle-aged boyfriend with various tattoos by now. She shipped Mike back to his grandpa.

The grandpa said, "Here you are again," and opened another bottle of whiskey and found a glass and said, "No one wants you, huh?"

Mike shrugged.

The grandpa handed Mike a can of tuna and a can opener.

He pointed Mike downstairs.

He said, "You mind the basement."

Mike said, "Okay."

This continued for years, a game of musical houses.

I cut the story from the original seven months to three because readers will believe a horror story but not a story of drudgery. The kid in the attic, drinking her own piss—you bet. The boy set on fire by his crazy uncle—definitely. The sensational lives of our white-souled victims and their outrageous perpetrators make for windows worth viewing, glimpses into worlds we are not. But the small horrors of daily survival are too tiny in their pain, too relentless in their repetition, and not large enough in their hope to hold the attention of readers obsessed with superheroes and super villains, a world divided into two parts, good and evil, cops and robbers.

My buddy Mike quit school.

He got his GED.

He joined the Army and never saw combat.

Now he works for Jiffy Lube as a manager.

You don't get to be a celebrity by waking up and eating Wonder Bread and going to work, no matter your age, so why read that shit.

Art as a mirror requires introspection, which requires change.

If you read the story of a kid in 1995, living on his own in a house with blankets over every window to lessen the autumn breeze, and how he sometimes cooks his food over a small fire at the bottom of the driveway, then you'd be forced to realize you could be his neighbor or his teacher or his aunt or his parent.

But you would not put Mike in an attic for years.

But you would not turn Mike into a torch for laughs and cruelty.

You, me, us, we're too good for that, obviously.

We read horror novels, we are not horrors.

Now, look at those losers working at Walmart.

Why are they so slow ringing my groceries?

The manager of Jiffy Lube is a crooked crook.

He wants to charge you for an air filter when you may not need an air filter.

Fucking conman bastard piece of shit.

MONEY-MAKING MACHINE

I could have made Gorilla Mike a pioneer and crammed his life into a couple hundred pages and sold him as a western hero.

Old men would have loved his ingenuity.

MY SEMI-RETIREMENT FROM WESTERN NOVELS

I haven't written a western novel in three years.

I'm proud of that, quitting cowboys and blacksmiths, quitting ranch hands and women delivering babies on beds stuffed with hay. Not that anyone notices or gives a shit about my artistic habits or dreams but walking away from writing that pays money, no matter how little, no matter how sorry, is a form of recovery because writing for money, for attention, to please, is an addiction and every addiction provides its own difficult kick.

When I quit writing western novels, my editor called and said, "You'll be back."

I said, "Maybe."

She said, "Oh, you will."

I'm not proud when it comes to earning money. If it paid enough, and I was desperate enough, I'd probably coach wrestling at a prep school, teaching rich kids the chicken wing.

A year later my editor sent a note that read, "Seriously?"

A week later she called and said, "You can write your literary novels and western novels. Western novels don't take that much time. Come on already."

I said, "It's not just time. It's more of a spiritual crisis."

"A spiritual crisis?" she said. "You really are a pussy."

"I'm just sensitive," I said. "It hasn't helped me much."

She said, "At least the patriarchy was run by real men. You knew who the enemy was. Now it's just a bunch of whiny cunts."

"I don't know what that means," I said, "but if I change my mind about writing a new western novel, I'll get back to you."

She said, "You're gross," and hung up on me.

My last western book, set in the years following the Civil War, followed a Missouri man, John Davis Eggert, a farmer turned reluctant soldier, a former confederate infantryman who never understood what he was fighting for or who he was fighting with. A pacifist by nature and religion, JD Eggert refused the war on both sides until the union passed through his farm and burned his house and killed his wife. The story ends up in Mexico, the same as a couple other westerns I'd written, but I thought this one, with its slightly more complex moral issues around race and class and geography, moved away from pulp and inched toward literature, even if a canyon of reading still divided the two genres. It was almost three hundred pages long, the length of a real novel. You couldn't guess the ending after reading the beginning.

Honestly, I was pretty happy with myself.

My editor said, "What the hell am I supposed to do with this piece of shit?"

"Publish it," I said.

"Publish it he says. We work in templates. To keep cost down, we need two-hundredish-page books. One-hundred-page books are better. This is a fucking trilogy or something. No old man will read this."

"Old men love this stuff."

"Is this novel true?" she said. "Did you steal this from a history book or something?" She said, "Am I gonna get sued over this bitch manuscript?"

"Of course not," I said. "I made the whole thing up."

"I think you're lying to me," she said.

But she published it.

After she edited away one hundred pages.

And sent me a bill for her editing services.

Which was fine.

I'd already been writing unpublished literary novels and teaching kids and dreaming artistic dreams, none of it while holding a welding gun in my hand or Honeywell goggles covering my eyes to block the sparks.

PART FOURTEEN

Berryman Follow-up

"One more question about that kayak trip," Berryman says. "Will we have to supply our own kayaks or will the kayaks be provided?"

"You're joking, Berryman," I say.

"I was thinking, because I'm going to back to New Jersey, and if the trip comes after that, because I have a kayak at my parents' house, we used to kayak on the lake when I was younger, so I could bring my own kayak if kayaks aren't provided. I could share it with the students or something. That's all I was saying."

I'm in my office, typing on my newest unpublished novel and arguing with an agent via email about my sixth unpublished novel, the one about Gorilla Mike. One of the brothers in *The Brothers Karamazov* said, basically, "The more I love mankind as a whole, the less I love man in particular." You could think for years on that quote. I have. I ponder it as Berryman stands there with his kayak face.

"It's a pretty good kayak," Berryman says. "Great balance, easy to roll through."

"Berryman," I say. "We are scheduled to take a kayaking trip with students from a community college, most of whom are poor, none of whom own kayaks. I neither own nor can afford a kayak. So—do you think kayaks will be provided?"

"Bad question," Berryman says. "My apologies."

"We will rent whatever shitty kayaks we can afford."

"Perfect, that's great."

I say, "The trip will probably get canceled anyway."

"That'd be a shame."

I say, "Do you read Dostoyevsky?"

"I do. I have. I had an AP English class on him in high school."

"You had a high school class on Dostoyevsky?"

"Russian literature. We read Turgenev and some Tolstoy and Chekov. A bunch of stuff. The poems of Anna Akmatova."

"The poems of Anna Akmatova, nice," I say, disgusted. Then, "No one will ever accuse you of being undereducated."

"You say that like it's a bad thing."

Berryman wears jeans today, nice jeans, not too blue but expensive. I see Brad Pitt in a similar pair on the covers of the tabloids in the grocery store, only Brad Pitt is skinny and beautiful. Berryman needs a belt. His jeans fit below his gut and they constantly need to be tugged to stay afloat around the bubbly river of his waist. He tugs his jeans now, awkwardly.

"It's about balance, Berryman," I say. "You never learned a trade."

Berryman stands there, thinking, failing at thinking, pulling up his pants.

THE AGENTS

Berryman leaves and I go back to the conversation I'm having with the agent. The last thing he wrote was, "Don't you have anything more high concept? It's obvious you can write but the market is very tough right now and high concept really helps."

I write back, "What's high concept?" and wait.

Thirty seconds later he responds, "Thanks for the opportunity. I'm not the agent for you. Good luck with your writing."

I told you about the novel I'd sent him, the Gorilla Mike story.

How do you take a teenager living on his own, working construction, using his wages to buy peanut butter and bread and the occasional Domino's pizza, and make it high concept without destroying the intention of the story, which was and is to show the pressures and successes of being a teenager living on his own, the impossibility of that, having to maintain your freedom and to stay out of foster care, to show the neglect so many of us experience from an early age? Then: oops, here's a laser. Here's a shotgun blast to the face.

I sent the same novel to another agent and he said, "Turn it into a mystery."

The next agent said, "More violence. Less insight. You keep talking about how your characters feel and their circumstances. Readers want to turn pages."

I sent it to a third agent, a woman. She represented a nonfiction book I loved about the building of the Brooklyn Bridge told from the perspective of the people who worked on the bridge, the men who dove deep and planted the base in the mud of the East River, the politicians who wanted it, the engineer who designed it, the women who rolled in with food carts selling jars of beans and sandwiches for lunch, the whole book a sort of oral history of what it was like to live and grind in New York in the late 1880s, what it was like to create a bridge of such size and importance when resources were so limited that the base had to be made of white pine trees cut and hauled in from Alabama.

I purposely ignored that this agent mainly sold chick-lit books about wealthy women in crisis over horrible and hot young men, whether to date or ignore or destroy them, and that her website, which featured the covers of books she'd recently sold, mainly looked like an ad for skinny jeans and the Eiffel Tower.

A couple months later she wrote back to say, "Yeah, but what happens when things really get bad? I mean, big bad mojo fucked-up bad."

I'm sure she wanted to sound friendly, yet be realistic about the market and my chances, not just in the market but for representation at all. I appreciate that and I understand her realistic approach but the commodities she deals in are books and books require intelligence, I want to believe that, it's on the dotted line, reading is not a search engine, it's the coal that fires the engine of your brain, and I didn't even know what "big bad mojo fucked-up bad" meant except that maybe she wanted Gorilla Mike to get stabbed or felled by a steel beam so I wrote back, less friendly but more precise, "Those Megan Tiara books you agent are really great. Literature needs another rich chick who loves to shop for shoes in Manhattan."

She wrote back, "Literature doesn't need you, asshole."

She's right, of course.

Literature doesn't need me.

But here it is, the 21st century, and I still need literature.

Turn Up the Misogyny

Some agents only take queries by old-fashioned mail. Jean Lessing was like that. Nine months after I'd sent her a query and some sample chapters, her assistant, a young woman named Lauren Hendricks, sent me a response.

Across my cover letter, in big curvy letters, she scribbled, "Love the misogyny! Turn it up!" then signed her name inside a huge purple heart.

Maybe she was twenty-one years old, an intern.

Maybe she was being sarcastic.

The purple heart, though, it looked so sincere.

I taped the letter to the wall over my desk.

I wanted it to remind me of something but I'm not sure what.

Writing

The next day I don't teach so I sit down to write. Nothing comes. I stand up. I sit down. Out on the back porch of my little apartment, I smoke a couple puffs off a joint. This doesn't help. I eat two huge handfuls of peanuts and chug some water. I want to write what I want to write and I do, I write my world, but I have these six unpublished novels and I wonder, repeatedly, what matters and where and how and why do I fail? I've sent out to forty-six agents and the best explanation I've heard came from an agent who said, "Willy Vlautin"—a contemporary writer I admire and one of the few successful writers talking about people with bad jobs and no money—"wouldn't have a book deal if he hadn't been in a band for ten years and written a bunch of songs and sold a shit-ton of records."

I considered that for days.

No band, no book deal.

But if you're not in a band, and I'm not, I'm tone deaf and can't play chopsticks, then the job of the publisher is to make you look like you're in a band, look like you're somebody, then people will read your books and you'll become somebody, a writer.

When did that die?

And why?

I sit down to write.

I push keys and listen to my memory and my imagination.

I have a steel mill novel I'm working on.

Braddock, PA, 15104.

Edgar Thompson Works.

One of the few active mills in Western Pennsylvania, it sits across the river and down the hill from one of the greatest amusement parks in America, Kennywood, and one of the oldest and best rollercoasters on the continent, The Thunderbolt, where kids and parents take the big drop at fifty-five miles per hour, arms up, blessed to feel the wood frame rattle and the metal rails ping. I know a woman who works in the mill. She has two kids and a husband with one leg. She's barely forty but he turned sixty last summer. He collects social security, is diabetic, is still drinking. He does not take his insulin. He smokes. He's fifty-percent legless with the doctors talking about taking his other foot. Every time I see her, she says, "You have to write my story." She says it joking but serious. Her dad reads my westerns. He's old and half-deaf and walks with a cane. She brought him to see me at the library when I gave a talk. I signed his books, dog-eared with broken spines. I said, "Thank you." He said, "What?" I said, "Thank you." He tapped his hearing aid. He nodded. He shook my hand. The woman thanked me profusely, more than necessary. She drove her dad home and came back to buy him a copy of my new novel as a gift. She thanked me profusely again.

Sometimes I see her in the bars around Turtle Creek and Wilmerding. She always says, "My husband gets drunk and weeps every year when I take the kids to Kennywood because he can't ride anything because of his leg. Tell that. Then tell about how I want to punch him in the face with an iron mitt." She says, "It's no fun living with a drunk, not when you're raising two kids and working full-time. I fucking love Kennywood."

I stand up in my apartment.

My apartment is in Wall, down the hill from Radform Tool. We used to have a strip club but it closed. Now we have a building filled with storage units.

I have a two-hundred-page draft based on the woman who works at the mill and takes her kids to baseball games on bobblehead night and coaches her daughter's softball team in Pitcairn and pours cold milk over her husband's head when he's too drunk to do anything but slur for another drink. I love the character she's becoming in my book, she's interesting to me, more interesting than TV or whatever won the National Book Award last year, and maybe she would be interesting to someone else but those people read Steinbeck from the 1930s and I can't get an agent who thinks a story about a steelworker and her kids and her stub-legged husband will sell to a publisher, let alone a publisher who thinks the story should be bound up in paper and shipped to warehouses then bookstores for the world to buy.

What would help, of course, would be for someone to lean too far on the Thunderbolt and fall out and over the edge and hit the pavement and wake up remembering ghosts or having stepped through time and into another dimension.

But everyone rides the ride, finishes safe, and gets in line again. People ride the Thunderbolt endlessly. If the cars jam on the top rail, riders look down and wave to strangers and family and friends until the electricity returns and the coasters roll down and back to the start for the next row of enthusiasts to jump inside and hang on.

So much joy, so little death.

The weekend fills up with fried food and lemonade and more rides, faster rides, helicopters, The Jackrabbit, then slower rides, Ferris wheels, carousels, then no rides, kids holding hands, adults holding hands, six high school bands walking through the park and banging drums and blowing horns, old men slamming anvils to win teddy bears.

Monday is a workday, that motherfucker.

SUCCESS

I stand up and pace around my apartment, all three rooms.

I said failure, and that's true, true and unavoidable, but failing as a writer also means success as a person, as someone who rejects the easiest and most obvious course.

Even though, of course, success couched as failure is still failure.

But failing as a person provides a direct line into the narratives that matter most.

So we are not binaries, winners and losers, but listeners and talkers of various and endless degrees, users of language to create meaning from the tragedy of daily living.

I've written the books I wanted to write, no matter if they're ever published.

The public world is so filled with explosions and perfect physiques, shouters and politicians, golden parachutes and houses the size of small planets, privileged people yelling at other people to acknowledge their privilege, that to be ignored for talking about the working poor is the greatest reward.

Until, of course, it isn't.

I want to publish a fucking book.

My desk is antique, or at least old, a huge wooden number with a roll top. I bought it from a man who wanted to move to Vermont but believed the desk was too heavy to travel. It was a yard sale, a picture of the desk on a card table with some knickknacks because he couldn't carry it down the stairs and into the grass. I told him I was strong. I told him I had friends. He wanted a hundred bucks. I offered him twenty-five and immediate pick-up.

The desk is the size of my bed.

I could sleep on it and sometimes do.

NO ONE READS GORDON LISH

I stare at the letter taped over my desk— "Love the misogyny! Turn it up!"

I once asked Berryman, "Do you think anyone really cares about poetry?"

He said, "Of course," then went back to eating an apple.

East Pittsburgh Downlow

Berryman knows how to eat. He chomps. He swallows. He chomps. He takes down an apple like a beaver takes apart a log. He loves food and eats like a man who can afford it.

He said, "The problem with apples is I can eat a dozen."

"What about the problem with poetry?" I said.

"There is none," Berryman said.

He'd been to school for poetry. He knows poets and those poets know other writers, journalists and editors and publishers, and those gatekeepers write about poetry in public places, newspapers and big websites and university journals, and they consider the implications of the sonnet and review published books of poems with blurbs from other poets, usually friends and colleagues and former professors, so poetry matters.

But I know waitresses and waiters and welders and plumbers, romance novelists and professors who teach classes in plumbing, and they love rock n roll, Led Zeppelin and Aretha Franklin, they love films, *Goodfellas* and *Star Wars*, and if they care about poetry at all it's as a memory of high school, a class to be endured like biology or playing dodgeball in gym.

I asked Berryman, "How many books do you sell?"

Berryman shrugged.

He said, "It's not polite to talk about book sales."

"Only if you don't need book sales to pay the rent," I said.

Because I've written books to sell, westerns, and see how little they sell, I'm not surprised how poorly actual literature sells, let alone poetry. In an interview right before he retired, after being asked about his impact on literature, Philip Roth answered, "I don't know. Maybe some. Maybe none. Maybe I don't care anymore. I'm old. Most of my books sell twenty-five thousand copies in hardback. Some sell a little less, some a little more. Every once in a while one of my books will cross over and sell big numbers. I have no idea how that happens or why. I no longer care."

I finished the interview and thought about Philip Roth selling twenty-five grand.

I think of Philip Roth as the most decorated author in America, even though he writes sex scenes like an eighth grader and I find most of his books over-written.

Twenty-five grand.

That's like a failed pop song.

That's like Guns N' Roses in a half-empty stadium on a rainy night with only one original member still in the band and the lead singer refusing to play the hits.

It was a scandal when a reporter revealed that a story collection nominated for the National Book Award a few years ago sold nine hundred copies.

Gordon Lish, who is a terrible writer and, from many accounts, a terrible person, but who was a wonderful editor and nurturer of talent, sells no books. I mean none. In the late 1970s, when normal people still read, before images completely punched a hole in what was left of book-life in an America already obsessed with TV, Lish edited fiction and poetry for *Esquire* magazine. He worked with, most famously, Raymond Carver, but he also worked with Barry Hannah, Amy Bender, and Mary Robison, all pretty brilliant writers. From *Esquire,* Lish moved to Knopf, one of the most prestigious and historical literary houses in the country, the press that discovered and published James Baldwin. Lish stayed at Knopf for years and edited hundreds of authors. His own books started to appear. His own books make no sense and often feel interchangeable with each other but so what—he lived in New York, the book capitol of America, and created literary stars by editing their paragraphs down to sentences. Claiming that his edits constituted co-writes or that his edits constituted full-on writes, meaning his edits were more important than the original text itself, only added to his prominence. The pages of print devoted to Lish and his crew have garnered him a huge amount of attention, maybe more than any editor ever and as much as most famous living writers. He's appeared in *The New York Times* and *The New Yorker* and *The LA Times* and *The Chicago Tribune* and every best-selling men's magazine in America and most of Europe, his stories crammed between fake tits and expensive watches, celebrity profiles and record reviews.

The talent, the mouth, the ego!

The endlessness of all three combining!

Book sales should soar when the amount of newsprint smeared across the western world is that high, when your name appears a few pages away from politicians and movie stars.

But Gordon Lish's last book, published in 2013, sold fifty-seven copies.

Consider that.

Fifty-seven copies.

Gordon Lish taught at Yale and Columbia and New York University.

He taught for thirty years.

His hardback, *Collected Fiction*, in its first year of release, missed selling an even one hundred copies by forty-three books.

If a writer both edits and teaches.

If you do the math.

If you're cruel enough to imagine.

Thousands and thousands of Gordon Lish's former students and writer friends and protégés did not buy his last book.

Ouch.

I turned to Berryman and said, "I'll wrestle you on the lawn if you tell me how many books you sell. I will wrestle you in a series of matches."

He said, "And if I don't say."

I said, "Then I'll really wrestle you on the lawn."

He said, "Five thousand."

"Bullshit," I said.

"I don't know," he said. "Maybe six hundred."

WRITERS WRITE

I start writing. Steel mill. Amusement park. The woman with her face flecked with ash and how she sits in her car after her shift at Edgar Thompson Works, smoking hand-rolled cigarettes filled with tobacco imported from India because it's cheap. Her daughter works at Kennywood. Her son plays soccer and made all-state last season. Her husband goes to the doctor in an Uber because she won't drive him anymore. The doctor wants the foot. The foot wants to stay. The woman keeps smoking. I ask her where she wants to go and she tells me, "Drive," so we leave the parking lot and head through Braddock and turn right and up and over and down until she sits on Route 30. Does she feel like cooking? She can get a medium Vincent's Pizza for fourteen bucks. It's greasy and good and right down the street and not crowded at this hour. The light turns green. She flips her turn signal.

I keep listening.

Characters talk in whispers even when they shout.

I want to hear.

Dostoyevsky said, "Deprived of meaningful work, men and women lose their reason for existence; they go stark raving mad."

The imagination is the force field that protects us.

I write until dinner then imagine this book, like my other books, at an agent, sitting on a desk in an office on Park Avenue. It's a success story. I allow myself to dream.

In the kitchen I eat half a bag of pretzels, a can of tuna fish, and a stale bowl of Honey Nut Cheerios because that's what's in the cabinet.

I write until midnight, until my spine feels compressed and impossible to align.

People should not live in New York City.

It damages them.

I went there once and got punched.

PART FIFTEEN

Smiley Faces For Grades

I have a night class on Thursdays that I am gearing up for, emotionally, meaning I'm thinking about myself and not doing work. I have not corrected their papers. They do not seem to care. They know the deal: the longer I hold their papers, the worse my guilt, the better their grades. I shuffled the papers on Wednesday night, moving my favorite students to the top of the pile. Then I didn't read a single line.

I may not read this batch.

I might just mark them with smileys and stars.

Many years ago, when I was a student at Pitt-Johnstown, very few of my professors ever handed back papers. You turned them in, they disappeared. It was like handing in an assignment to a black hole. Aside from the department head who taught the stuffy poetry classes, they all worked other jobs and carried their exhaustion around like a bag of books. They taught at other branch campuses and community colleges and worked summers for landscapers and pool companies and waited tables at bars and fancy restaurants. They tutored high school kids. They tutored illiterate adults. They came to class late, sweating. Classes were cancelled more than taught. I never complained. I always got an A or an A+. Everyone did.

I would have loved a smiley or a star.

ANOTHER AGENT

I'm twiddling in my office when an agent emails me about one of my novels. I know it's a rejection before I even open the email because they're all rejections but I still get excited because dreams are like that. I breathe deep and open and read and it starts with the usual rejection, blah blah, thanks but no, good writer, market is hard, and so on, but then she stops with the kind-hearted fakery and talks more specifically about my books.

She says, "People just don't read books set in Pittsburgh, except Michael Chabon's, and his Pittsburgh is like Oz or New York. I would read another draft of your novel if you would consider changing the setting to somewhere in Appalachia. Your Pittsburgh with its old mill towns reminds me of something out of West Virginia or Kentucky. Would you change the mills to coal mines? I don't mean to imply that there is a huge market for Appalachian literature, or even Southern Literature, but there are great traditions there that can be updated. Readers recognize the south as a viable place to set books, not in the same way they recognize New York, Los Angeles, or Chicago, but as a viable alternative."

How nice to be considered.

How obnoxious to be asked to change.

She continues, "I know these are tough choices, but it's a tough market. Please keep me in mind if you consider revising, or for any future projects that you think have market value."

I know I should wait at least a day to email her back and all I should say is, "Thanks for the thoughtful read," but I instantly start typing. I babble for a few lines, trying to sound kinder than I am, then I say, "I used to be a welder and I wrote Western novels under a bad pen name. That's an NPR story waiting to happen."

I re-read my response, know I shouldn't send it, then add, as a joke but not as a joke, "PS: I jog constantly and look good shirtless."

Then I hit send.

I do not expect a response, except how could someone not respond to that.

I stare at the screen and nothing arrives.

Then something does arrive.

I open the email and it says, "Still set in Pittsburgh," followed by a frowny face.

RIG, WEIGHTED DOWN

The campus security guard finds Rig sound asleep under a table in the library. It's midnight. By sound asleep, I mean nodding on dope. I learn this on the phone.

The campus security guard says, "He wakes up then passes back out."

I say, "I understand."

He says, "He's really underneath the table. Did I make that clear? It's like he was playing hide-and-go-seek and passed out. He looks like a little child, except huge. He's like a giant baby, like the baby of a giant. Man looks like he fell from a beanstalk. Whoever closed the library must have not realized he was still in here. I heard him snoring when I was making my rounds."

I say, "I'm glad you called."

I wear cut-off sweatpants and sit on my tiny couch. I'd been pacing, being my usual nervous self, trying to wind down and sleep, when the phone rang.

The campus security guard says, "He gave me your name."

"I'm glad," I say. "Thanks for calling."

The campus security guard says, "He's so big, I don't think I can move him."

"I just need to get dressed."

"I'd hate to send another brother to jail."

The campus security guard is black. He's also a Steelers fan. We're pals. When we bump into each other on campus, we talk football. He's also an ex-athlete, a former basketball player from Woodland Hills who got a scholarship to Robert Morris. Sometimes we humblebrag our past lives in sports, the tiny victories that sustained us and helped us grow, two jocks as far away from sports as we could be remembering when we could outplay everyone else.

I say, "That's Lawrence Riggins. He used to play right guard for the Pittsburgh Steelers. Do you remember him? He was the undrafted guy who used to wrestle."

The security guard says, "I know exactly who I have here. He was a beast. Do you remember the story about him driving his motorcycle with his helmet on backwards?"

"I do," I say, pulling on my shirt, reaching for my shoes.

"It's possible he's been concussed. These pro athletes are turning into zombie-type people. It's lucky you and I got out when we were young."

"I'm gonna leave in thirty seconds," I say.

"Good," he says, "big man is starting to stir again."

By the time I make it to campus, Rig is gone.

While the security guard monologued that everything was fine, that no one was in trouble, that while I was on my way, Rig shook off the dope, he sat up, he smashed his head underneath the table, he moaned, he scooted out and stood up, he rubbed his head, he rubbed his eyes, he appeared sensical if not pissed off, he blamed me for making him sleep in the library, he called me a crybaby pussy, he called me a fucking dictator, he apologized to the security guard, he called an Uber with his cell phone, he stumbled into the night.

When I arrive, we agree none of this happened.

The security guard and I shake on it, outside on the sidewalk, underneath a streetlight.

The security guard says, "Got an uncle who was a junky."

He says, "This might not have nothing to do with concussions."

He says, "That was an enormous gentleman."

He says, "Pro football all those years and now this."

"If I can do anything," he says, "just let me know."

Plans

I know I need to find Rig but there are so many people who need to be found and I believe that, in time, Rig will come back and find me.

PART SIXTEEN

Thursday, After Class

Brandon does not come to class so I do not have to return his compression which I am still pretending not to have read. I should email him a couple comments to clear him from my conscience but the idea feels like spoiling an already-spoiled child.

After class Megan says, "Are you coming to the bar?"

I say, "Not tonight."

She looks hurt.

I feel hurt. Her hair is a black wave, an ocean under moonlight. I'd like to be in a bar with her. I love bars. I love Megan. Or I have a crush on Megan. I crush love her. I'm backtracking. I love-love her. But I have papers to correct and my mother out there wanting to jog and Berryman wanting a beer and Lawrence Riggins dealing drugs or using his supply when he should be rich and retired and I need to see my grandmother most of all.

Megan says, "You don't teach on Fridays."

"I know but I can't."

"Come on, I miss you."

"That's sweet," I say. "You miss me. I think I just blushed."

"You did. You're actually red."

"I embarrass easily."

"Have a drink with me. I'll make you blush all night."

"I can't."

"I'll beg," she says. "Down on my knees?" and she makes her sexy face.

"Next Thursday, I promise."

"I thought you should get some you-know and then we could you-know and drink all night. We haven't had a Thursday like that in a long time."

"We've only had two Thursdays like that ever."

"Was it just two?" she says, and smiles.

She knows I'm not much of a druggie, even though I enjoy drugs (mostly weed), because drugs are illegal (weed won't be soon!) and illegal things scare me, especially illegal things with mandatory prison sentences attached. I think she's not much of a druggie but she's younger than me and parties harder. One time some drunk dude kept trying to impress her with his blow, how much he had, how much he could get, showing her his stash, so she took it, the whole bag, thanked him and kissed him on the forehead and pocketed his blow. He was too stupid and drunk to say anything, except, "Enjoy yourself, that's primo cut," before he stumbled out. Megan and I stayed past closing and pulled the shades down and tooted until dawn, something I hadn't done in ten years and maybe ten times in my whole life. We almost kissed that night, the air between us turned thinner, the space easier to close, but we didn't kiss, probably because I couldn't, nerves, ideas, all that, she's my student, maybe she doesn't want to, I had mat herpes on my elbow a dozen years ago, I haven't been laid in so long I'm probably terrible in bed, whatever. So I did another line and chugged another beer and we ate breakfast at Eat N' Park, followed by smiley cookies, then drove off to our separate apartments, the sunlight already cooking headaches inside our drug-tired skulls.

Now she says, "Come on, it'll be fun."

I tell her, "You get the you-know. Then we can gear up for next Thursday, after I've jogged with my mom, visited with my grams, and corrected my papers. And Berryman—I owe that dude a beer and possibly a wrestling match."

"I'm your student. I can't get it."

"You were my bartender before you were my student," I say.

She pulls out her cigarettes and says, "It's a good thing you're not the dean."

FISH AND FLOWERS AND THE ABSENCE OF DRUGS

On Friday I drive to The Wellness Home, a fancy senior living center, to visit my grandmother. I am, happily, not hungover. I do not teach on Fridays so I usually stay in bed later, late-ish, late for me at least, maybe nine o'clock, trying to remember different things that involve beer and driving, but not this morning.

It's barely eleven o'clock and I have already run seven miles. I am showered. I am clean. I have consumed copious amounts of coffee and a Mountain Dew and a bagel with butter. I read. I wrote. I paced. I read again.

I'd re-read some Faulkner recently and liked it better than I remembered, mostly for the dirt and the farmers but sometimes for the language and the people. I thought about re-reading *As I Lay Dying* but then I thought about the kid saying, "My mother is a fish," and how everyone who reads the book reads it in a classroom with professors who have all taken Faulkner 101 and how they have the same ideas about Vardaman, the kid who says the fish line. It usually involves Jesus Christ, who was a fisherman, who wanted his disciples to be fishers of men, who fed four thousand people with five loaves of bread and two fishes, and nothing to do with the actual book and the young kid with not a lot going on upstairs who is upset that his mother just kicked. That's why you can't read Faulkner anymore. Low-level intellectuals from high-rent masters programs have stomped all over the text.

Instead of Faulkner I started to read *The Heart Is a Lonely Hunter* by Carson McCullers, which I'd meant to read for years but somehow skipped. I brewed another kettle of tea and sat in my reading chair and plowed through the first thirty or so pages. So far, it reads great. But I guess a story that starts by referencing two mutes in a small town is bound for something like greatness.

Thanks, Carson McCullers.

Hello, parking lot of the Wellness Home.

I have purchased flowers for my grandmother from the local Giant Eagle, which means I overpaid but that they are beautiful. When did

Giant Eagle become such a complete rip off? I remember buying bubble gum and magazines there as a kid and now they want eleven dollars for a fistful of smoked cheese.

I climb from my car.

Later tonight I will see the bar and I will enjoy it more because I have been absent and productive, alone with my body and thoughts and skills for a dozen hours. To be productive one must be absent—no parties, no dinners, no drinks, no friends, no friends with cocaine and drink on their mind, no friends passed out on dope, no friends with gold cards and kayaks stored away at their parents' mansion, no family, no jogging with family, nothing.

My grandmother loves carnations.

Meet the Family

I call my grandmother Nona. Everyone does. Nona is seventy-one. Next month she will be seventy-two. Her hair is white, usually fixed in a long braid, and she often dresses in overalls and comfortable running shoes, a farmer's wife who doesn't make it to the field much anymore. She is fair skinned and wears a light pink lipstick called Spring Rose and no other make-up. I think she looks fifty-five or a young sixty. Nona says I am a good grandson but also full of shit.

My mother, Joanie, is still embarrassed of her mother, my grandmother, Nona. "It's the West Virginia thing," Joanie says repeatedly, a rant she's been cooking for years. "No one wants to admit that shit, that they're from West Virginia, it's like smiling with crooked teeth, but Nona dresses like a fucking hillbilly. She's actually proud to have grown up on a mountain, eating tripe. It's embarrassing. Do you even know what tripe is? It's cow's stomach, that's what."

Joanie does not hate Nona and Nona does not hate Joanie. When they fight, they start their sentences by saying, "I don't hate you," or, "I honestly do love you," or, "Who said anything about hate?" or, "I don't have to like you to love you."

My grandmother made my mother's clothes growing up. This is why my mother got knocked up then married my father the day after she graduated from high school. "Fashion and geography are both fuck-alls," Joanie says.

I do not know why my father disappeared before my first birthday and never returned. My mom says she kicked him out but she wavers sometimes then says he bailed without warning. Nona says my father was greasy. She says he was a moron who loved cars more than his family. He drank too much. He fought in bars. He robbed a bank. "Seriously," she says, "he robbed the Beckley Trust." That part is unverified. When he worked, he worked as a mechanic. Nona feels this is something to be ashamed of. She hates cars. She hates grease. "He had dirty fingernails," Nona says. "And he couldn't walk a quarter mile to the store for a gallon of milk. He drove everywhere, the moron."

His name was Billy.

Billy is a child's name.

I like to think he outgrew it.

I like to think he is alive somewhere, free of guilt.

If he died, I hope it was a good death, one surrounded by love.

I have one picture of my father. The photo is undated. Billy leans on his newly-polished Dodge charger, rag in his right hand. A cigarette splits two fingers on his other hand, the smoke barely visible. He smiles and his front tooth is chipped or half gone. His hair is longish and curly so it looks like a fishbowl on his head. Chest muscles fill out his t-shirt and his arms are lean and defined. Maybe he's eighteen. He looks like we all want to look but almost never do: happy to be alive, burning. It's the stance, the way he braces himself against the car without thinking about bracing himself, leaning without trying to lean. It's the smile, the messed-up tooth that he's not afraid to show. Maybe I am too small to be any trouble yet. Maybe I am not born. Maybe my mother took the photo. Maybe he still believed in her and she in him.

This is all I know of my father, one picture, one moment.

A moron and his car, Nona would say, or a man and his loves, I sometimes think, or a boy with a fucked-up tooth, Joanie says, whichever, probably all three, probably many more, one flash against one second, a tiny faded poster posing as a bible because those of us who do not have must learn to accept truths and false truths from the past as verses to guide us to the future until we don't need them anymore.

My dad looked like a savior until I didn't need saving anymore.

I do not know who he was but I can see that he was a child.

Now that I am not a child, I do my best to understand.

THE WELLNESS HOME

The visitor parking lot barely needs itself on Friday morning, three cars for forty or fifty spaces. The Wellness Home is huge, only a few years old, and has the look of a castle as imagined by a three-year-old girl: all happy knights and pretty princesses inside. There is a moat. There is a bridge. Koi fish swim in the moat under the bridge. The trees are perfectly manicured. The old people walk about, forgetful that they are at war with their own minds and bodies.

The Wellness Home pitches independent living and the happy later days that so many of our seniors have been saving for. I skimmed that in the brochure with my grandmother, reading it aloud over her shoulder. Nona said, "Sounds better than a barn." I agreed. A barn would be worse. Then Nona sold her house, the one where she'd lived since she'd moved to Pennsylvania from the mountains of West Virginia. She said, "The part I'm going for is basically an apartment with a bunch of oldies around. They have laundry service if you pay a little extra. It's better if I check myself into the home of my own choosing before I get any older and your mother gets involved." When I told my mother this, she said, "What was I going to do? Put her in a barn?" and sighed and lit a Marlboro.

This is the way it has always been between the two of them, mother and daughter. One operates well as water. The other operates well as land. At the beach they are always colliding, taking away and putting back.

MEET NONA

As soon as I come through the door, the young woman at the counter says, "She should be in the common area," and smiles and points.

I nod and wave.

I have the same thought I always have when I come to The Wellness Home, which is not a fair thought but still omnipresent: at least it doesn't smell like piss. In fact it smells like whatever potpourri tart they burn at the counter, maybe sugar cookie. The lobby looks like a modern hotel. The senior living homes I remember from growing up, when

Joanie would drag me somewhere, which we called old folks homes, were dark and dank and smelled like bleach and piss or just piss and old people dying on the installment plan.

Nona is not in the common room, a collection of couches and a big-screen TV. An old man, dressed in a tie and nice slacks, points to the glass doors.

I nod and wave.

Nona sits out back in a rocking chair on the porch that stretches the length of the building, a hardback book in her lap. Her hair is in a braid. She wears her glasses on a chain around her neck. Her dress is made from different swatches of fabric, mostly reds and blues. Even though she does not make her own clothes anymore (and hasn't for years), she is attracted to clothes that look homemade. My mother hates this. Nona wears sneakers with her skirt. My mother hates this too. She believes in high heels.

Nona sees me and closes her book.

She says, "You came!"

I always come when I say I am going to come. She knows this but does not trust it because I am the son of a daughter who hardly ever comes at all.

I say, "What are you reading?"

All of Nona's books, hardbacks like this one, get wrapped with brown paper bags to protect the covers like she's in fifth grade, like she'll have to hand the book back at the end of the school year. All of her books are romance novels.

I say, "Is that a dirty one?"

"It's only dirty when you read the dirty parts. I read the whole book. So it's only a little dirty with a lot of boring parts in between."

She gives me a kiss. She wears make-up, a rarity, but just the tiniest amount, some blush on her cheeks. Once, when we were in Macy's and I asked her why she still wanted to shop for cosmetics when she claimed to hate to shop for cosmetics, she said, "My lips are disappearing. I have to draw them back on."

"I got you flowers," I say, and hand over the carnations.

"They're absolutely beautiful," she says, and leans her nose into the bouquet and inhales. "You shouldn't have."

"Of course I should have."

"Of course you should have," she says, and laughs.

We hug for a minute, longer than normal.

An old man, a few rockers away, wolfwhistles at our relationship.

He says, "Where I can get a son like that? My son is a hobo. He lives in North Carolina and brews sour beers. Why would anyone drink a sour beer? Sour is old. It's nasty. Sour means it's gone bad. That's a good son who brings his mother flowers."

Nona says, "That's my *grandson*," and waves him off.

Nona thinks old people are idiots or lonely or lonely idiots who have lived their lives with not enough discipline and not enough gusto and now cling to whatever—tango dancing, vacations to Atlantic City, strangers with loose ears. "I like everyone," she says, "but I'm not going to sit on the porch and gab with some old regretful fucker who wants to learn to play Spanish guitar." Nona, like all of us, forgives her own transgressions, not that I name or judge them, but she has a swear jar in her room and I make her use it.

I turn her hug sideways and put my arm around her shoulder.

She is less than before. I feel this every time I am here, like she is slowly becoming a child, someone who will ride on my shoulders then fit in the cradle of my arms. Her face, lined with wrinkles, somehow looks more innocent with each passing year, the disappearing lips a more jubilant smile. We walk to the front of the building but take the side exit before we arrive at the main desk.

She says, "I want to buy you lunch."

"Someone should," I say.

We are supposed to sign her out when we leave the grounds but we never do.

"On principal," she says. "They're not paying me to stay here."

TAKE OUT

Nona only wants to eat at the Olive Garden. She likes the breadsticks and the endless salad. She does not like the entrees so she orders something she thinks I'll like then asks for a box and makes me take it home. I do not tell her I hate the Olive Garden. I am not morally opposed to the Olive Garden like some people but their sauce is bland and the garlic salt overwhelms their breadsticks, which is not a crime, but I go home bloated like I just ate a platter of sodium.

Nona is on her second bowl of salad.

I am on my fifth breadstick.

She says, "How's school?"

I say, "Good."

She says, "How's the students?"

I say, "They're all good. Busy. Most of them have full-time jobs."

She says, "I'm a big believer in community colleges. Your mother has a two-year degree in something. Accounting, I think. I always thought she should have kept going and got her bachelor's degree."

"I know. She's a smart lady."

"You're the first person in the family to get a four-year degree. Makes me proud inside to think of you with a diploma."

"Makes me proud I inherited your intelligence."

"You're just kissing my ass," she says. "Why don't you have a girlfriend?"

I cram the end of a breadstick in my mouth and mumble.

Nona says, "Very funny." She says, "Am I prying? I'm an old lady, we're supposed to pry. But I see people on the internet now and they get offended over everything. If you ask a thirty-year-old woman who doesn't have children if she's going to have a baby, it's considered offensive. You could ruin her life or something."

"I did not know that."

"Do you use trigger warnings in class?"

"I do not."

"Do you know what a trigger warning is?"

"I do."

"Is it like a rating on a movie? Sex and violence and nudity are about to appear, that type of thing, beware the human condition."

"Sort of," I say. "It's more personal, I think, like if sex and violence have happened to you, brace yourself because we're about to discuss it."

"How does sex happen? It happens to everyone, eventually."

"I think I meant rape, like if something terrible happens in your life you might not be ready to sit through a class where it's discussed in detail. But people are also offended by sex in general and the language sex brings. I don't know exactly. Trigger warnings are more of a big university thing. Community college students are tough. They just want to get better jobs and make some money. They mostly don't complain."

"Maybe you should just say: grow the fuck up, children. Do that once at the beginning of the school year and it covers everything."

"I don't need to say anything. I describe the books we're going to read and that's pretty much it. They can stick around if the books sound interesting. Community college students know the world is not a great place. A lot of them are older. They work while they go to school. They might not even know what a trigger warning is. They're not wired to complain like the students at Harvard or wherever."

"Harvard can kiss my ass," she says, but happy like it's something Harvard really needs to do for their own good, like homework, like a midterm exam.

I say, "You'd like the president at my college. I think she went to Harvard specifically to crush the kind of people who go to Harvard and expect to be Harvard-ites for the rest of their lives. The community college president has a huge heart for working-class people."

"Is being a Harvard-ite a thing?"

"I think I may have made that name up."

"Good," Nona says, and stares at her salad like it's an Ivy League student. "I always forget to ask for the dressing on the side. It's too much for me like this."

I say, "I'll sop it up," and stick my breadstick into her salad bowl.

She says, "It makes me feel good when I think of you being a college professor."

Nona saying that makes me feel humble and awkward so I say, "It's just a community college," but I'm proud too, unbelievably so.

Nona waves me off with her fork for being humble.

I wave her off with my fork to be funny.

She says, "You deserve everything you get."

"But lots of good people don't get what they deserve."

"There by the grace of God go I," she says, "and all that shit they taught us in school. It all starts to sound pretty true when you get old."

Nona had six older brothers and sisters. Of the seven only she graduated from high school. No one went to college. College, for Nona's family, was like Pluto is to an astronaut: cold and distant, impossible to reach, maybe not even a real planet. Two of her brothers died in a coal mine when the shaft collapsed. One killed himself from grief over his brothers' deaths by jumping off a cliff into the bottom of a stone quarry. Nona left West Virginia but her siblings all stayed and kept low-paying jobs until they died because they all needed money, including her older sister who collapsed from a massive stroke behind the counter at the 7-11 where she worked part-time when she wasn't on welfare or in a mental hospital. Nona came to Pittsburgh in her twenties and took all the bad jobs she could find and still struggled to pay her bills while raising my mom. Eventually, she made first teller at Mellon Bank, which she described as, "the kind of job where they pay you just enough to afford the outfits they require you to wear," but she stayed for years, often working a second job, until an executive from US Steel, a regular customer who deposited massive paychecks, fell for her charm and hired her as his secretary and treated her unbelievably well until she retired at sixty-two.

Maybe we are a family of lucksters, from the matriarch on down, me and my mom and Nona, forgetting all the suicides and early heart attacks and mine disasters, forgetting the gloom we inherited. My mom earned her associates degree when she was thirty-six years old after years of managing a dry-cleaning business. Now she fires people and dates veterinarians and limps around various tracks in fancy designer sneakers with swooshes sewn on in China. I am more than alive.

Nona says, "It makes me proud. I could have been a teacher—I guess that's what girls did back then—but I didn't want to do it because that's what was expected. I was young and stupid. I went to school to learn how to decorate cakes. Can you imagine that? Your mother's convinced I'm a product of inbreeding. I'm so glad I got away from West Virginia. That state is a death sentence to so many families. They get mesmerized by the beauty of the mountains and forget you need a way to survive. I like to love West Virginia from afar."

"My mother loves you," I say.

"Of course she does," Nona says. "And I love your mother."

The waitress brings our entrees. I have the chicken Alfredo, which looks a little like paste but not thick enough to be gross. Nona gets the chicken parmesan, a real chicken breast and not the oval patty made from minced meat they use at Eat n' Park, which is creepy but tastes better. I move my salad and finish my breadstick in a bite to make room.

The waitress must be in her late sixties or early seventies. She is thin with dyed black hair and highly tweezed eyebrows. She has on black tennis shoes that are covered in black polish. The polish has stained the white laces. Her feet must hurt all the time. She is not hunched but hunching, in the early stages of curving down.

Nona says, "I'm sorry but can I get that in a to-go box? All this salad, my God."

The waitress says, "It's a big portion."

Nona turns to me and says, "You'll eat that, won't you?"

I say, "Of course."

The waitress says, "Aren't you a cutie," and everyone smiles and one of us is moderately embarrassed by the compliment.

THE DIARY

We sit on a bench under a gazebo in the middle of downtown Ligonier, an hour from Pittsburgh, less from Youngwood, the small town where I teach. Nona likes to walk after her salad and breadsticks at the Olive Garden, then to sit for a while. Ligonier looks like a movie town, perfect-sized trees reaching from yards to streets and sidewalks leading anywhere you'd want to go. Most of the houses bump against the small downtown. Downtown fills out with a few restaurants and bars, an old movie theater, rows of shops. The shops sell antiques and coffee and sandwiches. Old people, dressed in clean slacks and short-sleeve shirts, long skirts and silky blouses, walk about, smiling. Younger people pass through but faster, still stuck with deadlines and jobs and unknown futures.

"Your great-great uncle, my father's brother, kept a diary," Nona says.

"Really," I say. "A diary?" and I picture a book written in coal dust.

"My uncle Loomis."

"Loomis?" I say. "I'd remember that name."

The only relatives I know are Nona and Joanie and I know very little about their histories except what Nona says and she is sporadic and random with her details on principle. She thinks I should learn about family from my mother. My mother could give a shit about our family history or she outright hates it, a thing to mock. Nona never mentions my grandfather, her teenage husband, except to say he got electrocuted while working for a mining company. My mother never knew her father. So I sit between them, Nona and Joanie, grandmother and mother, usually befuddled, usually hopeful. I imagine I have distant cousins alive but I don't know who they are or where they reside. The father I never knew was raised by a grandmother he barely loved because his parents abandoned him to move to Mexico and open a feed store. Nona's mother was a Baptist minister who died at forty of biscuits and fried chicken, a heart attack that dropped her to the rectory floor of the church she preached at. Nona's father was a coalminer. When he was not a coalminer, he drank corn liquor. "But a happy drunk," Nona said one time, before reconsidering and adding, "mostly happy." The Baptist minister allowed the coalminer to drink as much as he wanted as long as he kept his job and attended services on Sundays. Apparently the coalminer allowed the Baptist minister to preach and eat biscuits so long as she stayed clear of his drinking. Nona seldom speaks of either parent, but since she has moved into the Wellness Home, she talks more about her childhood and her family and her geography, the rivers and mountains of her youth, the people who swam and climbed and cooked and drank and believed in God.

"Why would a coalminer keep a diary?" I say.

"Why wouldn't a coalminer keep a diary?" Nona says, incredulous.

I shrug. I don't know. A coalminer keeping a diary is not so far away from a welder publishing westerns or, maybe, a community college professor writing unpublished novels.

Nona assumes I eagerly await her stories, that because I read and write and teach reading and writing, I should also be the family historian, the collector of tales, but her process frustrates me and the true description of my family, my own family, is small enough to fit into a shoebox, a few pictures, a couple news clippings, a seashell from a vacation from the summer when we had enough money to drive three hundred miles to the ocean. When Nona says family, she means generations. When I say family, I mean a triangle of Joanie and Nona and me across the bottom, trying to connect and hold.

Sometimes Nona says, "Write this down."

I seldom do but I listen.

Now we sit on the bench under the gazebo.

Nona says, "I want you to have it, the diary."

I put my arm around her and pull her in.

I say, "Thank you."

"It's important."

"Okay."

"I'm serious."

"Thank you," I say. "I'll finish it once I finish the chicken parmesan that you just willed to me from the Olive Garden."

She leans into me with the bird bones of her shoulder, a tiny jab, and laughs and says, "Why don't you get fat?"

"I run."

"Your mother gets fat."

"Not always."

"She porks up."

"My mother has started to run," I say.

"Why? Because she met a man who runs?"

"More or less."

"Exactly," Nona says.

An ice cream shop resides across the way.

Nona sits up and stares at the sign.

She says, "The older I get, the less interesting food tastes, except for sweets."

"What flavor are you thinking?"

"I don't know. I shouldn't have called your mother porky when all I want to do is eat ice cream until my eyes freeze."

Nona is not fat. She is old and sometimes she confuses this with being fat. Her arms are skinny but the skin is loose. Her neck looks wonderful but she's shocked that it is not the neck of a twenty-year-old girl. "I can't wear pearls anymore," she says, though she's never owned pearls. Her favorite flavor of ice cream is butter pecan.

I say, "I like their chocolate chip. They use the little squares of chocolate."

"I think I'll get a sugar cone this time," Nona says. "They used to have sugar cones at Sweet Williams. Now it's all soft-serve Dairy Queen shit.

Ice cream is supposed to be made with cream and taste delicious. Soft serve is poison. I don't care how many M&Ms you toss into it. Tell me who your mother has started to run with."

"She's dating a veterinarian," I say.

"Really," Nona says. "She's too fat to walk a dog, so she's getting in shape?"

"Joanie is pretty built for her age," I say, and it's true.

Joanie could be Marilyn Monroe or Betty Page, curvy but not thick, still with a waist even if it's held in place by Spanx. She ignores her age because she believes age should be ignored and she dresses to accentuate her hips, her sway.

"No offense," Nona says, "but your mother dresses like a slut."

"You're so almost charming then you just fall apart."

"Oh please."

"That sounds like ice-cream time," I say.

I take Nona's hand as we leave the gazebo. I know she worries about stairs, even these four small steps, though she walks like a much younger woman.

"The diary's back at my room," Nona says. "I have it in a box. Loomis was quite a storyteller. He wanted to write for the newspapers. When he was growing up, he was one of the few boys in the hollow who could read. He made sure all his children, even the girls, went to school until at least sixth grade and learned to read. That's why our family likes words. When I was growing up, at night, we passed around the *Beckley Gazette*, and each of us had to read a section. I read the funnies."

I say, "You lived with your uncle, who is technically my great-great uncle and Joanie's great-uncle, just to be clear?"

"Don't confuse me," Yona says. "Sometimes we lived with family, not always. Times were different. We lived where we lived."

"Do you say hollow or holler?"

"Hollow," she says. "Holler's what trashy people say."

"Have you read the diary?" I say.

She says, "Of course I read the diary. It's mostly about the mines. It's a lot about his brother, my uncle Shelby, who was more of a drunk than a miner."

The ice cream place is new but it's designed to look old. The sign is cursive with pink neon. A chalkboard describes today's flavors and the special: Okay Mocha, a coffee milkshake. The counter is lined with stools. Nona gets the rocky road, a surprise. I get the butter pecan because I know she will regret her choice and we'll swap cones. The kid working the counter barely speaks, maybe embarrassed by his old-timey uniform and soda-jerk hat. Nona lets me pay without much fuss and I drop a couple bucks in the tip jar.

"Everyone, even my daddy, loved Shelby," Nona says. "He could sing the old songs. He disappeared once and said he took a boat to Scotland. Maybe he did. Or maybe he was off on a bender and just made the Scotland part up. It sounded true. That's all we cared about. He said Scotland was filled with castles and sheep roaming the hills. He could sing 'Mattie Grove' and 'Old Barely Wine' and 'To The Hill We March' just like he wrote them."

"I thought we were mostly Irish," I say.

"Can you explain the difference between Ireland and Scotland?" Nona says, and before I can answer, she adds, "No you cannot."

"I'll make sure I read the diary," I say.

Nona takes a lick of her rocky road and wonders what's in there.

After she takes a second lick, I trade her my butter pecan.

"Why didn't you get the sugar cone?" she says.

"Why didn't you get the butter pecan?" I say.

"I get cold so easy," Nona says, not about the ice cream but about life.

The air is cool but the sun feels hot. I could sweat if we moved faster than a couple ice cream lickers on a small-town sidewalk. Nona stops moving and turns towards the sun, like a cat behind a glass window. She takes two more steps to a garbage can and drops in her cone without comment. I would have liked my butter pecan back. I would have liked chocolate chip. I lick the rocky road to keep it from dripping.

"Why don't you write a book about our family?" Nona says.

"Maybe I'll do that," I say, but not convincingly.

"You think you won't but you will. I know you get angry with me because I'm wishy-washy. It's just the way I am. All I've told you will come back once I'm dead."

"I hope so."

Nona says, "Oh, you do not."

Dave Newman

    She says, "Your cone is dripping."
    She says, "Lick faster."
    She says, "Families don't always have to like each other," and pauses to think out the rest and says, "They just have to be families."

PART SEVENTEEN

Cocaine

"**What if we don't do cocaine,**" I say, "but pretend like we did cocaine?"

I throw my hands up in a party gesture.

"I don't think it works that way," Megan says.

"But listen," I say, sort of joking, sort of flirting, "we'd have all the fun of doing cocaine but without any of the worry. It could still be a blast."

She squints to explain how irrational my ideas about drugs are. We sit in my office, door locked, voices not as hushed as they should be but still hushed. Night classes ended an hour ago. Even the lingering students have wandered off to their cars and bikes and buses. The night janitor will be here to empty my trashcan soon. Megan pulls a pencil from a mug of writing utensils I keep on my desk and twists her hair into a ponytail-bun combination then sticks the pencil into her hair to lock the ponytail-bun in place.

"I just need a break," she says. "I work, I go to school, I work, I go to school, I take care of my grams, I work, I go to school," and she rolls her hands to show the endless spiral of life.

"I get it," I say, then drink off my Mountain Dew and take a bite of Slim Jim.

"But you don't want to score it?" she says, articulating the obvious, which she probably sees as my rank pussydom.

I say, "Of course I don't want to score it. Scoring drugs is dangerous."

She says, "You know what's dangerous?

I say, "Eating processed meat sticks and drinking sugary sodas?"

"Yes!" she says. "Eating processed meat sticks and drinking that diabetes water you inhale, that's dangerous. That shit will kill you."

"I doubt it. And it definitely will not send me to jail."

"No one goes to jail for buying drugs anymore."

"I don't think that's true."

I bite off another hunk of processed meat.

I swig off my twenty-ounce soda.

I say, "It's your connection."

She recoils dramatically and says, "Connection makes it sound seedy."

"Exactly," I say, and point with my meat stick.

The last time we talked about this, Megan said, "It's my guy so you should score it," and I said, "I don't think it works like that," and she said, "How else would it work?"

Megan, who is young and hip enough to have connections, does not like to meet her connections because she is Megan, because she is beautiful, because she is a woman, because she is fun, because people love fun, because people love fun women, especially fun hot women, because she is a woman who treats her tits like capital, because tits as capital get weird, because dudes who deal drugs to beautiful women who treat their tits like capital grow massive boners and strange ideas about power and drugs because they are dudes who deal and because beautiful women are beautiful women.

I understand connections and I understand my lack thereof.

Now Megan says, "I own a bar."

"Right," I say, "so that makes you even more qualified to score drugs."

"That's not what I was thinking," she says, then removes the pencil from behind her head and twists her hair into another beautiful shape and re-inserts the pencil to lock the new style down. "I'm not complaining. I'm just being rational. I almost own a bar. It's my grandma's bar. It's our family's bar," and she really honks on family, sounding out her history. "If I get busted for scoring, three things will happen: cops, judges, jail. There will be fines. And newspaper articles. The Liquor Control Board will come in. I'd lose the bar. And so on and so on. Endgame: shitsville. I don't think you want that for me or for my family?"

"Really?" I say. "That's the card you're going to chuck on the table?"

"Yes. And you're a writer. If you get busted, it's a great story."

"I thought people didn't get busted for scoring drugs anymore?"

Megan removes the pencil from her hair, deposits it back in my mug of writing utensils, then shakes out her hair and sighs.

"I'm a girl," she says, "so you should score the drugs."

COCAINE AGAIN

I'm in South Greensburg, parked by the ice-skating rink. The guy with the cocaine is supposed to be here soon. Megan said so. I love Megan. I love cocaine. I do not love to score cocaine.

I hate to score cocaine.

But I love Megan.

I'll keeping saying all this.

Love demands it.

Years ago, when I was in high school, before I'd ever tried a drug, a cop found an eight ball in the glove compartment of my friend Randy's car. Randy was three years older than the rest of our group, already out of high school. He always packed a walletful of money. If our group headed anywhere, Randy drove. Randy paid for gas. Randy bought us food. We didn't know Randy did drugs, real drugs, drugs like cocaine. Randy drank bottled beer while he drove us around and he sometimes coasted through stoplights. He sometimes threw beer bottles at traffic signs. That was this night: Randy, beer, stoplight. The cop put his hand on the gun in his holster and asked us to step from the car. Randy climbed out. Everyone climbed out. I declined. The cop stood over six feet tall. Shirt tight around his biceps. Goatee. Shaved head. He said,

"Out now," and I said, "I didn't do anything," believing I had options, including not climbing from the car. The cop said, "Out," but reached for my face before I could respond and pulled me from the backseat by my hair. I knew not to fight. I said, "Sorry sorry sorry." He threw me to the rest of the guys who caught and straightened me. Another cop came. He stood six feet tall but looked skinny and mean. Goatee. Shaved head. The two cops lined us up and frisked our balls and put us in handcuffs. They shoved us over the hood of the car and frisked our balls some more and pulled out our pockets. No one had drugs. No one had money or anything. The skinny cop said, "You're fucking kidding me?" and the bicep cop said, "Empty as a trashcan on garbage day," and sighed. They uncuffed us. They shook their bald heads. Then they said, "Get the fuck outta here," and we started across the street. They said, "Not you, bud," to Randy and pulled him back as the rest of us continued walking, making freedom with distance and our feet. They re-cuffed Randy. Randy said, "What'd I do, man?" They smashed Randy over the hood of the car and frisked his balls. They pulled him up. They smashed him down. The skinny cop said, "Don't dent my hood," to the bicep cop who was doing most of the slamming. "You wanna be a hardass?" the bicep cop said. The skinny cop said, "He don't look like a hardass." Then they choked Randy and jacked him around like they were playing a game of toss-the-prisoner. They slapped the back of Randy's head. Randy stumbled. He found his legs and stood straight. He looked helpless. He looked scared. He looked like he'd never drive through a stop sign with a beer bottle between his legs again. The skinny cop said, "You ain't Scarface now, are you?" Randy stared at his shoes, like his shoes might explain his misfortune. The bicep cop said, "I picked up cats bigger than you," and took Randy by the scruff of the neck and shook him around. The skinny cop said, "There's some folks you're gonna wanna meet at the station." Then they stuffed Randy in the backseat of the squad car. We stayed and watched, too scared to leave, too scared to speak, too scared to help our friend. A man in greasy blue overalls showed up in a tow truck and chained up Randy's car and took instructions from the cops and headed to the pound in the Strip District. The cops chatted with each other and laughed then moved to their separate police cars and cranked up the flashers. Then they took Randy to jail. Randy nodded to us from the window, not cool but like: help please. One of my pals said, "Jesus." Another pal said something but I'd already started to move. I kept moving, directing my nervous feet, staying focused so I wouldn't tip over. I turned the corner and fired up my legs and ran home, full sprint, blazing from Oakland to Bloomfield, my shitty sneakers slapping the pavement, ducking those friends that night and the next and so on until I could finish high school, staying focused on wrestling, on studying, on avoiding, avoiding all of them, then ducking Randy forever.

Now I wait, still scared, still thinking about running.

The stress of scoring does more damage to your heart than the actual drug. Mine thumps like tiny bodies falling from an airplane have landed on my chest.

I lean on my truck and scan the parking lot.

Two teenage boys drink canned beer behind a green dumpster.

I have spent most of my life doing what women have asked me to do.

My spine is useless.

I climb back in my truck and wait.

I put in a Billie Holiday CD. I hated jazz for years, especially bop, maybe because I didn't have the time for instrumentals, but I've fallen in love with Billie Holiday lately. A newish friend, a colleague really, said, "Once Billie Holiday's voice was ruined, she learned to sing." It was a Berryman-type comment, passed around from people who think they're intellectuals. The colleague teaches at a Pitt branch campus, a step up from the community college. He likes to sound smart which, I guess, we all do, but I try not to think of him while I listen to Billie Holiday and, besides, my real love is bluegrass, because Nona loves bluegrass and grew up with bluegrass and maybe a little because my mother hates bluegrass. My mother likes Beyonce or whoever is popular. For years she loved Brittany Spears. Before that, it was Janet Jackson. I love bluegrass because every song has a breakdown that incorporates jazz but enough sense to pull back to a voice pushing a melody about love or work or alcohol or the downside of each.

Two Billie Holiday songs later the dealer shows up.

Did Billie Holiday do cocaine?

I know she loved heroin.

The dealer parks his blue Ford Taurus, which is as junky as Megan described. He steps outside into the evening, a nervous-looking white dude, maybe twenty-five, maybe thirty, on the fat side. He wears a blue suit, not a pimp suit or a gangster suit, but a normal business suit, exactly like the blue suit I wore to every interview for every job I tried to get before realizing I needed to go back to school and learn a trade.

The dealer straightens his tie.

He reaches down and pulls up his socks.

I like drug dealers who wear concert t-shirts.

What happened to those dudes?

I climb out of my truck and wave.

The dealer nods and waves.

He takes off his jacket and tosses it inside his very old Taurus, on the backseat. He leaves the door open, the engine running.

My door is closed, the engine off.

I think: damn it.

I'm never prepared for the getaway.

The dealer says, "Megan's friend?" and extends his hand.

"What?" I say, catching a good look at the white melon on top of his chicken-skinned neck. "No, I don't think so," I say, and try to sound confused, try to instantly shut this down, no drug buying, no conversation, nothing, smile and keep on.

He says, "Not Megan's friend?" and tilts, confused.

I know this dude and this dude is my former student.

I am embarrassed to be alive.

The dealer stands at my height but he's puffed up from eating lunches with people who will buy whatever he's selling when he's not selling drugs, maybe cars, maybe used cars, maybe ball bearings, maybe opioids and erectile dysfunction medicine. His black hair is thick on top. He has a goatee and a huge sore on the corner of his mouth, stress lines around his sunken eyes.

"You're not Megan's friend?" he says.

I say, "I had you in class a couple years ago," which is true, which Megan may have not known and definitely did not warn me about, but student faces come back, even the averages and the duds, even if their names do not.

"English stuff, right?" and his face shines up some recognition.

"Exactly," I say. "Creative writing, I think."

"You're not here for Megan?"

"Is that your girlfriend?"

"No, nothing like that."

"My nephew is playing spring hockey. You heading inside?"

He says, "No, thanks. I'm supposed to meet someone."

"Good to see you," I say.

"Yeah, you too," he says. "You still teaching down at Three Clowns?"

Three Clowns is the community college where I teach, Westmoreland County Community College—County Community College, three Cs, three clowns.

"Every day," I say, but walking away, moving to the skating arena, tragedy narrowly averted, if not tragedy then awkwardness, if not awkwardness then something else. I've managed to hold onto the dignity I sometimes imagine teaching brings.

"Stay golden," my nameless drug dealer and former student says.

"You too," I say.

"That's from *The Outsiders*," he says.

"I know."

"I read that book."

"That's great," I say, still moving, not mentioning that The Outsiders is a book for twelve-year-old boys that he should have read it in sixth grade, maybe seventh.

Inside the hockey arena, which is cold enough to fog my breath, I buy a soft pretzel and a large Coke with extra ice and start to sweat.

EXIT

Leaving the rink I stop outside by the main doors and look around. The teenage kids still drink beer behind the dumpster. One sports green hair. The other one sits on a basketball. They are maybe fourteen and I'm sure—I mean absolutely positive—they are cops.

Kids on skates inside the rink were cops.

The mom working the concession stand was a cop.

Cops scooch down in parked cars, waiting.

I want to run.

I walk fast instead.

Then I break into a jog like I need something from my car, which I do: escape.

BACK TO THE BIG MAN

I do exactly what I did not want to do when Megan mentioned getting coke for one of our Thursday night soirees but which immediately crossed my mind: I go to my office and pick up the phone and call Rig. It rings. I wish Megan would have asked me to score flowers.

He answers his cell phone and says, "Who's this?"

I decide not to ask for drugs.

"It's me, Sellick," I say.

"You checking in on me, brother?" he says, but happy.

"Just calling to say hi," I say, and concentrate on convincing myself of that truth: hi, hello, checking in, nothing else. I don't mention coke because I am embarrassed to mention coke, and coke would be the wrong thing to mention because it could trigger Rig, not that Rig doesn't trigger himself, not that being alive doesn't inspire illicit drug use. Or maybe it's self-preservation: Rig's phone is tapped and a squad of cops and DEA agents and FBI folks are listening and waiting to pounce. Only Rig's phone is not tapped, it's a welfare phone, which makes me even more embarrassed.

I want Rig to quit selling drugs.

I want Rig to quit using drugs.

I want Rig to be a millionaire with his wife and kids at home.

I wish drugs were legal.

I hate how the world starts with mistrust and jail.

He says, "We're not talking about the library, are we?"

I say, "Not unless you want to talk about the library."

The library, of course, means dope, enough heroin to take a three-hundred-pound athlete and put him under a table.

Rig says, "The less said about the library, the better."

"Fair enough," I say, relieved and not, concerned and not.

"You coming up for a visit?" he says.

"To Johnstown?"

"Yeah, to Johnstown."

"I was hoping maybe you'd come down here," I say, a lie.

Please Bring Cocaine, Or Don't

Rig insists he owns a car but doesn't want to drive it. I offer to come and pick him up. He politely declines, saying he loves the bus. It allows him time to think. I'm happy to be his friend, to grab a sandwich, to talk it out, which I assumed we'd do eventually, you don't pick someone up from jail then abandon them, but I imagined our next get-together would happen after the semester when he'd settled in to whatever he needed to settle into and I had more time to be a better friend and help with his problems.

But I picked up the phone.

But I dialed.

But I invited him down.

I don't know what I expected when I called Rig. For a tiny portion of his backpack of cocaine to magically travel to my hand from his home in Flood City? Maybe. I hadn't really considered a hangout. The world is so selfish. I mean me.

I say, "I bet Berryman would come and get you."

He says, "Your driver?"

"He's not really my driver."

"No shit, dumbass."

I say, "I thought I should clarify that."

Rig says, "He looks like your driver."

"He'll be happy to hear that," I say. "I'll make sure I tell him."

The Bus Station

Berryman says, "It's not every day you get to see the man who beat Kurt Angle for a second time," and cancels his afternoon class. He says, "I almost asked Rig for his autograph when I drove him to Johnstown but I was afraid he'd punch me."

"Why would he punch you?"

"He's big. He's angry. He was holding a backpack filled with drugs. I'm white. He probably hasn't had the best luck with white people in his life."

"That's some dumbass Ivy League talk."

"It's not if you look at the statistics."

"What statistics?"

"The rate of incarceration for African-American men."

"Who was incarcerated?"

"Rig."

"Rig was in jail."

"That's incarceration."

"For a night."

"Isn't that incarceration?"

I say, "You need to look up the word."

"What?" Berryman says, his neck turning red with embarrassment.

He knows the people of Western Pennsylvania speak a different language but it sounds similar to the language he grew up on, except all the meanings have changed because more is at stake. No one here quotes statistics or, if they do, they quote the correct ones.

"Berryman," I say. "Rig got popped for pissing in a garbage can. When the officer asked him to stop, Rig turned and wrote his name in piss-cursive on the asphalt."

"You think he would have gone to jail had he been a white man?"

"Yes."

"You're sure?"

"I'm not sure about anything. But I would like to see you try and piss your name in cursive in front of a cop who just asked you to stop pissing in a garbage can."

Berryman says, "Probably not gonna happen."

"That cop would slap the sweatsuit right off your body."

"I'm sure he would."

"I worry about you canceling classes," I say.

"You don't cancel classes?" he says.

"Never."

"All my old professors canceled classes. One professor, in grad school, taught one class a month from her home. The other three scheduled classes, we worked independently. The class at her house, she did as a potluck. Everyone had to bring something to eat and a bottle of wine."

"What kind of grad school did you go to?" I say.

"Ivy League," he says. "You know that."

"I just like to hear the words come out of your mouth."

Berryman nods and tries to roll with the teasing.

I say, "I don't even want to imagine what you brought for your covered dish."

"Usually hummus."

"I was figuring a kale salad but hummus works."

"Kale is a superfood."

"You're a superfood, Berryman. Go cancel your class with the secretaries or schedule a potluck dinner or whatever you have to do."

"The potluck dinners were nice," Berryman says, and turns and leaves.

BRANDON

The second Berryman walks off, Brandon steps into my office. He skipped our class today so I assumed I would be spared his mini-novels and his aggressive demands but he appears like a student ninja from the shadows of the community college hallway. He wears old jeans covered in mud splatters, what I hope are mud splatters, and a professional-wrestling t-shirt with the Undertaker on the front. The Undertaker was a huge wrestler in a black hat and trench coat who used to excel in steel-cage matches. Maybe he still does. His angle was death. He often made the gesture of cutting his throat with his finger. I haven't seen professional wrestling in years.

Brandon says, "You weren't in class."

I say, "I was in class. You weren't in class."

"I think you know exactly what I meant," he says, tone aggressive, per usual, and starts to continue, all the lines of his face stretching towards complaint.

But I step on his words with mine.

I say, "I don't have comments on your compression yet. I read it a couple times. It's good. I'll have it back with some comments soon. If you have another compression that you want to drop off, I'll take a look at it and get it back to you asap. I have a big meeting in Johnstown later today and I need to prepare. Glad you're getting so much work done. When you leave, can you close my door? Thanks."

He says, "That's it."

"Great, thanks," I say, and turn to my computer screen like it's important.

"You're really not going to talk to me?"

"I like your shirt," I say, fishing for some kindness to deliver.

He pushes his head down so his chin touches his chest and tries to see his shirt.

He says, "Undertaker?"

"Yeah, he's the steel-cage match guy, right?"

"Hell in a cell."

"That's what they call it?"

"Hell in the cell is completely enclosed. A steel-cage match is open up top."

"Good to know," I say.

He says, "Undertaker is a pussy in real life. I read that somewhere."

"Also good to know," I say.

The Bus Station

The bus station sits on the eastern end of downtown Pittsburgh, splitting the street, a building of glass and chintzy metal shaped like a five-story V with the terminal fanning out in different directions. The design is something a very talented kid with a build-a-block set would imagine. I'm sure the station has one address but, depending on the exit, you could step out into the city on at least three different streets. It looks pretty if you like modern, if you like space age, if you like a building designed to look like a mothership that births space rovers. Inside, it smells like desperation, like piss and cigarette smoke burned into winter coats and the dying dreams of travelers who believe in New York and Los Angeles without realizing the cost of those two cities. People who take buses are either running or coming home broke. They know the exact amount of money in their pockets, including silver change and pennies. People with money who want a similar adventure take the train. The Union Station, directly across the street, ten stories of calico-cat-colored bricks and beautiful archways, more condo than bus terminal at this point, is lovely enough for royalty. I roll down Liberty Avenue until I can turn left down a side street and dip into the edge of the Strip District then park in a hotel lot for five bucks.

Berryman and I pop out of my truck and walk around the corner. Business people finish their day and step from every imaginable corner and swinging glass door, lugging briefcases and heavy purses to oversized parking garages. Wait staff in white shirts and black pants and black skirts hustle for parking spaces in junky cars and climb from city buses, heading to high-end restaurants. All night they'll wait on customers who want dinner before catching a musical or the symphony or some ancient doo-wop group with one surviving member. Later, they'll sling drinks when the same cultured people stop back for a cocktail after the show.

We wait at the crosswalk by the convention center.

Berryman says, "You ever wait tables?"

I said, "I bussed a couple summers when I was a kid."

"You like it?

"There were lots of waitresses in their thirties to fall in love with."

"They fall in love with you back?"

"They humored me and tipped out pretty well."

Berryman says, "I always wanted to work in a restaurant."

"That's a fantasy I think we can make come true," I say.

The orange light turns to a white stick figure, walking.

Berryman and I move with the crowd.

I can feel the city underfoot.

I do not mean the concrete, I mean the vibrations of other people's steps.

Berryman says, "You ever wrestle down here?"

"When I was in high school?"

"Yeah, college, whenever."

"Not downtown—I don't think there's a public school here—but I wrestled all over the city. Lots of those schools are shut down now."

"What was that like?"

"What, wrestling in the city?"

"Yeah."

"Like wrestling in the country but with less trees."

"Come on, humor me."

"It was good," I say. "I won sections."

We stop and plop down on a bench of concrete finished in pebbles, cold on our backs, uncomfortable. Riders pour from the bus station, from the spinning door. We look for Rig but his bus is not scheduled to arrive for twenty more minutes. Berryman breathes heavy from our short walk. His gut rests on his legs like a round table he carries with him. It moves up and down until we settle in. He wears a blue sweatsuit, not fuzzy or velvety, and suede Pumas.

Berryman says, "I mean, what was it like to wrestle in an urban environment?"

"I don't know. The same as wrestling in a rural environment but urban."

Berryman nods.

"But was the competition different? Like the feel of the competition?"

I shake my head.

I am not answering his question effectively.

He wants to talk about race, about wrestling black people, but he is too embarrassed to ask, too scared to sound racist. We have some version of this conversation regularly, though usually it is about poor white people, what Berryman must imagine is my specialty. Over and again he wonders: what is it like to live in a world that does not end at a private college and a European vacation? Is happiness possible while ordering the #3 Value Meal and watching basic cable? The world is a myth to Berryman—black people, poor white people, welders who write western novels, a lineage of superheroes who survive an unimaginable America of low ceilings and moneyed bouncers pushing us down. He wants to apologize for our efforts and his lack thereof. The guilt pings his ears and tongue and he will, for always, vote against his own best interests, hoping some candidate may finally reach down with a policy or two and bring those beneath on up. Berryman wants to help. Berryman wants to bring the goodness, the fairness. It's sweet and kind and the opposite of racism and classism but it is untrue to his intentions, known or unknown, because his trajectory from birth is upward.

Have we discussed this?

We have.

Berryman will age a few more years and keep the same opinions and attitudes and intentions but he will lose access to what he wanted to understand about race and class and the structures that keep us in our place because he will get a better job at a better college, he will get married and move to a better neighborhood, to somewhere with good schools, because even people who believe in hope and change aren't willing to send their kids to public schools with metal detectors and weed dealers hanging in the hallways.

Berryman, in his intelligence and kindness, will remember us as we are at our best: people unable to get ahead but who try, desperately, who work harder than the people who think they create jobs by inheriting the world.

Berryman says, "What time is Rig supposed to arrive?"

"Soon," I say.

The smell of trash wafts from an alley and mixes with the exhaust of delivery trucks and steam puffing from a manhole cover. Downtown always stinks.

Berryman says, "What was it like to wrestle black dudes?"

"That's a very direct question, Berryman."

"I mean culturally speaking," he says, instantly embarrassed.

"Culturally speaking, of course," I say. "Otherwise, you'd be asking me what it was like to wrestle black athletes, implying some sort of genetic superiority."

"That's not what I meant."

"You sure? Because that's some Nazi shit you're talking, some early nineteen-hundreds faux science. Eugenics, even."

"Come on," Berryman says. "You know what I mean. I'm a rube from upper-crust New Jersey. I'm curious. Why do you always fuck with me?"

I say, "I fuck with you because you're fuckable, that's why."

"I'm just curious about things other than what I know. My parents kept me pretty safe and sheltered. I played for an ice hockey team in the summer. We skated around a fancy rink when it was ninety degrees outside. I know what I had and I know its limits. I grew up hanging out in malls. My best friend drove a BMW."

"What'd you drive?"

"A Volkswagen."

"Your parents drew the line there?" I say, sarcastic.

"Sort of," he says.

I say, "What kind of Volkswagen?"

Berryman says, "A station wagon."

"What? A Station wagon? Why?"

"I don't know. It probably had a good safety rating and was reasonably priced."

I say, "Volkswagens are not reasonably priced."

"German engineering and all that," Berryman says. "My parents wanted me to be safe when I was out at the mall. I don't know. What'd you drive?"

I say, "The bus."

Berryman nods.

Buses, obviously, did not stop in his neighborhood.

I say, "Or the shoe-leather express."

"Walking?"

"Walked everywhere. Sometimes ran. I wanted to get there when I was a kid."

We sit quietly.

I am always happy until I am bitter.

Bitterness is seldom fair to anyone.

I still sort of like it.

Berryman says, "What are you thinking?"

"Bad thoughts about you," I say.

"Don't think bad thoughts about me," he says. "I'm just sitting here."

"I apologize. My mind races."

"It's okay. I know I'm a douche sometimes."

"You're not a douche, Berryman. You're doing your best."

"You don't believe that."

"I do," I say, and mean it.

Berryman leans back on the bench, face up to the bit of sun not erased by the confluence of tall buildings. Maybe he's thinking about Volkswagens. Maybe he's thinking about black dudes in wrestling headgear. Maybe he's thinking about buses and their implications for poor riders' hearts and the toll that being crammed in a tin can on wheels takes on our souls. Berryman exhales. I can feels his guilt, his own perception of privilege and his confusion about what to do with it, his seriousness of self, the comedy of that, and the not-comedy of that, the energy he puts into considering his privilege, that he puts into considering everything, when at the other edge of consideration is more consideration, not action, but endless thought.

The river is great, it'll take you to the ocean, but sometimes you need to paddle.

Row hard, Berryman.

You may find the shore yet.

THE GRILLED CHICKEN STORY

Rig's bus does not arrive on time. I check inside and the board places it fifteen minutes behind schedule. I go back to the bench where the city has slowed and the restaurant workers have made it to their jobs and people in ties and nice skirts have started home and other people, people in fancier clothes who will be here soon to eat appetizers before a show, have yet to arrive for the evening. Berryman looks like he's swallowed the world and his body does not know what to do with the pain.

"Can I tell you a story, Berryman?"

Berryman sits forward, less tense, more happy-bumbling.

"I wish you would," he says.

I lean forward and spit on the pavement and tell him this story.

When I was a freshman in college, I was on a partial wrestling scholarship. The money paid half my tuition. No stipend. No meal plan. I worked construction as a laborer the summer after my senior year of high school and my mom took extra shifts as a waitress and Nona borrowed against her house. We paid everything that needed to be paid to get into and attend classes at a university. After I bought my books and my wrestling gear and signed up for the meal plan and shelled out for cable TV because my roommate wanted cable and insisted I pay half and I was too embarrassed to say I neither wanted, needed, nor could afford cable, I was as broke as broke could be. I mean zero dollars and zero-zero cents.

Joanie, who was enormously proud of me for getting any kind of scholarship, partial or otherwise, who was proud of me for going to college at all, said she'd put fifty bucks in my account after her next shift. Instead, she put fifty bucks cash money in the mail and the mail got lost or stolen, or maybe she never sent it because she was broke and under-tipped and too embarrassed to say so.

Reason irrelevant: my bank account flipped to negative dollars for not meeting the minimum dollar amount to have an account.

I snuck apples from the cafeteria in my backpack.
I overate at dinner so I wouldn't feel like snacking all night.
I was hungry all the time.
I'd been hungry my whole life and college wrestling made me starved.

A few days into the semester, heading to class, I spotted a HIRING sign outside the student union for their restaurant, a coffee shop and grill that kept long hours, early morning until late at night, where students could drop money and eat while they studied or when they grew tired of cafeteria food. I walked straight in and applied. A couple other wrestlers applied and we all got the jobs. The jobs paid minimum wage. They paid every two weeks and held our first checks for whatever reason companies hold checks so no one saw a cent for a month.

The boss, a middle-aged woman in a hairnet, owned us. Twenty years earlier she'd earned a two-year certificate from some off-brand business school and she believed students striving for bachelor's degrees were spoiled. She made late schedules, sometimes the day before a shift started, and we hustled to find out when we worked. After a while she grew to trust us, not like us, maybe still hated us, but she started to see we operated at a high level, that we were a crew who knew how to complete tasks with speed and efficiency. We cleaned the grill and smiled at customers and made sure the coffee poured fresh. We swept. We mopped. Because she was not much of a worker and felt that work was beneath her, she started coming in late and leaving early. When present, she hid in her office. We notched up our skills. We polished windows and cleaned the restroom before the university janitors arrived.

Eventually, wanting to leave before closing and arrive well after opening, she created two positions, first and second assistant manager, neither of which paid more than working the grill or cashier, so the titles were imaginary and the promotions fake, but it allowed us to have keys to the store and register.

I made assistant manager number one.
I was a hungry assistant manager.
I started stealing cheese.
I stole with the bravado of the young, arrogant, and frustrated.
Then everyone started stealing cheese.
Not everyone was as broke and hungry as me but we were all pretty

broke and hungry and exhausted from school and sport and job, and stealing felt empowering. Fuck you for beating me down, you corporate slops, and all that. The boxes marked American cheese product in the walk-in fridge lowered to a two-tier stack. As assistant manager numero uno my job was to do the ordering. So I ordered more cheese, extra cheese, pounds of extra cheese. When the cheese arrived, I marked the packing slip like the cheese did not arrive, not all of it. The company delivering the cheese ate the cost. It was a good plan. The university was filled with idiots. Food companies were filled with idiots.

No one would ever catch us stealing cheese.

I believed it, almost one hundred percent, like ninety-five percent, enough to keep stealing cheese, enough to start stealing chicken breasts, but not enough to tell the other guys that I was stealing chicken breasts because then they'd want to steal chicken breasts too and I couldn't risk that. Somehow chicken breasts seemed more inventory-able. Their absence in bulk would be noticed. My belly mattered most, more than other bellies, more than all the other bellies combined. I put the hush on my chicken theft.

I started at the restaurant in the off-season so eating a lot of cheese was fine, my metabolism was a jet plane, but as the season started, I needed to lose weight, to go down to a weight class where an upperclassman who was a schmuck, a guy with minimal skills who'd stuck around and waited his turn, believed his age qualified him to be a starter. I needed to lose fourteen pounds so I could pin the schmuck and take his position despite my age, young, and status, freshman. As a starter I could win matches and draw attention and maybe get a better scholarship the following season. I needed chicken breasts for that. I needed chicken breasts so that in the future I would not have to work with or live on poultry I'd not paid for.

So I stole chicken breasts and kept stealing them.

I stole them and lost weight and became a starter. I won matches, lots of them. They wrote me up in the school paper. They wrote me up in the local paper. I did not get a better scholarship. I asked once and the coach said he'd look into it and he didn't or he did and the news was dismal so he never bothered reporting back. I was too embarrassed to ask again. The season ended. I studied hard. I read and wrote. I kept my job at the dining spot. I stole more chicken breasts. I stole them for years. I stole them after the other guys quit the job. I kept stealing cheese. I stole bags of lettuce. I stole packets of sesame seeds. I stole sunflower seeds. I won conferences all four years, I won regionals three times, I placed second in nationals my junior year and won nationals my senior year. My photograph is in a glass case with three other athletes as you walk into the gymnasium and my name is on a banner hanging from the auditorium, the school's highest praise, like being famous.

Would I have done what I did without stealing what probably turned out to be thousands of dollars of frozen food from the University of Pittsburgh at Johnstown?

No, I would not have.

"Do you understand, Berryman?" I say.

"Yes," he says. Then, thoughtfully, "No, I don't think so."

"Keep trying," I say.

THE MAN ARRIVES

Rig steps from the bus station with the strap from a gym bag slung across his chest, the bag dangling around his back. He looks the same, still enormous, still in shape despite the enormousness. He wears a yellow polo shirt, nice jeans, and flip-flops. The travelers around him move like little birds, their arm-feathers flapping near Rig's cannonball shoulders and Himalayan chest and whale belly.

I stand and wave him over to the bench.

He sees me and smiles, the stress of a bus station so much less than the stress of stepping from the Allegheny County Jail. The sun is up somewhere but lost behind the cityscape so the light is dim. Rig throws up two peace signs like Richard Nixon. I throw peace signs back.

Berryman waves like a teenage fan.

I look at Berryman.

He says, "What? Rig and I are friends now."

Then I remember this visit started with a phone call where I was trying to get blow, not that I really forgot, but I sometimes allow myself to ignore my own garden of grossness while it grows things I don't need. I planted my drug seeds, now I need to reap my crop of cocaine.

Rig says, "There's Rig's main man," and takes me in his arms like a teddy bear.

Just for fun, as Rig releases me from his hug, I duck under and shoot a fireman's carry so my arm is between Rig's legs and I lift with my thighs and Rig, having a good time, being a sport, lets me, so he ends up across my shoulders, his huge body driving me down, my skinny body holding him up. I give him a couple spins then tilt so he slides off and lands feet-first on the pavement with much grace for such a large man.

Rig laughs and says, "You strong for a skinny fuck."

"I'll be feeling that tomorrow," I say.

Berryman says, about me, "We wrestle where we work, out on the lawn, and he tears me to pieces every time. And he's like half my size."

Rig looks at me and says, "You brought your driver." Then, to Berryman, after a significant pause, "How you doing, Berryman? I'm just busting your nuts."

"That's what people do," Berryman says. "Apparently, I'm very bustable."

The riders from Rig's bus have dispersed, save for a young punkish couple in denim and hoodies who appear to be fighting over cigarettes. The girl turns her pack upside down and shakes to show it's empty. The boy slaps his forehead, not comically. A homeless guy sitting with his back on a brick wall like a chair says something to them and rattles his change cup. The rest of the city has quieted enough so the river a couple blocks north sounds like wind and water fighting it out. A few people cross the street, jaywalking. I wonder if Rig still gets recognized as a pro athlete, if he has fans. Pittsburgh loves sports. I notice three people in Steelers swag when I scan the block, one a woman in a shiny black-and-gold jacket.

"Where to?" I say to Rig.

"Rig needs some protein," he says. "Then I need to meet some friends. No worries, gentlemen, I don't need a ride anywhere. They all downtown tonight."

"That's a shame," I say. "Berryman was hoping to drive you around."

Rig says, "When I get back on my feet, I'm gonna hire Berryman as my driver."

"It'd be an honor," Berryman says.

Rig says, "You really wrestle my skinny buddy, Berryman?"

Berryman says, "I do."

"And he destroys you?"

"Pins me in seconds."

"Mountain Cats, baby," Rig says, invoking our alma mater wrestling team.

Berryman says, "Can I piss really quick?"

"Hustle it up," Rig says, smiling, sounding like a coach.

Berryman says, "Got it," and heads into the bus station, maybe the first time he's ever been in a bus station, certainly the first time here in Pittsburgh.

"How's my little man?" Rig says to me.

"I got a favor to ask," I say, embarrassed, surprised to ask, my mouth stepping out on its own, staring at the gym bag across Rig's body, thinking: blow. I say, "I have this ladyfriend. She's a lady who's a friend, right now, but I'd like it to be more than that."

"She got a boyfriend?" Rig says. "You want me to beat his ass?"

"No, I hope not. And no, I don't."

"Good. Rig don't beat asses for hire no more."

"That's smart."

"I might back up a skinny fucker like you, though."

I say, "I appreciate that."

He says, "You want to introduce your new lady friend to your washed-up was-famous pro athlete pal Rig?"

"That'd be great but no."

"Explain."

I say, "She likes to party."

"Party?"

"Party."

"Party party?" Rig say, turning to face me directly, eyes wider.

"Party party, yeah."

"You party party?"

"I drink," I say. "It helps with my nerves."

"You always was a nervous fuck. I remember you puking before matches when I was coach up Johnstown. What you have to be nervous about?"

I say, "I'm just that kind of guy, I guess. I used to shake when I was a kid. If I went into a store with a dollar and a can of soda cost fifty cents and that's all I wanted to buy, I'd pace the store, worried I didn't have enough money."

Rig says, "There a medical term for that."

"Yeah?"

"It's called being a pussy."

Rig pops me in the chest with the back of his hand but not hard, just for fun.

I pause and pull away from the jokey kindness to get back to my personal request, meaning coke, meaning Megan who wants coke, meaning getting coke so I can be with Megan and we can talk all night and be drunk and keep drinking and talking and maybe start kissing, meaning two shy people pushing off shyness with drugs, otherwise this, me scoring blow, would drift down Liberty Avenue and end up in the cartoon museum, so I focus and ask, "But you have anything, like party-party, I can buy?" and I don't care about the answer or worry about the answer, only that I asked and can tell Megan I asked.

"You not buying nothing from me," Rig says, and looks appalled. "Come on. Your money no good. But I have something for you. I'll lay it on you when we get something to eat. Too open out here."

"I appreciate it," I say. "I feel like a douche for asking."

"Rig is off that stuff, in case you wondering. I don't even think you noticed but when we was in that bar in Pitcairn, I didn't touch nothing, not even a beer."

"Except you passed out in the library at the community college."

"That was a mistake," Rig says. "I also think I talked some shit on you to that security guard so I apologize."

"Not a problem."

"You gotta watch them opioids."

"They kill people."

"Stay clear, little man."

Rig nods towards the station. Berryman holds one of the side doors for a group of people, maybe a family, to step through. A middle-aged man in painter's pants tries not to step on an older woman hunched over a walker as they head inside.

Rig says, "He a good dude and all but don't mention this to your driver."

"Off the record," I say.

Rig says, "I can feel the stadiums when I'm downtown."

"Yeah?"

"Ah man, you feel that?"

He extends his arms so his body is a cross and leans back and reaches for the city to absorb whatever vibe Heinz Field throws across the Mon River and the Clemente Bridge and vibrates memories into Rig.

Rig says, "Feels good and bad, total fuck-ups at the end and big news from when I was knocking helmets at the beginning," he says. "Once I straighten out completely and get me some stability, it'll be all good. I'm proud of those memories. You know?"

I nod, I know, yes.

Rig is a man who had success, many successes, without being anointed for success, without seeing success at home or in the neighborhood, and now he's stuck wondering if all his blessings accidentally sprinted up his nose or fell into his throat like kids rolling down a huge grassy hill only to end up in a busy street.

Rig says, "Pro fucking football, who knew." He says, "Wish I coulda played a couple more years. I'd have me a nice fucking NFL pension."

"That's a fucking bummer," I say. "I never even thought about a pension."

"You got a pension for teaching?"

"They have a 401K you pay into."

"You pay into it?"

"Nothing. I'm still paying back my student loans."

Rig taps his own chest with his fist and says, "Not being sad is a shit-ton of work but I do it. We have to do it, all us." He says. "You get sad?"

"I don't stop moving," I say, the truth of my existence.

He says, "You on blow. That be some Speed Racer shit," and laughs.

Then, because I want to say thank you, because I want to be positive toward Rig, a middle-aged man lugging a bag of drugs around only weeks after getting out of jail, a man who could use some positivity, who deserves some positivity, who is working at positivity, because I want him to not be a person on a bus but a person who made millions through dedication and force, or I want to do something as payback for helping me to get closer to Megan, pathetic as that is, or because he is a middle-aged man lugging a bag of drugs around only weeks after getting out of jail, which I'm repeating for you and me both, or because I am encouraging that, the bag of drugs, because I'm hitting him up, or because I want to acknowledge that he has done things that no one I've ever known has done or will do, that he is in fact the genius of his own life or was and should be again, and because he needs a real fucking job and I am good luck with jobs, I say, "You ever thought about being a public speaker?"

"A public speaker?" Rig says. "You fucking kidding me?"

"I'm serious," I say, and I think I am.

Rig says, "I lived in Johnstown pretty much my whole life and I got a southern accent from living around black people who come up North to get jobs. I fuck up more grammar than I make. How Rig gonna be a speaker?"

"You got a story, that's how," I say. "No one gives a shit about how you speak, it's what you say. We have people come to campus all the time to talk to students. They bring in business people, entertainment people, B-list actors, shitty musicians, everyone you can imagine, but the ones who get the most attention are ex-athletes."

"For reals?"

"Ex-athletes. People love it."

Berryman steps up and says, "You two ready?"

Rig says, "This crazy motherfucker here is trying to convince me to be a public speaker. Wants Rig to talk to the children."

Berryman, straight-faced, a poet who loves athletes, a privileged gentleman who loves the stories of the downtrodden, even if the downtrodden are former millionaires like Rig, says, "You'd be great at it."

Rig says, "How much you pay to see Rig give a talk?"

Berryman says, "I don't know. A successful poet can make big bucks."

I say, "No one cares what a poet gets, Berryman."

Berryman says, "I know."

Rig says, "A couple hundred bucks? Five hundred bucks? And how many people come to these public speaks? Does audience size matter? Rig never played quarterback."

I say, "You don't get paid by the person. The university, or organization or whoever, brings you in for a fee. Speakers usually get five grand, minimum."

"Five grand?"

"Or more."

"Shit," Rig says, considering. "You help me write what I say?"

"I would," I say.

"You sure?" Rig says, looking for a tell on my face.

"Absolutely," I say, making my face positive and willing but still untrue.

I wanted my idea of a job, my suggestion, to be enough. I hate the thought of being responsible for anyone else's life, the time it takes, the chance for failure when you mean success, the way friendships crumble over bad advice, the way friendships crumble over good advice, and Rig is Rig, a man who could easily consume my tiny life without meaning or trying to. The man's personality is huge. He eats up rooms like cake then people bake him more cake because they love the way he eats. I'm the opposite. I like the distance between people best, the long gaps between goodbye and the next hello.

Rig says, "Talking to kids, huh," and closes his eyes to think. He says, "I saw Ice-T talk one time, right down the street at the Benedum. Bunch of blue-haired old white ladies ushered me to my seat. Lot a blue-hairs in the audience. Bunch a kids too, college kids. Not as many black folk as I expected. T talked about pimping and hoing all night. He used to pimp. Now he hoes by acting for TV shit. Everything was pimping and hoing. Some capitalism shit. It was okay. Not as good as his CDs. Or his TV show, the cop one." He looks at me. "You like rap?"

"Hate it," I say.

"You have bad taste in everything," he says. "What about you, Berryman?"

Berryman says, "I love it. All old school."

Rig says, "Berryman a culture vulture."

Berryman's face falls into his skull.

Rig says, "Berryman, take a joke."

I'm already disappointed in myself for encouraging Rig to be a public speaker, even though I think it's a great idea that he could cash in on.

"I'd have to memorize it," Rig says. "My reading aloud ain't for shit."

"I would help you write it too," Berryman says. Then, embarrassed, "If you wanted me too, I mean." He says, "I didn't mean to sound so forward." He says, "I'd love to hear you speak. You have an amazing story, like a Hollywood story. I'm just saying. I bet you could get movie people interested in your story. It's fantastic. I really don't mean to sound forward."

Rig says, "Berryman didn't mean to sound so forward," and laughs at the words.

I say, "You'd be great."

Rig says, "I'll think about it," and looks around the city, bus station, train station, convention center, river, bridge, football stadium, the truck in the alley, manhole cover, places a person could walk over and live in and ride and talk about with authority. He says, "Let's go get us some protein, medium, so it's not too bloody but still bloody enough."

FINDING PROTEIN, OLD MAYOR

Rig wants to eat at a fancy steakhouse. I've never eaten anywhere fancy, like absolutely never. When they serve wine and cheese at events sponsored by the community college, I'm too embarrassed to eat or drink. Sometimes I wrap some cheddar chunks and a couple crackers in a paper napkin for home then eat everything in the car because I'm starved. My favorite meal is a corned beef sandwich, regular with cheese, or a Reuben, though I also love a Rachel. I like breakfast foods, eggs and bacon and potatoes. Berryman probably grew up taking the train to New York so he could eat in Italian restaurants where they made sauce from plum tomatoes flown in from Italy. Rig, when he was a football player, probably ate all of Italy.

"What if we just got a sandwich?" I say.

They ignore me.

Do fancy steakhouses sell burgers?

Do the burgers taste like filets?

We walk through downtown, one of the few places in Pittsburgh on a grid or almost a grid. Some streets turn whatever way they want and disappear and re-appear later with the same name but most hold straight. Rig and Berryman walk along as pals while I stay behind muttering about Nico's Recovery Room and wings and karaoke. We could all sing

Michael Jackson songs or Journey. We could break chicken bones.

But they strut on, talking steaks.

Steaks embarrass me.

Rig says, "The best steak I ever had was in New Orleans, at this place called La Roca. Some Spanish dude owns it. The beef could make you quit everything but beef."

Berryman says, "I been there, I been there. I was at a conference and someone knew about it and that's where we ended up."

Rigs says, "Berryman a classy motherfucker, look see."

"Fuck you both," I say. "Steaks in New Orleans?"

"I'm not proud of it," Berryman says, still walking.

"I am," Rig says. "Money for food, for good fucking food, I wanted it my whole life."

I tail along, thinking my thoughts about food and money, how it pisses me off, how much money you need for good food, if good food is even good food, or how food that costs serious money somehow means something, like a poem means something, like it's a special language, hating that, remembering stolen cheese and chicken breasts, but realizing I could spend twenty or thirty or even forty bucks on a steak, I have it, my bills are paid, I have a job, a decent job, I still eat noodles three times a week and hit the Taco Bell drive thru, and hmm and hah, and I don't know, and I could use a drink. Drinks help with all this.

"I'm not dressed for anything fancy," I say.

Rig turns and stops hard and says, "Look at my feet. You see that, man? Flip flops. Rig's not talking fancy. I'm talking good. You need to learn the difference."

"Someone's going to bring us a wine list," I say.

"Who gives a shit?"

"I do."

"You don't," Rig says. "So stop your nonsense. You broke? I got money. Rig is buying tonight. I'm the treat-er. You be the treat-y"

Berryman says, "You don't have to pay for my dinner."

Rig says, "Berryman, you want to drive my ass around all night?"

Berryman stands there, not sure how to answer.

Rig says, "Onward, gentlemen."

So onward we go.

Grant Street is a brick river between buildings meant to last forever. The old post office is now a courthouse. The old Kaufmann's department store is soon to be million-dollar condos. We pass insurance buildings, steel buildings, bagel shops, Fed Ex, a tavern inside a lobby, the mayor's office with a statue near the steps of Richard Caliguiri, the mayor of my youth.

Caliguiri was an Italian guy from Greenfield, a Catholic neighborhood on a hill slopping into the Monogahela River. His dad was a milkman. My mom and Nona loved him. He was handsome in a shy way. He pushed for cultural things downtown when hookers still legged the corners of Liberty Avenue. Caliguiri governed for eleven years. Nobody in the city had jobs, industry took a nosedive, and big name companies headed for California, but the air was suddenly more breathable and things turned pretty but still kept their grit. He took our wonderful soot-covered bridges and painted them all yellow, the safe color for public restrooms and the psych ward, and somehow made it look beautiful. All anyone cares about is money, unless you can make something lovely, then you'll be loved. Caliguiri did pretty and he did smart and he sort of fucked over the downtrodden, hoping they'd become fancy because he thought fancy was the future and anyone could be fancy, which is a lie. Outside the mayor's office they built a six-foot bronze statue of him dressed in a suit, both hands jammed in his pockets like he really might listen to what you say, like he genuinely cared.

Sometimes I talk to the statue.

Sometimes I walk on by.

STEAKHOUSE

We decide to eat at Ruth's Chris Steakhouse. By we, I mean Rig, with Berryman nodding along. I admire Rig's confidence, the way he bulldozes forward, even if I disagree with what he plows.

Ruth's Chris Steakhouse is more legend than restaurant, an upscale chain charging for premium beef flown in from the Midwest, cooked at one thousand degrees, then dabbed with butter handed down from God. They throw a plate of asparagus spears on the side for an additional fifty dollars and rich people cream in their upscale knickers. When I was a welder, I heard industrial salesmen mutter about taking important clients to Ruth's Chris, both elated at the food and made miserable by the prices, but I've never seen nor actually talked to a person who has eaten there not on an expense account but by paying hard-earned cash. I know this particular steakhouse exists downtown somewhere but only as a myth and not somewhere to consider or seek out because I worry that I eat too much Taco Bell and too many bowls of soup from Harry's Bar when I should be buying groceries and cooking more at home to save money.

Rig says, "We almost there."

Berryman says, "I've never been in this part of Pittsburgh before."

I keep my yap shut to avoid ridicule.

Ruth's Chris is located in PPG Place, a whole bunch of skyscraper-esque glass buildings filled with a whole bunch of businesses I know nothing about. Between the buildings sits a sort of courtyard with a small ice-skating rink for winter and some jets to make water gush from the ground during summer so little kids can cool off and soak their parents. Joanie dragged me here to skate a couple times during Christmas when I was in elementary school but I was too scared to let go of the wall and she hated all the happily married yuppies and their kids in new winter coats so we quit coming and she started taking me to Ross Park Mall to visit Santa and eat Sbarro Pizza at the food court.

I can't remember the last time I walked around downtown Pittsburgh, let alone came to PPG place, but we've moved into a corner of the world that looks like it was made by superheroes who possessed ice powers and threw up these buildings to block out heat-seekers and the humans who don't make a quarter-million dollars per year.

I break and ask, "You two sure you want to eat here?"

Rig slows down and takes me under his huge arm and says, "You gonna love this, so quit being a crybaby pussy."

"Yeah," Berryman says, happy to get a knock in against me.

Rig says, "You a professor. You deserve a good meal."

"This better not be as expensive as I think it's going to be," I say.

"That's crybaby pussy talk," Rig says. "What I say about that?"

Wood and White Table Clothes

We step inside the front door and a coat rack lines the wall and a nice-enough hostess, a twenty-something skinny blond who would not be out of place bartending at TGIFridays, asks us how many in our party.

Rig says, "Three but we like a big table if you have it."

"Absolutely," she says, and marks our seats on her dry-erase board and leads us into the dining room.

I expected people in suits and wedding parties and middle-aged success stories enjoying a birthday filet. I expected doctors celebrating anniversaries with their wives, other doctors sneaking out on their husbands to meet their twenty-five year-old boyfriends, and dentists with gleaming white teeth dragging their families here for whatever reasons dentists celebrate. But the room is half-packed at best and the people are so normal looking and underdressed as to be unidentifiable. The bar is old wood, not broken in but certainly not fancy. Everything is wood, dark, a little mysterious. The tablecloths are white as cartoon clouds.

The hostess stops at a six-seater near the middle of the restaurant.

"How's this?" she says.

Rig says, "Rig thinks this perfect."

"Glad Mr. Rig likes it," the hostess says, smiling.

We take our seats, Rig in the middle on one side, Berryman and I across the table, a chair between us so we don't have to touch.

Ordering

The waiter is barely of drinking age, or he's a plastic surgery miracle, so terrifically handsome and fit, same as everyone who works here. His skin is the color of the brown masks rich women use at spas, a creamy beige. He either loves the sun or loves a tanning bed or both. His hair is almost completely shaved on the sides but the top is twisted into tiny gelled spikes. He wears glasses with some kind of an emblem on the side, maybe a subtle G for Gucci or maybe a C for some brand I can't name.

He says, "I'm Marcus and I'll be your waiter."

Rig says, "I'm Rig, and this old pal is Sellick, but everyone call him Professor because he a professor, and this is his driver, Berryman."

Marcus says, "Berryman, like the poet?"

Berryman smiles.

Rig says, "No, Berryman like the driver."

Marcus, maybe slightly frazzled or at least surprised that Rig introduced us all, including my driver, while ignoring Marcus's waiter-ly knowledge of poetry, says, "Have you gentleman had the pleasure of dining at Ruth's Chris steakhouse before?"

"Many times," Rig says.

Marcus says, "Fantastic," and puts his hands behind his back and rocks on his heels in a gesture that is supposed to be authentic.

He, like all the staff, appears to be terrifically trained in the art of comfort, in the ability to put people at ease with the money they are about to be separated from so they don't feel regret and never return.

Marcus says, "Let's start you gentleman with some drinks."

Berryman starts to speak but gets cut off.

Rig says, "I'll have water with lemon, coffee back. Sellick will have a beer, domestic, your choice, something shitty if you have it. He grew up without a dad and his mama worked hard but they didn't have a lot. He drinks cheap. Get Berryman the fanciest beer on the menu. He's a driver but he comes from money."

"Sounds great," Marcus says. "I'll be back with your drinks and your menus."

"No menus necessary," Rig says, and he starts to order. "These two will have filets. I'll have the T-Bone. We'll have mashed potatoes, the lobster mac 'n cheese, and the grilled asparagus for sides. We talk desserts at the south end of this meal."

"Excellent," Marcus says, using his brain as a tablet. "I apologize but we're all out of the asparagus spears tonight. Could I suggest a substitution?"

"No," Rig says, "you may not offer a substitution," and looks at Marcus like it would be appalling or worse to accept a food suggestion from a waiter, especially one as young and tan as Marcus. Rig says, "We'll have the sweet potatoes, two orders."

Marcus says, "The sweet potato casserole?" sounding know-it-all.

"That's what I said," Rig says, not friendly, barking back.

"Excellent," Marcus says. "I'll return with your drinks."

"We gonna need an appetizer too."

"Excellent. Do you have something in mind?"

"Seafood."

Marcus says, "Anything in particular?" and it's obvious he's already learned to zip the recommendations and wait.

"Seafood," Rig says, repeating. "Lots of it."

"Lots of seafood," Marcus says.

"Work harder," Rig says. "You not charming."

WAITERS

I say, "You should be nicer to our waiter. Those guys work hard."

Rig says, "This ain't Applebees."

I say, "You should still be nice to the guy."

Rig says, "I tip the fuck outta service. I ain't gotta be nice," but he smiles and the laughter in his voice makes it sound like he could be nice going forward.

Or not.

Rig says, "What's the fanciest place Sellick ever eat?"

I sit there, thinking, looking at my napkin-wrapped silverware.

Rig says, "Exactly. I'll handle this."

RENT VS. SEAFOOD

I'm seated facing the front door so I see everyone who comes in. It's a slow weekday night but a few stragglers show up and the hostess seats them. I sip my beer and try to keep my skin on. Not seeing the menu, meaning not knowing the prices, doesn't help. Despite his semi-dickatudeness to our waiter, Rig seems happy to be chewing through a pile of shrimp and crab legs and lobster tails. The lobster tails appear more perfect than a photo in a food magazine. Our appetizer surely costs more than my weekly food budget. I'm afraid to eat because it will probably—absolutely—taste delicious and once the deliciousness is confirmed my brain will release chemicals to acknowledge how good this is and I will spend the rest of my life blowing my salary on food I can't afford or starving myself from things so tasteful I'll never be satisfied again. Berryman peels shrimp like his fingers are knives made for this. Rig hands me a crab leg.

He says, "Quit being a pussy and eat."

"I ate a shrimp," I say, but still crack open the crab leg and a huge hunk of meat pops out, no digging, no additional cracking, just crab meat, so I pull it off and dunk it in butter and pop it in my mouth and it's better than I hoped for, so sweet and tender I want to slow my chewing to make it last, except Rig has ordered piles of this and will, I think, order more if necessary. I finish my crab leg and discard the shell on a clean white plate and I go right for a lobster tail, the smaller one because I've heard those taste best.

Rig sees my face and smiles and says, "That's what I'm talking about."

"Fuck you, Rig," I say, sliding my finger between the lobster meat and shell.

Rig says, "Look at you, seafood boy. Rig showing you the goodness of the world."

Berryman says, "In Maine, you can go to the harbor when the fishing boats come in and they'll sell you a lobster for five bucks and cook it right there."

He dips a shrimp in butter and pops it in his mouth.

"Maine?" Rig says. "Don't be arrogant, Berryman," and he holds his pissed off face for a good three seconds before he smiles and says, "Rig likes you. You got the illusion of style."

"But no real style?" Berryman says, enjoying the attention.

"Not yet," Rig says. "But keep eating."

STEAK, FINALLY

We eat our steaks, which are so pink inside but somehow still warm. No one talks. We understand talking diminishes us, that every bite is less of a bite when mixed with words. Our knives quietly clink against our plates as we cut and repeat. I quit drinking beer, fearing it may lessen my taste buds and fill my belly, and switch to water. Rig takes one of the remaining lobster tails, pulls it from the shell with his hands, then tears it into three pieces like the flesh is bread and he is our Christ. He places the first piece of lobster on top of a chunk of his T-bone and spears both with his fork and guides it to his mouth, a speedball of farm and sea. He looks up and nods at me to verify I have noticed, that I have learned a new lesson. I have but I am not ready to repeat his feat of decadence. The amount of seafood and beef a person would have to consume to realize they can be combined like peanut butter and jelly must be astronomical. I stick with the filet, carving off smaller pieces to make it last, until only a light pink swirl of blood and butter remains on my plate.

Then I go for the mashed potatoes.

Then everyone goes for everything.

Rig says, "Beef and seabird," meaning lobster, "repeat after me."

STUFFED

Rig orders us desserts to go, lava cake and pecan something and crème brûlée. All the other plates have been scraped clean and we have licked the serving spoons, literally, each of us choosing our favorite side.

Marcus brings us warm washcloths filled with lemon chunks and tied with a ribbon to clean our hands. For a second I think they are another dessert.

Rig thanks him and says, "We ready for our check now."

Marcus says, "Nothing else?"

"Not a thing," Rig says.

"A little more coffee," Berryman says.

"You bet," Marcus says. Then, "I don't want to overstep my boundaries here and make any assumptions but it appears that you gentlemen enjoyed yourself?"

"Very much," Rig says. "It ain't Spain but a man can eat good, right here in Pittsburgh, that's for sure. I'd kiss Ruth right on the mouth were she alive."

Marcus says, "Excellent. I was hoping you enjoyed everything. I'll be right back with your check and some coffee for Mr. Berryman."

Marcus walks off.

The three of us sit, food-stunned.

The level of joy I feel to have eaten so well has turned my brain from a thinking control panel into a second stomach, another satiated spot unable to fit anything else.

Berryman says, "I need a nap."

"Berryman," I say, "you are so fucking fat."

Berryman says, "That hurts my feelings."

Rig says, "He meant it as a compliment."

Berryman says, "Fair enough."

THE BILL

Marcus comes back with our check, which I assume is huge, huge beyond my comprehension, possibly the size of my bi-weekly paycheck after taxes. He smiles in his professionally-trained way of appearing intimate and happy, unfazed by Rig's gruff sense of command and all our overzealous eating or, perhaps, he is genuinely happy, three experienced eating machines with no sense of decorum lighting up an otherwise uneventful and boring shift like a batch of insane and lustful reality TV stars. A huge tip will be in order for Marcus but, here in Ruth's Chris Steakhouse, all tips must be huge. Or the tips must be beyond huge when customers who are drinkers and orderers of wine bottles and cigars cash out. Newbees celebrating big events pay their bills and are so filled with joy and shame they plunk down everything to share the happiness. There is no reason not to tip beyond comprehension. Money rolls like trucks on an interstate in restaurants that charge twenty bucks for mashed potatoes.

No waitperson goes home broke.

Most go home loaded.

I love that, a reward for working people dealing in ridiculousness.

Marcus adjusts the paper receipts inside the carrying case and opens the thin black book of our debit and sits it on the table so it stands up on its own, like an apartment building, like something you would own and not consume.

Marcus says, "I'll take the bill when you're ready," and walks off.

I go for my wallet, assuming we'll divide this three ways, hoping so at least, not remotely expecting Rig to pay like he offered but praying I am not expected to treat, that the check standing in front of us is not mine alone.

Then, suddenly and horribly, I realize I am about to treat.

This was a joke, I am the punchline.

What do you call a community college professor in an upscale steakhouse?

Poor as fuck.

Berryman reaches into his pocket and pulls out his wallet, a blue slice of folding suede. I wait for Rig to go for his wallet but he does not. I sip my water. At least Berryman will pay for half. Then I think this is a joke on Berryman, that Rig is about to make him pay—come on white boy, you privileged piece of shit, put that Ivy League education to use and buy some real wrestlers a meal of farm and sea.

I pick up my lemon washcloth and rub my hands like seafood and filet are dirt that may have gotten under my fingernails.

Rig leans back in his chair and touches his belly with both hands.

Berryman says, "Can you pass me that check so I can see what I owe?"

"Me too," I say, appreciating Berryman's lead, his comfort with money.

Rig says, "Nah," and pushes the check down flat without checking the bill so no one else can even sneak a look at the prices.

Berryman says, "I want to pay my share."

Rig says, "Like forty acres and a mule?"

Berryman says, "What?" and turns red and bows his head.

Rig says, "Fucking with you, white guy."

Berryman says, "I knew that."

Rig says, "No you didn't."

I say, "I still want to pay my part."

Rig says, "Poorest of white boy, please stop."

I say, "There are white boys poorer than me."

Rig says, "Nah, there ain't."

Marcus immediately appears like he has been scouting our payment plans.

Rig reaches to the floor and picks up his backpack. He goes inside with the shovel of his hand. He pushes things around, clothes, drugs, whatever else is in there, looking for his wallet or his money clip or a couple gold pieces, I don't know.

Marcus looks at Berryman and me and he nods, patient. He smiles, so fake it's sincere, so sincere it's fake. He's seen rich people dig for money before, no rush. He's used to being tipped but he also knows Rig will verbally slap him down if he speaks.

Rig finally pulls out his hand. His hand is so enormous it covers whatever he's pulled out which is not a wallet but at first appears to be a clear plastic bag of money. He places his hand on the check and moves his hand away, leaving his payment—not cash or gold or plastic but three oversized eight-balls of cocaine—on the black carrying case. By oversized, I mean twice as big as an eight-ball used to be when the cop pulled us over in Randy's car when I was still in high school. Maybe these are double eight-balls. Or triple eight-balls. I don't know the math. I never learned the language. Berryman sighs the word fuck like it's leaked from his lungs then catches himself and reaches for cream to dump into his new coffee. I try to make eye contact with Rig. I make my eyes say: no, don't do this, are you insane? Rig ignores me and stares at Marcus. Marcus looks around the restaurant, less panicked than I expected, less panicked than I am and Berryman is, less panicked than a man should be who has just been offered blow to cover a tab for steaks and shellfish.

Rig says, "We good?"

Marcus scans the room one more time, sly but confident, like he might need a sommelier or some other high-end help, a bartender with three hands, a waitress with three tits, and he subtly palms the eight-balls and removes the check from our table like it's a dirty plate.

He says, "Yep, we good," and walks off.

Rig reaches back in his bag and pulls out another oversized eight-ball and slides it across the table so I have to grab it before it falls from the edge. It's more coke than I've ever seen and the amount leaves me clueless and scared and with no choice but to drop my hands, one filled with a whiffle ball of drugs, underneath the table and recalibrate my face into something less paranoid.

Rig says, "For you and your lady."

So much for keeping Berryman on the downlow.

I squeeze the coke in its tied-off sandwich bag and nod.

Berryman says, "We should leave."

Rig says, "Gentlemen, grab your desserts."

The desserts are packed in three separate Styrofoam containers, all stacked together. I stand and stuff the coke in my front pocket like it's car keys and guide it towards my crotch so it looks like I have three testicles, one of them a miniature planet made of cocaine. Rig walks away. Berryman walks away. I grab the stack of desserts and make sure they don't tumble. Berryman immediately moves for the aisle and powerwalks to the front door.

Rig says, "You enjoy yourself?"

I think I nod an affirmation as Berryman moves like an eel through customers and waitstaff and out of the restaurant's main doors. I check the kitchen but Marcus knows enough to not re-appear. The hostess hosts at her station. I do not recognize anyone who is obviously a manager. Or a cop. Or the FBI. I carry the desserts so they cover my crotch.

My crotch is a ball of blow.

The cops and sirens and jails are all in my head. I know that but I still can't stop my imagination. Every breath drops bars and chains and guns on my life.

Rig puts his arm around my shoulder and I can smell his breath, the after-dinner coffee. We step outside, still trailing Berryman.

I enjoyed myself enormously, I mean to say.

Berryman turns and says, "Where'd we park?" but keeps moving.

Rig says, "Berryman never gonna be woke."

I say, "You scare me sometimes."

"I scare myself," Rig says. "Make sure you enjoy that dessert."

I raise the dessert to carry it belly-high and instantly smell the coca and vanilla and burnt sugar. The more distance we put between us and the restaurant, the more I want to return, the more I want to take my Nona here and Joanie here, maybe both at the same time, mother and grandmother together again, learning to love each other over one hundred dollar steaks.

Thanks Rig, for the insight and education.

And thank you too, Berryman, for whatever reason, for being rich, for being Berryman, for recognizing a good time, for knowing steaks, for knowing seafood, for knowing to be scared enough to run us outside while I bumbled desserts and practiced saying crème brûlée.

Rig says, "Hmm ha," like those are words.

I say, "You big fucker."

He says, "You little bitch."

I'll be back with my whole family once I get the money, or sooner because this dinner cost me nothing. Rig paid for it like a big shot. He is the genius of bigshots. He rolled blow across the table like solid gold dice, his fuck-off to everyone so he could be a king again.

And he deserves to be king.

We all do.

PART EIGHTEEN

WCCC

Sometimes I park in the back lot, which is really for delivery trucks, and cut through the gymnasium to avoid people and polite conversation on the way to my office when I'm behind on my work. I try that this morning, the sneak-around, but a student sits on the loading dock, waiting, her feet dangling in combat boots, real ones from Ralph's Army Surplus and not Doc Martins, her heels kicking the wall. A stack of binders rests in her lap. Her name is Tessa and she dresses punk rock, rips in her clothes, concert t-shirts. She's sweet and tough and watches MSNBC and reads the *NY Times* on Sundays and attends rallies in downtown Pittsburgh and marches for causes. Instead of paralyzing her, the awfulness of the world seems to focus and energize Tessa. She's twenty-two. I hope she keeps believing and swinging but the fight and belief business is tough to grow into. Last year she had green hair. Next year she'll be wearing jeans without holes. In five years she'll be in a business suit, too tired to crank up the Pussy Drops, her favorite punk band, let alone her Clash records and her *Nuggets* boxset. Her concerns about the living wage and mountaintop removal in West Virginia will slowly wilt as her bills pile up and the hours at her job become endless.

Days she finds time to take an uninterrupted hot shower will be great days. Her expectations will become so low, they will be unrecognizable as expectations.

All of us, adults, our expectations become so low.

I hope I'm wrong about all of it.

Right now she waves and smiles as I approach.

I wave and smile back.

She says, "I knew I'd find you here."

"Nope, you didn't," I say.

"I did," she says.

"Am I that obvious?"

"Everyone knows you sneak into school when you're hungover."

"Everyone does not know that," I say.

She says, "I think they do."

I consider this.

I'm seldom hungover on campus. When I'm hungover on campus I make sure it does not show. I've never been drunk on campus, ever. I usually dress in khakis and a Gap tie to appear professorial and yet my students think I wobble in the back door with a booze head. Through speculation and guesswork I've turned into the cool professor or, possibly, the greatest professor of all time, the drunk professor. Should this information reach my colleagues, which are few here because of the campus size and our copious use of adjuncts, I shall be made an intellectual mockery, to which I say: who gives a shit.

I love this job.

I'd fight and lie for this job.

When I go cynical and dark, I imagine the president who hired me disappears and the fanged doves who generally run institutions of higher learning suddenly appear and ask me to leave for not having a master's degree and for being comical in class, for getting along with the students, for teaching books where people fuck and love and fall down from war and anxiety and poor wages, and—now that I know my reputation—for being the drunk guy on campus, hungover and sneaking through the alley.

I repeat my previous argument, "I'm never hungover on campus."

Tessa says, "Everyone knows you drink at Harry's Bar."

I say, "They probably know that because I don't hide it."
She says, "I'm not judging."
"Harry's Bar is great."
"I'm sure it is."
Tessa slides down from the loading dock.
She says, "I'm not judging you, Professor Sellick."
I say, "That's because you're a good person."
"I try to be."
"Spread some good rumors about me," I say. "Tell people what a thoughtful professor I am and how I use the back entrance to clear my head."
"I will do that," Tessa says. "Aren't you cold?"
I check the sky. Black clouds in the distance. White clouds overhead. The sun like a hundred-watt bulb behind a lampshade of fluff.
"It's spring," I say.
"I need eleven letters of reputation," Tessa says.
"No, you don't."
"I do."
"Really? Eleven letters of recommendation?"
"Is that what they're called?"
"Yes," I say, "though I like letters of reputation better."
"It's like a song lyric I've been garbling. Reputation. Recommendation." She stops and sings those two words. She says, "Hmm. Thanks for the correction."
"No problem."
"I'm a dumb cunt," she says, sort of sad, sort of happy to say cunt.
"You're not," I say.
"I feel like it."
"We all do. I often wake up and my first thought is: I'm a dumb cunt. You're a sweetie and super-smart. And involved."
"Thanks," she says. "Can you write the letters?"
"Sure," I say. "But eleven is an enormous amount."
"I need to get out of this shithole, no offense."
"None taken."
"Can you do it? Write eleven letters?"
"Are these all for schools you're applying to?"

Tessa says, "Ten of them are, and one's for an internship."

"So, really, one letter for ten schools, and one letter for an internship."

"That sounds right, I think, yes."

"You decide on a major?"

"So I'm getting my RN now, it's a two-year thing here, and I work as a secretary for a doctor in Irwin. I'm thinking of majoring in psychology. Then I'll be a nurse psychologist. Is that a thing? Nurse Psychologist?"

I consider that.

I say, "I don't think so but maybe it could be," and I raise my voice.

High-end career counseling is not my specialty but I aspire to help all who need employment to be employed at the best jobs possible.

My English degree landed me a construction job.

My construction job landed me a gig as a western novelist.

My western novels landed me here, at the community college.

I say, "If nurse psychologist is a thing, you'll be great at it. Can you ask the doctor you work for? Doctors know stuff like that."

"Maybe," she says. "He's busy and kind of a dick."

I say, "To be a psychologist, I think you have to have a master's degree and maybe pass a licensure test. You might have to have a PhD."

"How long does a masters in psych take?"

"Usually two years, after four years of undergraduate."

"Fuck," she says, "you kidding?" and instantly looks discouraged.

"Did you check with career services?"

"Do we have career services?"

"We do."

"Where's it at?"

I say, "In the student services wing," and point through a brick wall.

She says, "Shit, how'd I miss that," and she twirls but mad at herself. She says, "I'm always so busy. I don't know anything about this place."

"I'll walk you there," I say. "Then I'll write your letters of recommendation. What's the internship for? It's better if I make the letter specific."

She says, "Did your mom name you after Tom Sellick?"

"She did," I say.

"Your mom must have loved mustaches."

"She did."

"But you spell your name different."

"My mom wasn't much of a speller."

We both climb on the loading dock to avoid walking to the steps. Tessa is tiny, maybe five feet, but she leg-kicks up like a gymnast on a horse.

"The internship is for the nuthouse over at Westmoreland Hospital."

"Okay," I say, "maybe I won't call it a nuthouse in my letter."

OFFICE WORK

I finish Tessa's letters in half an hour. I have three templates I use for letters—pretty good, great, and off-the-charts. Tessa gets the highest recommendation. I give my phone number and encourage the people in charge to call. I make more copies than Tessa needs and, of course, she doesn't stop back to pick them up, not because she's irresponsible but because she probably rushed to class then to the doctor's office where she works then, shortly, to another class, then home to eat a bowl of ramen noodles.

I think people don't understand how working-class kids operate.

Their lives are clusterfucks of employment, learning, and shot-y self-care.

Such is why I love them.

I close my door and un-pile my stack of student papers and do not shuffle them or try to arrange a system but take a pen and start correcting. I fuel with coffee from my thermos. My thermos reminds me of welding, which is work, which is what I do here, work, building better students from the raw materials of their papers. I correct three assignments then take a break. I stand up and walk my office, a tiny square, but I do not step into the hall where I can be distracted. I correct three more papers. I take a break. I correct three, I take a break, I drink more coffee, I correct three and don't stop, I correct four more, I take a break, I move like a ninja to the soda machine and buy three cans of Mountain Dew, I correct ten while I chug Mountain Dew, I walk my office, I correct five, I move for more Mountain Dew.

I do this until all papers have been corrected.

I open my office door and the students smell like flowers.

NOT NICE

Within seconds Brandon puts his face in my door. He wears the look of a student who wants his life handed to him like a computer program he can run to generate success, meaning lost and hopeful and overly stressed around the eyes.

I know I have avoided him for too long but I also know I was incapable of listening to him because I sometimes have a hard time listening to students who are unlistenable.

And now, somehow, I am ready.

I say, "Hey, I have your first compression completed. You want to sit and talk for a minute? There are some comments on your paper. You can just take it and go if that's easier. Let me dig it out," and I push aside my stack of finally-graded required papers and dig out Brandon's extra story-novel-thing.

I smile, confident.

Brandon stands there, leaning, only his head and neck and shoulders visible in my door like half his body has been sliced away.

I say, "You want to come in?"

He says, "You know what? Fuck off."

"You want to just take this?" I say, and wave the paper at him, ignoring his bile, ignoring that I wrote thoughtful and encouraging comments on a story filled with hate.

"It's bullshit," he says.

"Actually," I say. "I thought you made some very interesting moves."

"No!" he says, holding the word, stretching out the one vowel, veins popping in his neck and forehead as his face flushes, a heavy metal singer on stage.

Death death death, growl.

I am the reaper and you are the reaped.

Be doomed, motherfucker!

That's the sound of Brandon performing his life.

"Are you okay?" I say. "Should I call someone?"

"Call yourfuckingself," he says.

"You said that."

"It's truth," he says, furious.

"You want to have a seat?" I say, still calm.

"Call yourfuckingself," he says, and his whole body appears in my doorway.

"That's probably not going to solve anything," I say, calmer than calm.

Brandon extends his arms in the doorway so he's pushing out against the frame like pillars he can knock down to make this place crumble.

I lean forward at my desk in a way I know makes me appear powerless, showing neither anger nor disgust, nor my usual emotion when Brandon is near: go the fuck away. I want to convey the accident of this situation: oops, we bumped.

No one is in trouble.

No one is being reported.

No one is being arrested.

No one's grade has been affected.

No one is offended or threatened.

It's fine.

We're fine.

I see your un-fineness and say: it's okay, you're fine.

I'm fine too, not that you give a shit.

This is me tolerating someone who needs to be tolerated while trying to make tolerance look like decency and kindness.

But Brandon, not feeling my call to kindness and compassion built on necessary lies, says, "Call yourfuckingself," and again, "Call yourfuckingself," and again, but worse, "Call yourfuckingself, you cunt," then back to, "Call yourfuckingself," on a loop, like a skip in a song.

I say, "Okay," and breathe out, useless.

He says, "Not okay!"

I say, "Just breathe. Relax."

He says, "Just fuck yourself."

I say, "I'd like to help you."

Clearly, he does not want help and I know this but I both want to help and want to be someone who helps and want to be someone who succeeds at helping.

Brandon says, "No and no!"

He says, "No, no!"

He says, "No fucking way!"

He says, "Fuck no!" like he's spitting.

Then he clears his throat and spits on my floor.

I star at the gob, a tiny bug splattered by a laser.

It is grotesquely yellow and green.

I say, "Come on, Brandon, that's just gross."

He says, "Fuck you!"

He says, "Fuck no!"

He says, "No!" and looks like a child stuck in a very young man's body, pouty and harmless but with random and underdeveloped facial hair.

He says, "Fuck off!" so the last word rattles his throat and hangs on.

He says, "Dick cunt!"

He says, "You're a dick cunt! You know that? Double bad. Dick and cunt. You're the fucking worst."

I lean back in my chair, nonthreatening.

This is the best I can do.

I had a psychology class once and we talked about riot reduction.

I make my hands visible and not like weapons.

I keep my palms flat and not shaped like fists.

Brandon says, "What the fuck are you doing?"

I say, "Nothing."

He says, "I see what you're doing?"

I say, "Being calm."

He says, "The fuck you are!"

I show him my hands.

I stand up.

I breathe like I'm a yogi to show I am zen and will stay zen.

Brandon, panicked, more than panicked, says, "Don't you hit me," and starts to back away. He says, "Don't you dare hit me," and shakes his pointer finger at me.

I sit back down and say, "I'm not hitting anyone."

He instantly steps back to my door, emboldened, and says, "That's right, that's right, you're not hitting anyone, no one."

He says, "That's it, you're sitting."

He says, "Stay down."

He says, "You're a cunt."

I say, "I get it. I'm a cunt. I'm fine with that."

He says, "You're fine with that because you're a cunt."

I say, "Exactly."

I lean back, mellow, so mellow.

He says, "Don't get up, don't you dare get up," like I've been knocked to the ground and not like I've made myself comfortable in an office chair.

I stand up again to walk to the door, not out of fear but out of obligation, to make sure the other students are fine, that they are not scared, so I can look in the hallway to see if there is order, to see if security has been alerted or if other professors have arrived.

Does anyone hear Brandon?

Where is my security guard pal?

I wish Berryman was here to crush Brandon.

Here is a young man Berryman could pin to the ground.

I say, "Brandon, you're a good dude," and I say it so sincere it must be true.

He says, "So says the professor cunt."

I say, "Come on, you can do better."

He says, "You can do better, cunt."

Before I can take two steps around my desk, Brandon says, "Listen to me, Mr. Professor," and he is panicked. Panicked like a fox in a trap. Panicked like everyone who has ever been panicked. A disaster. He says, "I said: fuck off!" He says, "Did you hear me?" He says, "I said: fuck and off, fuck off. Stay still. Sit back down. Sit down and fuck off. Did you hear me? I'm not threatening you. I'm commanding you! Fuck off, you jagoff, you fucking jagoff, you fucking cunt, you hairy cunt, you dick, you dickface," and he steps back from my office door and turns and starts to sprint away but his shoes are boots with slick heels and he stumbles and slides and almost falls but catches himself then finally runs and I hear his feet as he bursts down the hall, the slapping of toe and heel, bowlegged and awkward.

I say to myself: thank God.

When I make the hallway, I see other students, a few stopped, most moving slowly, none scared, most laughing, though a confused laugh, the kind of pinched smile that might turn grimace or worse. Kids know other kids can be awful and sometimes show compassion to it.

No professors have appeared.
No cops either, thank God.

Who Here Can I Help?

I call Berryman. Berryman knows university bullshit and academic procedure. I'm here, at a community college, which maybe means nothing. I have a trade. Berryman holds a master's degree. He's taught at three different schools. I press the phone to my ear and stand at my desk in case Brandon decides to return. Berryman picks up after a dozen rings because he never set up his voicemail to answer and he sounds like he's been sleeping in his office again. Berryman loves to nap in a chair.

"Hey," I say. "I have a problem."

"Rig's in jail?" he says.

"What?" I say. "No," I say. "Nothing like that."

"That was one of the best meals of my life," he says, "until Rig messed it up with that drug stuff. That was insane."

I say, "Don't judge Rig."

He says, "Did I sound judgmental?"

I say, "You said: Rig messed it up."

He says, "I'm a white asshole."

"Stop talking," I say.

"Obviously," Berryman says.

I explain Brandon and his breakdown.

Berryman says, "Take him to the counseling center."

I say, "He's gone. He ran down the hall, screaming."

Berryman says, "I'd still go and talk to someone at the counseling center. That, or I'd call campus police. It's a tricky world. You want to cover your own butt."

"I'd rather report him to the counseling center than security. Nothing good comes from telling the cops. I'm pals with Jerome, the security guy, but I'd hate to push Brandon on him. He might flip. He's mentioned what a douche Brandon is before. The other security guards aren't as nice. Where's the counseling center at?"

"I assume in student services."

I consider that.

If the counseling center is in student services, I've never seen it.

I say, "Do we have a counseling center?"

Berryman says, "You'd know better than me."

"I don't think we have a counseling center," I say. "That sounds expensive."

"Call the school nurse," Berryman says. "I had to get a band aid from her once. I know she exists. She gave me a flu shot last fall."

I say, "Berryman."

He says, "Don't be mad at me."

He says, "Flu shoots are important."

EDP

I walk to student services, a long hall in an old building, looking for a door plaque that says something about counseling but it's mostly employment and advising and closets for janitors to store their stuff. I walk the hall again, the gloss of the tiled floor reflecting the overhead lights, to make sure I've not missed a therapist or a psychologist or whatever they're called. My shoes quietly squeak and I hear my pants brushing at the knees so I broaden my gait. Very few people sit at their desks. The ones who are present work diligently or at least mess with their computers in a serious way. The oldness of the building makes the quiet in the hall feel like a haunting. I finally stop at the nursing station. The nurse's name, according to the sign on her door, is Nurse Patty. No last name, unless her legal first name is Nurse.

Two students, both young girls, both in jeans and sweatshirts, sit in the small waiting room, playing with their phones, their skinny bodies contorted into the office chairs at odd angles with their legs pulled up and under.

I say, "Are you two waiting for the nurse?"

One says, "We work here," and smiles.

The other one doesn't look up from her phone.

The first says, "Can I help you?"

I say, "I was looking for Nurse Patty."

Nurse Patty, from some unseen place in her office, says through the open door, "I'm back here," in a voice that sounds like a landslide of gravel.

The student worker whispers, "She's gruff but she's sweet."

The other one, not looking up from her phone, says, "No, she's not."

The first says, "She is."

The grumpy chick lowers her voice and says, "Are you kidding me? She's an A-1 bitch."

I thank them both and step inside Nurse Patty's office, with its desk and a computer and three metal bookshelves filled with medical textbooks and manuals. The office opens to a hallway that leads to a couple of bathrooms and maybe a supply closet then an exam room filled with bright light and a half-visible exam table and a rolling blood-pressure machine stuffed in the corner like a friendly robot.

Nurse Patty is maybe five feet tall, probably shorter, skinny, with black and gray hair cut in the style of a small boy. She wears jeans and an old gray sweatshirt. Over everything she wears a doctor's smock with her name, Nurse Patty, written in cursive on the left chest pocket.

She stares me down and unleashes that voice.

"You're an older student with the flu?"

"Not quite," I say.

"You're a dad looking for your sick daughter?"

"No."

"A young doctor doing research?"

"Not even close."

"A creep looking to rape?"

"Not at all, but thanks?" I say.

"Don't leave me hanging," she says.

She takes a seat at her desk and motions for me to grab a chair.

I say, "I teach here."

She says, "You look too happy to teach here," and smiles.

"It's a good place," I say.

"It is," she says. "Let's not keep it a secret."

She pulls out a pair of reading glasses and positions them on her nose.

I start to say, "I have a student…"

But Nurse Patty cuts me off and says, "White male, working-class, frustrated. He gave you some lip and you're not sure what to do."

"Basically," I say, "yes."

"EDP," she says.

"What's that mean?"

"Emotionally Disturbed Person. It used to be Emotionally Damaged Person back when I was in nursing school. Stuff changes. They might not use either version any more. Too insensitive. Too truthful or whatever. But I like it. I'm a sucker for acronyms."

"I don't think that's actually an acronym."

"Really?" Nurse Patty says. "You teach English?"

"Writing," I say.

"Good. We need those too. You write books?"

"I wrote some western novels but I'm trying to write something less formulaic."

"Less formulaic," she says, and scoffs. "What's wrong with western novels? My dad only read Louis L'Amour books. I think he might have read a couple Zane Grey books but it was mostly Louis L'Amour. He lived to be ninety-five and was sharp as a whip right up until the end. God bless that man. He was my hero. You above writing westerns?"

"Westerns are fine, they were fun to write," I say. "I just want to write about something else now, people with bad jobs, people without jobs. That type of thing. I feel like very few writers talk about that anymore. It's all shoe shopping and baseball players."

"Jesus," she says, "you're earnest."

"Thanks?" I say.

"You read Steinbeck?"

"I have."

"You read *Grapes of Wrath*?"

"I have."

"You know it's great?"

"I do."

"Tell me the main character."

"Tom Joad."

She takes her glasses off and stares at the lenses like they've quit magnifying from exhaustion, like the job of fixing vision was not worth the pay and Nurse Patty knows this, she can see it in the glass, but she puts them back on her nose anyway and sighs and says, "You know *Grapes of Wrath* is great, you're okay. I believe Steinbeck actually gave a shit about the world. Believe it or not, we were required to take a literature class specifically designed for nurses back in the day. Now it's all math. They don't think about people. People quit believing in art. That was a mistake." She pauses to consider that. She says, "Tell me about the kid who flipped his lid in your class."

"It wasn't really in my class," I say, and go on with my Brandon story, his snap in my office, the rage in his face, his previous weirdness in class, his short novel compressions which are graphically violent, the way he wears his hoodie so his eyes are hidden, the fuck and you of it, the fuck and you of everything, the running away when he thought I might hit him.

Nurse Patty stands and removes her white coat.

She shakes it out like a rug and hangs it on the back of her door.

"Ten years ago," she says, "I would have shrugged and thought you were being hysterical. Twenty years ago I would have asked you to quit being a scared-y cat and told you to leave my office immediately. I don't know any more."

She stops.

Nurse Patty thinks before she speaks, a rarity.

She closes her eyes to imagine her years at the community college, the slow deterioration of students and the world in general. She rubs the corners of hers eyes again with her thumb and pointer like the answer might be pinched out.

I say, "I'm sure he's a nice kid."

She says, "Maybe, maybe not."

I say, "He's not really a kid. He's twenty-four or so, I think. Maybe older. Closer to thirty."

She says, "Nice?"

I say, "Honestly, not at all."

She says, "Does he have access to guns?"

"I don't know," I say. "He's not very knowable. He loves science fiction and he seems to hate all the books I teach. It's almost like he wants to be my friend so he can bully me and explain why I'm wrong about everything."

"It's important to know if he has access to guns."

"I don't have a clue."

"Is he suicidal?"

"I don't know. He's mean. He criticizes everything."

Nurse Patty says, "Does he write about hunting? Hunting knives? Rifles? That kind of thing? Stories where animals get killed?"

I try to pull up Brandon's stories in my head then scroll down the pages. The world he consistently creates is science fiction and zombies and soldiers and versions of superheroes and spoofs of other books. How do I explain to Nurse Patty that Brandon's last story was about a man who whittled his dick into a sword and butt-fucked his oppressors to death?

I don't, that's how.

I know Brandon works at a grocery store because he sometimes talks about that in class and other students have mentioned it but the world he lives in is not the world he writes about or, if it is, the stories and images and characters have passed through so many metaphors and prisms that they are no longer recognizable as real. Lettuce never appears in his stories. No one makes minimum wage. He never mentions organic vegetables. He never mentions groceries or customers or the people he works with.

Or maybe his boss is really named Zultar.

Maybe the produce section he manages at Shop N' Save resembles Green Planet Zoon.

I have no interest in speculating on what writing means about the writer, not in the student writer who can't control language and story or the serious writer who can control both.

Those thoughts end with art dying.

I'm completely fucking serious.

If we blame the reality of art on the artist, art dies.

I go back to zombies and fake Iranian prisons and refuse to make much of it.

I try to explain the polite parts to Nurse Patty.

She pulls down a huge book, the DSM, the *Diagnostic and Statistical Manual*, where all the mental illnesses of the western world come to be defined and locked down. She starts to flip through the pages, looking for a specific diagnosis, then stops.

Then starts again.

Then stops.

She closes the book like a building she's about to abandon.

She says, "I honestly don't know. I might not know anything anymore. They've made the rules and changed the rules and broken the rules and re-made the rules so it's a big deal if I prescribe an aspirin to a student with a headache. I'm not joking. It's a mess. I'm so disappointed in everything. I don't think I'm too old to understand the world but maybe I am because I don't understand the world at all. Your angry student probably needs a girlfriend. Or a boyfriend. Or an in-between person, a transgender, whatever they're called. I support that. It's a lonely world. I could give you some kind of psych bullshit but unless he comes to see me and wants to be helped, it doesn't matter. At all. Not a blip. It's all bad news."

I say, "I hope you're not right."

She says, "You got a sad angry kid in your class. That's my very humble medical opinion. Diagnosis: pissed off young man with no opportunities to speak of."

WALK ON WOOD

I sit in my office, half waiting for Brandon to show up in a ninja outfit and toss throwing stars at my head. He doesn't. The halls bustle in their usual way, kids with backpacks slugging cans of Red Bull while rushing to classes and cars. I dial Berryman but he's in class or eating a sandwich somewhere. I pull down my favorite Robert Frost book, *Mountain Interval*. I read the first poem, "The Road Less Traveled," a couple times. I'm not sure if the book, or even the poem, is any good anymore but I read it to remember high school, to remember how much I loved books, to remember the librarian handing me what she thought I wanted and what she thought I needed, that perfect balance.

I am here because I love books, nothing else.

"The Road Less Traveled" says don't be afraid, the difficulties and how we handle them define us, but what does that mean when almost everything is difficult for almost everyone?

Am I a twat for loving Robert Frost?

Is Robert Frost a twat for being Robert Frost?

He can't be.

I love him so much, the poems, the life, how he loved to beat people at tennis.

I love him for writing about choices and how they save and break us.

Brandon tries to be brave by shouting me down, by enrolling and enduring classes he believes are wrong, classes that promote the worst in literature, what he believes is the worst in literature. If the community college appears to be the road less traveled to creativity, if this is the difficult path that makes all the difference, then Brandon wants to tear down trees and walk on wood until his writing is the only path, and the only path means he's walking through Hell and wants to tell you about it.

That seems fair.

But all his stories are so awful.

I hope I'm wrong.

I hope Brandon is a genius and succeeds at everything.

I hope he is the best of the best.

I know he's not.

GET ON THE WATER

Dr. Bronse, the president of the college, passes my office, looking rushed, dressed in her blue business suit and sneakers, professional and athletic. She bolts by then changes gears to reverse and appears in my doorway, still inching away, revving.

"You look like you're rushing somewhere," I say.

"I am," she says. "You look stressed."

"Not much," I say.

"Don't burn out on me," she says, smiling, sincere, so sincere.

"I won't."

"I need you here. I probably don't tell you enough because I think you know it but I'm telling you now. I appreciate what you do. So do the students, even if they're too embarrassed to tell it. These kids love you."

"Thanks," I say. "I appreciate that," and I do.

She says, "So."

I say, "You look twenty years younger than you are."

She says, "You're a sweetie."

I say, "You're the best boss I've ever had."

"I have a meeting," she says. "I'll see you soon. Okay?"

"Okay."

"Kayaking got canceled."

"Again?"

"It's a long story. We'll replace it with something else. These kids need nature. So do you. So do I. We're turning into robots. We can do better."

"You're right," I say, "one hundred percent."

She nods and starts to walk away. She stops and adjusts her pile of books and stacks of papers and what appears to be a bunch of brochures. She does this thing with her legs, flexing, stretching. Her calves ripple with muscle. She blows her bangs from her face. Her gray hair is down and wild like she's pushed it around all day to think.

The whole world should be Dr. Bronse.

Dr. Bronse is the fucking best.

She says, "I'd like you to help me with planning. Would you be willing to do that? When was the last time you had a raise? Help me with planning."

"Absolutely," I say.

"We'll come up with fun smart things, then gather up students and chaperones."

"We'll find chaperones for the chaperones," I say.

She says, "I'm so glad I read about you in the newspaper. I knew you'd be a great professor. You're a good guy. The world hates guys. I know you're great."

I say, "Thank you."

She says, "If you were on my rowing team, we'd never lose."

STEADY

Brandon disappears from campus, three classes in a row, no office visits. I scan the halls for his hoodie, for his angry eyes. I ask about Brandon's disappearance in class and one student, a boy who grocery shops where Brandon works, says Brandon quit his job.

I say, "That's too bad," half-hoping Brandon has quit school too.

The boy says, "That guy is off his rocker."

"He's doing his best," I say.

"I'd hate to see his worst," the boy says. "He's a real dick."

I teach for a week like this, lighthearted, hoping to remain lighthearted, feeling bummed out, trying to feel lighthearted, trying to focus, waiting for summer, waiting for long days built from my own thoughts and hours.

I call Rig once but he does not return my call.

I discuss this with Berryman.

Berryman wants to plan an adventure to Johnstown, to float around Flood City in my truck or his fancy Ford until we wash up on Rig and whatever he is doing to rebuild and redesign and get legal and make greatness.

Berryman says, "What do you think?"

"Rig would hate that," I say. "He's private."

"He's not private," Berryman says. "He tells his life story to everyone."

"That's the truth," I say.

He says, "I love that guy."

"We all do," I say.

Student papers pour in, the last batch before finals.

I said I would not get behind.

I am drowning in words again, grandma stories, please help.

I see Megan but I do not do drugs with Megan because I am running and writing and waiting for summer and thinking about Rig and my mom and Nona and one thousand other things, including Megan, always. I do not dream about Megan but I take her into my nighttime thoughts, when I wait for sleep and when I wake from sleep, restless.

I see her in the parking lot and she asks me when we're going to do the blow.

I say, "What blow?"

She says, "Come on," but light and playful. Then, "Save it for when we really need it."

"That's a good plan."

"That's the best plan."

Now that we have the blow, we treat the blow with less urgency. Neither of us wanted to score. Both of us love the comfort of having drugs, of knowing cocaine fits inside a medicine cabinet, same as aspirin, same as cough syrup. Here is the common cold of being alive. Here is the powdered prescription for relief.

Megan says, "The bar is booming."

"That's great."

"I know but it makes me hate the bar."

I want her to show up at my apartment. I want her to step through my front door without knocking. She does not. She invites me to the bar every time I see her. I go to the bar. I eat a sandwich. I leave early. She tells me not to go. I tell her I'll be done teaching soon. I want to tell her: love me. I want to tell her: I love you.

I feel a terrific drunk coming on.

I try to jog with Joanie once a week.

Her progress is minimal.

One Friday morning I take Nona to Burger King.

She says, "Not as good as McDonalds but I liked it."

Most mornings I wake with the desire to bury myself in blankets.

Yesterday, I heard a city bus skid into a stoplight.

This evening I run nine miles.

PART NINETEEN

Good Messages

I show up early to my office, intending to correct papers, smileys or comments, I'm not sure which, probably both. I write for an hour on my novel. Hammers pound rocks. A woman in an uncomfortable business suit goes to an interview for a job she is grossly overqualified for. I ignore the flashing light on my campus phone. No one ever leaves a good message on a work phone. I write for another hour. I break and check the messages.

Joanie says, "Can we run tonight? I need to know soon. Otherwise, I'm going to stop at the gym on the way home and run on the treadmill. I joined a gym. Did I tell you that? It was ten bucks a month. Call me, please, and not at five o'clock either."

I think about my mom and gyms and hope none of this is LA Fitness.

The next message clicks on.

It's Fat Bill.

He says, "I just wanted to make sure we're still on for next week. It's okay if we're not on. I know you're busy. Sorry to be a pest. Thanks, Professor."

Fat Bill is my former student. At some point he logged six weeks on a military base and turned into a soldier. I need to think more on Fat Bill before I can explain him to you. Five years into this job and students have started to blur in a way I assumed they would not. I mean, I know Fat Bill is Fat Bill, that he was a student I cared and still care about, I just can't remember who Fat Bill is, exactly, except for his voicemails.

Joanie clicks back on.
She says, "Do you really even work here?"
Joanie hangs up.
Fat Bill clicks on.
He says, "It's Fat Bill. Just checking in."
Next message is Joanie again.
She says, "Quit being a jerk and call your mom."
The final message is Brandon.
I know it by his breathing.
I am tempted to erase him without listening.
He clears his throat and starts tentatively.
He says, "I apologize for calling so late."
He pauses.
He says, "I am truly sorry," and stops and wheezes.
He continues to wheeze but does not speak.
I wish Brandon were present so I could say, "No apology necessary."
Extended apologies are for attention seekers.
He says, "I'm apologizing," and stops to consider for what.

His voice is slow and thick and sometimes slurred. Twenty years ago I would have assumed he was drunk. Now I assume his psych meds need adjusting.

He clears his throat again and says, "I apologize for clearing my throat." Then he says, "No, sorry, I apologize for calling so late, sorry." I wait for the punchline, the twist where he tells me to fuck off or die in flames, but he continues, slowly, thoughtfully, trying to enunciate. He says, "I just lost it this semester. I want to apologize. That's why I'm calling. I actually want to apologize." Again, a slowdown. He says, with slightly more emotion, "I'm reading this off a piece of paper. My therapist suggested I write everything down, that it would be easier than remembering it. It's all smudged. I lost my job at Shop N Save. It's fine. I live at home."

He says, "I got a therapist."

He says, "So that's good news."

He continues with his script, saying, "I actually want to apologize. I know I've wasted a lot of your time and the class's time this semester. I acted selfish and, for that, I wish to apologize. With your permission, I'd like to apologize at the beginning of our next class. Which is tomorrow, I guess. It will only take three to four minutes, max. As you know, there is a great deal of shame associated with mental illness. I'd like to help everyone by breaking through that barrier. Maybe my courage to speak out about my struggles will help others."

He says, "Thank you."

He says, "I understand if class time is unavailable for my apology. I would also be willing to write my classmates an email."

He says, "Thank you."

He says, "This is Brandon, your student from Creative Writing. I think I forgot to say that at the beginning. I'm the one who writes compressions."

He says, "Thank you. I look forward to your response."

He pushes a couple wrong buttons on his cell phone before hanging up.

The message clicks off.

I pick up the phone and call Joanie.

Her voicemail picks up.

I say, "I'll meet you at the track at five o'clock. I'll be all juiced up on Mountain Dew and Red Bull. Congratulations on the gym membership. Let's run."

COME TO THE SHITSHOW

Berryman stops by my office. He wears jeans and a three-button polo shirt that hangs down to his knees. I've never see him in anything but track suits. His gut looks like an astronaut's helmet underneath his shirt. He still wears suede Pumas. His hair is styled in a professional manner with mousse. No Kangol. No ballcap.

He says, "Just stopping by to see if you're interested in a wrestling match on the back lawn. I'm feeling pretty fit today."

"You're not even dressed for wrestling," I say.

"I'm not," he says. "I was just messing with you."
"Are you getting a sense of humor?"
"I think I am," Berryman says. Then, "You look stressed."
"I think I am," I say.
"Can I sit down? My back is killing me."
"Please."
"So what's the stressor?"
"I don't know," I say. "I just can't shake off the job lately. My crazy student called and left a message saying he'd like to apologize to the class for being disruptive this semester. I'm going to let him because every time I tell him no, he flips out."

Berryman says, "Are you talking about the student who writes the crazy little novels about killing people?"

"That's the guy."

"And he wants to apologize for disrupting the class by disrupting the class?"

"That's it."

"That," Berryman says, adjusting his shirt so it better fits his gut, "is everything that's wrong with college these days."

"That," I say, "is everything that is wrong with the world."

"It's a shitshow," Berryman says.

"Maybe it's always been this way."

"I don't think so."

"It has," I say, "but there's always beauty buried in the shitshow."

"People hate beauty."

"They hate beauty in the shitshow, unless the people in the shitshow are rich and famous celebrities or rich and famous criminals."

Berryman says, "Everyone loves that shitshow."

"I think it was better when people didn't have to go to college," I say.

Berryman stands up and says, "You going to let him speak?"

"Probably," I say. "You want to get a soda?"

"Chemicals aren't good for you," he says.

"Sugar is," I say.

SO LONG, BERRYMAN

Near the soda machine, Berryman, suddenly twitchy and pop-eyed, says, "I have a date. I completely forgot."

I say, "Like a date-date?"

Berryman says, "Exactly."

"In the afternoon?"

"It's a lunch date."

I say, "When did you start dating?"

Berryman says, "I always date."

"You?"

"Yeah, me."

"Lunch dates?"

"They're more comfortable."

"God, you're gross," I say. "It almost makes me jealous."

He reaches in his back pocket and pulls out his wallet, a denim blue river of leather folded in half. He checks for bills. Bills appear plentiful. He ruffles them then rearranges them by denomination so the money is easier to count.

I say, "Who's the date? Where are you going?"

He says, "I'll tell you about it when I get back."

I say, "Is it a student?"

He says, "Come on," and looks genuinely offended.

I say, "Your wallet matches your jeans."

He says, "I know," and smiles.

"Is this why you're wearing big boy clothes instead of a track suit?"

"A track suit is big boy clothes," Berryman says, and slowly jogs off, beltless, holding up his jeans with both hands so they don't fall from his hips.

THE DATING MACHINE

I always thought of Berryman as a troll, romantically speaking.

SODA

I buy three Mountain Dews and stop to chug the first can as I walk to my office. It goes down in a gulp. I make no eye contact in the hallway. I focus on floors and ceilings, alternating. Students gab. They bump each other and laugh. The air smells of piss, like the bathrooms have flooded, like the plumbing barely works. I toss my empty can in a recycling bin.

I stop and crack another soda. I take a sip and need to burp. I walk until I make my office. I immediately close and lock the door. Brandon can apologize but I refuse to see him before class and I plan to be wired on caffeine and sugar when he slurs whatever gobblygook his therapist wants him to slur.

And Berryman is on a lunch date, holy shit.

Meditate

I close my eyes and breathe deep.
I tried yoga once but my hangover made stretching difficult.
Thinking with my eyes closed, though, I dig that.
I like running better.
Look out, Joanie.

Sad or Mad?

On my way to class I stop by the snack machine to buy a huge stick of beef jerky or some cheese crackers or some salt-and-vinegar chips. My stomach is raw from soda and worry. I feed two dollars into the money slot and try to decide what numbers to push.

Megan appears beside me and leans on the plastic window of the machine.

She says, "Hey."

I say, "Hey back."

"You happy to see me?"

"I always am."

She wears a yellow polo, almost like Berryman's shirt but infinitely sexier.

I say, "Jerky time."

She says, "I have to miss class to work at the bar. I apologize. The afternoon bartender called off like ten seconds ago. In a text. Texts are for cowards."

I push the buttons for an extra-large, extra-spicy Slim Jim.

The Slim Jim falls into the trap with a thud.

"Not a problem," I say. "I'll share my jerky if you have time."

"Slim Jims aren't jerky."

"I know but they're delicious. I'm a jerky expert. I need to get to

Bundy's."

"Where've you been?" she says.

"I have been swamped," I say.

Megan stays with her left shoulder pressed to the machine like she might drive it through the wall but gently and with great intent. The plastic window curves to her weight. I close my eyes. I know I am wrong with her and she knows I am wrong with her but we both know I am not wrong enough to create static. I open my eyes. My eyelids are weighted with everything I want and am embarrassed to see. Megan touches me and I pretend I am not being touched. I'm thinking of a metaphor for love. It's the ocean. It's the bar. I worry about drowning. I worry about drinking too much and drowning. Drowning, always.

I stare at my Slim Jim waiting behind the snack gate.

Megan knocks on the plastic with her right fist so I turn towards the noise.

She says, "Are you mad at me or something? Did I do something?"

"I'm not," I say. "You did not."

I bend and reach into the mouth of the machine and pull out my Slim Jim like a disposable tongue the snack monster chewed off and discarded for two bucks.

She says, "That's it?"

"I'm not mad, really."

"Are you sad at me?"

"I am definitely not sad at you."

She says, "Then what?" and pushes her hair out of her face and over the front of her head and down the other side of her face but out of the way so she is more beautiful than she was a second before when she was already too beautiful to look at straight on.

I say, "Can I come see you at the bar?"

"Yes," she says. "I was going to ask you that." She says, "But you have to look at me first because I'm standing right here."

I look at her.

I say, "I'm sorry."

She leans away from the machine and scans the hallway, nearly empty this close to the start of class. She waits for a boy in a knit hat and combat boots to walk past.

"All clear," I say.

"All clear," she says, and takes my face and pulls it to her face until our lips touch and we stay like that until the pull of her missing bartender and my students separate us into two people who would rather be one.

I know.

I know.

I know.

Brandon's Apology

Brandon sits in my spot at the head of the classroom, next to the podium, in front of the chalkboard. His backpack rests on the table, partially unzipped, papers oozing out. Brandon reaches inside the bag. I look for a gun because I am useless with violence and scared and would like not to get shot, but he pulls out a Monster energy drink, the huge M on the can written so it appears dripping with electric slime. I turn sideways in the doorway and let a couple students pass. Brandon wears a white oxford, wrinkled but buttoned up. A tie with Bart Simpson on it hangs around his neck. His hair is very styled with gel, wet-looking and pulled forward to cover his receding hairline.

I wait in the hallway until other professors start to pull their doors shut.

I leave our door open.

I count heads: seven students.

Then I count Brandon: eight.

At the front desk, I kneel down and ask Brandon if he's okay.

He nods.

"You're sure?" I say.

He nods.

"This is very brave," I say.

Sweat pours down his forehead like he's leaking courage.

He could turn and run.

I've seen him turn and run.

I say, "Take all the time you need. I'll be in the corner."

I plan to say more but my knees lift me up.

I lean over the desk.

"You'll do great," I say.

Brandon says, "Thank you."

I walk to the corner of the room and lean into the wall, the smooth yellow paint, the cool cinder blocks against the warm spring air.

Brandon does not speak.

He reaches into his backpack and pulls out a notecard.

The other students start to notice the strangeness.

A few go quiet.

Brandon still does not speak.

I clear my throat and notice the Slim Jim in my hand, a foot-long meat stick wrapped in plastic. I address the whole class, pushing out the words.

I say, "Hello, welcome, we're almost done."

"For the day?" someone says.

"For the semester," I say. "But an excellent try."

I step away from the wall.

The Slim Jim looks like a wand, like a pointer, like I might touch a globe with the tip of it and say, "You are here." Brandon continues to sweat profusely. Most of the class turns to face me in the corner, still clutching my meat wand. They look so young. They always look young but today they look like a class of second graders.

I say, "Before we get started, Brandon has something to say."

The class neither moans nor mutters, good signs.

Brandon turns to me and says, "Thanks," then he turns back to the class and coughs.

He coughs again, a real thunderstorm, followed by an extremely loud clearing of his throat. He clears again. Something comes up with the next cough and he holds it in his mouth.

I say, "You okay?"

He ignores me.

I say, "Do you need a minute?"

He turns his head and leans and clutches his Bart Simpson tie to his chest.

I hope he is not going to spit on the floor.

I say, "Do you need a Kleenex?"

A student says, "He's going to spit on the floor."

I say, "Does anyone have a Kleenex?"

Then Brandon spits on the floor.

It's a very long drip hanging from a very leaky faucet.

I look at the class, over their heads, pretending not to see Brandon's gob.

The whole class collectively moans.

Someone says, "Gross."

Someone else says, "Here we go."

Brandon barely acknowledges the mocking of his peers.

He straightens back up and looks down at his notecard and says in slow motion, "Thank you, everyone. I really appreciate your time on this already busy day," and stops.

I wait for another cough, another buzzsaw throat clearing.

Someone says, "You just spit on the floor, dude," in a voice so offended it sounds doused in stringy spit.

A girl in the front row, more compassionate, says, "You okay, dude?"

Brandon says, "Thank you all for coming."

A boy in the back row says, "He's fucked up," and laughs.

Parts of the room laugh, uncomfortable.

Brandon's ears barely catch sounds.

He starts again and says, "I really appreciate your time on this already busy day."

His entire body speaks of absence.

If a person can sink under his own voice, he touches bottom.

SWEAT

Brandon does not say anything else.

He continues to sweat like his scalp is a cloud making rain drops fall across his forehead and down his cheeks.

He stares at his notecard.

SLIM JIM

I set my Slim Jim on the desk. I mean to offer it to Brandon, to say, "You want some Slim Jim?" but I think the gesture, putting the Slim Jim in front of him, is enough. It matches his unopened Monster energy drink perfectly.

I nod.

I push the Slim Jim forward.
He does not acknowledge the Slim Jim.
I do not use my voice.

LATER

Later, weeks, maybe a month, I will remember that Brandon's last words were, "I really appreciate your time on this already busy day."

Before that, for the semester, for the year, for years, for his entire college career, for his life, his main words were fuck and off or, if inspired, fuck and you. Limited vocabulary. Unbelievable commitment. He opened his mouth and coughed hate. It was always and only fuck and something else. Fucking hell. Fucking shit. Fucking cunt. Fucking professor. The rest was filler. "Go fucking die," he said once to another student writer then argued that he'd been talking to the student's characters, to the story, to the people on the page.

No one believed him

I said, "You can't talk like that in my class."

Brandon said, "I was talking to myself."

Go fucking die.

I really appreciate your time on this already busy day.

NOTECARD

On the notecard, which Brandon holds with both his hands and curves into a windshield, a hand-drawn gun, pencil and black ink, slightly smeared, slightly erased, covers the entire space, three inches by five inches. None of us can see the drawing. The words he appears to be reading from the card are improvised. I really appreciate your time on this already busy day. Or the gun is a symbol only Brandon can read and what it says has nothing to do with what he speaks.

Later, a cop will pick up the notecard and say, "He was no artist, that's for sure."

His partner will say, "I could have drawn that."

I'll be in the hallway, answering questions, trying to explain.

Blood will have speckled the back of my shirt.

APOLOGIZE OR NOT

Brandon turns over the card I've yet to see and places it face down on the desk.

Someone says, "Speak already. These classes ain't cheap."

Someone else says, "Actually, they are."

A few muffled laughs.

Someone says, "Is this like a speech for a grade?"

Someone else says, "I hope not."

I think the students, always sick of Brandon, always sick of being humiliated by Brandon, always sick of the potential threat, might rush the front desk and pound him down into the puddle he tries to make everyone drown in.

Someone else says, "I think he's retarded."

I say, "Stop, come on."

The same person rearranges his words and directs them directly at Brandon, saying, "I think you're retarded, guy. You have some brain problems or something."

I step away from the wall and towards the rows of chairs dotted with students and say, "Stop now," and, "That's it," and, "Come on, show some respect," and I use my wrestling voice, meaning: shut the fuck up.

Meaning: I will take you down.

GUN

Brandon reaches into his backpack, forearm deep. I assume he pulled the wrong card before, that the card he's been staring at is blank or half-worded, an early and incomplete draft. The card with whatever he wants to say is still inside, mixed with compressions and old tests and empty packs of cigarettes and cans of warm energy drink.

His arm stays in his pack like it's being eaten, like the pack has teeth to clamp and hold.

I step to him slowly, gently, and say in a soft voice, "You want to try again next class?" I say, "You did great." I say, "You can try again next class." I say, "Don't stress yourself out about this," and I try to make eye contact, some connection to reduce whatever fear or anxiety holds his tongue in place so he can barely speak.

I bend at the knees to whisper more thoughtful remarks.

Brandon slowly pulls out a pistol but not like he's pulling out a pistol. He pulls out the pistol like he's pulling out a notecard or a puppet, some prop for his speech. He stops halfway, the barrel still in his backpack, to make sure he has the right thing.

I instantly stand up and step back like I've been popped with electricity. Brandon's hand and the pistol move like his voice until the gun sets on the table, his hand touching the metal but resting and not near the trigger.

My first thought is: I don't know any pistol names but Glock.

Then, instead of moving, I think: Luger, Derringer, six shot, Smith & Wesson.

GUN NAMES

But I'm pretty sure this is a Glock.

I've seen Glocks in movies.

I've seen Glocks in bars.

One guy who I worked construction with, a middle-aged white guy from Iowa who insisted he played fullback for Iowa State, who I shared a motel room with for weeks when we were working on a power-plant in Montana, an electrician and card-carrying member of the IBEW, owned a Glock.

He kept it in a locked box.

He cleaned it once but put it right back in the locked box.

He never took it to work.

He never took it to bars,

I asked him why he needed a gun.

He said, "The ammo's cheap."

KNOWLEDGE

I know Brandon is here to kill himself, I know it like some people know God, I know it like parents know their favorite child. The sound of a drugged hand on a loaded gun resting on a table is silence until it is not. The gun goes up, the gun goes down. I know that we are all safe, that this is not a massacre. I know that we are doomed to relive this for our entire lives, like we've become the soldiers we never wanted to be, but our bodies will still be bodies and not burned-up meat when Brandon finishes his goodbye.

I am not afraid when I stand in front of the desk, even though the gun is not yet pointed, even though bullets sometimes think for themselves.

FEAR

I am so scared, even my tongue aches with fear.
I lied about being unafraid.
I lied to you.
I lied to myself.

RE-THOUGHT

I know Brandon will shoot me.

ME, THE COWARD

I could grab the gun. True, Brandon's hand holds the grip now but it stills rest on the table and he appears more confused than before when all he wanted was to apologize.
I could slap the pistol away.
I could pull the gun from Brandon's dumb hand.
I could own it.
I could shoot Brandon.
I could not shoot Brandon.
I could take the gun and hold the gun or throw it to the floor or down the hall or out the window or stuff it in my jeans like a badass.
I could shoot Brandon.
I could shoot him in the face.

RULES

I have many rules for living.
First, do not kill.
First, do not die.

ONE

One student, a girl, says, "Holy shit, he has a gun. No one tease him." The class makes the sound of a cloud dissolving.

No one teases Brandon.
No one speaks.

THE EYES MATTER MOST

I say, "Brandon, you don't have to do this," and my words rush into him as opposites.

His dull eyes go lit. The fear pumps off him. He pulls the gun closer, only a few inches across the table but closer, almost to his chest. He wakes from whatever stupor he'd paused and thought and drugged and notecarded himself into and he stares into my eyes and he nods.

I say, "You're a writer. You don't have to do this."

He says, "I do."

I say, "You don't," and I make my voice into heaven and money and the sun and every drop of whatever keeps us alive. Oxygen. Kindness. Love. I'd be his mother if I could make the change, if he had a mother worth changing into. I'd be my mother for him.

Brandon says, "I'm sorry."

He puts both hands on the gun but still not the trigger.

I say, "You're a writer, that matters."

He says, "No one cares."

"They do."

"No one even cares at all."

I say, "They're good kids," and motion to the students.

He says, "Maybe."

I say, "You're not sweating anymore."

He says, "I wrote because I wanted to be famous."

I say, "You can still be famous."

He says, "Everyone hates me. Please stop talking."

He guides the gun with his left hand to the edge of the table and picks it up with his right hand and holds it to his chest like he's about to say the pledge.

He says, "I don't even know how many bullets are in here."

I say, "I'm going to turn my back to you," and I turn my back to him.

I feel the first bullet before it's shot.

I tell my students, who I love, who I love more than anything in the world, whose lives I can see, their careers and marriages and children and homes made of wood and brick, their apartments, their trailers, I tell them, "Turn around now, turn around and close your eyes and cover your ears and close your eyes and don't open your eyes."

Their chairs and desk all pound and scrape the floor, frantic.

Your eyes matter most.

They show our hearts the world.

Not seeing this will mean you can still see the rest.

Eyes

I keep saying, "Turn around and cover your eyes."

Turn around and cover your eyes.

Close your eyes.

Cover your eyes.

I don't stop.

Close your ears.

I mess it up.

Shot

It's two sounds, the sound of the gun, a crack that echoes around the room like an explosion of fireworks, but also the sound of the bullet entering Brandon's head through the roof of his mouth. The sounds are pushed together so closely as to be indistinguishable but I hear them as distinct. The bullet exits Brandon's skull and goes through the ceiling tile and leaves a tiny maroon mark above the classroom that I will sometimes stop back to view.

Maybe that's three sounds: gun, body, ceiling.

The Fourth Sound

The fourth sound is Brandon's body leaving the chair and hitting the floor. It's a slow sound, one mixed with the previous three, but also the gun falling and the chair tipping back. I wait for a fifth sound: struggle. When I don't hear anything, I feel a great relief.

I push my hands up like I am surrendering or like I am reaching for heaven.

I look at the backs of my students' heads.

No one has turned back around.

Most of them have pulled their heads near their knees so they appear fetal.

REMOVE THE STUDENTS

I have to say something to exit us all from the room, to remove the students from the scene without them having to see the part of the scene that will cause damage. I assume Brandon has fallen behind the desk and so is hidden from view.

A girl, in a voice filled with tears, a voice filled with hope and fear, two emotions I never considered friends, let alone siblings, and who I will consider forever as twins, says, "Is it over?"

Someone else says, jumpy, "He killed himself, didn't he?"

"No one turn around," I say.

"I'm going to turn around," I say.

I say, "You don't turn around, no one."

I say, "Okay?"

I hear some affirmative sounds.

I turn to the front of the room.

Brandon's body lies behind the desk. His head, which is leaking blood, which appears to be wearing a blood-painted wig, extends just past the desk like a prop at a haunted house. I do not want to keep looking but I have to keep looking to see what to do. I stare. I am calm. I am so calm. A dead head will do what you think it cannot: put you at ease.

But I am also scared at my calmness.

This fear allows me to speak.

I say, "No one turn around yet."

Someone, scared, voice warbling, says, "Is it gross?"

"Just don't think about it," I say.

I pivot to my students and they are still backwards to the classroom, faces turned away from tragedy. How smart they are to listen and not look. I want to praise them and I will but I don't know when and, really, I may not.

I turn back.

Brandon's body.

Brandon's head.

The blood on the floor looks like the wrong kind of jelly.

But the bullet has removed the lines from Brandon's face. The stress and meanness and the hate and all of the terribleness that he lived with and embraced exited with his life so that his face could find peace and serenity. He looks like a movie star. He looks like a wax figure of a movie star. He looks relieved to be dead.

And thankful.

No one has turned yet.

They still face the back wall.

One of my students says, "I'm going to throw up."

Another student says, "Don't puke or I will too."

FROM THE NEXT CLASS DOWN

No one throws up.

"Everyone okay?" I say. "As good as can be?"

I say, "Considering?"

They nod.

I say, "I know this is awful. We're almost done."

No one speaks.

I stay, "Stay where you are."

A student from another classroom, a boy in a blazer and jeans, handsome, comes to our classroom door, obviously sent by his professor, and says, "We just didn't hear a gun go off, did we?" and he says it like a joke, like he's embarrassed to ask, then he sees Brandon's body and, I assume, from the angle, the bullet hole in his head.

The student looks at me.

I admire his blazer.

You see so few students in blazers.

I forget what I was never taught to say about these things, public suicides.

He says, "This isn't like a Halloween thing in spring?"

The student's eyes are the size of screaming mouths but he never screams.

He says, "I'll go call the cops," and runs away.

A girl student in my class says, "Who was that?"

I say, "A kid from another class."

She says, "Was he scared?"

"Yes," I say. "I think so."
I say, "Still don't look."
A boy says, "No one is looking."
A boy says, "We're all fucking scared."
A girl says, "Do something, please."
So I do.

BLAME

I blame movies. I blame TV. I may say, out loud, "Fuck you TV." I understand this is a crime scene. I understand that cops will arrive, that they will poke and prod for answers, that death is precious and should not be touched, that life turns to evidence once completed, but I also don't give a shit. What happens at the crime scene of a suicide when there are witnesses should be irrelevant to the crime. If asked, we will stutter details into an exact picture.

A student says, "Are you doing something?"

"I am," I say.

I start thinking cop shows: *Dragnet*, *Hillstreet Blues*, *The Wire*.

I love *The Wire*.

I remember *Dragnet* reruns in black and white.

There was that cop in *Hillstreet Blues*, the dirty undercover guy. He wore a knit hat and sometimes grew a patchy beard and he always called the criminals, once he blew his cover, once he busted them down to nothing, dogface.

I make myself stop.

Kids are here.

My job is to save them from what they have already been scarred by.

How many thoughts can one man have in the moments leading up to and the moments after having witnessed a young man pump a bullet into his head?

Millions or more, and I am conscious of each.

I step to the desk like I am a mover, like my job is to carry and adjust furniture, and I pull the desk towards the door so that Brandon's head is hidden and only his feet appear from the other side, thinking, logically, dead feet in sneakers are nothing compared to blood wigs and leaky brains and I step back to look, to see and not see. It's imperfect. It's a fright but maybe less. I've accidentally pulled one desk leg through the blood and it's made a paint streak of suicide on the floor. I step back to the desk and adjust that, pulling the edge forward.

I had a girlfriend who managed a Pier 1. She built displays from couches and chairs. I used to watch her. She'd pull and fuss, make it all pretty. She was great with pillows and baskets and candles. I am not making furniture displays except I am and how thankful I am for that girlfriend. I pull the desk again, the sound as scratchy as metal legs have ever sounded against linoleum floors, and I make the angle so it is impossible to see the wreckage of Brandon's death even if you are a scared nineteen-year-old leaving the classroom with orders specifically not to look and still you turn to see.

EXIT

I say, "Everyone stand up."

A student says, "What?"

I say, "This is almost over. Everyone listen to me and do exactly what I say. Everyone stand up slowly and don't be afraid."

They all stand up.

I say, "We are going to exit from the last row. So just stay standing. Back row, that's Larry's and Donna's row, just file into the aisle by the corkboard and keep facing the corkboard wall and walking sideways and don't look anywhere else and walk out of the room and down the hall to the secretaries' office and wait for the rest of us."

I say, "Ready?"

Their heads nod.

I say, "Back row only, start walking slowly."

I say, "Everyone is safe."

I say, "This is almost over."

They move like scared penguins and shuffle against the wall, some with their backpacks, some leaving everything behind.

I say, "Britney's row."

I say, "Tom and Lily's row," and that name, Lily, it brings me flowers.

PART TWENTY

The Cops, The President, Hugs

The state cops act like state cops, very serious. They wear uniforms. They wear fancier uniforms. I blame their careers on TV and movies too. They act like actors. They fake compassion. It's a sort of real compassion so maybe not fake.

I don't need to say anything else about them.

The details are in our collective terror.

The recovery is so endless and haphazard, it barely needs to be described.

Newspaper people come around. They are nice enough. I talk to them. They are all fat. They look poor. Their clothes are rumpled, their hair a mess. They sweat, all of them. The man with the beard drips tears from his bald head. The woman with too much make-up ruins her eyes. The make-up from her neck smears on her collar.

Another reporter shows up.

A dude from the *Tribune Review* named Sean Stipp shows up with a camera.

I think we went to high school together.

He used to wear those round John Lennon glasses.

I thought that was cool as hell.

Cops in suits show up.

A woman with a pen and notebook says, "What was he like?"

I say, "I don't know."
She says, "What was his writing like?"
I say, "Student writing."
She says, "Describe student writing."
"You were a student," I say. "I bet you know."
Other students, students not in the classroom with Brandon, come around and hug the students who heard the crack of the gun. So much hugging happens. I get hugs. I get so many hugs. The students keep coming. They keep hugging. Then they are asked to leave campus but nicely and without force. They hug as they walk away.
One of the cops says, "Who's the dean of this place?"
A kid says, "Dr. Bronse, the president?"
The cop says, "They have a president here?"
The kid says, "What do you think, cop?" to make the cop feel small.
Dr. Bronse has been here the whole time. She appeared in the hallway minutes after the shooting. She helps me with the cops. She helps me with the reporters. She does not tell me what to say. She sometimes holds my hand. I hold her hand back. I think of her rowing. I think of her defeating the world.
She says, "I'm sorry I brought you here."
"This place is the best," I say. "You make it that way."
She puts her arms around me and rubs my back in a circle.
She stays with me during the day and later calls my phone. She is so lovely and kind-hearted, I talk to her until I don't want to talk anymore.
She says, "I don't want to keep bothering you, I just want to make sure you're okay. You did an amazing thing."
I say, "I think I am going to sleep in then get drunk tomorrow."
She says, "I'm not sure that's what the psychologists would recommend but you do what you need to do, sweetie. I'm here for you."
"You're a sweetie," I say. "People should tell you more often."
She says, "You can call me if you get too drunk."
All of us, me and my students, stand by the secretaries' offices.
This is right after the shooting.
I'm jumbling this, minutes and hours and days, but that's death, that's guns, that's college, I think, that's college, that's how we learn now, from terrible things.

Someone should write a book called: *It Takes a Shooting*.

You wouldn't even need words inside.

Various people, students and teachers and staff, walk by and say they've tweeted and facebooked and snapchatted and emailed and whatever else so no one comes to campus, so the kids know to stay away. The college security guards, who probably like to be called cops and not security guards, especially since they carry guns, walk around and thoughtfully guard us, pretending, thankfully, not to guard us. They are simply a presence, a wall. My ex-athlete buddy who found Rig passed out under a table in the library is off today, maybe sick, maybe at the dentist. I love him for his luck. I am jealous of his luck. I know I have luck too. The remaining security squad stays with us. They pace, hands on pistols but not aggressive. The state police could learn from these folks. One guy, a big fat dude, black skin, high and tight hair, trimmed beard, goes and buys a bunch of sodas and bags of chips and hands them out to the kids.

He has the best Pittsburgh accent.

He says, "Yinz must be hungry."

He says, "Yinz should eat."

PART TWENTY-ONE

The Bar, My Papers

Night arrives. **This is after the shooting,** two weeks. The president of the campus suspended classes for a couple days. Then classes resumed. They changed all my classrooms. I went back to the bullet hole in the ceiling just to look. We made the news then disappeared. This probably has something to do with the difference between a suicide and a murder. A woman from the *Tribune Review* contacted me about a follow-up interview then never followed-up after I returned her call. Joanie never called. Nona never called. Both are indifferent to the world, to newspapers and the nightly news, so their obliviousness was expected. I called neither, relieved to think my thoughts and not explain my thoughts to them. Megan knows. She tries to make me talk. I would talk. I have nothing to say. Megan talks. She says, "Oh sweetie." She says, "That crazy fucker." She says, "Fucking guns." I should have referred Megan to the *Tribune Review* while they were still interested in the story. Megan would have given great quote. When I start classes, I say, "Everything okay?" but like I'm asking about the weather, about traffic. The students nod. An army of counselors invaded the campus but very few students talked to the counselors so the counselors wandered off.

I am teaching more or less like a teacher.

Tonight, I am drunk but steady, a good place.

Everywhere away from campus is a good place.

The bar is crowded with old men and the Seton Hill girls' volleyball team. The Seton Hill girls' volleyball team is legion. They have won a big victory over the boys at St. Vincent's in a scrimmage and now they are drinking like soldiers. Pitchers and shots are lined up on tables and the bar. There are howls and high fives. Boozy energy floods the room. Megan is too busy to talk, pouring shots, mixing drinks. She knows I am here to get loaded. She knows I consider getting loaded medicine. And therapy. And recovery. I called her earlier and said, "I'm coming to your bar to get fucked up," and she said, "Good, it's about time."

I have drugs in my pocket.

I have my briefcase on a barstool.

I have decided to correct my students' papers, to finally catch up.

The first paper, a response to James Baldwin, starts with the line, "I think this dude is black, and that's why he had a hard life growing up."

Sometimes a simple observation is the truth.

James Baldwin was black and lived a hard life.

I turn the paper to the last page and write: nice job, A+.

VOLLEYBALL

I have done three shots with the Seton Hill girls' volleyball team. Shots are not my thing, the mad rush, the inevitable sloppiness. But these girls have money. They attend a private college and appear to be thriving. I accept their generosity, mostly because it would be more effort to swat the shots away. It keeps going. They buy me and the old men rounds, many rounds. The old men, especially Vinnie with only five teeth, are smiling. The popcorn machine works overtime. I just saw Harriet—owner of Harry's Bar, in case you forgot—give William, another old drunk, a disbarred lawyer, a mug to keep forever. Harriet does this. She sneaks pieces of the bar to her favorite patrons. I want to be a favorite patron. I want Harriet to give me something too: a mug, a stool, the bar. I want Megan to write her story, to keep writing her story, to turn her ten pages into a novel, and I want to be a character in it. I want someone to succeed with writing in a way I have not, and by someone I mean Megan, and by success I mean us both.

Writing makes me greedy.

I include myself in everyone's books.

One of the volleyball girls, a brunette with a long ponytail pulled back on the top of her head like a genie, says, "I wish you were my professor."

A boy, maybe their trainer or a student coach, says, "We have nuns for professors. Not all of them but I have a nun and a priest for two of my classes."

Another volleyball girl, younger, a blonde wearing only her shorts and a sports bra, says, "I should transfer into one of your classes."

I say, "It's a community college. People transfer out."

She says, "Whatever." She thinks about that. She says, "Do you teach at that community college where the kid just offed himself?"

"I do," I say.

She tries to think again but a second thought would be too much.

She says, "Ka-blewy, huh?" and points her finger at her temple.

I say, "Pretty much."

She says, "The world is messed up. Terrorists, and now students."

I nod.

Another volleyballer, who is behind me, who I can't see, says, "I was at Franklin Regional when that dude was stabbing people. Kitchen knives! Crazy!"

The girl in the sports bra ignores her.

She turns to her pal, the brunette.

The brunette says, "Put your jersey back on, you slut," and laughs.

MEGAN, THOUGHTFUL

Megan says, "How are you holding up?"

"Really well," I say. "It feels good to be getting drunk."

She says, "Happy to be of service," and kisses the tips of her hand then touches my head with the kissed fingers.

STILL PARTYING

An hour later, Megan says, "When do you want to start you-know?"

"Soon," I say. "I'm getting shitfaced."

The volleyball girls are now playing volleyball with a bunch of wadded up napkins that have been taped together and a pair of sweatpants stretched across the table as a net. Vinnie, still smiling, still drinking, still showing his five teeth, is the referee. The ball hits the net and falls backwards to the server.

Vinnie says, "I don't know. Who gets that point?"

"We do!" a girl squeals.

Vinnie makes a football gesture like they've roughed the kicker and awards a point to the girl who squealed.

"Hit it again," Vinnie says. "Keep it in the air."

Egg Sandwich

Harriet winds down for the evening, her rounds and tasks complete, sleepy but not ready for bed. After the popcorn popped so it filled the machine, she unloaded it into a couple brown paper grocery bags then she popped another machine-full and served everyone and plenty of popcorn is still left and now she has called the night. She's swept a little, given away some merchandise, poured a couple beers. Megan made her a fried egg sandwich that she eats in the office at the back desk, relaxing. The girls' volleyball team still plays out in the bar, screaming, drinking. Harriet likes them but they are loud, too loud for her old ears that sometimes hear only sounds and not words. I sit on a couple cases of beer stacked near Harriet and her sandwich. The room is cool, damp like a basement.

I offer to turn on a space heater.

Harriet shakes me off and says, "Close the door. It'll warm up."

I push the door with my foot so it clicks shut.

The volleyball sounds instantly lessen.

Harriet says, "Better."

I say, "You sure you don't want the heater?"

She says, "Those things start fires. I'd rather not go out in flames," and turns away from her sandwich and smiles so I know it's a joke.

I drink a draft and listen. Harriet takes small dainty bites of her sandwich, barely bites, mousey nibbles. The office is mostly boxes of booze that won't fit in the storeroom and metal file cabinets that look like skyscrapers that failed at being skyscrapers.

Harriet says, "I always forget your name."

I say, "That's okay."

She says, "It can't be helped," and laughs and accidentally spits a little egg. Her front teeth are as yellow as corn flower. She says, "You're the journalist, right?"

I shake my head.

She says, "The doctor?"

"Not even close."

"The volleyball coach?"

"No," I say, "but I used to wrestle."

"You're the teacher."

"That's it," I say. "I'm trying to be."

She says, "You were at the college when the boy hung himself."

"Pretty much," I say, not bothering to explain the difference between a noose and a bullet, blue bodies and red.

She says, "You're okay?"

"Pretty much," I say.

She says, "There's always been tragedy. I don't mean to sound insensitive but some people have always wanted to leave the world on their own schedule. We should quit being so surprised. Better that they go than kill someone else."

Harriet puts down her egg sandwich, the crust remaining like a freestanding fence. She wipes her mouth with a crumpled paper napkin. Her dress, blue cotton, is loose on her body. Her hair is completely white. One minute her eyes are there, sharp, the next they turn to a dreamy puddle of milk. I keep thinking of my grandma, my Nona. My mom is out tonight with her veterinarian. I would rather own this bar than teach. I love to teach but I worry I am failing as a professor constantly. It would be easier, spiritually, to pour drinks and fry eggs. I could have Nona live upstairs. Joanie could visit us. Seeing her would make me worry less, though I would still worry. She lives on her looks and body and those years are finite and they end well before death. I worry that Joanie will not grow old because she does not know how.

Harriet says, "I used to swim in Indian Lake with my husband when we were fifteen years old. He always wanted me to take my clothes off but I never would." She smiles when she says this, the sexiness still present. She pushes her plate away. She leans back and stretches out her legs like she wants to make sure they haven't fallen away somewhere in the bar. I can see the thick blue veins through her pantyhose. One of her slippers is missing. The office chair creaks. Harriet closes her eyes and breathes the breath of accomplishment, of working well.

"Was he handsome?" I say.

"He was so handsome," she says.

TIME TO THINK

Harriet says, "You go help Megan. I'll stay here and do the thinking."

"Let me know when you want to go upstairs," I say.

"By the time I'm ready to go upstairs, you'll be too drunk to help me along."

"Not a chance," I say.

"You had three beers while I ate an egg sandwich," she says.

"That's what doctors do."

"I thought we decided you are a teacher."

"A man has a right to better himself."

Harriet opens the bottom drawer of the metal desk and pulls out an open bag of sourdough pretzels. The pretzels have all been scraped free of salt.

Harriet says, "You're pretty funny for a man with no name."

FUCKNUT

Some of the volleyball players have left, including the one who relentlessly talked about spiking and sounded like a bullhorn. A hipper bar waits up the street. The girls have stumbled there to meet boys and drink flaming shots and the infamous Pittsburgh Klondike, a drink named after an ice cream sandwich but loaded with booze. Our bar mellows a little but still sounds like a jukebox of chatter. Three girls throw darts in the back. A couple more drink at a table. Vinnie, the old man with five teeth, watches the dart game and collects free drinks. His gray hair is a mess. He wears a girl's warm-up jacket, a gift from one of the volleyball players. The girls hand him a dart. He points at the bullseye. The girls point to the same spot, sincerely, not mocking. Vinnie does a throwing motion. The girls nod. Vinnie looks seventeen years old all around, the body, the energy, except for his face, where he looks eighty, a leather bag lined with bad teeth and a cross-punched nose. He throws perfectly and the girls applaud. Vinnie bows.

I sit at the bar, believing in nights like this.

Nothing is supposed to happen then everything does.

Beauty accidentally flows like drinks.

Or: dreariness is supposed to arrive like a tidal wave but instead trickles back to the ocean so all we feel is the rain and mist of sadness.

It's pretty great, a little sadness mixed with a lot of fun.

Megan says, "Where's Harriet?"

I say, "Eating stale pretzels."

"Without salt?"

I nod.

She says, "Good. Her blood pressure is up. She's a suicide pretzel eater." She stops and drops her bar rag and says, "Not the best choice of words."

"What?" I say. "I'm not offended by pretzels."

"You're still funny," she says.

"I need to correct more papers," I say. "I fell way behind this semester. I just couldn't face them. Then I caught up. Now I don't want to face them again but I have to."

"You could get away with not correcting papers."

"I want things to be as normal as possible."

"Normal is good."

"Normal is good," I say. "It's surprising how fast things go back to normal."

Megan, teasing, says, "We could get you to be a normal professor."

I say, "I think that'd require more education."

She says, "You should be stricter in class. Start there."

I say, "I am strict in class," a total lie.

"You brought in pizzas during finals week last year."

"Students get hungry."

"You take late work all semester."

"I want students to do well."

She says, "The sick part of me wishes I was there when fucknut offed himself. I could have helped you somehow."

"There wasn't much to do," I say.

"You know what's weird?" she says. "When I fantasize about this, and I do, I have this idea about how it all should have gone down. I know that's creepy but I've thought about all of this and I have this hero dream and it's like: I'm the one who does right. I handle it. I'm the hero. I want to be the hero. I'm willing to risk my life. But it never involves saving Brandon. I just like shield you and the rest of the kids. I don't even worry about him. He's nothing. He could be any killer, any person in the world doing awful. I hate to say this but he's a piece of shit. Was a piece of shit. Is a piece of shit wherever he's at, in whatever afterworld there is for pieces of shit. I know you shouldn't say that about people who are mentally ill but he hated everyone and everything. You can't spin that into something good. I think about him being near you with a loaded gun and I get fucking furious. I want to kill that dead motherfucker."

"I was worried he'd shoot me," I say, "but not that much."

She says, "He was the worst person I ever knew."

I shrug and sip off my beer, not wanting to acknowledge such an obvious truth.

On Megan's Nerves

Megan looks down the bar and says, "Those bitches are getting on my nerves."

"All the crazy ones are gone," I say.

She says, "I hate bitches with red hair. Blondes, too. And brunettes. That one at the end of the bar says she's the captain."

"She looks like the captain," I say.

Megan flicks her rag at me and says, "She looks like a chick in a sweaty t-shirt."

"Look at this line," I say.

I am committed to correcting papers, even if I need to find new ways to complete the task, like working drunk, but my stack of papers still looks like a paper sandwich no one, least of all me, wants to eat. I used to hear people talk about burnout and I'd think: lazy. They'd say exhaustion and I'd think: lazy. I worked hanging from a bridge with rust falling on my forehead. I was happy to be paid. Now I want to crawl in bed and not hear another human voice for days. Be quiet, my lovely students. Your voice-hammers smash my spirit.

Megan says, "What's the line?"

I point to the paper.

The line says: you, sir, are an asshole.

Megan says, "Is that supposed to be directed at you?"

"Could be."

"Fail him."

"It's a her."

"Fail her."

"It's looking like an A paper," I say, then mark it as such.

Megan says, "At least a B+."

"You're right," I say. "The A has been completely devalued. I shouldn't add to the confusion. The A+ is my most sincere grade. If a student gets an A+, they know they've done something special. A is fairly sincere. A- is less sincere. B+ is not sincere. B is below average. B- means you shouldn't have been awarded a high school diploma, let alone come to college, but since you have, I am going to encourage you."

Megan says, "I don't think that's the scale other professors use."

"You have to be flexible," I say.

FAT BILL

Megan goes off to pour beers and get tipped. I glance at the TV above the bar, a square mounted to a stand. The TV is probably twenty years old but the picture is fine, color, no lines. During the day the regulars watch old Westerns and Humphrey Bogart films or ESPN. Now, a woman in a blue sweater dress holds the remote. Customers do this. It's fine to change channels if you ask. She flips around. She stops. She flips some more. She hits the news. She stays on the news. We can't hear the news because the volume is off and the jukebox is loud. The reporter on the TV is in the Middle East somewhere.

I have a horrible thought: I am supposed to meet with a former student who dropped out of college to enlist in the military. The student's name is William but everyone calls him Fat Bill.

I mentioned Fat Bill before.

I've yet to sort him out.

Fat Bill sent me an email a month or more ago, saying he was back from basic training, getting ready to ship out to Afghanistan. I can't imagine fighting anyone in the desert so I generally believe we shouldn't be in the desert fighting. Those are my politics. My politics are minimal.

I think Fat Bill has come to the same conclusion: politics suck, death in the desert sucks. I mentioned that he was calling but before I could call back he started emailing. His last email was sketchy and confused, like he was afraid someone else might be spying on what he said, but the undercurrent was: oh shit, and help, and fuck me. Basic training complete, the reality of his commitment ahead, he sounded like he wanted to go back in time and chose again, to re-imagine his life without guns and boots and a desert looming.

Maybe he never wanted war.

He wanted someone to pay for his college.

The Army said they would do that.

The rest sounded like white noise and adventure—communication skills, world travel, helping your country, be a patriot. Bill wants to be a writer. Maybe he thought the Army would provide him with a great story then he realized that being alive provides more stories than we can ever write down. You don't need war to be creative. The stress of waking up provides enough juice to make you want to scream and tell and speak and story.

In the last email he sent his phone number, which he'd already left in a message.

He wrote: can you help?

I knew what he meant—save me, please—then I thought about that and re-read the email and started to wonder if it was me, if I was imposing my views on his email, if that's what I would have wanted—save me, please—but maybe he wanted something completely different. He was a young man, I was an adult, maybe we disagreed on politics—had we ever talked politics?—then I didn't know what he meant by help, if I could help with the war, or keeping him from the war, or teaching him to write something about the war, or if he just wanted a care package with socks and some good chocolate and a couple packs of cigarettes. People are often confused about the powers professors possess. They think we are millionaire wizards with endless knowledge and a direct line to whoever is in charge, including presidents, journalists, and professional athletes. Maybe Bill thought I could call his commanding officer or hide him in my office at school or ship him to Canada in a wooden crate.

I wrote down his phone number.

I put the scrap in my fancy-ass satchel with everything else I use for teaching.

It took a day but I finally decided to call.

Before I called, I needed something to say.

Nothing came.

I remembered Fat Bill but not his actual writing. I paced my office, staring at the phone, thinking. He was a lover of Charles Bukowski, the alcoholic poet who worked as a mailman for years, the one writer all the poor kids who find books on their own love, but I think Bill wrote in a denser style, more literary, lots of description. He disliked the stories other students wrote about vampires but he was nice about it. I know I gave him a good grade because I give everyone a good grade but I wanted to say something personal on the phone. I wanted to say, "Remember that story you turned in," and somehow spin his dread of going to war into hope, something to keep his mind straight while he's parked in the desert, hating the sand. I wanted to say, "Remember that essay about—" but I couldn't remember any of his essays. What Fat Bill wrote felt like a mystery novel I hadn't finished or even paid for. On the first day of class I asked if he wanted to be called Bill or William and he said, "Fat Bill. Please."

I remember that.

Only I never felt comfortable calling Fat Bill by his nickname to his face and since he doesn't like to be called Bill or William, I never addressed him except to say, "Hey," or "What's up?" or I nodded and smiled. It added to the dismal fog.

But I still picked up the phone and dialed, hoping his voice would punch up a memory.

Fat Bill said, "I'm sorry about the email. I've just been very nervous."

I said, "It's a not a problem at all. It was good to hear from you."

He said, "You're not mad?"

"Of course not."

"I called you a lot."

"You didn't."

"I left a lot of messages."

"That was fine."

"I thought you'd be mad."

"Why would I be mad?"

"I don't know. I'm just mixed up. They yell a lot during basics."

I said, "I'm sure you could use some quiet."

He said, "My dad thinks I'm doing a brave thing. He keeps saying it at least. My sister says I'm fucking nuts. I think I'm with my sister on this."

I said, "I wish I could do something for you," meaning I don't know what to do for you. The line stayed quiet.

I said, "Is there anything I can do for you?"

He said, "Could I write you?"

"Of course," I said. "Absolutely."

He said, "Could I see you before I take off? Or maybe we could go out for a beer or some pancakes? I have a little time before I ship out. I could come by your office or whatever. I know that's a lot to ask. I know you're busy. Your class meant a lot to me. I never had anyone to talk books with before I took your class."

"I'd love to see you," I said. "I'd be honored."

The world is too easy sometimes, too easy to trick kids into doing what they don't want to do, like war, and too easy to comfort the kids who have been tricked. I told Fat Bill to come by. I told him I would buy him a beer. Beer is comfort. I told him I would give him some books if he wanted books, if he was allowed to have books, if he planned to read while he was away. Books are comfort. Fat Bill said thanks and we made plans and I was so happy to be useful, so happy to help out that I didn't write anything down, not the day or date or hour. He called again to verify our get-together. I erased the message along with various messages from Joanie about running and Brandon about apologizing in class.

I should not have erased the messages.

Fuck me for being me.

DO YOU KNOW FAT BILL?

Megan serves me a beer.

She says, "You're putting them away."

I say, "Yes."

She says, "Do you want to do a shot?"

I say, "Yes."

The longer she works, the crazier her hair gets, the more beautiful she becomes.

I say, "Do you know Fat Bill? Was he in your classes?"

"Everyone was in my classes," she says. "I've been taking classes for years."

"You know who I mean?"

"Yeah, the big guy. He was sweet."

"I'm supposed to meet him for lunch or a drink."

"He's going to Afghanistan."

"I know," I say. "I'm supposed to meet him before he takes off and now I can't remember when he wanted to meet. We have plans."

Megan opens a bag of peanuts and puts the bag to her mouth and pours. She chews and swallows then swigs from my new beer to wash down the nuts.

She says, "You want some nuts?"

Before I can answer, she says, "D'ese nuts," and does a hatchet move to her crotch with both hands so it's clear which nuts she means—basically her ovaries.

I say, "It's like your brain is part eighth-grade boy."

She says, "I know where Fat Bill lives. It's a dump. You want to go see him?"

"I should probably go see him," I say. "He sounded scared."

"Well, no shit," she says. "He's going to the desert with a bunch of whackos."

"They shouldn't send kids to fight wars."

"Who else would go?"

"Bartenders?" I say.

"No fucking chance," she says.

"I'll go see him in the morning," I say. "That's the right thing. Do you have his number?"

"No. He's been in here, though, right when he came back from basics. I'm surprised he hasn't shipped out yet. He's not fat anymore. He's built. I think he was looking for you. He mentioned your class. He's really sweet and desperate."

"Why would he look for me here?"

"Everyone knows you drink here," she says.

"Another student just said the same thing. Why is that a thing?"

"That you drink here?"

"Yes."

"Because professors are supposed to be robots with pretend liberal political views who drink scotch and smoke pipes or whatever. Don't worry about it. Think about Fat Bill."

I don't worry about it.

I think about Fat Bill.

I say, "I think I have his number somewhere."

Megan says, "Don't give him any books about war if that's what you're thinking. There are no good books about war. Seriously. I mean, no books make war sound good. If that's what you're thinking, don't. No poems about war. No novels. Nothing. Not that Hart Crane book. Not those Bruce Weigl poems. Not the Tim O'Brien stories. None of those fucking Russians you read and especially that story where the guy's head rolls across the ground like a sun or whatever. Fat Bill doesn't need to see any of that. Do not give him anything that has been written about war, ever. War is shit. Books say so. Don't give them to him."

"I wasn't thinking that," I say, but that's exactly what I was thinking.

Whiskey for My Horses!

Megan says, "What about the you-know?"

I smile and sort of nod-shrug in affirmation.

You know, yes, sure.

I am drunk enough to think that snorting blow all night will keep me sharp enough to be sober and attentive when I show up at Fat Bill's house in the morning. I am drunk enough to wish I could do one of the things I imagine Fat Bill wants: call the President, get him to Canada, call this whole war off. High on blow I could imagine myself going back in time, rolling through thousands of calendars until I stood with Jesus and Muhammad, and I would tell them to speak clearly on war and killing, that both are abominations, that those who commit either act should be sentenced to walk the earth for twenty years, stopping only to feed the hungry with their bones and witness the beauty of the sunrise and the joy of solitude. Blessings on you both, I'd tell them, demand your disciples speak only your truth about death and destruction.

Then I'd offer them both a bump.

I turn to Megan and say, "Will you come to Fat Bill's house in the morning?" which was my original plan for getting high: to stay close to Megan.

"Of course, I will," Megan says. "I was planning on it."

"I wish I could do something for him."

"You're going to his house," Megan says, "that's doing something."

"Is it?"

"Yes," she says. "Now let's get the party started."

I say, "Harriet is still in the back room, eating stale pretzels."

"One of us needs to put her to bed."

"If I had any money, I would buy this bar and move my Nona in upstairs and then I would quit teaching, even though I love teaching."

"You can't buy the bar. It's my bar and I wouldn't sell it to you because it's not worth owning, mostly because it's a bar."

I say, "Technically, it's Harriet's bar."

Megan says, "Only when she's not binging on pretzels."

The captain of the volleyball team yells out, "Whiskey for my horses!" and twirls her warm-up jacket over her head so it looks like a pizza made of cloth.

Megan says, "You see. This is not a bar worth owning."

"You love this bar," I say.

"Like you love teaching," she says.

Don't Be Sad

Megan goes to gather shot glasses and bottles from the customers she most hates, like the volleyball team captain, and the ones she most loves, which is the majority of the bar despite her grumpy attitude tonight. The coke in my pocket waits. Such a huge eight ball. I should have crushed half and brought a bag of powder. The beer is cold. Cold beer never hurts my stomach. When I drink like this, I know I will never quit drinking because I do not ever want to quit drinking, not meaning the lifestyle, but the session I'm involved in. I want to use alcohol to avoid whatever responsibilities await at the end of this drunk. Drinking lessens my responsibilities or allows me to feel like my responsibilities are manageable and not like dumbbells tied to my ankles. Sometimes, when I close my eyes, I see the hole in Brandon's head but the graphicness of the hole does not cause alarm or nausea or even appear graphic. It's just a hole in a young man's head, one he put there for a specific reason, like a tattoo. Once, I imagined putting a golf ball into the hole like dead Brandon had turned into a round at Monster MiniGolf.

Then I opened my eyes and he disappeared.

I correct another paper to distract myself.

The paper is an essay about a job interview with Pizza Hut.

In the essay the student describes how the store manager made him wear a Pizza Hut ballcap during the entire interview to see how comfortable he was in a uniform.

The essay is fucking great.

It's by this kid who is not a kid but a young man, Adam Matcho.

He manages a Spencer's Gifts at the mall and is trying to get a business degree so they will promote him to manager. I think he has a new baby, a little boy. He writes so fucking well.

I read it twice then give it an A+.

Then I invent a new grade, +A+.

I hope the grade makes him a million dollars.

Or at least thirty grand and the occasional weekend off.

I pull out another paper.

I read it and can't tell what it's about, maybe being happy or how to become happy or techniques to maintain happiness, something. The only coherent moment appears to be about smiling into the bathroom mirror while brushing your teeth.

I write some comments.

Mostly the comments say: yay you!

And: read Kurt Vonnegut!

I set it aside without a grade, knowing I'll come back later tonight or tomorrow and scribble another overtly positive mark across the top.

My stack of to-be-corrected papers becomes smaller.

If I had to grade these, meaning to give them real grades, Bs and Cs and Ds and Fs, grades that a committee could investigate and verify, I would quit and go back to welding. I am not capable of gatekeeping. Education is different than that. Education says: read this, be smart, you're busy, read this, keep trying, keep trying when you can't try, when you're overwhelmed, when the world that is your world collapses, stay true, read this, pat attention, look up.

Megan walks by and says, "Don't be sad," and keeps moving to gather more empty bottles and glasses. She says, "You're not any good when you're sad."

It's true.

I'm better at being happy, even when I fake it.

I lift my beer.

I shuffle my papers.

My previous stack of papers must have weighed three or four pounds. This is nothing, a balloon, a collection of air. And yet I know these papers will multiply. Students are like Jesus with the loaves and fishes, they cannot help but feed the multitudes with words, only I am the multitude, one man on the shore, and I'm not really hungry anymore. I'm actually stuffed and sick. Their new papers will be about suicide. Their new papers will be about guns. Their new papers will be about bullets and how they sound. I fear this and believe it to be true.

Megan walks by with a shot glass on her finger and a bottle of lemon juice in her other hand and says, "Happy happy, be happy. Be happy."

I am old enough that I can't imagine being in the Army or Marines or Navy or whichever branch recruits from the community college. I can't imagine getting ordered around. I can't imagine giving orders. A bugle or a screaming sergeant as an alarm clock would be death in my ear. I can't imagine marching in time with soldiers who can't keep up. I can't imagine marching. Or soldiers. Or keeping up. Even though I am speed incarnate. But tomorrow morning I will tell Fat Bill that I think he's doing a brave thing and I'm really proud of him.

I lift my glass and drink.

Now I am done thinking about Fat Bill until morning when I knock on his front door.

Now I will focus on getting fucked up.

It's Not Bedtime

I look at a guy I barely know, a pizza shop owner who has a tattoo of a black rose on the back of his neck, and I raise my beer.

He raises his shot glass and smiles.

I sip.

He slams.

I salute him for slamming.

Harriet opens the office door and steps into the dim bar light. She gets a bag of pretzels from behind the bar, hands the bag to Megan. Megan stops pouring a shot to open the bag. Harriet takes the bag and starts back to the office, taking mini-steps, her feet barely leaving the floor. Megan will soon tell Harriet that bedtime is near but Harriet will not be ready for sleep. Harriet is tough on sleep, doing it when she wants, regardless of sun or moon or people in her bar.

Harriet shuffles and eats pretzels.

She waves at me and smiles.

I wave back.

The volleyball players know me. The old men know me. I want everyone to know my name and I know this is impossible but I hold the dream. To be named. To be loved. I hope this is not why I write. It may be. But it may not be. I am happiest making kind gestures no one sees. Harriet steps in the office and closes the door. A clock shaped like the top of a beer can, the long hand dragging foam, hangs above the bar. When it's almost full, I will help put Harriet to bed. I will do this by standing in the hallway while Harriet undresses and climbs under the covers and says, "Go away now, doctor, I am fine enough to sleep," and I will take comfort in her confusion or, if not confusion, her practiced un-remembering of my name and career.

Right now, behind closed door, Harriet eats her pretzels, the new ones covered in sea salt, ignoring her blood pressure, and I am remembering that happiness is a choice. Do it.

I will be happy.

I want you and everyone else to be too.

JOHN GRISHAM

Megan serves me a beer. She gets beers for two of the girls at the bar. A man in a suit walks through the door. He has brown hair, a warm face, and glasses. He looks like John Grisham, the lawyer who writes novels about people who end up in court.

Megan nods at the John Grisham look-alike and says, "That guy once tipped me one hundred bucks on a twenty-dollar check."

"Don't trust that guy," I say.

"A hundred bucks is a great tip."

"Not on a twenty dollar check. It's creepy."

"I know but it's still a hundred dollars."

"I think he wanted to do bad things to your vagina."

"Like impale it with a vampire spike?"

"Possibly."

She says, "He kinda looks like Stephen King."

"What?" I say. "He does not. That guy looks like John Grisham."

"What's the difference?"

I say, "One writes scary books that get made into decent movies and one writes shitty lawyer books that get made into shitty movies."

Megan says, "Let me get him a beer and then let's start doing that cocaine."

BLOW

I palm the blow from my satchel and hand it off to Megan in a discreet move, part prison shake, part loving touch. She holds my hand so I can't pull away.

"Your hand feels good," she says.

"Your hand feels good," I say.

She leans into me and touches my lips with her lips in the smallest way, not like a kiss but like her mouth is passing a secret to my mouth.

She leans back and says, "That was nice."

"That was," I say. "That was nice."

I am so clumsy with words in the clutch, too aware that what comes out of my mouth can't be revised and how that makes me safe and not passionate when what I want is passion, when what I want is to accept foolishness as a condition of love.

Megan puts her hand on the bar, the hand holding the blow.

She says, "What did you just hand me?"

"That's a big eight ball."

She nods and blows up her eyes to show how big.

I say, "I know, right?"

She says, "It's huge. I'll pay you for half."

"I got it free," I say. "It's a long, embarrassing story."

"Good," she says. "Since you didn't pay for it, I'll go start this without guilt and you can put Harriet to bed. Toot for me. Sleep for her. You be the good saint."

"Will she give me trouble?"

"She loves you."

"She doesn't know my name."

"She knows more than your name. Tell her you're my boyfriend."

I say, "I'm going to tell her you're in the back somewhere, doing toot."

"Bah," Megan says, washing glasses, always working.

Her dedication to motion is endless and admirable.

I want the same thing, to always be doing.

I miss physical work.

I miss tasks.

I miss knowing the definition of a good job.

I forget all that and look at Megan's hand holding the blow.

I say, "You just bah-ed Harriet."

Megan says, "Oh, come on. I bah-ed you, obviously." She makes a look that says it would be impossible to bah Harriet. Then she says, "You can't nark me out. One, Harriet wouldn't even know what toot is. And two, when she was younger, she was a pothead. All her brothers grew weed in Kentucky. She was a smoker."

"Seriously?"

"She's a mountain woman. She made her own butter, her own ice cream, smoked her own meats, all of it. Anything you could do for yourself, she did, right up until a few years ago. She wouldn't even drink store-bought iced tea. That's still why the popcorn machine is just corn and oil and real butter, none of that greasy fake stuff. She used to serve homemade pretzels that were like eating salty delicious air. She grew up in Kentucky, right? I know I said that. Her dad raised pigs. That's what he did for a living, raised pigs. It wasn't a pig farm. He just raised a few pigs and they ate them and sold some and traded for the rest."

Megan pauses to consider the feats of her grandmother, the history of her family, Kentucky and pigs and working but not having a job. The tenderness comes across her eyes and smooths her face into something approaching tears but still proud.

I try to make a joke and say, "A weed-smoking mountain woman."

Megan says, "She was really lovely. When you and I die, we won't leave anything behind. Everything we know how to do, everyone else knows how to do. When Harriet dies, she'll take things from this world that will never be done again, not in the way Harriet did them."

"That's why we write," I say. "I hope so."

"I hope so too," Megan says. "Harriet is my story."

"Harriet, you're a story," I say, an echo.

Megan says, "You're a story."

I say, "Everyone is a story."

"But you're brave."

"Everyone is brave."

Megan says, "Only brave people think that."

"Bah," I say.

"To Harriet," Megan says, and shoots the rest of my beer.

I consider Harriet, stoned, smoking marijuana grown on a mountain in Kentucky, how lovely she must have been, how fun and outrageous, and how lovely she is now, still, even as she mostly worries about giving away her bar and finding heaven.

"We're all so useless now," Megan says.

"I hope you're wrong," I say.

"I hope I'm wrong too," Megan says. "You have something in you. It's perfect. I'm glad you're too blind to see it. If you saw it, you'd be obnoxious."

"A star quality?" I say.

"See," she says. "Always with the fucking jokes."

"Don't make me take my shirt off and strut around your bar."

"Don't make me chase you and tackle you from behind."

I take her hand and she takes my hand back.

So it is, how damaged people flirt.

And, honestly: who here is not damaged?

Who here is not overcoming damage?

I'm asking.

I want more kin.

QUIET DOWN NOW

Megan reaches for the volume button on the jukebox so a silence comes over the bar like a sun setting on high speed, on fast forward. Everyone turns to look.

Megan says, "I have to make a phone call in the back. Does anyone need anything before I go? Drinks? Popcorn? Hugs?"

She waits.

The bar shakes its head no, fine, thanks for asking.

Megan says, "No one? Okay. I'll be ten minutes tops."

TITS

One of the girls' volleyball players wants to show me her tits. Her name is Tasha. Tasha is maybe twenty-one or twenty-two. She is short and athletic and happy to be drunk in a bar with such weird old men and good dart players. I like her ponytail. She likes fun and wants it to continue, to escalate the fun to something else, maybe rapture.

Tasha says, "They're not huge but they're shaped great."

She says this like she's selling candy door-to-door.

She says, "They're a B-cup but that's because I'm short."

I keep drinking, fake drinking, glass held to my mouth for a few extra seconds, no beer coming out, while I consider what gesture to make, what words to speak. Tits in a bar are not my thing, especially young tits. I am a man of great embarrassment and awkwardness and minimal promiscuity. No boobies here, thanks. Keep your tits to yourself.

Tasha says, "I always wear good bras because I don't want to have low-hangers when I get old. Old ladies with low-hangers are gross."

"Gross is a strong word," I say, paying attention, pretending to pay attention, but mostly looking for Megan, knowing she will return but that her return is not imminent because she needs to cut and smash and line and inhale and rewire and maybe repeat.

Tasha smiles playfully and says, "You're a good age."

I say, "I'm not sure what that means."

She says, "I bet you do."

I know to be flattered that Tasha has offered to show me her tits and that tits, both seeing and showing, are one of the world's small but essential engines. Except not exactly. Tasha is too young, too giddy, too sure of her power, but she is also too young, too serious, too unsure of herself. She reminds me of my students who are not my bartenders, the ones who are not Megan but who need to be reassured and encouraged and lavished with endless praise. Tasha deserves praise. She deserves an enthusiastic man-child, some twenty-one-year-old guy with a hard-on poking through his sweatpants. She should show tits and be fucked exactly as she wants. I support that. But I don't want to be that. That, to me, is horror. I am a good age but I am also old-ish, very old-ish, and too worried about too many worlds to be consumed by tits, even Tasha's, Tasha who does not know I am a man who once suffered mat herpes and carries a very small but very real fear about all things sexual.

Please don't rape my face, young lady.

I turn on my stool and face Tasha.

She says, "Do you want to see them?"

"I don't think so," I say.

"Oh come on."

"Maybe another time?"

"Don't be a pussy," she says.

"Since you put it that way."

"They're exceptional."

"Sure," I say. "Are there three? I've never seen three tits on one chest before."

Tasha says, "Just two."

I say, "I probably don't need to see two. Two are pretty common, no offense."

She ignores me, completely.

I say, "Go find a young guy who is gung-ho for tits."

She says, "Here's goes," and jiggles and leans forward so the tits get some gravity then she leans back and lifts her sports bra. Tits fall forth.

"There you go," I say, and use all my nerves and muscles and drunkenness to pinch my face into something happy. "You look great."

"Really?" she says, flattered.

"Absolutely," I say, not remotely meaning it because what are tits without love? Tits, yes, but really just skin and fat and a couple of pink nipples.

She says, "I knew you'd like them."

I nod, sure, yes, tits, hello.

She says, "Did I tell you my cup size?"

It's a brave thing to show your tits in a bar and I want Tasha to know she is a hero, if not to me then to someone more in love with young tits because, I think, the world really wants to believe there is a place for tits to appear without reason, for women to show themselves for fun.

Berryman would love this.

So would Rig.

My mom would probably think it's hilarious.

Tasha stands there.

I sit here.

Enough time has passed to put the tits away, mission accomplished, but her scrunched-up bra still rests at her collarbone, leaving the rest exposed. Tasha bends at the neck in a very chiropractic way to see what I'm seeing. She smiles. I tilt my neck slightly and look at her feet, her fancy Nike sneakers. I look back up. She moves closer, extending her chest. I think I am supposed to touch or maybe suck a breast but I'm struggling to keep my eyes open and not even considering contact. Contact would be gross, that strong word. I'm not down with chicks I don't know. That always sounds like humiliation.

Tasha says, "Well?"

"Great," I say.

She smiles and gives her boobs a shake, using her shoulders to make things jiggle to the music playing on the jukebox. She sticks out her tongue and twirls it, either like she'd blow me or lick her own nipples, I can't tell. I keep looking because I feel like looking away will hurt Tasha's feelings. Hurt feelings mean anger. Anger will mean violence. Tasha cups her boobs but does it with spread fingers so her nipples poke through. Even drunk I feel my neck turn red with embarrassment. Nipples. Tits. Nothing I want.

I look up at Tasha's face, not her eyes.

I say, "It's definitely something. You should wrap it up."

She says, "You want to take a picture."

"I don't even have a camera-phone," I say. "I'm completely analog."

She says, "Take a good hard look before people start gathering around. These are tits you're gonna want to remember," her voice sounding like a horrible wink.

I scan the bar, hoping someone gathers around.

I hope someone appears to love these tits.

But nothing.

No Megan.

No one paying attention.

Tasha says, "Spank material."

I take my good hard look to make it stop.

The lines from Tasha's bra are so pronounced it's actually hard to notice the tits in a fun tittie way, it's more like an examination. She's cutting the blood flow off by wearing a tight bra, that's my medical opinion, and her nipples look a little crinkly from being tucked away during the big volleyball game, one nipple completely dripping down like a sad brown-pink teardrop.

Loud voices sound from the sidewalk, then a group of volleyball players, ones not here before, walk through the front door and directly into our private semi-topless party.

One girl immediately says, "Oh my God, Tasha!" and sounds shocked.

Another friend says, "I should bite that titty, you whore," and laughs.

They are very loud women: pointing, clapping, stomping.

Vinnie walks over from the dartboard and his eyes lock on Tasha's tits like heat-seeking missiles on a jet plane and he stands so close it feels creepy.

"Settle down, old man," I say.

Vinnie turns to me and says, "That's the craziest thing I've ever seen in my life," and his eyes keep popping with tits and craziness. He rubs his face. He messes his messed-up hair and reaches down and zips up his girl's warm-up jacket.

One of the girls says, "That old man is loving your tits, Tash," and points and smiles at Vinnie who barely looks up.

Tasha pulls her sports bra back down.

My eyes feel released so I turn and check the bar. Everyone else drinks and stares at their drinks. Megan is still off, tooting. I am ready to escape to Harriet, to help her prepare for bed. The new John Grisham sits off to the side, drinking a shot with his beer.

Tasha says, "What do you think?"

I say, "You win."

"God, you're so weird. I love it."

"Well," I say. "I really do need to correct some papers," and I stand up and walk into the women's bathroom and do a line of blow off a tiny mirror, standing next to Megan, crammed in the stall, my brain instantly ablaze and pumping joy.

Megan says, "Put Harriet to bed tonight. I'm too emotional."

"I will," I say. "But I need another line. Or two. Or ten. I don't need it. I want it. I feel so much better already, instantly. I forgot how great this is. I'm all for cocaine."

Megan takes my face and kisses me.

I kiss her back, our bodies above the toilet, pressed against the stall.

BEDTIME STORIES

Harriet is tired. Megan is not. Megan is, as she said, emotional. She stands here with her rag, near the tip jar, wanting to run a better bar, wanting to finish college, wanting her grandmother to live forever. I am not tired and I am not thinking about my family. I am purposely oblivious to my own life so I can help Megan and be happy to do the task. I checked in on Harriet and she said, "Five more minutes," then I checked again and she said, "I could sleep in this chair," and I said, "Probably not," and she said, "Five more minutes."

Megan says, "Harriet would sleep standing up."

"It sounds like it," I say.

"Then she'd fall over and break her hip."

"Not on my shift."

Megan says, "Go check on her again. We have work to do."

Maybe it should feel dirty to do blow in a bar owned by an old woman who misses her husband but it does not and I am grateful for the straightness and clarity provided by a couple lines after hours of drinking. I want to be needed but, more than that, I want to be of service. I walk to the back room. Harriet holds a salted pretzel and thinks her faraway thoughts. I never see her drink but Megan says Harriet drinks wine with dinner, bourbon for her colds. All those pretzels require something, a better companion than A&W Cream Soda.

"Are we ready for bed?" I say.

"We are not," she says. "But I am."

"Good," I say.

She says, "Was it a good night?"

"I think so, yes," I say.

"I don't mean sales. I mean the people."

"It was good, I think."

"You think they were good people?"

"Yes, they were good people, all kinds but all good."

Harriet says, "The college girls get rowdy but they're nice. Girls are stupid like boys now. I guess that's progress. It used to be all working men in here. I'd encourage them to bring their wives on the weekend and sometimes they did. Mostly they did not. I don't know why men and women have such hard feelings for each other. I get along with both fine. Of course, I had brothers. Do you have any siblings?"

"Just me," I say. "My mom raised me by herself."

"Your daddy was a cop-out?"

"My daddy was a cop-out."

"Don't blame him too bad."

"I don't blame him at all."

Above the desk a group of bills and messages and old Post-It notes hang together on a single thumbtack. In the upper right-hand corner a black-and-white photo of a man in an Army uniform, but casual, holding a beer, laughing, hangs from what appears to be a cufflink. He could be a movie star with his hair combed back, his shirt unbuttoned.

I touch the picture and say, "I bet that was your husband."

"That," Harriet says, "was my boyfriend."

"Your boyfriend?"

"Boyfriends before husbands, it's the law."

"Did he go to the war?"

"He went to Korea but he didn't fight. He was useless as a fighter. He was too loving for that, as gentle as could be. Korea wasn't a real war. It was just terribleness they did behind people's backs. But we wanted to get out of Kentucky and, back then, the military men used to come around in good-looking uniforms, recruiting, promising boys all kinds of treasures if they enlisted. They always made it sound like a vacation."

"That's what they do."

"Lied about his age," Harriet says. "He was only sixteen when he enlisted. A child. Drove a car once. Drove a car with no license, a big Buick.

Left for war at sixteen. How awful. Imagine that. Could you even?"

"I can't," I say. "I was a sophomore in high school at sixteen, wrestling and working in a restaurant, hoping the waitresses tipped out. I didn't even know people went to war. I wanted to buy fancy jeans so I'd be cool. Sixteen. That's too young for anything."

"If you went to sixth grade in Kentucky, you were lucky. My father made sure I made it through the middle grades because he thought I was smart but they needed me at home. Everyone worked, all the kids, the adults, everyone. My grandma shucked peas with her old arthritic hands. We were needed."

Harriet digs in the pretzel bag, very seriously, like some of her story might be in the bottom, like it could be lifted out in one braided piece.

I say, "You like those pretzels?"

She says, "I like the salt. We used to keep all our foods fresh in salt when I was a child. Salt or smoke. I never lost the taste for it. I couldn't care less for refrigerators. I'd take a smokehouse any old day."

"I think you are a wise woman."

"I think I am an old woman," Harriet says, and laughs. She pulls out a pretzel, examines it, then drops it back in the bag. She digs in for another and keeps it. She says, "You started me on a story. Now I have to finish. Where was I?"

"Korea."

"Yes, Korea. My beau never had to kill anyone. He wasn't a killer. Wouldn't even kill an animal. His brothers killed all the meat. But he fixed things and the Army gave him training. He was a worker. Me, too. We had bigger dreams than those around us. Maybe that's why we fell in love, the way our dreams mixed together. We made it out of Kentucky, both of us alive, and he became a welder and electrician, two trades, both from the Army because he was smart. He was a good welder. He could make a child a bicycle from old scrap, fire up that torch and just build it. He was a good electrician too. He rewired this whole bar, got everything up to code. We came to Pittsburgh in 1955 and he always had a good job in the mill. He never had to carry the coke, never had to work near the blast furnace. We had a good life together. What a handsome man. I see him all the time now. I see him more than when he was alive, those last few years. I am not occupied with all the care it takes, all the pills and baths and bedsheets and things, so I can think about him and me when we were young. It's so real how he comes to me."

I say, "He sounds like a wonderful husband."

"My one true love," Harriet says. "Maybe Megan is like that for you?"

"I think so."

"I think she knows so," Harriet says, smiling. "She's beautiful but she's mine through and through. She will work you over if you let her. I was rough on my beloved when we were young. You be tough right back."

"I'll be tough," I say.

"We women in this family tend to wear the boots."

Harriet stands up and dusts her dress so the crumbs and salt fall away.

She says, "Megan thinks I have old-timers' disease."

I say, "She just worries about you."

"I worry about her. I worry about her more than I should. Vanity is one of my many sins. I can't imagine how anyone will live without me."

"Would it be okay if I helped you upstairs?"

"I'm slow but steadier than I look," she says, and takes my arm, like we are a prom couple, like I am her beloved from decades ago. She says, "You'll have to wait in the hall while I change into my bed clothes. And I'll need some water splashed with juice by my table for when I get dry in the night."

"Of course."

She says, "I'm not crazy. I miss my husband."

"I know that."

"I believe you do, yes."

Past Bedtime

Megan says, "Did you put her to bed?"

"I did," I say.

"Should I go up and say goodnight?"

"I think she's out already."

"No problems?"

"No, she's wonderful."

Megan stops working and nods.

I say, "She's you with wrinkles."

"You think I'm that wonderful?"

"I think you're that wonderful, yes."

MEGAN MAKES SENSE

Megan says, "I don't think we should sleep. I think we'll be happier if we don't sleep. My dad will come by tomorrow morning and check on Harriet and she'll still be sleeping or she'll be up, watching her programs, and grumpy that he showed up at all. She hates to be checked up on. We should just keep on until morning and have breakfast and go see Fat Bill and just stay sharp and focused. I was sad before but it passed. I'm so happy, I want to stay happy, but I'm mad at the world too, which is normal, I'm always mad at the world, but I'm really happy and I want to use that. Am I making sense?"

I say, "Completely."

A VERY FOLKSY JOHN GRISHAM

John Grisham waves to me from across the bar.

I give him the double-eyebrow raise.

John Grisham smiles then gives me the double-eyebrow raise.

There are only eight papers to correct and, frankly, I wish there were a hundred more. Or a thousand. Or a million. I want to be a great teacher, the best. The Muhammad Ali of community college professors. But how? To judge myself or to be judged as a teacher often feels like an impossible task, a list of subjective nonsense, but correcting papers can be measured in words and pages and pounds. I do this many and I say these encouraging things and give these encouraging grades. Then add it up. Correcting a million essays and stories means greatness, means I'll be the champ, the paper champ, the teacherly champ, the creative hero, though I am also thinking in terms of booze and coke, like I can correct this stack in five beers and three lines, and should I run out of papers, would the booze and coke diminish me or will I still be the do-gooder I aspire to?

I wave to John Grisham, an invitation.

His entire demeanor is kinder than I originally described.

He stands with his beer mug and shot glass. He takes a step and the shot spills over the edge. He stops to sip his shot down then starts to walk again and spills beer on the hard wood floors which probably have absorbed hundreds of gallons of beer over the years. John Grisham wears a nice olive green suit and some fancy brown shoes. He sips the beer as he moves. It appears he is an excellent, albeit clumsy, drinker.

He says, "I saw you doing some paperwork and it just got me curious. Is it okay if I have a seat? I'd like to buy you a beer."

I say, "I would very much like you to buy me a beer."

"Good, my treat."

"A beer doesn't mean I'm going to sleep with you."

"I would think not," he says.

John Grisham drinks his shot in a very thoughtful way, the opposite of slamming, and extends his whiskey-soaked hand. I shake it. He wipes his mouth with the sleeve of his suit coat and takes a seat. John Grisham is very folksy, like the real John Grisham, like he too was raised poor in the South but has money now but knows that the money will never mean as much as being poor. I love good manners. Joanie raised me right, not to be fake but to start with kindness, though she is more inclined to fuck-off and pisser than please and thank you.

John Grisham says, "So what's your profession? What's all this paperwork?"

I say, "I teach at a community college. These are my students' papers."

"What do you teach there?"

"Writing."

"Like research papers? Like science or something?"

"No," I say. "Not so much like that."

"Like poetry?" John Grisham says.

This is what people say who ask about teaching writing: oh you teach them to write research papers, oh you teach poetry, oh I get it you ruin their lives with sonnets, oh you make them read the speeches of Gandhi and look for typos. Nobody understands the possibility of the written word and how it's not mastered by sixth grade like it appears to be and, of course, it's not their fault, we were all raised on TV and now it's worse than TV, it's computers and an endless stream of half-assed news programs, gangsters, gangstas, and genitals. Do I teach writing? Yes, but only as well as students teach themselves how to live, which includes writing but which also includes other classes as well as their families, friends, lovers, careers, and the blessings and curses of their geography.

Do I teach writing?

In theory, yes.

What I really teach is word collection to the few students who are willing to acknowledge their own pain and intelligence and who want to take responsibility for the horror and beauty of the world. I give these students maps and as many good books as they can carry and I send them into whatever place they want to be in or the place they have to be and I tell them to come back once they have enough words for a good sentence.

Then I tell them to do it again.

ONE HUNDRED

John Grisham puts a one hundred dollar bill on the bar. He doesn't do it dramatically or for attention but he goes into his wallet, looks, counts, and pulls out the hundred and sets it on the bar to pay for the next round once Megan returns from serving the captain of the volleyball team who is still as rowdy as ever, beer for her horses and all that.

I say, "That's a hundred dollar bill."

John Grisham says, "I know. I was at the bank. It's payday."

I say, "That's wildly inappropriate for a dive bar."

"Really?"

"Maybe."

"I don't have anything smaller and I wanted to buy you another drink. I've never met a writing professor before. This is a great honor for me."

"You're old fashioned for a middle-aged man. I like that."

Megan comes back and says, "I can't break that right now."

John Grisham says, "Can I run a tab?"

Megan says, "Can I hold that hundred?"

John Grisham says, "Sure."

Megan says, "You can run a tab."

John Grisham says, "Thank you. I really appreciate it. I usually don't carry hundred-dollar bills on me but it's payday and I didn't think to ask for anything smaller when I was at the bank. I'm forgetful sometimes."

Megan says, "You still go to the bank on payday?"

John Grisham says, "Of course."

Megan says, "There're these new things: they're called money machines."

John Grisham says, "I hate the fees. I'm old-fashioned, like your friend here just said. I have one credit card that I never even use."

"You're a Luddite," I say.

"I apologize," John Grisham says. "I don't know what a Luddite is."

"Allow me to educate you," I say. "A Luddite is someone not interested in technology. I think the original Luddites smashed their weaving machines as a protest against the Industrial Age. I might be making the last part up."

"That sounds right," John Grisham says.

"The fee is one beer," I say.

"Agreed," he says.

Megan drops the hundred in the cash register.

She turns to me and says, "Someone wants to see you in the bathroom."

COCAINE, COCAINE

I head to the bathroom and wait for a dude to piss. I lock the stall and I do two lines. It's not as sexy as doing a line in the women's bathroom but the men's bathroom has its own appeal, like the mirror above the sink is partially covered in Andre the Giant stickers. I close my eyes and focus on my nose, how great my nose feels.

Why is this stuff not legal?

Head shrinkers should dole it out.

THE REAL JOHN GRISHAM

John Grisham wants to understand how a professor corrects papers from community-college writers. He keeps buying me drinks. Drinks are the plan.

"This is a good first line," I say, and circle the line.

The line says: No one was home, so I turned on the TV, and lit a joint.

John Grisham says, "Are they allowed to talk about joints in college classes?"

"They are encouraged to talk about whatever they want. The whole point of college is to lift restrictions. They speak freely and we give them good books."

"What about trigger warnings and all that? I've read a couple articles about students being offended by everything."

"Not community college students," I say. "They're tough. Being born is their trigger warning. They know the world thinks they're stupid."

John Grisham points at the paper and says, "So this is a good sentence because it's controversial? Because it's sort of edgy?"

"No," I say. "Is smoking a joint edgy?"

"I'd say not."

"Exactly," I say. "This is a good sentence because it's a young writer accurately describing the details of his life in a very specific way. It's something that appears easy but which is almost impossible to do."

I draw a star next to the circled line. I go to the last page. There is a long typo-filled paragraph summarizing the whole story. I write in the margin: don't summarize; end on an image; trust the story; watch out for typos; great work. I use three exclamation points.

John Grisham says, "And what? You like speed-read the middle stuff?"

"More or less," I say. "I'll go back to it later but students tend to deliver on the beginning and the end. Or you have to read for a while to find the actual beginning. Sometimes they have to talk it out. And sometimes the ending is buried in the middle. I'm trying to present you with a formula but there is none. The whole point of writing is to say something and be willing to mess up how you say it then come back to it and fix the words as many times as necessary."

"How many times is that?"

"Hundreds," I say, "maybe thousands."

"Fascinating," he says, and downs another shot.

Three more shots sit in front of him.

"Are you the real John Grisham?" I say.

"What?" John Grisham says. "Like the movie star?"

"No, like the writer who writes legal thrillers that get made into bad movies starring shitbirds like Tom Cruise and Tom-Cruise-type actors and other actors who have talent but who also want a lot of money for very little work."

John Grisham sips his next shot to the midway point.

He says, "It could be very hard work, acting in those films. It's possible they're only watchable because the actors worked so hard to elevate very horrible material to a level that is at least watchable and sometimes entertaining."

"I hadn't considered that," I say, "and I'm not going to argue it."

He lifts and finishes the rest of his shot.

I say, "You really love your whiskey."

"Bourbon," he says. "That's all they serve here."

"The woman who owns the bar grew up in Kentucky."

"That makes more sense. I love bourbon."

"Order us a couple. I'll buy."

"Let's keep it on the hundred in the cash register."

"Deal," I say.

He says, "I wish I were the real John Grisham. I would use some of that movie money and buy this place. I'd love to own a business. It's a beautiful bar."

"You should tell Megan, the bartender. She needs to hear it."

"I'm uncomfortable complimenting women. I'm always afraid they'll take it the wrong way. That's why I overtip to the point of obnoxiousness."

"You're an old-fashioned gentleman."

"I may be," he says. "I've always wanted to own a bar. Or a racetrack. But a bar seems more reasonable."

I finish my beer in a long, not so graceful, swallow.

I say, "I'm glad you're not the real John Grisham because I read one of your books once and it was really fucking terrible. I was jealous it'd been published."

"Thank you," John Grisham says. "I think."

LAST CALL

Megan says, "Last call. You don't have to go home but if you stay here I will punch you in the throat as hard as I can."

She says, "Last round on me, even volleyball players."

She says, "Beer only, no shots."

She says, "I love you all."

She says, "Thanks for coming and good night."

COCAINE, COCAINE, COCAINE

The bar emptied, the blinds on the windows pulled completely down, the front door locked, Megan and I sit at the four-top table by the office, as far from the street and the outside world as we can be without leaning through the back wall and into the alley.

Megan is sweating, occasionally dabbing her forehead with a napkin.

I admire women who sweat.

I'm not sure I knew this until now.

She has done the inventory and wiped the tables and washed all the glasses and polished away the fingerprints and dust from the jukebox with a vinegar solution Harriet mixes in the morning to still be a part of what a working bar needs. I have promised to sweep the floors and put the chairs up before we leave.

I was talking about Fat Bill going to the Middle East but Megan asked me to stop. She was right so I stopped. Now I start again. We think Fat Bill might have written the story where the lawnmower dies and the man digs up his front lawn with a rake. If so, Fat Bill is a pretty good writer.

The nearly fingerprintless jukebox plays Etta James because, years ago, I brought in an Etta James disc and asked to put it in the jukebox and Megan allowed it. Now I spend dollar bills playing Etta James songs I've already purchased. The price meets the need. Her voice and soul and the horns and the back-up singers chase away all the other music in the jukebox that is not Etta James. What a fucking hero her music is to a bar.

Megan says, "Let's talk about you."

I say, "Let's."

She says, "Seriously," and folds up her wet napkin. She says, "You talk to students all day and you're here tonight talking about Fat Bill. You graciously helped put Harriet to bed. You probably called your mom because I know you worry about her. I saw you talking to John Grisham. Let's talk about you for a change."

"Good," I say. "Someone should talk about me."

Megan says, "Why aren't you famous?"

I think about this.

There are many reasons, perhaps millions, but I say, "I've never been on TV?"

"Come on."

"I've never been on the internet. I don't pull my junk out and photograph it. I don't immediately feel compelled to digitally take up every cause in America. I don't casually refer to strangers as racists and sexists. I don't photograph my sushi. I don't eat sushi."

"Stop it," she says. "I mean book famous. Like known as an author."

"For starters, I don't even have a book, not a real one. I have westerns I'm proud to have written but sort of ashamed of too. They were written under a pen name anyway."

"Slim Howdy," she says, and laughs.

I say, "Not Slim Howdy but close."

We're saying fame but she means—what we mean—is success.

Time off and more money and no debt.

We want to die less each day.

We want to find more moments to pause and breathe.

The cocaine is on the table and we are trying to cut it into a winding line. We think this is funny, the winding line, how it looks like a wagon trail. We take our debit cards and the chunks of cocaine and smash the chunks into powder and move the powder into a white river of blow. Then we put our debit cards away and all we have to do for the rest of the night is inhale.

Megan says, "I love to read."

I say, "Me too."

She says, "I don't think anyone else loves to read but us."

"That's possible."

"You have poems and stories in magazines and you've written novels and you can't get a book published, even though you've published western novels. It doesn't make any sense. I know I don't know anything about that world but that seems wrong."

"You're depressing me," I say. "I know I can't get a real novel published. I can't even finish the novel I'm writing."

"It's not depressing. It's brilliant. Those fuckers don't know."

"They know what they know, same as everyone else," I say, but I don't believe it.

There's not a less well-read class of people in America than the agents and the publishers at the major presses, except for maybe fans of NASCAR or car racing in general.

I feel bad for thinking that.

NASCAR is a fine sport.

Making a left turn at high speeds must be difficult.

Literary agents and publishers are fine people.

Should I be accepted into their club with a manuscript of my own that is not a western novel, I will acknowledge their intelligence and good taste, save for their obsession with the celebrity books they agent and publish and the memoirs by conservative talk show hosts that keep appearing on bestseller lists and the liberal newscaster books written by TV journalists who are as rich as a movie stars and better looking than models.

"Trust me," Megan says. "Those people are ridiculous. You're a genius. They publish books by The Sweet Potato Queens." She stirs her whiskey and coke with her finger and says, "What's wrong with you is really what's wrong with them."

"I'm not even sure that makes sense," I say.

I swig off my beer. I go down to the cocaine and inhale a small line from the river. I touch my nose. The broom waits behind the bar. If Megan doesn't quit talking about my failures as a writer, I'm not going to sweep, or I am going to walk outside and sweep the sidewalk to show the world it needs clean sidewalks free of boot tracks.

She says, "I have been reading about Andre Dubus. Andre Dubus was great."

I say, "Andre Dubus is great."

"The dad, not the son. I haven't read the son."

"They're both pretty amazing, completely different but both awesome."

"I love the dad. He's dead."

"He's still great. As a writer, he's still great," I say, and I go for the broom.

The broom is new but too small. I know brooms. I've swept restaurants and stores and hallways and gymnasiums back in high school and college. I swept when I was a welder. I always left my work-space impeccable. I'd like to leave this bar impeccable. You need a wide broom to be effective but I'll make this place shine nonetheless.

Megan says, "Andre Dubus couldn't get a book published. Nobody wanted Andre Dubus' books and now they make movies out of his books and everyone reads Andre Dubus. So fuck them. You're as good as Andre Dubus. You'll get a book and you won't have to teach at a crappy community college anymore."

I say, "I am not as good as Andre Dubus."

Nobody, no one writing in America for years, has understood the heart and all its twisted ways like Andre Dubus. It's a great compliment but it makes me sad because it makes me think Megan will say anything and I want her to be more than that.

She says, "You are too as good as Andre Dubus."

I take the broom and launch a fallen pretzel at her feet, hockey style.

She says, "Stop that."

I say, "No."

She says, "I'm not being nice. I'm being honest."

I say, "I like to teach at the community college. I would like to teach fewer classes and grade fewer papers but really, this semester, aside from the openly racist chick and the crazy guy writing novel spoofs who ended up shooting himself in the head, it's been pretty great. I met the school nurse. She's great. I love the president. She's great. The security guard, Jerome, really bailed me out and helped my pal Rig. All the campus police have been amazing since Brandon killed himself. They've been really sweet and attentive to everyone. I'm just a little burned out, I think, maybe a ping of numbness. There are so many personalities coming at me all the time. And then the one with a gun. The world should have a mute button. And a pause button. And a stop button. I don't mind people but they're constantly moving around, which makes me nervous. And they won't shut the hell up. People should shut the hell up. I try to."

She says, "It's bad. The community college is not a good place to teach."

I say, "Working at Walmart is bad. The community college is pretty awesome."

She says, "Owning a bar is not bad."

I say, "Owning a bar is great."

She says, "Why didn't you ever try to kiss me?"

"Because you were my bartender and, after that, you became my student."

"I'm smart."

"And pretty, too," I say. "Maybe I was waiting for you to kiss me."

"I kissed you already," she says, "multiple times."

I go to kiss her because I am not thinking or because I am thinking, because the cocaine is doing what it should, or Megan and I exist outside of cocaine and bars and community colleges, which is what love should be, a step outside with someone who knows that being inside and alone is only the answer when love is not the question. She comes with me. My lips are numb from all the coke but I still feel it, her tongue, soft and wide in my mouth. She feels it, the way she reaches. We stay with it. Etta James sings to us with her saintly voice, a trumpet of soul. The broom falls to the floor. I climb on Megan's lap and we both start to laugh.

DAVID FOSTER WALLACE

You know what's great about people like me and Megan?

We never talk about David Foster Wallace.

MARY KARR

David Foster Wallace was Mary Karr's lover for a spell. In interviews, when people mention their relationship, Mary Karr acts offended. Not acts, becomes. She calls the interviewers misogynists then rants and whoops. She walks out. She comes back. She swears she will never answer questions about David Foster Wallace again. She insists that David Foster Wallace's dick is the least interesting thing about him. She swears she's quitting interviews, quitting publicity. Does she need this shit? She does not.

But I don't know.

If I banged Mary Karr or David Foster Wallace, I'd play it up, I'd make it sexy and smart, I'd make it an advertisement, a resume, a pitch, especially because I like Mary Karr's memoirs, the booze and Texas dirt, especially because I hate David Foster Wallace, the do-rag and abundance of words that critics confuse with quality.

Megan hates Mary Karr.

She hates her books. She hates that Mary Karr is offended when interviewers want to ask her about sleeping with David Foster Wallace, the fake outrage. She hates that Mary Karr talks about how poetry needs to be more accessible but writes horribly overblown and inaccessible poems.

I once taught a Mary Karr memoir.

Megan, who almost always loves the books I teach, said, "This is a bunch of fake bullshit. This is a college professor talking about poor alcoholics like a college professor would talk about poor alcoholics. She's supposed to talk about poor alcoholics like poor alcoholics would talk about themselves. It's just fucking fake."

That's why Megan and I don't talk about Mary Karr either.

JAMES BALDWIN

I am better than Andre Dubus. Megan has convinced me. My unpublished novels are better than his published novellas. At the very least my unpublished works are longer than his published works. I will accept that.

I am longer than Andre Dubus.

We both agree that I am inferior to James Baldwin, how he could make a sentence read like a bible, how he wrote arguments and lectures that never sounded like either, just a steady flow of story from the corners few people walk past. No one was ever able to articulate what it means to be outside—through race or class, orientation or desire—to insiders, to famous musicians and actors and writers and critics, better than Baldwin. Everyone loved him, from William Styron and Marlon Brando to Nina Simone and Ray Charles. A black man who lived most of his adult life in France and who was also gay and knocked by all the roughs who called themselves revolutionaries, Baldwin moved through all structures and belonged to almost none. He existed where he needed to exist, fought with all, and above it, loved. I can't imagine having to read Baldwin in a class, to have him contextualized, to have him explained, to have him turned from a writer into a hammer, a politician, away from the music and story. I hope I do not do that to the books and writers I teach and maybe it is not possible to destroy books like that at the community college level. Students are so new to books. They barely grasp story.

They want to understand story.

They know their lives are stories above all else.

They are in my class and gone so fast.

Megan says, "Who is the Turkish writer in that documentary?"

I say, "Which documentary?"

"The one about Baldwin."

"I didn't know there was a documentary about Baldwin. I missed that. Is it like a Public Television thing? A thing they'd show on PBS during a pledge drive?"

She says, "Not the new one on Netflix, the old one."

"What? There's two documentaries about James Baldwin?"

"Yes, one is out now, on Netflix or something. The other one is old."

"The PBS one?"

"I don't think so. It's not hokey like a PBS thing. Baldwin is so pissed off but he's so beautiful. He's pointing and yelling and you can feel the love coming off him. It's that smile. He knows things other people don't know and you can see how happy it makes him but he's not arrogant about it. He includes you, even white people."

"I need to see that. How did I miss that?"

Megan says, "Who's the teacher now, my young learner?" and rubs some blow on her gums and uses her eyebrows to make it funny.

"Did you read Baldwin in one of my classes?"

"I think I read him in the library. Did you teach him?"

"I tried."

"How'd it go?"

"Bad. The kids here are too poor to recognize anyone else's poverty."

"They're nice kids."

I say, "We're all nice kids."

Megan says, "Next time we do this, we need books, stacks and stacks and stacks of books. Then we can read to each other. I'd love to read some Baldwin outloud. I would absolutely love that. I would read a couple lines and kiss his book."

"I would kiss all his books."

She says, "I would kiss all his books."

"Except a couple novels. They get really dense and hard to read sometimes."

"Stop it."

"It's true. We don't have to love everything a writer writes."

"Like I hate *Travels With Charley*."

I say, "How can you hate a Steinbeck book?"

"Fucking dog book," Megan says, and laughs.

"And *The Red Pony. It*'s written for teenagers or something. Grade school."

"But Baldwin," she says.

"Those essays," I say. "I'd kiss those."

"I'd kiss them better," she says, drinking. "Next time I'm bringing a library," and she goes down to our river of blow and inhales with a tiny drinking straw.

Then I go down and huff.

Megan says, "A whole huge library."

"That'd be perfect," I say, meaning the books and meaning next time we come together but not like this because I am done using cocaine forever, not because of cocaine but because I just looked at the door amidst our conversation about writers, amidst the kisses and the moves we make for affection, and I imagined a cop coming through the wood and glass, a cop pulling his gun, then handcuffs and jail cells and whatever happens in jails cells, not because we've done anything wrong or hurt anyone but because someone somewhere said cocaine is wrong and those who do it are wrong and should be gathered up and put behind bars and held until a judge can decide how they should pay back their time spent breathing coke and talking—should they pay in dollars or years in prison? Neither works for me.

I hate when I scare myself out of joy.

I promise myself to sing along until at least morning.

"James Baldwin," I say, and raise my beer.

"James Baldwin," Megan says, and raises her beer.

MORE BEER

Beer tastes so good like this. Maybe it's the cocaine or maybe it's the joy but my throat catches fire then the beer turns the heat to a breezy day and I stroll.

It must be close to four in the morning now. At six, maybe seven, no later than eight, we are going to Fat Bill's house and we are going to drag him to a diner and I am going to buy him breakfast. I am going to buy him eggs and bacon until he thinks he's conquered a farm.

Megan looks at me and says, "You're thinking about Fat Bill."

I say, "I'm thinking about you."

I would like Megan to live with me. I will look for the right moment to say this, which will probably not be today but which could be. We kiss again and again.

Someone knocks on the glass, on the front door. The tick of my heart instantly goes boom, a kick drum. It's the cops. I know it's the cops. I can hear their bullet-proof vests and guns. I so hate guns, all of them, the Glocks and the shotguns, the automatic and the semi. They are going to shoot without asking. They have heard our noses and know our noses are happier than their noses and now we must pay with our lives. Megan and I stop. I put a finger to my lips. Should we run? Hide? Head upstairs and bury ourselves under Harriet's blanket?

Cops, be still.

Cops, be not cops.

Perhaps you've read about me recently in the *Tribune Review*.

I am Western novelist, Montana Jones, the man who averts children's eyes.

Would you really want to shoot a Western novelist, Mr. Policeman?

Or a man who almost blocks suicides?

Before I can complete our deaths in my head, we hear John Grisham's voice, cheerful, friendly, coming around the cracks of the front door.

John Grisham says, "Hello." He says, "I just saw a light in there." The shadow of him moves along the front glass, the blinds, pushing his face against what he can't see.

Megan says, "Oh God, John Grisham."

"I think I like him."

"Really?"

"He bought me all those drinks and he was interested in how I correct my students' papers. It felt really sincere. Nobody is sincere anymore."

"I think he's lonely," she says.

"We all are," I say. "Let him in."

"What if he's a cop?"

"He can't be a cop," I say. "He writes very bad legal thrillers."

John Grisham says, "Can I come in?" He says, "I have money."

Megan says, "We should kiss again," so we do, and it is better than all the previous kisses which were also pretty great and we lean into this one like the others but more.

Megan starts for John Grisham and the front door. I look down at the table. We have been kissing and talking but not doing a very good job of breathing up the rest of the cocaine though, in our defense, it is an enormous amount of marching powder.

I say, "What about this?"

She says, "Put it in the backroom until we see if he's okay."

"It's all cut," I say.

"The whole table," she says.

Megan smiles and turns.

I pick up the table like it was a blanket filled with china. It is not an easy thing to transport, cut cocaine, but I do it well, even though I would rather watch Megan walk away, her ass and everything else, just the way I like it, which is that it belongs to Megan.

PART TWENTY-TWO

Get Up

Fat Bill doesn't live in a house. He lives in a trailer. The trailer is yellow, faded to dirty mustard, the color of a dying sun on a rum bottle. Out front, over the door, a small wooden porch supports a sagging green awning. Around the trailer is property, lots of it, woods and leaves and flowers that have barely bloomed. It's a magical forest where the elves all live on weeds and jaggers, except for the rose bushes, except for the manicured shrubs.

We sit in my car, all three of us, me and Megan and John Grisham. All three of us are drunk but clear because we have finished almost all of the cocaine. It was a lot of cocaine but we approached it with great seriousness, especially John Grisham who insisted he hadn't seen a line in more than a decade then transformed himself into a starving anteater who treated the grains of coke as ants. The time is past seven, seven-ish, eight-ish, six-ish. Probably seven-ish. I don't want to look at my watch. I'm going by the sun. There are clouds to consider. And wind too. It's a game we've been playing, guessing time, and now it's turned into something else. The roads we took to Fat Bill's trailer swerved a lot and we needed a good joke, something about sunshine and minutes and how confusing clocks are.

Trailers depress me.

Once, when I was very young and Joanie was working and trying to put herself through school, we lived in a trailer, just like Fat Bill's, but we didn't have the woods and leaves and flowers and weeds. It was a city trailer park and it was awful. Beside our trailer was another trailer and, beside that, another trailer and so on, like someone had planted a garden of trailers then abandoned the seeds to grow wild. Our trailer park was muddy with crabgrass and gravel and potholes. I didn't bring any friends home from school that year, even though I was allowed, even though Joanie said it was okay, even though we'd lived in apartments she'd been embarrassed of. None of my old friends knew I lived in a trailer. I told them we moved in with my Nona to take care of her, though Nona was healthy and took some pleasure in knocking Joanie for ending up in a trailer, however temporary.

Megan says, "Should we knock?"

"Maybe we should come back around noon?" I say.

"Maybe," Megan says. "But then the sun will be too hot."

"The sun will be behind those trees by noon," John Grisham says. "It's the way the earth's axis tilts at seventeen degrees."

"Earth's axis?" I say.

"True," Megan says. "I trust the lawyer when it comes to reading the sun."

She sits beside me, shotgun. John Grisham hangs in the back, on the hump and leaning forward. The top of his head fills my rearview mirror. His hair is thin. My truck is huge. We could fit a classroom of students in here.

John Grisham says, "I don't think I can make noon. I think this is a super nice thing you're doing, seeing this kid off, and if you get him out here, and we get him to a diner, I'll buy everyone breakfast, but I don't think I'll make noon. But maybe I will. I'm more tweaky than sleepy. I don't know what I'm talking about. This is why people do drugs then quit drugs."

"I'll go to the door," I say. "You two stay here."

"Really?" Megan says, surprised but thankful.

John Grisham says, "I'm sort of scared to be here."

"Maybe I should stay in the truck," I say.

It's the sunlight, it's the drugs, it's the trailer, it's the shame, it's the trailer.

"You've got this," John Grisham says. "No reason for both of us to be scared."

Megan says, "Maybe you should write a note and leave it on his door. I have a pen and some paper in my purse."

"Do you have tape?" John Grisham says. "He'd need tape."

"Stop it, both of you," I say. "Allow me to breathe and I'll be fine."

I close my eyes and inhale through my nose.

I breathe out my mouth.

I repeat until calm appears like a breath.

"Your breathing is very calming," John Grisham says.

"You just knocked me out of my calm place," I say.

"Sorry," John Grisham says.

Megan says, "Let's all just breathe and not talk."

"Exactly," I say, and inhale.

If you're going to do right, do right.

If not, okay.

My job is education. I still believe that. I teach. I listen. And will take students on a kayaking trip someday. When I'm alone in my office or my apartment or drunk enough in Harry's Bar, I correct student papers. Will I shove a shot-through student's head behind a metal desk to shield students from horror? Yes. I also show up to all my classes on time and work to make them interesting and accessible to as many people as possible. I say encouraging things and I lend out books knowing the pages will come back torn and waterlogged or not at all. I accept readers of all levels, even those who don't read, as intelligent human beings with life experiences to back most of their thoughts and beliefs, and I believe everyone who makes an effort with a book, with books, will become a more complex and thoughtful person. I write letters of recommendation on a one-day notice. I make office hours. I listen. After class I stick around and answer questions unrelated to my job because sometimes students need an adult to talk to.

I am doing more to make the world better than I am doing to make it worse.

I hope so, at least.

I pray so.

I hope and pray so all the fucking time.

But Fat Bill is going to fight a war he doesn't want to fight, that I wouldn't want to fight, that he signed up to fight so he could get money to go to college to do something that does not involve fighting, probably because I told him going to college was a great and holy thing, we should all be learners, everyone needs English, and whatever.

I'm doing the math here.

I hope it does not add up to me being a monster.

I get out of the car.

Megan says, "Don't knock too loud."

John Grisham says, "If you smell meth cooking, run."

Megan says, "It does look meth-y. I thought that and tried to forget the thought then thought it again but I was afraid to say it."

I say, "There are flowers hanging from the awning. It does not look meth-y."

John Grisham says, "But a lot of the property looks weedy."

Megan says, "I saw jaggers."

I say, "Stop it."

I close the car door.

I open the door.

I lean back inside to speak.

I say, "I'm afraid his parents will be pissed I'm here, like I'm being intrusive."

Megan says, "You are being intrusive."

John Grisham says, "That's the point."

I close the door.

They both give me the thumbs up through the glass.

The road is paved, the driveway dirt covered in gravel, the sky blue and dotted with clouds. Empty flowerpots of various sizes and shapes line the wooden porch. The awning is covered in leaves. But blooming flowerpots do hang and add beauty. If I knew which window was Fat Bill's window, I would throw a small rock. A rock could knock this place over. The front door doesn't have a doorbell. I try to remember if my trailer had a doorbell. I remember Joanie coming home with a man. He wore a tie and slacks. He had smart glasses like Clark Kent. He looked at the trailer. He looked at me and my toys. I didn't have a lot of toys. There was a train. The tracks were starting to rust because I took them in the bath, my favorite place to play. The man attended community college with my mom, with Joanie. He looked scared and embarrassed. I knew.

I was maybe seven, eight, and I knew. People looked funny when they heard we lived in a trailer, let alone stepped inside. I said, "Have you ever been in a trailer before?" and he said, "Oh sure, yeah, lots of times." The guy never came back. I asked Joanie what happened to the man with the Superman glasses. She made her hand into a jet and moved it towards the ceiling. "Whoosh," she said. "He flew away."

I knock on Fat Bill's door. The knock is barely audible. I can feel my fingers but all the cocaine has shaped my fist into something that resembles a fist but feels like a feather. If I try again, it could be a wrench. It could be a wrecking ball. I peek inside. A small window cuts through the top of the door and the window is partially covered by a cloth, like a checkered green napkin. I accidentally bump my head on the glass. It makes just the right sound.

I step back.

The door opens.

It's not Fat Bill.

It's Fat Bill's father. He wears khakis and a polo shirt and looks like he manages an office supply company. I thought he would have brown teeth and a gray beard and more hair on his chest and back than on his head. I'm terrible sometimes with the things I feel. I should stop. Fat Bill's father is maybe in his early fifties. He sips coffee from a mug, blowing it to cool, and he does not seem like the kind of father who would encourage his son to go to war. He seems like a man not rushing to go to work and unafraid to open his door to strangers.

He says, "Can I help you?"

I give him my name and say, "I had William in class last year at the community college, I teach there, and he contacted me recently, and I know he's going to the Middle East, and he wanted to see about getting together, and I have a class this morning, but it's late in the semester, and only two of the students showed up, they're over there in my truck, that's Megan and that's John Grisham, and we thought we'd come and see William, and maybe talk about books and writing and wish him the best before he ships out."

Fat Bill's dad looks past me and into my truck and says, "John Grisham, like the romance novelist?" and takes a loud sip of coffee.

"Same name, different genre," I say.

"Okay, come on in," he says. "Bill's sleeping. I'll get him up."

"I'll just be in the way," I say. "Just send him out when he's up."

"Okay," he says. "You sure?"

I say, "I don't want to be intrusive."

He says, "I knew Bill had a couple nice teachers down at the community college that he cared for. Thanks for stopping by."

"It's not a problem," I say.

He says, "I don't mean to pry or stir anything up but are you the one from the newspaper I read about? With the kid who, you know, offed himself?"

"I think so," I say.

He says, "You did a brave thing."

"Thanks," I say.

"This fucking world," he says, sipping his coffee.

"Parts of it," I say, taking my tiny jab at cynicism, defending hope.

The dad says, "Well, thanks again for coming by."

"I'm happy to be here," I say. "William is great."

Fat Bill's dad says, "He really is."

I wait for him to walk off to wake his son.

He keeps nodding.

I nod back and smile.

He says, "You look a little rough."

"It was a long night," I say.

"Nothing else?"

"Just a long night."

He says, "I trained to be a counselor but didn't have the money to finish the degree. So if you ever need to talk is all I'm saying."

"Thank you," I say. "I'm good."

"Long night?" he says.

"That's it."

"I've had a few of those," he says, and he stops to remember those nights and smiles as the memories come back. He says, "Good times when they're far away," and shakes his head and laughs. He turns to walk off.

The trailer looks nicer than my apartment but more cluttered. Framed photographs of family line the walls. Magazines are piled on a glass coffee table. The kitchen is part of the living room, the two rooms divided by a long counter and some cabinets. Newspapers are stacked on the floor by the kitchen garbage can and a recycling container filled with blue Pepsi cans. A neatly folded blanket rests on the arm of a checkered couch. A big screen TV quietly talks the news. Neatly lined throw pillows go across the couch from arm to arm. The colors and styles of the pillows do not match—checkers, plaid, peach.

Fat Bill's dad turns back and says, "You sure you don't want some coffee?"

"I'm good," I say. "Thanks. I had four cups this morning. One of my students brought me an expresso. It tasted terrible but worked."

"It's a good wake up," he says.

He walks towards me, not aggressive but not what I expected.

I start to step off the porch. The dad steps from the trailer into the world under the awning by the flowerpots on the ground that are filled with dirt and leaves but not yet flowers.

He says, "Thanks for coming. I know I said that already but I mean it sincerely." He's almost whispering. He says, "A lot of Bill's friends said they were going to stop by but not too many have. He's pretty scared. It's a nice thing, what the three of you are doing. The sweetness is appreciated. Bill is worried a lot, as you can imagine. I know he would have rather stayed in college and maybe done something else but this is what he decided to do. I encouraged him to get a trade, maybe work a job for a few years, then go back to school, but he said he wasn't good with his hands, and he's probably right. I asked him to fix a leaky shower and that was nine months ago. The shower still drips. It's like an old tick-tockey clock in there, keeping time with the drips."

"I couldn't go over there," I say, meaning the Middle East.

"Me neither," he says. "I'm an assistant manager of a tire store."

"I used to be a welder."

"I bet that's a whole other story, welder to professor."

"It sort of is."

"You sure you don't want some coffee?"

"I'm good," I say.

"Thanks for coming."

"It's a pleasure. William's a good guy."

"William," he says, and smiles. "I think you mean Bill."

DINERS

I refuse to eat at Denny's because the place smells like burnt coffee and the glasses are always cloudy from the dishwasher. The tears in the booths are covered with duct tape. The busboys all have acne. The waitresses look overworked and underpaid but kind. But needy. But exhausted. Unless I quit drinking and doing blow or get a better job or publish a book, I can't afford to tip them what they deserve, which is a couple hundred percent or more.

John Grisham says, "What about Eat N' Park?"

Megan says, "What about Ritter's Diner?"

"In Pittsburgh?" I say.

Fat Bill, riding shotgun, still wearing his pajamas and some hi-top sneakers, skinny and pimply-faced and looking like a kid, says, "I like Pittsburgh, over where Ritter's Diner is. What is that? Is that Bloomfield?"

Megan says, "I think it's sort of East Liberty, Shadyside, and Bloomfield all rolled into one. Maybe North Oakland too. It's an odd location."

"Odd location, terrible food," I say.

"Their food is fine for a twenty-four-hour shitstain," Megan says. "They even ruin eggs. Their bacon tastes like asphalt. And they charge for refills on drinks."

"That's to keep the hobos out," John Grisham says.

"I like hobos," I say.

"We all do," John Grisham says.

Fat Bill says, "Why'd you suggest it if you hate their food?"

"Not everything has to be great," Megan says.

Fat Bill says, "I'm not sure choosing a shitstain diner, as you called it, is the right choice. I think you only accept the suck when you have to."

"Spoken like a prophet," I say.

Megan says, "It's the nighttime talking. I'll never eat at Ritter's Diner again. That's my promise to everyone in this car. That place is the diarrhea of diners."

The whole truck lets out a collective gross.

Megan says, "I stand by it and my dad is a plumber."

Bill says, "That's a line I'll remember."

John Grisham says, "I lived in Detroit for like two days. They had hotdog places everywhere. Chili cheese dogs galore."

Bill says, "I love hotdogs."

Megan says, "I love a chili cheese dog."

She sits in the back, driver's side, sometimes reaching up to touch Bill or me to punctuate her points with affection.

John Grisham rides the hump.

He says, "Pittsburgh it is. We'll find somewhere to eat."

"Bill," I say. "Is it okay if I don't call you Fat Bill anymore?"

"You never really called me Fat Bill."

"I know."

"I'm pretty skinny now," he says, and looks down like his gut might reappear.

Megan reaches up from the backseat and touches Bill's shoulder and says, "You look great. Don't they feed you in basic training?"

"Oh, they give us food," Bill says. "Then they run it off us."

"Where'd you do basic?" John Grisham says.

I turn onto the Parkway and head towards Pittsburgh.

I would rather eat at Fat Head's than Ritter's Diner, than almost anywhere else in Pittsburgh, but Fat Head's doesn't open until eleven and I was just there with Joanie and after seeing a trailer and remembering what it was like to live in a trailer and now thinking about Joanie dating a veterinarian who is younger than me, I can't suggest anything, especially a delicious Cuban sandwich and some fancy beer.

Bill says, "I was at Camp Lejeune."

John Grisham says, "I was at Fort Bragg."

Megan says, "John Grisham, you were a Marine?"

"Army," Bill says. "Fort Brag is the Army. Lejeune is Marines. They made us crawl through the mud on our bellies like king snakes."

John Grisham says, "Are you one of those Marines who looks down on everyone? I don't mind if you are. Marines are tough motherfuckers."

Bill says, "I like everyone. Marines, Army, Navy, waitresses, community college professors, bartenders, the guy who built this car, every last person in America, and people around the world who don't shoot at me. I'd much rather be a waitress or a college professor or a bartender than a fucking Marine. I'm scared fucking shitless if you want to know the truth." Bill laughs uncomfortably to himself and looks out the window. He says, "If you hold a gun, you really start to understand that other people are holding guns too. Boot camp turned me into a fucking pacifist, that's what." Then, quietly, "Oorah."

"Can you not go to the Middle East?" I say, which I shouldn't say because the answer is obvious and probably feels like a taunt.

"Hell no," Bill says. "Not unless I go to jail. Jail would be worse than the desert. I think so at least. That's the odds I'm banking on. I'm scared to death to get fucked up the ass in the shower or whatever. Guys get knifed for their dick size and stuff." He pauses. "It don't matter. I'm okay with it now. I prayed about it, as much as a guy like me prays. God didn't answer me back or nothing, whatever, but I'm gonna go there and be bulletproof and not kill anyone and not drink the water and not fuck the women or worship Allah or nothing. I'm gonna dig a fucking foxhole to China and poke my head back out when my tour is over. I might fire a couple rounds in the air so it sounds like I give a shit about something other than coming home alive. I've thought this through. It's not figured out but I have ideas. I'm only firing or fighting if one of my pals is in trouble. That's it. They can chop my head off or whatever but I'm a good pal. I stand with my fellow grunts."

"You sound like a man with a plan," I say.

"Can I write you letters?" Megan says.

She leans forward and touches Bill's shoulder.

She always leans forward and touches Bill's shoulder.

If I could drive and kiss her hand on Bill's shoulder, I would.

"Letters would be great," Bill says.

"I mean, will they get there?" Megan says.

"I think so," Bill says. "From what I hear." He reaches up and touches Megan's hand. He turns his head and smiles and looks at Megan then he turns the other way to look at John Grisham. He says, "How long you in for, John Grisham?"

John Grisham says, "I was a soldier a lot longer than I've been a lawyer."

I say, "I didn't know you were a real lawyer, John Grisham."

John Grisham says, "These fancy suits don't pay for themselves."

DETOUR

Rush hour has started but the traffic is still fast and not clogged. People jump lanes without thought so taillights flash and blur. The sun is bright and burns through the windshield. Four bodies are not enough for my truck so passengers tend to slide and my air conditioning never works. I'm guessing it's nine o'clock. I turn the air conditioning on anyway. It smells like dust. Megan and John Grisham are too cold even though they are in the backseat and I have all the vents pointed at me. Cocaine heats me up, more than exercise. The radio sings. We all agree that radio is terrible.

Bill says, "You guys are pretty drunk. You sure you want to get breakfast?"

He says, "We could get a beer."

He says, "I don't really have anything to do today."

He says, "If you're going to get your ass shot off in the desert, you might as well have a couple beers with some friends."

He says, "Right?"

JACK'S BAR

Jack's Bar on the South Side opens at seven. It stays open until two in the morning. Fat Head's, still stuck in my mind with images of Joanie, is eighteen blocks away. No one is hungry for Fat Head's anyway. Jack's Bar is open every day of the year. I like that. Everyone in Pittsburgh, in the bar, at this tiny table in the backroom, likes that.

We are serious drinkers who love our city.

We embrace drink specials and the early hours.

Bill says, "You mind if we talk about books?"

"Sure," I say. "Whatever you want."

"Books and writing," he says. "No guns."

Megan and John Grisham play pool.

Neither one is very good.

Bill and I drink.

I feel a second buzz coming on, different than the buzz I've had all night, more like a runner's high. I said the blow was almost gone, meaning I have a little powder twisted into a balled-up napkin in my pocket. For emergencies. Because I need to be sharp. Because at some point I will have to drive us home.

A bottle sits in front of me.

Bill drinks from his own pitcher.

His pajamas do not look out of place here.

An old man in a ratty cardigan sweater and a blue bowtie sits at the bar and sips a shot. Lots of people with blurred eyes fill stools. Two frat guys, both handsome and bloated, stand by the jukebox. One is black, one is white. The sides of their heads are shaved. They both wear oversized polo shirts. They are not bad for frat guys. They neither shout nor punch nor paddle each other. Above the bar a row of beer bottles lines a long shelf with their labels facing out like a menu. Neon is everywhere, lots of it red. There are mirrors advertising beer and mirrors to see our reflections. The bartender is a woman, maybe thirty, looks forty, has wild hair, wears a tight red v-neck t-shirt so her tits stick out. She has a friendly smile and gets hit on by everyone every time I am in here because her energy is lovely and her bartending skills are impeccable.

Bill says, "Thanks," and raises his glass and pitcher and pours himself another.

"It's nothing," I say.

"Not this," he says. "Everything."

"I wish I could do something for you," I say.

"You are, trust me. Teaching, talking, all of it. It's nice to get out and have a beer. I've been staying up all night watching fucking *Star Wars* on DVD. I've been watching them since I was five years old. It's the same thing. I hate Luke Skywalker. I'd punch him right in his force-filled head. I love Princess Leah. She at least has a sense of humor. She knows she's going to be saved so the whole thing is a joke. The droids are unbearable. The fighter pilots are worse. When Chewbacca talks, I want to punch him in his furry face. At least Han Solo is the coolest guy ever. He's like a cowboy in space." Bill looks at me like my face is a map with a star on it and says, "You like *Star Wars*?"

I say, "How can you hate Luke Skywalker?"

"He's a pussy."

"He's a Jedi."

"He sees everything in black-and-white, good and bad."

"What? No."

"Yeah," he says. "Dude is a one-dimensional space cop."

I say, "I politely disagree. Luke is the only one who sees the good in Darth Vader. Everyone else thinks he's evil but Luke understands you can do evil your whole life and still come back and be decent. How can you call him a pussy?"

"He's got that feathered hair."

"The feathered hair doesn't help but he always walks into dangerous places alone and takes on whole armies. He killed Jabba the Hut and beat Darth Vader's ass. He's a tough guy who just happens to be sensitive and have feathered hair."

"Shit," Bill says, "you could be right," and finishes his pitcher. He wipes the beer slobber from his chin. He says, "I don't own any other movies on DVD and I hate watching movies on the internet. My computer is like nine hundred years old and the screen is so small and shitty. I'm probably just sick to death of Luke Skywalker and his whole galaxy."

"The world usually forces popcorn movies down our throats. It gets tiring. I should show more movies in class. Students love movies."

Megan sets down a full pitcher. She touches Bill on his shoulder and walks back to the bar with the empty pitcher then resumes her pool game with John Grisham.

Bill says, "Everyone buying me beers?"

"I hope so," I say.

"I appreciate it but I'm military rich. I still have part of my signing bonus and I'll get combat pay starting soon enough. If I stay alive, I'll be trailer rich too. Might buy me a used Kia or something. I can buy you guys a beer. I want to."

"I will graciously accept your offer," I say.

"Good," Bill says. "All my green friends are home somewhere else, Georgia or Ohio or wherever. Bunch of fucking privates, the bunch of us. All my high school friends are working. All my college friends are working and going to college. I hate being bored."

"Read," I say.

"I know," he says.

"Seriously," I say. "Read."

I say this because it's true.

I say this because I think he wants me to say it.

I say this because I am too old to be Bill's friend and I want to offer something sincere, something useful against desperation, an adult choice, reading.

He says, "I went to a bookstore the other day and I just can't find anything. It's either Nathaniel Hawthorne or some book with a pink fucking cover."

"Nathaniel Hawthorne is okay," I say, which is a lie. All Hawthorne's books are sin and guilt and symbols, little worlds that only hint at the real world, characters that are ideas and not real characters.

They made me read Hawthorne as an undergraduate.

At least they showed me what not to love.

Bill pours another from his pitcher. He's playing catch-up but he can't catch us unless one of us collapses and he keeps going for another twelve hours.

He says, "I think I had to read Nathaniel Hawthorne in high school."

"Not unless it was a smart high school," I say.

"Who wrote the story about the fire going out in the wilderness?"

"Jack London."

"Did you read that?"

"In high school," I say.

"Did you like it?"

"I loved it. I love Jack London. I had good high school teachers. They made Jack London sound like a rockstar. He was a tough guy and it appealed to my wrestler side."

Bill says, "Jack London was a tough guy?" like he doesn't believe me.

I say, "He grew up poor in Oakland, California. He was raised by a woman who was a former slave. He did his homework in a local bar. He supposedly beat up a bouncer who made fun of him for writing in a notebook. He went to Canada during the gold rush. He worked as a sailor. He was a genuine tough guy."

"Jack London?"

"Keep writing," I say. "Maybe you'll be the Jack London of your generation."

"He go to war?"

"I don't know. I don't think so."

Bill says, "I wish I had a better attention span. I spend too much time on my phone. I go to do something and I check my phone for a second and an hour later I'm still checking my phone. You have that problem?"

"No," I say. "I have a crap phone. I usually don't admit to having a phone."

The jukebox changes the song. I don't know this one, or the one it played before. The frat guys are making more selections. I would like to hear something with an acoustic guitar, though a horn could bowl me over if blown by the right mouth. I would like to hear a lyric that includes the word love and another one that includes the word heaven and a third one that makes references to some dirty bar in New York City or even Mississippi or possibly a song about tramping. Or fire in a can. People create songs so we can sing and be saved. The songs the frat guys play were written for money and only appeal to people who love jewelry and clubs and want to shout their own names. The world keeps flipping itself so wrong feels right, even though it should be impossible to fuck up music.

Lesson one: everything can be fucked up.

Why do I have to keep learning that?

Bill says, "There's this book at Barnes and Noble. It's right out front, first thing you see when you come in the store. It's called *Bright Lights, Big Ass.*" Bill drinks his whole beer then sets down his glass. He burps, hugely. He says, "*Bright Lights, Big Ass,*" and he makes like he's holding the words up on a marquee.

"I've seen that book," I say.

"Have you read it?"

"In high school."

"Really?" he says.

"No," I say. "I'm just fucking with you."

Bill says, "Thank God," and laughs. He says, "There was a subtitle. I wrote it down on a piece of paper but I left it at home. It was something like: *A Sorority Girl's Guide to Why Everyone Else Sucks.* Who the fuck would read that?"

I say, "The question to ask is: who the fuck would publish that?"

Bill says, "The whole fucking world is stupid as shit. I signed up for the Marines to get money to go to college so I can live in a world where people write shit. It doesn't make sense. Why do we like to eat so much shit? People are stupid. I know I'm stupid but I'm trying to read my way out of it. I want to be better."

"I have to piss," I say.

IS IT OKAY TO ASK?

Bill returns with a bottle for me and a pitcher for himself. He slides the bottle across the table and I grab it before it jumps over the edge.

He says, "I said I wasn't going to ask this but I have a buzz now and I feel like asking. Tell me if I shouldn't ask. Is it okay to ask?"

"Is it okay not to have an answer?

"Sure."

"Then you can ask," I say.

"What happened with that dude blowing his brains out in your class?"

"Pretty much that."

He says, "Yeah, just, you know, how did that go down?"

"Did you read it in the paper?" I say.

"I saw it on the news."

"It was pretty much like that."

Bill nods. He picks up his pitcher and, instead of filling his glass, puts it to his mouth and slowly takes a long and deliberate drink, careful not to spill any beer.

He says, "And you got everyone out?"

"After he was dead," I say.

Bill wipes his mouth on his sleeve.

He says, "That's hero shit."

"I was scared," I say, "and I didn't want everyone to be as scared as me."

Bill says, "I can see you don't want to talk about it. That's cool."

I say, "I would talk about it but I don't have anything to say."

Bill nods and goes back to his pitcher.

I nod and lift my bottle.

He asked because soon he will go to a place of dead bodies and possibly make it so.

I would talk about it but I don't have anything to say.

I would talk about it but I don't have anything to say.

WHEREFORE ART THOU, ANSWERING MACHINE?

In the bathroom, which is small but not a bad bathroom for a bar that opens at seven in the morning and never skips a day, I dial Berryman on my crappy cell phone.

With his endless curiosity and his desire to be around working-class folks, Berryman would do great in a place like Jack's Bar.

He'd listen.

He'd learn.

He'd fall in love.

He'd help Bill.

I lean in the stall, feeling good, buzzed and thoughtful, but also scared and empty.

Berryman's voicemail picks up.

"Berryman," I say. "I'm drunk and in Pittsburgh and with a former student who just finished his Marine basics and is shipping off for the Middle East soon. We could use your indomitable spirit here this morning. Can I count on you?"

I say, "I miss answering machines, Berryman."

I say, "I wish you could hear my voice."

MY FRIEND BERRYMAN

I walk out of the bathroom and see Fat Bill and Megan and John Grisham all together by the pool table, laughing, a group of cousins at a family reunion.

I turn and go back into the bathroom and wash my face in the sink.

I dial Berryman again and again and always get his voicemail.

"You're a good friend, Berryman," I say.

I say, "I don't think I tell you that enough."

I say, "I don't think I've ever told you that."

THE SPEED OF DYING

I think about death and the world accelerates at a rate I find hard to manage.

POOL TIME

I play pool with Megan while John Grisham and Fat Bill do shots at the bar. Megan destroys me at pool, which is not difficult, but she really does it with impunity. I sink one ball in two games. She drops bank shots twice and jumps a ball.

She says, "You're beautiful when you shoot but the balls don't go anywhere."

"Now you're just being lovely," I say.

Frat Boys Juking

John Grisham is back at the pool table with Megan. I sit with Fat Bill and he talks and I listen and he drinks me two or three beers to one. John Grisham brings us shots and Bill drinks both. Megan brings a pitcher. Bill finally appears drunk. A lot of the old men have disappeared or moved to the other room to avoid the sound of cracking pool balls. The music changes again, playing some pop song that sounds like a computer.

Fat Bill turns and looks at the jukebox, at the frat boys.

I turn and look at the frat boys. They are children. They have bad taste in music. Megan is not a child. John Grisham is not a child. Bill is a child. I think about what he says, about books, about stupidity, and I try to remember if I said something like that in class, if he is echoing me, if I attacked a crappy novel or the publishing world or any of it. I have. I do. I should stop. I should be more positive. My actions are a crane, my attitude a bulldozer. I'm building replicates when I mean to build individuals. The frat guys bounce around like they are dancing but without understanding the concept of dancing. Maybe they are trying to fall but don't understand the concept of falling either. Megan looks happy with John Grisham. John Grisham looks white and pasty, like he could roll himself into a loaf of bread but won't because he finally has new friends. The pool balls smack with the authority of skulls banging into skulls. The jukebox plays a rap song, not hardcore but poppy butterfly. I can feel the bass in my forehead, the yeah uh yeah.

Bill says, "What's the purpose of writing if people don't read books?"

"Writing is a spiritual pursuit," I say. "It doesn't matter what gets published."

"Do you believe that?" Bill says.

"No," I say.

"Yes," I say.

I say, "I don't know. Maybe. It sounded good when I just said it. I use the word spiritual a lot, usually to justify things I love that don't end up being monetized. I hate wastefulness. Saying something is spiritual means whatever has not been wasted. I've been drinking since early last night and haven't slept in over a day."

Bill says, "You maintain pretty well."

I say, "Thanks."

He says, "If it doesn't matter what gets published, how can it be a spiritual pursuit? It can't be. Those are like oxymoron things."

"What do you mean?"

The bartender comes around the bar. She picks up Bill's pitcher and shot glasses and my empty bottle. We all nod and smile. Bill could use her touch. Touch is essential, more than medicine. That's science. I read it in a medical journal. Maybe the bartender read the same medical journal. Maybe she will notice Bill's need for touch. She is a great bartender. I have seen her helping drunks out the door when it would have been easier to call the cops.

Bill says, "If they publish shit, and all there is to read is shit, then how can it be a spiritual pursuit? You can't read shit and find it spiritual." He says, "Can you?"

I say, "I think you're on to something."

I'm thinking I should finish off the cocaine soon. My attention wanes by the second, by the minute, by the drink. Bill deserves more attention. I would like to talk to him about books but I talk about books all day and now I don't want to talk about books anymore. I want to write books. I want to read books. James Wright, a beautiful Ohio poet, said, "I have wasted my life." I feel that every day but I never say it outloud. Then I feel the opposite, which is what James Wright meant when he said he wasted his life. The bartender brings a bottle and a pitcher. She touches Bill. I knew she would. She puts her hand on his shoulder and asks if we need anything else. We don't. I smile and look down. The floors are clean. I can see where the mop left streaks. She rubs Bill's shoulder for a second and walks away.

Bill says, "Why don't you write a book?"

"I'm trying," I say.

"Didn't you write cowboy books? The community college president said that. She really likes you. My grandpa reads cowboy books. My dad reads self-helpy shit."

"Cowboy books don't count."

Bill shrugs and says, "They should."

It is no good to be a writing teacher and not have a real book. It's embarrassing. It should be illegal and yet there are thousands of us out here, teaching writing, and writing, not ever getting a book deal, some of us not writing at all, just teaching the same books we were taught, happy to be paid and have benefits. Maybe the colleges where we teach should publish our books. Maybe someone somewhere should believe what they say.

One of the frat guys stumbles back. The other one shoves him. They push each other a couple times and laugh. They are louder now. They are not so handsome. They have on the same jeans, clean and blue. One has on a large ring and I am sure he wears it so his punches are backed by something solid.

Bill says, "I really liked your classes. They were the only college classes I ever really liked. I liked my history classes too. And I had a cooking class that was great. We ate cookies a lot. But your classes were the best."

"Thanks," I say.

He says, "I had other teachers I liked but I didn't care about their classes. You take chances. You really let the students talk. No one does that."

"I appreciate that," I say.

"I can't tell you the impression you made on me, you and the books you taught. A lot of people didn't get it but I really did."

"I'm glad," I say.

"Do you like rap music?" he says.

"Not much," I say.

"No?" he says. "Then I'm going to kick the shit out of those two frat faggots," and he stands up and, as I reach for his arm, he shrugs me off.

PART TWENTY-THREE

Bill's Nose

"**Jesus,**" **Bill says,** "that's a lot of books."

I stand outside, the door open.

Bill stands inside my apartment. His voice is nasal, a handkerchief jammed up his nose which makes a honking sound. The rag is starting to shine through with blood. Everything Bill sticks up his nose to stop the bleeding turns crimson and needs to be replaced. He looks around. There are maybe seven hundred books on three large shelves, more in my bedroom, some stacked in closets.

Bill says, "Did you read all of these?"

"I think so," I say. "Except for *Journey to the End of the Night* by Celine. He doesn't use periods. He uses ellipsis. Drove me nuts. I think I read about half the book. But I tell people I've read it so they think I'm smart."

"I don't know who that is."

"He's French."

My key is stuck in the front door. It's an old front door and the handle is tarnished with rust. I give it a jiggle. I lift and twist.

Bill says, "This is like a bookstore without the pink books."

"Look out for the Hawthorne," I say.

Bill turns to me. The white in his left eye is all red but the other eye is blue and shiny. He takes the bloody handkerchief from his nose.

Outside, a motorcycle roars.

Motorcycles often roar in Wall, my town.

The bar up the hill hosts biker nights where beer and spaghetti are cheap.

Bill says, "Do you have anywhere I can throw up?"

"The bathroom," I say, and point and my key falls from the lock.

Bill bolts, thundering across the room with his hand over his mouth.

I step inside and close the front door.

Bill wretches like he is trying to scare small animals.

I've quit looking at the sun and gone back to the clocks. It's almost noon. My stomach is sick from drink and drugs. I have to eat soon or I'll turn in on myself. I hate coming down from anything but cocaine most of all. I imagined I'd been catching a second buzz but those last beers felt like broken glass. They were cold but they cut me up inside, my stomach rawer with every swallow. I hear Bill in the bathroom. Pause, gag, wretch. I hope his nose is not exploding while he throws up in my toilet. What a good, stupid kid.

We dropped John Grisham and Megan back off in Greensburg.

Megan drove home to sleep it off or to walk around in her bathrobe and drink orange juice until she can close her eyes. I am supposed to meet her later this afternoon so we can have dinner or watch a movie or come back here and kiss or more than kiss. When I close my eyes, I see her, and I can feel her through everything that has happened and everything that is going to happen for a long time to come. I believe this like no other thing.

John Grisham needed to meet with a client. He was a sweaty mess but coherent, happy to buy us all beers at the last bar we visited, a dive which kicked us out when we asked for a bag of ice because Bill's nose started to gush on the floor.

FLASHBACK TO THE BRAWL

Back at Jack's Bar, the frat guys had not wanted to fight. They wanted to apologize. They wanted to admit their drunkenness. They wanted to confess their lack of taste in music. They said, "We didn't know you guys didn't like rap, honestly." They said, "We're just having fun." They said, "It's cool, seriously, no problems here." But Bill was pissed and tired and already a soldier, but also a pacifist, so he pushed but did not punch one dude, then the other, then the first one again. Shove, shove, shove again. He acted in the horrible fight-no-fight mode that young people arrive at sometimes when they are angry but still scared, when they will risk fighting to make other people back down, even though they never really wanted to fight, even though fighting might not be within their skill set. It gets stupid quick when everyone is loud and afraid and young. Bill threw out another round of tough-guy pushes and said, "Is that so?" and the frat guys said, "We don't want to fight," but Bill sort of did but not really.

The bouncer, unfortunately, wanted to fight, no joking around.

He said, "Fucking enough," and waddled over from the door in the front room, wearing a tight John Cena WWE t-shirt. His arms were Easter hams. He pointed and repeated himself, saying, "Fucking enough, you mouthers with your fucking mouths."

The t-shirt said: hustle, loyalty, respect.

Those are all fine qualities, I thought, especially hustle, which is often underrated.

I turned from the bouncer, who stood six feet tall and five feet wide, and looked for the bartender who usually worked her sober and rational magic over these moments to calm down drunks and save them from arrest but she'd disappeared to the bathroom or to get another case or to change a keg or to find a clean rag, the practical needs of her job replacing the spiritual component she so excels at.

There it is again, spiritual.

The bouncer said, "I don't want any more tough guy shit."

No one noticed the bouncer but me.

Megan said, "Calm down, everyone," but she clutched her pool stick and stood in line with the frat guys, probably planning on swinging at their heads like cue balls.

John Grisham, looking scared, said, "Guys…" but stopped before he could figure out what else he wanted to say.

I touched Bill's shoulder and said, "Maybe we could just get some breakfast."

Bill ignored my thoughtful suggestion.

The frat guys, maybe seeing the bouncer and feeling protected or maybe tired of Bill, moved forward in a tandem strut and said, "Back off, man, we didn't do shit."

Bill pushed the white guy in the chest, hard.

He lost his balance and stumbled back.

The other frat guy caught his pal.

Then the bouncer stepped up and popped Bill.

It was some kind of special punch, a punch they teach in bouncer school, fast and hard but not too hard, a punch meant to sit you down but not knock you out.

Megan said, "Ouch," and cringed but did not raise her pool cue.

Bill fell to one knee and started to bleed and said, "Shit, I'm bleeding."

I should have punched the bouncer out of loyalty or respect for Bill's military service but John Grisham already stood between us, saying, "We'll leave, we'll leave, not a problem, we're leaving," and I couldn't have hit anyone anyway.

I am both a coward and a natural peacemaker.

People assume I am a tough guy because of my wrestling past but I've never been in a fight. To be as strong and fast as I could be on the mat, I always needed the referee, an older person in a striped shirt with a whistle, to make sure wrestling stayed a sport and never became a brawl. I was always scared of brawls.

I still am.

The bouncer said, "We done here?"

The frat guys backed out the side door, fast, without complaint, hands up in surrender or as a request not to be hit. The bouncer stood there, chest out, gut in, fists still clenched. Megan still clutched her pool cue. I looked at her and shook my head: please don't. John Grisham gathered us up. His olive green suit looked magnificent despite the wrinkles. He helped Bill stand. Bill bled a little then got his legs. He straightened up then bled a lot.

Megan said, "Does he need a doctor?"

The bouncer looked at Bill's nose and said, "You okay, kid?"

Bill said, "I'm fine," but muffled from his hand and the blood.

The bouncer said, "I just wanted to clip you a little and settle you down." He said, "Sorry I called you a mouther. We all get mouthy sometimes."

Bill said, "My teacher was on the news for saving people."

The bouncer looked befuddled.

I said, "He's fine. We're leaving."

John Grisham said, "No problems here. We're all good people."

The bartender, who was still beautiful, emerged with a case and a bottle resting on top to re-stock her station and she stepped behind the bar and said, "I leave for three fucking minutes."

The bouncer said, "I misjudged the punch."

The bartender said, "You think?"

Megan looked at the bartender then at the bouncer and said, "It was a cheapshot."

The bouncer said, "What? Bullshit," but like sad and embarrassed.

The bartender said, "Honey, cheapshots are his job."

John Grisham said, "We're leaving right now."

The bartender said, "You seem like nice people. Can I suggest you guys leave the city, just in case those frat guys call the cops? I don't trust frat guys. Those ones were from Duquesne. Catholic frat guys are the worst."

John Grisham pulled out a wad of money and paid our tab.

He was very generous and I felt inspired.

I threw a twenty on the pile to make sure everyone understood that we appreciated the service and did not need to be arrested.

The bartender said, "Take care of him."

"I will," I said, and meant it.

We walked out of the bar and drove east, straight on to Electric Avenue, then walked into the Hollywood Show Bar and drank a few more drafts until Bill's nose started to gush again and he dripped blood in his mug of beer then the floor and the bartender said, "I can't have this."

FLUSH

Now the toilet flushes and Bill, shirtless, steps from the bathroom with my one clean hand towel, my only hand towel, period, on his nose. Blood drips down his chest. His pajamas are filthy with beer and blood and dirt from the barroom floor.

He says, "My nose is an eggplant."

"I think we should go to the hospital," I say.

"You're probably right," he says.

He takes down the towel and it looks worse, some unknown vegetable that grows from seeds of pain and misunderstanding.

BILL'S NOSE

He says, "An eggplant right?"

I say, "Sort of."

It's more of a tool that a congested alcoholic might purchase then apply to his face then drop one night in the middle of a bender then never be able to get back in the right place, a purple and crooked mess that's not very useful for what it was meant to be used for: breathing.

PTSD

Bill and I sit in my truck, waiting for it to cool off, which it never does. I recline and tell Bill I need a minute, two minutes, three minutes tops. I close my eyes and a summer breeze blows from the vents but dusty and gross.

Bill says, "We should put the windows down."

"That sounds good," I say, and I move my hand and my fingers but nothing else and touch the buttons for the power windows.

Bill says, "I think you may have PTSD. They talked to us a little bit about it during basics. You don't have to be in war to get PTSD."

"Thanks," I say, "but I don't."

"You'd need a psychologist or a psychiatrist, one of those, some kind of shrink, to diagnose you. You can't diagnose yourself. It has to be a medical person."

I say, "I looked it up in the DMS."

"What's the DMS?"

"It's a big book of mental disorders that doctors and shrinks use. I don't fit any of the criteria for PTSD. I'm clear."

Bill says, "Maybe you're depressed."

"Not even close."

"You saw a student blow his brains out. You have to have something."

"I didn't see a student blow his brains out. I heard it. Then I saw the hole and the blood."

"That sounds like war."

I say, "It sounds like college."

He says, "What if you have PTSD and don't even know it?"

"I'm tired," I say. "Not everything has to be a medical diagnosis."

Bill takes the hand towel from his nose and sets it in his lap so the blood slowly trickles down like a leaky garden hose into the grass of his chin and neck and shirt.

"Well," Bill says. "I'm scared I'm gonna get PTSD. I'm scared I'm gonna get it and I'm gonna tell someone and they're gonna say: nope, you're fine. They're gonna tell me I'm fine and put me back in the same spot that gave me PTSD. I'm gonna see horrible shit and not know what to do with it. My dad wanted to be a shrink when he was young. He knows some stuff. He used to watch the news and talk about PTSD then he quit talking about PTSD once I signed up for the Marines. He quit watching the news too."

I un-recline my chair and open my eyes.

Bill says, "I'm not crying."

I say, "Let's fix this nose then go from there."

He says, "I'm too fucking sensitive to be a Marine. I can't kill anyone."

"I know," I say. "I just need to clear my head," and I pop my truck in gear and pull onto the backroad that leads to the front road that leads to the main road.

McDonalds

Bill insists on going to the Veteran's Hospital in Oakland, back in Pittsburgh. I tell him he can go anywhere but I don't know what I'm talking about and he insists he can only get care at the VA up on Cardiac Hill. He's the Marine so I do what he says.

I turn my truck and steer that way.

Bill says, "Remember when you mentioned breakfast, right before the bouncer re-arranged my face?"

I say, "I do."

He says, "Could we get some grub?"

I nod and say, "Sure."

Grub sounds great, a saving miracle.

I'd do anything to stop my insides from chewing their way out.

Bill says, "Somewhere cheap, if that's okay."

I drive through McDonalds and get the fish sandwich. Bill gets a large Coke and a large order of fries. The smell of grease fills the cab of my truck. Bill offers to pay but I won't take his money. Fry by fry, he feeds himself under the towel while keeping pressure on his nose. I think about calling off class but maybe I can make it back and stay awake. I hope I do not need more cocaine. I do not have any more cocaine.

I could probably get more cocaine.

Rig is somewhere.

I would not ask Rig.

Where is Berryman?

He never called me back.

And I may have told him I love him.

And I probably do.

We sit at a stoplight. I can hear Bill's breathing. The breathing is jagged, like Bill is drinking air through his nose and the air is too thick to swallow. The stoplight turns green. I tell Bill I am sorry. I tell him I should know better.

Bill says, "I should be apologizing to you."

Bill says, "You have a job."

He says, "I could have gotten you arrested."

He says, "I'm really not crying," and continues to cry.

He hands me his box of fries, which are a little bloody, then he rolls down his window and tries to get some air, a shaggy dog in the wind.

He says, "Thank you."

He says, "This is the best day of my life."

THE DOCTORS

I pull up to the Veteran's hospital and pull inside the parking garage, a six-story concrete behemoth. A security guard in the booth sees the bloody towel covering Bill's nose and waves us through. I park in a handicapped spot by the first-floor doors and hope no one gives me a ticket. I should write a note and toss it on my dashboard but I don't. I should have showered away the smoke and booze and drugs but I didn't.

Bill says, "I heard this place used to be a shithole back in the seventies but it's really nice now. I got my face medicine here for free. I get really zitty if I don't use a special soap and medicine. The pharmacists are all really nice."

I put my hand on Bill's shoulder.

We pass by the elevators and through a huge revolving door and into the lobby, a hall-sized room filled with comfy chairs and mostly old but some younger veterans waiting around. They wear jeans and all kinds of shirts—sports teams and camo and button-up and emblems and mascots naming their hometowns—and lots of them wear ballcaps naming the branch they served. An inordinate number of ears are filled with hearing aids. A guy my age or younger walks by on crutches, one leg gone below the knee but no prosthetic. The president's photo is on the wall, framed but tilted like it's been bumped and straightened so many times it can no longer hang the way framed photos should hang. The lighting is bright but not obnoxious. A janitor walks by with a mop and bucket. An unexpected grand piano sits off in an open space, a man in a suit playing some boogie woogie and having fun.

Bill says, "They have a pool table in Heroes Hall," and motions towards a waiting room that is filled with comfy chairs and TVs and men having a good time playing pool.

"That's pretty sweet," I say, "but I think pool got us into this," and I touch Bill on the back so he knows I'm joking.

The sign-in desk sits like a huge hockey puck in the middle of the lobby. A man and woman, both on rolling chairs, move from computer to computer, signing people in. We stand in a short line until it's our turn.

Bill says, "Hi," and waves.

"Oh sweetie," the woman receptionist says.

"You get clipped?" the man receptionist says.

They are both in their fifties, black, dressed in professional clothes.

Bill says, "I think I fell."

She smiles and says, "Okay, okay. Bumped your nose?"

"Yes," Bill says. "I think I bumped my nose," and he laughs a little, despite the towel, despite the blood and the way his left eye is almost shut from the swelling.

East Pittsburgh Downlow

The guy receptionist moves to another veteran, an old guy in a Vietnam baseball hat, who holds himself upright with a cane.

The woman receptionist says, "Are you his dad?"

I say, "Just his friend."

Bill says, "He's my writing professor."

The woman receptionist says, "A writing professor? Isn't that interesting."

I shrug and say, "We think his nose is broken."

She says, "Can he breathe through it?"

Bill takes the towel down and nothing gushes.

He sniffs some air but gently.

He says, "I think I can breathe, maybe a little through my left nostril."

The woman receptionist says, "That a good sign." She says, "Are you active duty?" She says, "Do you have your insurance card?"

Bill says, "I don't. I probably do somewhere but I don't have it with me."

She says, "Okay, how about last four."

Bill says, "Okay," and gives her his last initial and what I think are the last four digits of his social security number.

She types this into the computer and says, "There you are." She prints a couple forms and puts them on a clipboard and hands it to Bill with a pen. She says, "Have a seat and just look this over. Make sure your address is correct and your medical allergies sound right. We don't want to give you the wrong medicine."

Bill says, "Thank you," and takes the clipboard.

We move to a seating area.

Bill says, "They're nice here."

"They are," I say.

Bill reads the forms, squinting with his one good eye.

I say, "Do you want me to read that for you?"

"I've got it," he says.

I lean back in the waiting-area chair and kick out my legs and stretch and let go of some sort of elongated yawn sound. How I would love to be on a track somewhere, running, sweating, punishing myself to clean up, finding the perfect pace. I crack my knuckles all at once then again, individually. If I don't get some orange juice soon, my feet and legs will cramp. I need a banana. I need a bunch of bananas, anything with potassium. My eyes are dry as paper towels, probably red as lava. Little tanks roll around the inside of my forehead, making tracks, adding to the overall throb. I un-stretch and sit up straight. At least my stomach feels better from the fish sandwich. McDonalds is evil and they pay their hourly workers an awful wage and they poison children with fake grease and artificial sweeteners but nothing soothes an aching stomach like a Fillet O' Fish and its flaky goodness. The yawn sound comes out of me again.

I am so thirsty, I can't spit.

Bill says, "You getting sleepy?"

"Is there a cafeteria where I could get something to drink?" I say. "Are you thirsty? Do you want an iced tea or a Coke?"

The woman receptionist hears me and says, "There's a pop machine right outside the door." She points and the flab underneath her arm jiggles. She's the shape of a large truck tire but very pretty. She says, "Do you need change? I have change," and she smiles.

What perfectly straight white teeth.

My teeth are the teeth of a man who grew up without dental insurance.

How clean and pressed her uniform is and her necklace has a cross dangling down into a hint of cleavage. I am jealous of it all, her professionalism and beauty.

Bill looks like he fell off a bullet train and bounced.

My head is a dying sun.

Sergei Kuzmich wrote that about working on a farm in Russia.

It feels worth stealing.

Bill says, "Go home. I've been enough trouble."

"I'm not going home," I say.

"Seriously," Bill says. It is not easy for him to talk. Maybe his tongue is as messed up as his nose or his mouth is as dry as mine. He says, "You've done too much. I feel guilty. Go home. You're the only person who came to visit me since I been home from basics. You're the best."

"I don't have to work until tonight," I say. "I can stay a couple hours."

The secretary says, "Are you family?"

"Not really," I say. "I'm his teacher."

"That's right. You said that," she says. "What subject?"

"Writing," I say.

"Oh, you said that too," she says. "I'm sorry. It's been so busy here all morning and into the afternoon. I was always good in English."

Bill says, "You should definitely go home."

"Spell definitely," I say.

The lady receptionist says, "I'll spell it," and she does. Then she says, "You should d-e-f-i-n-i-t-e-l-y go home. We'll take care of your student and make sure he gets healed. We have a shuttle that runs to Greensburg. It will take him directly to his house, no worries."

Bill says, "He's a great professor."

I say, "Thank you."

The secretary says, "I can see that," and smiles.

Bill says, "He was a hero too. He was in the newspaper."

The secretary, not biting, says, "I believe it."

Bill says, "He's great."

She smiles at me and says, "Okay, great professor hero, it's time for you to leave so we can help your student and our soldier and get him back in shape."

PART TWENTY-FOUR

Who's in My Kitchen

I took Tylenol PM and ate a bowl of cereal and drank some juice and now I am on my bed, naked, except for a light purple blanket I bought at Walmart covering my ass and thighs. The fan blows across the room, swirling warm air. I open my eyes. I wish my apartment had air conditioning so I wouldn't turn it on and know I was saving money. The overhead light is off but the room glows with the late afternoon sun. The numbers on my alarm clock flash red. I tripped over the cord on my way to bed and was too tired to set the time after I plugged it back in.

I'm guessing it's four o'clock.

Someone rattles around in my kitchen, opening cabinets, clanking dishes.

I'm guessing it's Bill.

I'm guessing he couldn't go home to his father with a mashed-up face and asked the VA shuttle to drop him here and my door was open because my door is usually open.

I roll from bed and find my boxer shorts. I stand stupid in my bedroom. My brain freezes, unfreezes. I am in pain. The pain starts at the top of my head and goes into my toes then back up the other side and into my brain. This is the kind of pain that requires more pain, the kind of pain that requires punishment. I find some shorts and running shoes and a shirt. Seven miles, I think, maybe eight. Bill can sleep on my couch and breathe through his mouth. He can live here. I may turn my apartment into a dormitory for damaged students, past and present.

I step into the living room.

Nary a Bill in sight.

"Hey Mom," I say.

"Joanie," she says. "Knock it off with the Mom shit."

I sit down on the couch. Everything is on but my shoes. My shoes sit in my lap like a puppy. I hold them like they matter. I'm going to need to brush my teeth.

"What are you doing here, Joanie?" I say.

"You look a mess," she says.

"Thanks," I say. "You look lovely."

Joanie says, "I thought you were dead in there. I thought you weren't breathing and then you started to snore like a rhinoceros."

"It was a rough night," I say.

She says, "It sounds like it, rhino."

Joanie eats a bowl of Lucky Charms but without milk. She uses a spoon. This seems a long and tedious process and it adds to the dryness in my throat. She is here to check on me because somehow she learned about the suicide, either through cultural osmosis or she stumbled on a news story in a waiting room, and now she is another person I don't want to talk to because I am not in need of talk though, in her defense, she probably has no desire to discuss death when she can barely stand the thought of growing old.

I say, "Yeah, but what are you doing here?"

"I came to see you," she says, and crunches.

"Come on."

"One of your students popped his head off in class. That's horrible. It's as horrible as this horrible world gets and the world gets awfully fucking horrible. All the time, lately. No one loves each other anymore, even in a friendly way. But we can discuss that later. You're sensitive. You're very very very sensitive. And you're my beautiful son. It's my duty as your only parent to stop in. Besides, I stop in for lots of reasons."

I start to speak and she stops me.

She says, "I know you're fine and don't want to talk about it. Look at me, I'm not exactly a fucking counselor. This will pass and all that so just let it go and don't be whiny. No one likes whiny. The whole fucking world appears to be hypocrites because that's all they do, act like whiny twats, but whatever. I stopped by. I'm here. I love you. Get over it."

"Okay," I say, "but speak quiet."

The cereal box sits on the counter. A can of diet Coke sits there too. A sponge and some cleanser, usually underneath my sink, are out. I think Joanie was scrubbing my counter and sink, which doesn't make sense because she never scrubs her own. She pays a maid—some twenty-five-year-old meth-ed out white chick with cornstalk hair and a minivan that says: Maids Are Cheap—to clean her apartment.

Joanie says, "You didn't throw up blood, did you?"

"Of course not," I say. "I didn't throw up anything."

"There was blood in your sink."

"That was my student."

"You're beating up your students?"

She puts down her cereal bowl and spoon. She puts the box back in the cabinet. Her hair is different, a slight color change, maybe a different length. Men do this to her. They take her on dates and she morphs into different versions of herself. It is either to please or alienate them, I don't know which. I'm not sure she knows which. Though this time she bought a poodle then tweezed her eyebrows into an arch. Now she has bangs which fall into her eyes and are jagged as chipped ice. She looks weird. She usually looks great. Time slaps all our faces. Fashion does worse.

I say, "I am not beating up my students."

She says, "Of course not."

She gets out the cereal and pours another bowl.

I say, "Do you have bangs?"

She touches her hair and says, "Do they look stupid?"

"They look good."

"Eyebrows?"

"Look great."

My kitchen cabinets, which are not real wood, which are the cheapest fake wood you can buy, are covered in photos I've cut from magazines, mostly writers and musicians and actors who never picked up a gun in a movie. I used to tape everything but the tape didn't stick so I bought a can of spray varnish and now everything stays in place and shines. When I move out the landlord will keep my security deposit.

"I need to run," I say.

I lift my shoes from my lap.

"You need to sleep," she says.

"One of my former students is going to the Middle East."

"Army or Marines?"

"Marines," I say. "That's his blood in the sink."

"Does he want to go?"

"No," I say. "He wants to stay."

"Write him letters," she says.

"I will. He's in the VA Hospital. We were at a bar last night, this morning I guess, and he got angry and tried to beat up some frat guys."

Joanie thinks about this. She chews some cereal. She points with her spoon and starts to say something and stops. She puts down her spoon and finds a marshmallow with her fingers.

She says, "Have you thought of not going to bars with your students?"

I say, "Have you thought of not dating veterinarians?"

"Yes," she says, and raises her spoon to acknowledge my point. "I have been considering lots of things and first among them is not dating veterinarians. I'll run with you if you want to run. I need the exercise."

"You don't have any clothes."

"I have stuff in my car."

"Why aren't you at work?" I say.

"Do you know what time it is?" she says.

I say, "There's Tylenol in that cabinet. Can you get me some? And a glass of Gatorade from the fridge. I would greatly appreciate if I didn't have to move for at least another couple minutes. I am genuinely a mess." I hear that and say, "From last night, not from anything else."

She says, "Take aspirin. Tylenol is bad on your liver if you've been drinking."

Joanie opens the cabinet. She moves some things around and finds an old bottle of Bayer aspirin, the brown and yellow label fading. She opens another cabinet and gets a glass. My head has grown an inch or so inward and it's squeezing my thoughts so they feel strangled. I need to call the secretary at the community college and cancel or I need to be prepared to teach my night class in running shorts, covered in sweat, my dirty sneaks hot on my feet and my skin stinking like booze. I think this can be forgiven. People have been generous lately.

Joanie fills the glass with orange Gatorade. I like the red better but I drink the orange sometimes so I won't get sick of the red.

I wish I had a big Mountain Dew with crushed ice.

The world would be better if I bathed in Mountain Dew.

Joanie looks at my kitchen cabinets, all the faces and bodies of people I have read and listened to and watched and loved, and she says, "That's kinda high school for a grown man."

"I don't know," I say. "It feels right."

"Who's this ugly guy?"

"Isaac Babel."

"How'd he get so ugly?"

"He grew up with gangsters in Russia."

"He looks like a wimp."

"He was brilliant," I say.

"Who's this black guy?"

"Etheridge Knight. He's a poet."

"Who's this black lady?"

"Sonya Sanchez. She's a poet. She was married to Etheridge Knight."

"You like black people and Russians," she says.

"I like all people," I say. "That's the point."

She points again but more like a touch and doesn't ask.

It's a picture of Howling Wolf, the greatest blues singer who ever lived, but there's Townes Van Zandt too, a white guy from Texas, the third greatest songwriter who ever lived, and one of Yuri Nagibin, a Russian short story writer. Above the sink is a black and white photo of a poet I always teach, Gerald Locklin, who the students love, also a white guy, and in the photo he sits in the bathtub with a can of beer and a rubber ducky. It goes on. There's Nicanor Parra from Chile. There's Mohammed Mrabet from Morocco. There's Tennessee Williams, white and gay and southern, drunk. There's Mohamed Choukri, a Moroccan who loved Tennessee Williams. There's Billie Holiday, an orchid in her hair. I like to look at my kitchen cabinets. I like to imagine my face up there, meaning someone else's kitchen cabinets, or on something somewhere, being admired by someone for what I've written.

"I knew you were smart, growing up," Joanie says, "but I had absolutely no idea you were so weird and artsy. I thought you'd outgrow books."

"I love writers," I say.

"Both are good," Joanie says.

"Both what?" I say.

"Blacks and Russians," she says, and walks to me with her hands full. "I can do a mile, maybe a mile and a half at the most, then I'll have to walk the rest."

"That's fine," I say, and take the aspirin with the orange Gatorade.

RUNNING

Joanie is in better shape than before. I'm not sure how this is possible because I cannot imagine her running on her own, even with a fitness-minded young boyfriend who loves poodles. I do a slow first lap and she keeps up. She has on black yoga pants and a gray sweatshirt, not her usual hot pink Nike sportswear, and she looks like she cares more about her lungs and heart than meeting hot men.

I love my mom.

I hope I've been clear on that point, one of the few facts of my existence: I love my mom.

I am eternally grateful that she raised me, that she refused my desire to retreat and sit quietly and weep at the world. She is wild as the weather but less predictable, her flaws are her strengths even if I need to remind myself of that sometimes, and she is constant as gravity. I feel her inside me, same as my heart.

She says, "Pretty good for an old broad, huh?"

"Pretty good," I say.

I want to outrun her but I don't, not yet, I keep coasting.

The sun still hangs in the sky but barely. I could throw up on the side of the track if I thought about it and maybe will but not long enough to break my pace. Puke and go. The walkers take the outside lanes. Most of the walkers are old women and fat middle-aged men. They would be sad to see me barf.

I'd like to be a fat middle-aged man.

I'd like to be that slow and powerful.

Joanie says, "How's work?" while puffing for air.

"Okay," I say. "I got caught up on my papers."

"How's writing?" she says.

We start the second lap.

I up-shift to second gear.

Joanie keeps pace.

She says, "You're still done writing the cowboy books?"

"Pretty much," I say.

"Writing poems?" she says.

"No," I say.

"No one reads poems," she says.

"Berryman does."

"Berryman sounds like a wimp."

"He's a good guy," I say.

"Please don't become a poet," Joanie says, fully huffing now.

I upstep but only slightly.

I am not becoming a poet.

I am working on a novel because I am always working on a novel, because America is filled with people who have full-time jobs that diminish them and literature is not filled with those people. The novels I work on are filled with those people.

Joanie says, "Write a scary book."

I say, "No."

Joanie doesn't read, not really, just my western novels and the occasional romance novel or an Elmore Leonard novel that's already been turned into a film. She started that *Fifty Shades* book about the woman who likes to get tied up or spanked or whatever but never finished it because the movie came out and got bad reviews.

But Joanie is happy that I write.

She believes in me like fierce mothers should and do, like she did when I wrestled, when I attended college, when I became a welder. When I was growing up, she used to buy me books and give me gift cards to bookstores when she made extra money, even though she only read magazines in the bathtub and resented that Nona believed in books and West Virginia, like those two things were incompatible, words and mountains. When I wrote a book, meaning a western, she would make everyone she knew buy a copy.

Joanie says, "What kind of book are you writing?"

I say, "A book where all the characters have jobs."

"That sounds hard. Just kill a bunch of the characters. That's easier."

"Nona says I should write a book about the family."

"How is my mom?"

Nona is always good.

Joanie knows this.

I need to read the book that my great-great uncle wrote or Nona will be sad. She will say I'm just like my mom, her ultimate insult. I don't know why my great uncle's book fills me with dread. Maybe his story will confuse mine.

I like to be the teller of my story.

The rest of the world is often forfeiture.

"Nona's Nona," I say. "She always lovely. How'd you get in such good shape?"

I could say more about Nona but my mom wouldn't listen.

Joanie says, "I joined a gym. I've been on the elliptical."

"That's a big word," I say.

"Yes," she says. "My ass was getting so elliptical it was starting to block out the sun. I needed to bring it back down to size. Running around this track is better than the elliptical. That skiing in place gets so f'ing boring. I wish I was good enough to run trails. I love those commercials where women book it up mountains. Do you know what fascia is?"

"No," I say. "Is that like cancer?"

"No," she says. "It's ass fat. Women think it can't be broken down but it can. I'll explain it later. I need to focus on my breathing."

"Ass fat?" I say.

"Ass fat," she says, starting to gasp.

I can run six miles and make my class on time with a few minutes to towel off. I've never taught in running shorts before. The president wouldn't care. She'd find it earthy and accessible. Most of the evening faculty is part-time. No one notices anything. They are too broke to pay attention to wardrobe. I need to run seven-minute miles which is fast when I've been pounding my body into oblivion.

Joanie says, "I should come and see you teach sometime."

"You did," I say, "when I first got hired."

"That's right," she says. "You were great."

Years before that, when I was welding, my mom took a week's vacation and drove to Missouri where I was working and we drank in the worst bars in Ripley County, the poorest place in the state. All the truckers passing through loved my mom and the locals drinking at the Cow Patch loved my mom. All the waitresses loved my mom. My mom once left the bar with a truck driver and helped him unload his trailer at a Walmart two counties over and came back covered in sweat and trailer dust and thirsty for vodkas on ice and light beer. Another night she wanted to unload another trailer with another trucker, a little woman with a peach fuzz beard who wore a huge mesh hat, and Joanie dragged me along and we threw some boxes and rolled some carts and she smoked a lot of cigarettes and took a lot of breaks and made a lot of friends. One old guy, a warehouse manager, who Joanie kept calling Rock n Roll Ted, said, "Is your mother always this charming?" and I said, "Yes, she is."

I would like to say to the world sometime, "This is my beautiful mother," then I would sit back and watch and hope they'd lift her up and they would.

Joanie, speaking words between breaths, says, "Don't you breathe?"

"Zen," I say.

Joanie says, "I don't know," and gasps, and says, "what that means."

Neither do I.

Running helps but I feel like I'm running from someone, from something, to somewhere, away from somewhere that feels a lot like a punch, a gun, a busted nose, a hole.

Joanie looks down at her watch and hits a button, some stopwatch or calorie counter or pulse tracker or jetpack to make her take flight.

I feel a sudden and terrible presence.

Joanie says, "You look white," and gasps, and says, "like a ghost."

"I'm fine," I say.

I am really sweating now, booze and drug stink pouring out.

I can smell Jack's Bar.

My eyes set themselves ablaze.

I focus on Joanie.

Joanie's watch is pink and green with lots of lights and straps. She touches a button a couple more times, eventually squeezing and holding until it beeps.

"That's a fancy watch," I say.

"It monitors my heart," she says. "It tells me I'm not dying."

"I'm going to take off now," I say.

She says, "I knew you would," and she starts to sprint ahead of me but, despite the elliptical and her showiness, she's not very hard to pass.

Dinner Plans

I am so stinky and soaked in sweat, it looks like I showered in my clothes then dumped beer and ash on myself for effect. I take off my shirt. Joanie looks sweaty but I don't see any sweat on her face or coming through her clothes. Maybe it's grease. She stopped running once I took off and walked the rest of her laps. I ran six miles. I am okay with six miles. I wanted more. I would have taken less. Joanie and I lean against my car. I have calmed. I am not calm. I am breathing like a monk, telling myself: breathe like a fucking monk. I need more Gatorade, gallons. I need God, some version of it, maybe cocaine. Not cocaine. Real God. Light. Joanie gets her purse and finds her cigarettes, Marlboro Reds.

"I thought you quit smoking," I say.

"I did," she says and lights up.

"How's your poodle?"

"Poodley," she says, and blows a cloud of smoke the size of one lung, maybe two.

I take the air like I am stealing it from the sky. I hold it. I exhale. It's loud and obnoxious. I think about Tibetan monks. I think about nervous wrestlers waiting on the mat.

"I'm proud of you," Joanie says.

"Thanks," I say. "I'm proud of you too."

She says, "I'd like you to meet my veterinarian."

"I would like to meet your veterinarian."

"Good," she says. "We can have dinner."

"Good," I say. "I have someone I would like you to meet too," and I think of Megan and I start to doubt myself and I stop it and wash out the doubt with the best thought I can manage: kissing Megan, Megan in my lap, me in Megan's lap, Megan with a pool stick, ready to crack some frat boy heads.

Joanie says, "Really?" and flicks her cigarette like a small rocket into space.

"Really," I say.

"Really?" she says, super excited.

She turns and grabs my face and kisses me, a loud smacker. I feel it in a way that is like feeling but not feeling, an impersonation of feeling, which is okay, better than no feeling at all. Joanie is always lit even if it's laced with cynicism and sarcasm so it's surprising to see her find another level of joy and I try to focus on that: joy, Joanie's joy, the way she radiates joy for two. She releases me then comes again with both hands and her lips. I want to kiss back but accepting is difficult enough. I accept. I keep accepting. She lays the puckered smooches on my cheeks, on my forehead, on my hair, then back to my cheeks.

She says, "Meet someone?"

She says, "Meet someone?!"

She says, "You big boy!"

I say, "Come on, I'm not twelve," the best joke I can manage.

She says, "Wonderful!"

She releases me and settles herself.

She says, "You reek of booze and smoke."

I say, "Sorry."

She says "You never introduce me to anyone."

She says, "I assumed there'd never be anyone, that there wasn't anyone."

She says, "Which is fine, I'm not judging."

She says, "Nona told me you were gay."

She stops and punctuates that, a little too happy to sell out her mom.

She says, "Maybe that was just her opinion."

I say, "What?" and feel distraction taking over and hope it takes over.

I say, "Why would Nona tell you I was gay?"

I say, "When did you talk to Nona?"

I am supposed to take Nona to the Olive Garden soon and she has been talking to my mother behind my back about my romantic life and telling her I am gay. Now, if I write a book about my family, I will have to say terrible things about my lovely grandmother, about what a gossip she is, what a neb and shittalker.

Joanie says, "There's nothing wrong with being gay."

"You are absolutely right about that," I say.

She says, "I'm for the gays."

I say, "I'm sure the gays appreciate that."

She says, "You know what I mean."

I toss my shirt in my truck and look for something to dry off with.

I need a towel with nails to wipe away my skin.

Joanie says, "I'm assuming this person is a woman but she could be a man."

She says, "A man is fine, too."

She says, "I'll be happy either way."

She turns and hugs me and I hug her back with all my sweaty body. I lift her off the ground and give her a swing. Being able to swing my mom is not unlike winning a million dollars or a state championship, such is my momentary resistance to the rest of the world.

Joanie says, "Oh my, you're strong and sweaty."

The old women start to come off the track. One looks at me and waves. She is short, like a troll, in a pink fuzzy jumpsuit, green designer sneakers, with gray frizzy hair. Her face is enormous with the successes, with being alive and still able to move. I lift my hand from my mother and wave back. The old woman takes one of her friend's hands and swings it in an exaggerated way and off they go.

Joanie says, "My baby's all grown up," and kisses me again.

"Maybe even more than his mom," I say.

She takes my shoulders and says, "Tell me then—is it a boy or a girl?"

"It's a Megan," I say. "And she is beautiful."

DRIVING

I roll the window down and roll the window up and turn on my dusty air conditioning and roll the window down. I stick my face in the wind and feel smashed by the wind. I am so very happy to make my mother happy, to let her know that I am okay, that I feel, that love is not fear, that at the end of birth and years of raising a son, a mother will be rewarded with another woman, a woman to love her son and someone she can love through her son, a new intimacy, and yet I could jump from my moving car and eat pavement and rise and run as far and fast as I can.

I do not mean a bite of pavement, I mean all the pavement.

My Brain

I know that there is a force trying to kill me, even as I know there is no force.

My brain is not right.

It appears to be thinking on its own.

The air is bullets that, when confronted, denies having been fired from a gun.

Class

I'm in the hall at the community college with Joanie. The hall is empty. We are five minutes late. There are lockers here, like in high school. The lighting is dim, like a dive bar, like a suck apartment, like any place that is worried about the electric bill.

"There," I say to Joanie in a whisper and point to Megan.

Joanie says, "Is she a student?"

"Yes," I say, "but older. She used to be my bartender and still is."

"So what if she's your student," Joanie says. "It's all bougie crap, who cares."

Megan wears a skirt and a spring sweater, more fancy than usual, just as lovely. I managed to rush home and pulled on a clean shirt and jeans but I didn't have time to shower or even wash up. My hair is dried with sweat to crispiness. My skin is tight as a sheet on a military bed. I hope I don't smell like stale booze. I cake-decorated my pits with deodorant then added a swipe across my chest. Joanie still wears her running clothes. She drinks a can of diet Fresca through a straw, lipstick on the plastic. I am still breathing deeply but doing it so it does not look like I am trying to calm myself or steal everyone's oxygen.

Joanie says, "She's gorgeous. Do I get to talk to her?"

"After class," I say.

"You stink like booze and baby powder," Joanie says, and walks into the classroom like she's been a student all along and takes a seat in the back row with the stoners and shybirds.

I count kids. Most of my class is here, nineteen students. Twelve students are better, easier to manage, but this is fine. Most of them have met with counselors they didn't want to meet with, only to tell the counselors they didn't want to meet them anymore. I look for Brandon, his ghost, his energy. I step inside the room. Joanie shuffles her desk, trying to get comfortable in a seat made for a nineteen-year-old. I try to imagine her in college all those years ago, lugging books around, rushing from class to her job, taking care of her family, her bills, her ever-complex love life. I try to remember her complaining. I can't. Bitched, yes. Complained, no. I would have complained. I would have written letters and made phone calls and cried out to God, help me please, for you know I am being crushed. Not Joanie. Never Joanie.

I wish I could be a pisser too.

I love her toughness.

I need her toughness.

The amount of toughness in the world is deeply underreported.

Because the complainers sing the loudest.

Because the complainers complain about toughness.

Megan is a tough motherfucker.

She sits in the front row, like always. I wave and she does something with her eyes, a stare without force, that makes me want to kiss her and not stop. It is hard to believe I am in love because I have spent most of my life avoiding love, I have spent most of my life fearful, I have spent most of my life trying to be a good son and grandson and friend and teammate and worker and now teacher, not knowing if any of those things connected to romance or how to make romance something connected to my life. Fear is more solid than any element. We hold it because we need something to move around and run away from and to be blocked by and then we don't. Then there is love and we take it and hope we can still move, still accomplish what fear motivated us to be.

But then other fears appear.

I decide to teach tonight to impress Joanie.

Or: I decide to teach tonight to impress Megan.

Or: I decide to teach.

Or: I decide to not run from the room.

I am not making decisions.
I am accepting what is offered, whatever that is.
I reject air as bullets.
I reject blood holes that open ceilings.

To the students I say, "Everyone still okay?" which is how I start all my classes, post-shooting, but I say it mellow and calm, not dramatic, like we're all mourning a Steelers' playoff loss to Baltimore or Cincinnati or New England, those fucknut teams who do not hold guns.

Maybe post-shooting is all our lives now.

By all, I mean everyone in America and parts elsewhere.

"I have your papers," I say to the class.

"I probably flunked," someone says.

"No one flunked," I say. "Everyone did an admirable job."

"Does admirable mean A?" someone else says.

"Sometimes admirable means A," I say. "Sometimes it does not."

A girl, maybe nineteen, maybe a high school dropout working on her GED, dressed in a waitress uniform, says, "Are we doing anything today? Like anything serious? Because I have to work at seven thirty."

"No," I say. "We're not doing anything today at all."

Someone else says, "Really?"

Another person says, "He's joking, douchecanoe."

This is Creative Writing. We do a little of everything and watch movies when we're bored. I like this class. It's better than Comp because I've had some of the students before and they understand my requirements, minimal as those may be. They know they have to try a little and read a couple books and revise their papers to get an A or quietly and respectfully disappear to get a C and pass the class.

My mom looks at me and she beams.

I try to beam back, to show I am a man with a mother who worked to make a son.

Joanie says, "What's due today?"

One kid says, "Are you new, lady?"

I say, "You were supposed to read 'The Waitress' for today."

Half the class looks away in unison.

Academically speaking, these classes are the dead zone.

The semester has stumbled past the middle but it's not close enough to the end, an academic purgatory. The students are bored. I don't blame them. They've written some poems. They wrote a two-page TV script. They wrote an argumentative essay. They all argued that marijuana should be legal. Now we're doing fiction. I have Malcolm Barth lined up. I do not like Malcolm Barth. Most of his stories are too obscure and the ones that aren't obscure are only half a page long and the characters are only there to serve the language. But I love "The Waitress" and how it shows students that a story, that art, can be built around what happens in a single day and, during that day, no one needs to get shot or punched or kicked in the genitals. None of the characters are zombies or vampires or mutants. The waitress starts her day at ten in the morning with coffee and orange juice then a cigarette then a shower. The rest of the narrative follows the waitress from her apartment to the grocery store then to work at a diner in Southern Ohio where she is scheduled for a double shift, lunch and dinner. The waitress has held the same job for years and today she either gets tips or she doesn't but it means a little more than other days, how one moment or one day can represent thousands of moments and days. She either goes back to the grocery store when her shift is over to get the diapers and heartburn medicine she forgot or she doesn't. She either decides to watch *The Fall Down Starlet* on cable for the thousandth time because it was her mom's favorite movie or she decides to turn the TV off and get a good night's sleep for a change. Malcolm Barth must have had an accident when he wrote this story, or maybe an out-of-body experience, or maybe he took his head from his academic ass and looked around and cared about someone's life as much as he cared about language, because the characters in "The Waitress" are believable and flawed and in crisis. He does not mock them or make fools out of them or any of the terrible things he usually does to his characters so he can sound intelligent. When I read "The Waitress" I feel like the world is going to explode from the drift of being alive and become something else, a new level of consciousness, because it should explode and seldom does. We should know more than we do. It should be in stories.

"I read that waitress story," someone says. "And it's like nothing happens."

"Obviously, you've never been a waitress," another woman says. "Everything happens in that story. She has enough money to buy diapers and heartburn medication."

Someone says, "So what."

Erin, who is twenty years old and works part-time for UPS in the warehouse because they pay for three credits a semester, who wears her brown uniform, raises her hand, furious, and says, "What do you mean, so what? Have you ever been broke? Have you ever had to make a choice about what to buy?"

And they are off, talking, racing to talk, and I am happy not to speak, happy to focus on them, happy they need focus.

A boy student says, "Why'd she buy diapers? She doesn't mention having a kid."

Megan says, "I think it's too painful for her to mention the kid. I felt like her ex-husband or lover or maybe her parents have her kid because she did something or they think she did something wrong. I think she only has the kid on weekends or a couple days a week. It could be worse. Maybe the kid died."

The boy student says, "That's too sad if the kid died. Ten seconds ago I didn't even think there was a kid or that the kid was real. And now he's dead."

Erin says, "I don't think she can afford the kid. I have a nephew and I buy my sister diapers sometimes when I have money and they are so expensive."

I pull out the chair from behind the teacher's desk and quietly drag it around so I can sit and not be blocked off from the students. They keep talking. I wait for a moment to step in and add some perspective but the better students keep straightening the more confused students out and I am able to nod along without speaking, maintaining focus, trying.

Paycheck aside, this is why I teach.

I love to hear people read then speak about what they read.

It saves the world.

Or, at least, it saves my world.

I hope my world is saved.

After a few minutes psycho Brandon appears at the door. I understand that psycho Brandon cannot appear at the door and that he is not at the door but he is at the door, as sad and furious as ever, death not the glorious retreat he'd imagined.

His appearance is unwished for but not unexpected in an unexpected way.

I feel so fucked up but, because I know that I feel fucked up, fucked up feels manageable.

The students keep talking.

Brandon stands there, radiating Brandon.

This is my brain setting fire due to my having witnessed a tragedy but I reject it. I do not reject that it is happening. I reject the loss of function. I reject death as something other than death, as a scar and not a memory. Is it a tragedy if someone who wants to die takes his own life? I refuse to feel the same as a combat-fucked soldier or a rape victim or any number of people who have had their lives pushed against violence. I have not had my life pushed against death so I focus and try to force the Brandon who is not here to leave.

I catch him in the corner of my eye and pretend not to see his hoodie, his rage.

He stays there long enough to make me turn.

I wave him in, casually, late student, it's fine, you're dead, so what.

You were always dead to me, Brandon.

My imagination gave you life and I'm glad it did and now it will kill you again.

He extends his arms like he's holding the doorframe to keep it from collapsing.

He leans forward with his chest.

I speak over one of the students and say, "Brandon, do you want to come in?"

I think I say this in my head.

I do, I'm sure.

But the class turns to him.

I think the class turns to him.

We all wait.

I look at Megan.

She shakes her head but like a question.

Brandon flicks his tongue like a snake.

I say, "Come on, Brandon. You're welcome to come in but you can't stand in the doorway and distract everyone."

By come in, I mean I'm inviting him into my memories, which is different than inviting him to stay present and as a distraction.

Brandon looks over the room and says, "You people believe this asshole?"

No one in the class speaks, though I wait for Joanie to rush the door and knock Brandon out for infringing on anything involving me, her son.

But Joanie cannot see Brandon.

Maybe Megan can, or maybe Megan understands I am seeing Brandon.

Or not.

Brandon says, "I feel sorry for you motherfuckers."

"Okay," I say, "close the door and leave."

I draw the line at motherfucker, especially if my mom is near, even if she is oblivious to ghosts and generally uncomfortable with other people's pain and loves the word motherfucker.

Brandon leans back, still holding the door frame, and says, "I'm not in your classroom so I can do what I want. I'm here. You're there. You're bothering me. You're in my hallway. You're in my world. You leave."

He flips down his hood.

A hole dots his forehead, not gruesome, almost healed.

I say, "I am not actually in your world."

He says, "You're a mothermotherfucker."

I say, "That's disappointing."

Brandon triples it and says, "Mothermothermotherfucker."

I stand and put myself between Brandon and the rest of the class and walk toward the door, not knowing what I'll do if Brandon stays, if he holds on to the frame, if he releases and tries to fight. I accept his brutality. I accept his presence as both a non-presence and a presence. I keep stepping. Maybe I'll have to jack him in the chest or whisper something cruel or maybe something kind or maybe I'll just stand there like a second doorway, one he can't walk through, or I'll suddenly become a fighter and pop him in the nose so he looks like a post-clipped Fat Bill without the charm. I hope I can do these things without motion, a thought fight. Minds create realness and realities more real than realness. I live so much of my life with and within my imagination that this makes sense—visions, creations. I keep stepping to Brandon, Brandon who is dead, Brandon who I have created, the Brandon I neither worked on nor wanted to publish but who is here, real as a book. He growls. Maybe I'll slap the teeth from his mouth. Maybe I'll apologize and run and hide, a grown man afraid of spirits with huge mouths and bullet scars.

Brandon rocks forward like he's going to turn himself into a missile but I don't stop. He instantly pulls himself back so he's in the hall and not holding the door.

He says, "You don't know shit," and points at me with the bony finger of the Grim Reaper and starts to walk away at his usual coward's pace. He keeps pointing, shaking his finger like a stick, speed walking, saying, "Nothing, you don't know shit, nothing, you'll never know anything, teacher my fucking ass," and his voice warbles from anger or like he's started to cry.

"You're always welcome in my class," I yell, and I hear it clear and clean outside my head, circling back into my ears, circling back into anyone's ear who wants to hear.

I do not turn to see what the class is doing, thinking.

I could be talking to anyone in the hall, a live person, a devil.

Brandon stops.

I wave.

He does not wave.

He points.

Then he raises both hands to chest level and flips me off.

It's a very slow, profound gesture.

He backs into the main doors and starts to push his way through the metal and glass.

"Still welcome," I say, and I really would have him back.

Not What You Saw, What I Say

I turn back into the classroom and stay calm and I shut the door, making sure I don't slam, that the door quietly clicks. Megan stands up, her face a mask of worry, hands at her side, clutched into fists. Joanie sits in the back, confused. Another boy student, also in a hoodie, stands in the back with some kind of extend-a-club device in his hand. He looks righteous and kind and worried, like he's been trained to police my worst thoughts and now is ready.

I touch Megan so she knows it's okay to sit.

I smile at Joanie, no problem.

I nod at the boy student with the club and say, "Thanks, I appreciate the backup, but nothing is here. No problems. I got confused."

He says, "Who was out there?"

I say, "No one important."

He says, "You sure? I thought we might have another shooter."

"No shooters," I say.

He says, "Shooters suck."

"Absolutely."

"I'm not going out like that."

"You're not going out at all," I say. "What is that?"

He pushes the club so it de-extends and says, "A head knocker."

I nod to acknowledge the accuracy of the name.

I say, "Sounds about right."

I take my seat.

I look at Joanie.

She raises her hands, asking if I need help.

I shake her off.

I say, to everyone, "Sorry about that."

I say, "Let's continue."

THE SILENCE

We do not continue.

No one, understandably, talks.

Most of the students stare at their desks. A few pull out their phones and subtly text. I hope no one snapped a picture of me while I followed what was in my head, what I expected to be in my head but which was not in my head and now is gone from my head for good, I hope.

I hope no one took video of the inside of my skull.

I hope no one turns the video into something else, a short film, a cartoon, a skit.

For the fucknuts among us need the most love.

I think Jesus said that.

Kindness takes enormous numbers and compromise.

For the cruel shall inherit the earth and they mostly have.

I Turn My Attention

I turn my attention away from myself.

Attention

I turn my attention away from myself.

It's the advice I give my brain.

It's also the advice I give you, and your brain, though I am not much for giving advice and I apologize if I've overstepped my boundaries.

Bill

Bill, Fat Bill, Bill who got clipped by a bouncer and bled all over Jack's Bar, is probably home from the hospital, is probably in the trailer where he lives with his father who works in tire store, but maybe not quite like that, the father may still be at his job, Bill may still be at the VA hospital and his face may never recover from getting punched.

I close my eyes in front of the classroom.

I never pray because I never learned how but I say something to Bill.

Then I say something to Rig.

Then I say something to myself.

Then I say something to Joanie and Megan and my students because you should never end a sentence with your own name.

Star Gazing

I tell the class they are dismissed. The class is not sure I am serious. We have not finished discussing "The Waitress". I have not commented on the story or provided a summary. The prose has not been explained, nor the cadences, nor the details. They have learned a new name, Malcolm Barth, and read his story and argued about the meaning and they will take it with them and the rest is theirs. Forget it, love it, memorize it, whatever.

I have not given them a story.

I have shown them a star they didn't know existed.

That's why they hired me: to be a telescope.

OUTSIDE THE CLASSROOM

Joanie looks confused but keeps quiet. Joanie knows the know and the not-know and the cracks and the fissures and the notes between the notes.

She speaks without speaking.

I answer the same.

Megan whispers, "You okay?"

I say, "I am."

She says, "Okay-okay?"

I say, "I had a bad thought. It passed."

She says, "We can talk about it later."

I say, "Or not at all," and that is it, my truth.

READERS

Readers sometimes get mad when you write one-sentence paragraphs.

Those are not my readers.

They have never heard death.

PARKING LOT

Megan and Joanie huddle together, talking. They are so different. We hang in the parking lot, under the streetlights, the asphalt still warm from the sun and the day's heat. Megan holds her cigarette down and away. Joanie's cigarette barely leaves her mouth. Megan has long hair, her natural color. Joanie has neither. But kindness passes between them as kids pull from their spaces and rush home or to work or the bars and I stand like I've always stood.

Or: I feel like I'm standing like I've always stood.

The adult students linger and talk, knowing the rush is futile.

Erin, who works at UPS, the woman who loved the waitress story, walks toward her car which is a couple rows behind my truck and it's clear she has something to say so I walk with her and chat while Joanie and Megan talk running and cigarettes and firing bad employees and bartending and mothers and grandmothers, but not boyfriends and sons who have visions.

I ask Erin, "You've probably told me before but are you going to work or did you come to class right from work?"

"Going to work," she says. "I'd be a sweaty mess if I came from work."

"Throwing boxes," I say.

"It's only a four-hour shift so that helps."

"You okay with everything?" I say.

She stops and turns herself older somehow, like she mindflexes to the future and pushes out a wise and lined face, and she says, "I'm twenty-three. My big brother od'd when I was twelve. My mom is in jail for drugs. When she gets out, she'll do more drugs and go back. I'm okay. I wasn't in class when Brandon killed himself. I sort of hated him. I take care of myself. You need to learn to do that. Take care of yourself. Make sure you're okay. If you need to walk around the class and wave your arms, do it. Feel better. Cancel the rest of your classes. Everyone will understand. Think about you for a change, okay?" She leans in and takes my head and holds it and kisses my forehead. She releases me and gently touches my shoulder then lets her hand fall away.

"You're a smart lady," I say. "Thank you."

She nods across the parking lot, towards my truck, and says, "Who's that crazy lady in jogging clothes, talking to Megan? I don't think she's supposed to be in our class."

"That's my mom," I say. "She just came to watch me teach."

Erin turns the color of red wine, a deep purple coming out on her neck and face.

"I'm so sorry," she says. "I didn't mean that. I was just…"

"It's not a big deal," I say, and laugh. "I should have said something, made an announcement or welcomed her."

Erin says, "I just… We were talking about Brandon and crazy people and I just sort of hung that on her. Totally unfair. I'm so sorry. I am a bonehead."

"You're not a bonehead."

"I was sounding smart for like two seconds and I blew it."

"You didn't. You're great. I'll let you get going so you can get to work."

"Totally and completely sorry."

To change the subject I say, "Is this your ride? This is nice."

Erin says, "No. My ride is over there. I'm completely embarrassed of it. I usually wait until the parking lot clears out before I try to start it, in case the battery is dead."

"You want me to wait until it starts? I can give you a jump. I have cables."

"No, but thanks. I'd rather you not watch which car I get into."

"Deal," I say, remembering some of that shame, junky car, living in a trailer, stealing food, and I say, "Thanks for everything in class. I really appreciate it."

"Sorry about saying that about your mom," Erin says. "I'm going to school to be a nurse. It's taking me forever. Why is the world so shitty?"

"I'm trying to pretend it's not."

"That's a good plan."

I start to walk back to Megan and Joanie in her jogging clothes then turn back and say, "You'll be a great nurse. You'll make a bunch of money, you'll have a cool car, and you'll help a lot of people. Don't hurt yourself throwing boxes."

Erin says, "I know what that waitress story means," like she wants to explain it.

"I know you do," I say, and keep walking.

JOANIE AND MEGAN

I glance towards Joanie and Megan. I hear Megan say John Grisham's name. They both laugh. I know Joanie is asking questions about the blood in my sink, the night at the bar. I know Megan has the right answers, the right tone. She will hide the darkness and change the sounds. They will decide I am not a madman because they know me and I am not.

Joanie says, "The jukebox? Really?" and they laugh again.

I'm not ready to laugh yet. Everything will be funny when Bill's nose heals, when he comes back from the Middle East, alive, safe, when I come back, alive and safe.

Joanie has her hand on Megan's shoulder.

I need to get back to bed.

I've known this for many hours now.

HOTNESS

A boy student stops me next to his muscle car which is most definitely his car and not a decoy because he talks about it in class and his stories always have cool cars in them.

He says, "Who was that new lady in class?"

"The one in jogging clothes?" I say.

"Yeah," he says, "the cougar. She was fucking hot."

"Thanks," I say. "That's my mom."

Instead of being embarrassed he says, "Dude, set me up."

LUNCH

Megan says, "Your very sweet mom just very sweetly invited me to lunch," and she appears to be very happy with the invitation.

Joanie says, about Megan, "She is absolutely lovely."

Megan says, "You are absolutely lovely."

They are giddy with each other, their new connection.

The moon hangs above us, a fresh-cut lime.

The farm across the road from campus smells like dirt and grass and hay bales still in the field from last fall. The first light in the parking lot clicks off. Every fifteen minutes another one will go dark. I hope this is not a metaphor for the world.

"You're both lovely," I say. "I need to go to b-e-d."

"Thanks for spelling it out for us," Joanie says.

Megan says, "I'll take your mom home."

Joanie says, "Really?" even though she has her car.

Megan says, "Do you want to get some coffee?"

Joanie says, "That's so sweet."

I kiss Joanie on her lovely cheek and Megan on her lovely lips and I say, "B-e-d. I am going home to sleep," and I climb inside my truck and turn the key and roll down the windows.

Joanie walks close to my truck.

She says, "You just kissed Megan and she's your student. Is that okay?"

I say, "Is it okay that you're dating a veterinarian?"

"You said that already," she says. "And he's not my boss."

I say, "I meant that rhetorically. Or maybe metaphorically, like: is it really okay for anyone anywhere to ever be dating a veterinarian?"

Joanie makes a face and says, "Don't be weird."
I blow Megan a kiss.
They say, "We know you don't want to talk to us but you can, anytime. We love you because you're sweet and brilliant."
I hear them like that, as one voice, because I need to.

PART TWENTY-FIVE

Nona

Nona **wants to eat at** the Olive Garden again. We share the front seat in my truck, driving around aimlessly, gabbing, gossiping. I want to tell her I have a girlfriend. I want to ask why she thinks I'm gay, to tease it out of her. I want to ask how often she talks to Joanie and if we can be a family like other families, together and not brawling, or together and brawling but out in the open so everyone knows when to duck.

It's Thursday afternoon and bright.

The trees bloom along the road.

I roll down the window halfway so the wind hits my face. Nona holds her blouse against the wind. I lean into it. I don't feel like pretending to enjoy the Olive Garden and Nona doesn't eat the food so I am thinking we can go somewhere else and eat something we want to eat that is not a salad and a breadstick.

Nona says, "Where's Italian that's not too spicy?"

"It doesn't have to be Italian," I say.

"We always have Italian," Nona says. "I hadn't considered that we could have something else. Garlic is good for you."

I take backroads until we end up in North Versailles and ride Route 30 for a couple minutes. I talk a lot as we pass King's because Nona likes diners and I don't know if I feel like meatloaf and mashed potatoes, though I love meatloaf and mashed potatoes and King's has delicious apple pie with cinnamon ice cream.

Nona says, "There used to be a steakhouse along here somewhere. I think it burned down. Is the movie theater up there still discounted?"

"It is," I say. "They share their building with a snowmobile dealership now."

"Who snowmobiles?" Nona says. "Assholes, that's who," and she smiles. "The theater was always six bucks, not just matinees either."

"It still is," I say.

"It's four dollars for seniors."

I am supposed to meet Megan tonight for a movie. If we want to see a movie we can talk about, we have to drive to the one artsy theater in Pittsburgh. If we want to see a movie where stuff blows up, we can stay close to home or go right here, where the lobby of the theater is filled with climbing walls and another room off to the side is filled with trampolines and mats for kids to bounce and land on.

Nona says, "Talk to me about teaching but don't be embarrassed about it."

Nona does not know about bullethead Brandon.

"I'm not embarrassed about it," I say. "I'm proud to teach."

Nona says, "Then talk like it. You always downplay everything. Talk like a big star, like you know some things. You're too old to be shy."

"I'm not shy," I say, which is a half lie.

"Take me through your day," she says. "Just like the Beatles song. Start with when you woke up and got out of bed and ran a comb across your head. Or just start with when you get to campus. Do people accept you?"

"People accept me," I say. "Most everyone is nice."

"It's important to be accepted. Your mother fights with the world."

"The other teachers are nice. The janitors are nice. The nurse is nice."

"Good," Nona says. "Be nice back. Now tell me details."

I start telling Nona about my day.

I say, "This morning I talked with Berryman in my office for an hour."

She says, "Berryman," like it's a brick she's building a scene with, something she can see and understand and remember. Then she says, "And the other one is Rig?"

"Exactly," I say.

She says, "Rig played football."

"Yes."

"And Berryman writes rich people poems."

"Basically."

She considers this.

I go back to my career.

I make it sound like Berryman and I discussed lesson plans even though we mostly talked about Rig until we realized there was nothing to talk about, that it was just a feeling, a man out there in the world, doing what he wants with a purpose that is his alone.

This morning I wrote on a Post-It note: call Rig.

Then I stuck it on the edge of my computer screen.

Maybe I'll look at it and I'll call Rig.

Maybe Rig will call me.

Nona says, "Keep talking."

I say, "Berryman and I made plans for the kayaking trip which had been canceled but which we may do with his fancy kayak and without students."

Nona says, "Berryman is the rich one."

I say, "Right. I've told you this before."

She says, "Sort of but not with much…" and she pauses, thinking about our kayaking trip, and says, "Bravado. Good for you boys, you and that Berryman, for taking the students on a trip."

I say, "Berryman and I were actually going to ditch the students and kayak alone."

"Don't tell me that," she says.

I say, "It's a community college."

She says, "Say things with bravado like in the movies."

I don't mention that Berryman asked me to teach him to weld because, in my head, it either sounds like too much bravado or not enough. Berryman said, "Please teach me to weld, please," and I said, "Welding's not like that, like I could just teach you," though everything is like that, I guess, if you need it to be. I said, "Let's fish. I'll teach you to fish," and he said, "You fish?" and I said, "Of course I fish," and he said, "But you grew up in the city," and I said, "The entire city is built around three rivers. I used to pull catfish from the Monongahela."

I tell Nona that Berryman wants to learn to pull carp from a river.

Nona says, "You talk about fishing in the office?"

"Of course," I say. "We both teach writing. Everything applies to a writing class."

Nona says, "How so?"

I say, "Because it all applies. Language and experience co-exist."

"Language and experience co-exist," Nona says. "That sounds smart."

"Very," I say.

Nona pats my leg.

I pat her leg back.

Earlier, after I talked to Berryman, I dug through the bookshelf in my office. In my next class I read a chapter from a Dmitri Smirnov novel aloud. The chapter was about a young boy working as a fisherman for his stepfather. His real father died from tuberculosis and his mother, a peasant, married her husband's brother. It was set in Siberia, on the edge of the Sea of Okhotsk. The boy lived with his mother and his uncle, the stepfather. The men in the family fished all summer. The women smoked the fish. In the fall the family traveled south by wagon to the edge of China to sell the fish and to trade for flour and beans and vodka. The stepfather hated the boy. He wanted the boy to pay rent, even though the boy was barely twelve and still attended school in the winter whenever school was available. The part I read was set on the journey south, when the family stays the night in a village, and the stepfather tries to rent the boy to an innkeeper. "Keep him," the drunk stepfather says. "He's good at work but not good enough to pay much." The mother weeps. The boy refuses to weep. The scene is about the boy refusing to weep. I flipped a hundred pages ahead and read a section from the end about the boy net fishing, rowing his own boat, pulling in fish for his family, his new wife and his daughter. The kids at the community college in Westmoreland County all fish more seriously than the people in Allegheny County, where I fished when I was growing up. Kids out here tie their own flies and lures. We used dough balls and corn, whatever was easiest, when I fished from the edge of the Mon. My class looked attentive and thoughtful. I said, "How is this story like where you grew up and how is it different?" I let them talk on that then I dismissed them early.

I am counting the weeks until the semester ends, not angrily but hopefully, the summer waiting, then wanting to start teaching again next September and do better.

Earlier in the semester, one of my best students, Shenorah, who wants to be called Shay, also from Wall, where I live, but a better part of Wall, up on the hill, asked if she should transfer to a bigger college and major in English. I never know how to answer that question because I majored in English and it was so useless I ended end up welding on bridges but then I became someone who teaches English. Shay works as a waitress. She has a kid and no partner to help. She skipped all her classes this week, maybe the last two weeks. She's been spotty all semester. I never answered her question about majoring in English. I didn't want the responsibility so I talked around majors and college and careers until she looked confused but now I think she should write a novel about a waitress with a kid, the sadness and success of that, the importance of coloring books for parents who can't afford to buy their kids iPads or whatever new electronic gizmo is popular. The kid is four but Shay can't pay for preschool. Preschool isn't cheap. Neither is daycare so Shay's mom watches the kid and complains that she's being taken advantage of. The mom still works two evenings a week at Target. Sometimes Shay brings her daughter to class and gives her crayons, three at first then another color every few minutes. The kid works quietly, diligently. Shay floats there, motherhood, student, daughter, thankful daughter. It's something special, the way Shay lives, and it looks impossible to maintain.

Nona says, "That sounds like a very full day."

I turn the car towards DeNunzio's Restaurant, where Shay works.

Nona says, "I don't like real Italian food. It's too spicy."

"Olive Garden's real Italian food," I say.

"Olive Garden is not real Italian anything," she says.

I roll down the window the rest of the way.

The breeze messes my hair and opens my eyes.

I should call Megan and we should run for the beach, for a couple days, a weekend. When I think that I have money, that my bills are paid, that I can afford an offseason dive, I always think it twice, say it twice, so it feels realer, because for many years it was not. When I say many years, I mean my whole life. The light today is blinding, the same sun over Western Pennsylvania as over every beach everywhere, Atlantic City, Morocco, Cannes, Ocean City, Maryland. The tourists won't be out for another six weeks and Megan and I could have the boardwalk to ourselves, the warm breeze, the cold waves, fluffy pillows at a motel.

Nona says, "I heard from someone else you're quite the teacher."

"Oh yeah?" I say. "Who says that?"

"Your mother."

"Since when are you talking to Joanie?"

Nona says, "I am always talking to your mother, sometimes more frequently than others. She might call me just to insult her upbringing then mention what a special boy you are." She reaches for my leg and gives me a pat. She's in a patty mood.

Nona wears a pretty blue dress, not her usual denim overalls and turtleneck. I am dressed the same as always: jeans and a golf shirt. Nona's hair is styled. It is pulled back and held with a fancy blue clip. She has on sneakers and white tube socks. Her fancy shoes are in a plastic grocery bag she clutches like a purse. I will probably want to run after lunch, miles and miles until I can barely breathe.

I say, "If you really want to eat at the Olive Garden, I'll turn around."

Nona says, "It doesn't matter. I never eat anything but a salad."

"That's true," I say.

"I thought you liked the Olive Garden," she says.

"Just the breadsticks."

"Roll the window up," she says. "It's messing my hair."

Pasta

DeNunzio's has a sunroom. The air conditioning kicks on. Every other table is taken, people chatting, pretending they don't have to be back at work. The waitresses wear black pants, white shirts, black bowties. The customers are mostly young businessmen with huge guts and bad ties. A few old people sip soup. I like the sunroom. Upstairs, the walls are stucco and hand-painted with grapes but it's closed during the day. One of the owners, Ronnie or Jimmie or Donnie DeNunzio, is at the bar, smoking a cigar and drinking scotch. He looks like a man who loves to own a restaurant.

Nona orders chicken parmesan.

I order a bowl of wedding soup.

Nona says, "That's it?"

"That's it," I say.

The waitress is not Shay but she looks like Shay. Every waitress in Western Pennsylvania could be a student or former student of mine.

If I didn't already grossly over-tip, I would feel pressure to over-tip.

My politics are, basically, over-tip.

Also, be kind.

Vonnegut said that: be kind, babies.

The waitress looks at me then at Nona. She smiles but not fake.

I should write an entire book about waitresses who take writing classes at the community college. The intended audience would never have time to read it or would rather read a thriller that has nothing to do with their lives. Those who read my book about waitresses trying to better themselves through education would be angry that I used dirty words.

Nona says, "I think you should get more than a bowl of soup."

The waitress says, "Maybe he's just not that hungry."

She winks at me. I haven't been winked at in years. Nona opens her menu again. The waitress takes her pad and pen from her apron.

The waitress says, "Maybe he ate a big breakfast."

I am starved but I know Nona will not eat her chicken parmesan and I have to meet Megan before I can put the leftovers in my fridge and the food will spoil or at least turn to mush in the heat of my truck and I can eat it now if I only have soup.

Nona says, "He'll have the chicken parmesan, too."

"I'll have the homemade pasta," I say.

The waitress says, "Good choice," and goes to get us some bread.

Nona says, "Tell me about this girlfriend."

BOOKS

I tell Nona about Megan. Nona thinks she sounds great. She claps her hands, quickly and closely, like she's cheering at a talent show, a version of Joanie's response. Everyone is shocked I can get a date. I think this makes me pathetic, except I am so happy to have Megan, I feel like rejoicing. Nona keeps clapping. A few customers look at the crazy old lady applauding and smile. One guy raises his glass of red wine. Nona waves him off for noticing her loudness.

Nona says, "I'm so glad you found someone. We are not a family that finds partners very easily, as you may have noticed."

"I never noticed," I say, and tear a piece of bread from the loaf.

I ask why Nona has been gossiping about my sexual orientation.

She says, "What's orientation?"

I explain orientation.

She says, "That's a new word to me."

But Nona doesn't think I'm gay.

"I never thought that," she says.

"Never?" I say, smiling.

Nona says, "It wouldn't matter if you were but it never occurred to me. I know how busy you are with your job and your writing, your mother and me. If someone would have asked me what you were, I would have said busy. I did think your daddy might have been a fag."

I say, "I think you're just being mean."

"That's probably true."

"People don't say fag anymore."

"Why not?"

"It's not nice, that's why."

Nona says, "I'm old. They'd forgive me. There's an old queer back at the home who calls himself a fag. Calls himself an old queen too."

It's not a conversation worth having at this point in Nona's life but I say, "It's okay if he calls himself that but not when you do."

"Now I know," Nona says, "so shoot me."

The waitress swings by and says, "Your food will be up soon."

Nona and I both thank her.

Nona says, "I may have said you were funny, like funny ha-ha, but not like funny gay. I think maybe your mother has been teasing you."

"I think you've been teasing me," I say.

She says, "When I was growing up in the mountains, there was this lesbian, I guess she was a lesbian, everyone called her a girl-man. We didn't know the word lesbian. She was nice, a farmer. She raised pigs and smoked meats. She lived with two pretty women, both younger than her, and they lavished themselves on her. I don't think they did any work at all. They just kept themselves pretty and available. One day I was picking berries in the woods, really deep in a patch, and I saw Joe, which was the lesbian's name, her real name was Margaret Joe but everyone called her

Joe, and she dropped her jeans to take a pee. She had lady parts, which sort of surprised me, I thought she might've had man parts, or some combination of inee-outee, but it was woman parts. When she went to pee, she didn't squat down like a woman. She had a very little metal funnel. She put the wide end, which was maybe as big as a silver dollar, she put that to her ladyparts and out came the pee in a stream, just like she were a man. It was sort of magical and confusing."

I say, "You saw all this from a berry patch?"

"I did," she says, and drops it. "When will I meet this Megan?"

The restaurant fills out with more businessmen and a few families in fancy clothes, little kids in suits and dresses. The waitresses carry trays the size of small cabinet doors. I'm glad I ordered the pasta, even if the chicken goes to waste. You want to know if an Italian restaurant is any good, order the pasta and a meatball.

Nona wants to write a book.

She says, "It doesn't have to be a big one," and thinks about that and adds, "but it could be a big one, nothing colossal, just decently big."

She would like Joanie to help her write the book. I could help too, if I have the time. She adjusts her blue dress. I can tell this is important, the making of a family book.

She says, "It seems like a wise thing to do."

"It does," I say.

Writing is contagious and Nona has caught it from me. The cure for writing is, of course, writing, the medicine masquerading as the disease, how doing it and realizing the difficulty of the act, let alone the chance to publish, will make almost anyone stop and go back to binge-watching cable TV shows while eating fluffywhip.

"But you're awfully busy," Nona says.

"I'm never too busy to help," I say. "Maybe you could take my class."

"Are classes expensive?"

"They're reasonable at the community college. Or you could just sit in."

She says, "I'd want the credit if I took the class."

"Then you'd need to pay," I say.

Nona says, "I just think you're the best. I'm glad you're doing so well in the world. It was hard being a welder, even though you never complained. I worried about you up on those bridges, all laced up in stretchy ropes. And you stayed in those dumpy motels. You could have caught AIDS or HIV or whatever. Herpes from a dirty bathroom. People don't even vaccinate anymore. Measles is coming back. Pretty soon we'll all have polio again." She stops her cynicism and smiles and says, "It's good you turned out so much better than the world. I feel warm from it," and she hugs herself and laughs to show how warm.

Nona still has on her tube socks and sneakers, the tube socks pulled so far up her legs they almost look like stockings. I think we are celebrating something, my coming out as a viable romantic partner, my ability to teach, my escape from the trades, my lack of an autoimmune disease or my skill at dodging herpes. Nona wants to love me up today, to show her pride and to make me proud of myself. It's better here at DeNunzio's than at the Olive Garden. Here, the whole room smells of sauces and garlic and olive oil and not garlic salt. Garlic salt is a sin. The waitress sets a salad in front of Nona, wedding soup in front of me. She tops both our dishes with ground pepper and parmesan. We thank her for her delivery and skill.

Nona says, "I've read a lot."

"I know you have," I say.

"Not all bad romance novels either, if that's what you're thinking."

I was thinking that, exactly.

Nona says, "My book won't be anything fancy. And the size can't be large. I don't know why I said that. My book will be small, like a gift book. It will mostly be a book of wisdom with some stories about growing up poor mixed in."

I know those books.

They sit on the counter, right by the register.

They are passed around by church folk.

Last week Nona saw two women, two sisters, twins, eighty-nine years old, on *Oprah*, her favorite TV show and internet website, and they'd written a book. It was a book about how to live to be eight-nine years old. They were young looking for their age, their teeth colored the fake Hollywood white everyone has now. They wore sneakers with their dresses, just like Nona does. Oprah laughed a lot and gave them hugs. She handed out copies of their book to the audience.

Nona says, "All they had going was old age. Who wants to read about that?"

"I don't know," I say.

"Your great-great uncle wrote a book," Nona says.

"I remember," I say.

My great-great uncle, the coal miner, the drinker, the reader of the *Beckley Gazette*, the author of the handwritten book Nona passed to me like it was the constitution of her own personal country, the book I meant to read and have not. I look at Nona and I think that she is old enough to forget certain things and I hope maybe this one.

She says, "I know you. You haven't read it. Don't make any excuses."

"Sorry," I say. "I meant to read it."

"This is a good salad," Nona says, a small leaf of lettuce hanging from her lips.

I love the bread here, that it's not breadsticks, that the loaves are fresh baked. I can eat and chew and not consider what I haven't read. I have eaten the whole loaf with my soup and now I need another loaf and more butter. I could live on loaves.

I scan the room again for Shay but nothing. Some of the waitresses are her age, some are ancient. Very few are middle aged. No men wait tables. The bartender is a guy. The bus boys are all young, maybe nineteen, sweating through their nice shirts. Shay is probably home with her kid or attending some class that I am not teaching. Nona chews her salad and starts to talk about the book she wants to write again, how she'd like there to be pictures with captions.

Maybe I could write the captions?

Maybe the captions are all her book really needs.

The waitress brings me another Coke.

I'd rather it be a Mountain Dew.

Nona is almost done with her salad. The lettuce is deep green. Nona has been eating around a slice of hardboiled egg and a very purple beet.

I feel better in a sunroom.

I think less terrible thoughts, though I feel thankful to sit with my back to the wall so I can face the door and beware.

I say, "Why don't you just write it yourself? What do you need Joanie for? Or me? We'd only eat up your profits."

Nona gives up on her salad. She puts the fork in the middle of the bowl and pushes everything to the side.

She says, "I don't know why I like the Olive Garden. I know it's not any good. This is a very nice restaurant. Local is almost always better. This is good stuff." Nona touches her mouth with a cloth napkin, the whole mouth then both edges, and says, "Joanie is very wise. And she's always making mistakes. Young girls could learn from her."

"Interesting," I say. "Why don't you just write a mystery?"

Nona says, "I could but I don't know anything about guns anymore. Nobody uses rifles, let alone a single shot. I think they use Glocks."

ERIN

I finish eating and push one more slice of bread around the leftover sauce. The meatball was great. The homemade pasta was better. Nona's chicken fills out a huge styrofoam box sitting on the table. She holds the check. I would like to pay but she would swat at my hands. The waitress waits while Nona looks for her card. I ask her if Shay is working.

"Shay Holmes or Shay Cartwright?"

"Shay with the skinny dreads?" I say.

I want to save everyone but I can't remember their names.

"Shenora, that Shay," the waitress says. She sports a huge floppy ponytail that has been swaying like a pendulum since business picked up and she started to rush around the dining room. She says, "I think she works tonight. Do you want me to check the schedule?"

"That's okay," I say.

Nona gives the waitress the bill and a credit card. The waitress walks off. The back of her head could be a horse but tiny.

Nona says, "Who's this Shay again? Was she a student or another girlfriend?"

"Shay is my student," I say. "She works here. We were just talking about this. She wants to know if she should major in English and be a writer."

Nona says, "She should be President if it makes her happy."

I ask Nona for a pen. She digs in her purse. I can't write on a cloth napkin so Nona digs some more and finds paper and an old envelope. I want all of my students to be rich, to have jobs that fill their bank accounts like furniture fills up a fancy house.

I write, "Shay, you should major in whatever makes you happy, and read a lot."

I look at the words. The ink is too blue and wet. It will smear when I fold the paper to fit in the old envelope. I look at the words again. When I need to be profound, I never am

Being a waitress, a good one who makes customers happy and who knows how to do her taxes, meaning don't pay taxes, pays as much as being a community college professor, maybe more, but I have summers off and long holidays and as many sick days as I want.

But I have health insurance.

But I'm not working at 12:30 on Friday night, asking drunks to go home.

Shay has a kid.

Kids trump everything, I think.

I write, "You're great with words. Let me know if you need anything. Be a nurse. That's a good job. That's a great job. Seriously. Write a brilliant novel about nurses."

I fold the note and try to seal the envelope.

Nona says, "What if she thinks it's a tip? What if she thinks someone left her a big wad of cash? Some big spender came back and dropped a hundred dollar bill on her? Men do that, you know. They can be very generous to young attractive women."

"Oh shit," I say. "Why'd you go and say that?"

Nona pulls out two twenties and a couple fives and stuffs the money in the envelope.

"This'll help," she says.

THE LAST BOOK OF WISDOM

We stay seated and finish. Nona doesn't feel like the park today. She feels like coffee. The sun is too bright and she burns so easily and she didn't moisturize her arms with the cream that doubles as sunscreen. She could have an iced tea in the shade, drink it at an indoor table. Or maybe the park would be nice, get a little sun but not too much. She doesn't know. Today, Nona is older than the last time we ate Italian food but the next time she may be younger.

Or maybe her days of turning younger are over.

I'll read the first couple pages of my family book, the coal mining book, and three or four lines from the middle and the last paragraph. I'll say something nice no matter what I read.

Nice things are important.

My phone rings.

I answer and it's Megan.

She says, "I have to work tonight. The part-time bartender called off. Will you come and see me? I'll say pretty please."

"Just come back to my place," I say.

Nona says, "Is that Megan?" Then, louder, "Hello, Megan!"

Megan says, "Is that Nona?"

"That is Nona," I say.

Megan says, "Is she beautiful?"

I say, "She's being ornery today."

Nona says, "Hello, Megan."

Megan laughs and says, "Call me later, promise."

"Promise," I say, and hang up.

Nona says, "She sounds lovely, I bet."

The sun shines but the wind and sky wash out the heat. I have Nona on one arm, my other arm holds the Styrofoam box of chicken parmesan, her purse slung over my shoulder. During the summer the days will cook us. We should enjoy being outdoors now and Nona hates coffee shops anyway, the way people linger with their computers.

"What about some ice cream?" I say.

"I don't think I'll write that book anymore," Nona says. "Your mother would never do it and I think I've been watching too much TV. Fucking Oprah. She's so great."

PART TWENTY-SIX

Rig

Rig shows up at my apartment. I answer the door in running shorts, shirtless, clutching a can of Mountain Dew in my fist. Rig wears business clothes, slacks and a nice shirt and a purple power tie covered with paisleys. He looks thinner, healthier, or the clothes have slimmed his appearance and made him look like a professional athlete at a press conference or a CEO or banker or high school principal or a preacher before the lord commands him to loosen his tie and sweat his savior's name. I am not surprised to see him so handsome and together, though I would not be surprised to see him in a coffin, lips sewn shut, either.

Perhaps he imagines me the same.

Rig says, "You ain't got a lady in there?" and pokes his face into my apartment like he's trying to grab a smell or eat the oxygen out of my small kitchen.

"Nothing," I say. "I was writing. Now I'm going running."

Rig says, "Why you drinking that Mountain Dew? That shit is poison."

"It tastes good," I say. "Did you get my messages?"

"Rig did," Rig says.
"I was worried about you."
"The messages sounded that way."
The breeze blows in and ruffles my one set of cheap drapes.
Rig says, "You ever get sick of Rig?"
"I haven't seen you in ages," I say, avoiding the question.
"You get sick of Rig."
"I get sick of everyone."
"You a diplomat," he says.
I say, "How'd you find my apartment?"
Rig looks at me crooked, happy.
Maybe it's a Sherlock Holmes outfit that he wears.
"Just did. Rig knows you, Sellick."
"You look like a man on the fast track to success," I say. "You look like a man about to accept an award. Look at that tie."
He says, "You gonna invite me in?"
"I am," I say, and step aside.
He says, "You live in a place called Wall."
"I know."
"Wall," he says. "What kinda town name that be?"
Rig walks into my apartment, his huge feet in new black oxfords leading the way around the kitchen and living room, one open space divided by some linoleum. He comes back to the kitchen and starts again. He touches my refrigerator then runs two fingers across my cabinets then my walls like he's checking for dust. He stops and reaches up and touches my ceiling, which is pathetically low. The apartment barely contains his size. He holds his hand in place, palm to ceiling, stopping the world from collapsing on us.
He says, "You got people pasted on your cabinets."
I say, "They're my heroes."
He lowers his hand and turns to the cabinets.
He says, "No wrestlers?"
"Just artsy people."
"Look like an art project for school. Like sixth grade."
"Don't hurt my feelings," I say.
He says, "I don't get it."

I say, "What?"

He says, "I thought you were doing well."

"I am doing well."

"You own this building? Collect rent from folks?"

"Nope."

"You a professor?"

"I am," I say.

"Then you ain't doing well," he says, but smiling.

"Well enough," I say. "Why are you all dressed up?"

"Coming to see a friend," Rig says, "who I thought was doing well." He says, "Come across this shitty little apartment and give Rig a hug. God, you white trash. I love you but you are stuck in shitsville. Your mother ever see this place?" He pauses to think about my living conditions. He says, "I hope not. She probably thought you was successful too." Then he says, "Come on over here no matter what, you big failure."

So I do and I jump into his arms.

He carries me like I'm his son, his only child, like he's going to toss me in the lake and teach me to swim so I don't drown.

SPEAKING

I keep the light dim in the apartment. The window air conditioning from my bedroom clanks and hums. A candle burns on the kitchen table but just for the smell, lavender, my favorite. Rig sits on the couch, which is really a loveseat, and fills the whole thing. He starts to talk, serious but relieved. For days he's thought and made decisions. Those decisions are private. This one is not. Rig wants to become a public speaker. He wants to rise up and tell. He throws up his arms to show how he wants to rise up. His arms are huge, a cannonball and an anvil. He wants to talk about his successes and his failures, football and booze and wrecking motorcycles. He keeps rambling, mostly sideways but sometimes straight. I know the story but I like to hear him piecing it together outloud, reaching back before he was born and ahead to the successes he plans. He'll need a podium. He'll need notes. Pictures. Video. People will love him for his public speaking.

But he wants to fight a couple mixed martial arts matches, too.

He wants to get into the octagon with the best. With the worst. With

Collin whatever the hell his name is, that Irish prick, and any local yinzer too. He doesn't care. He leans forward, elbows on knees, drinking a bottle of water. He repeatedly straightens his tie, like it might untie itself and escape.

He says, "My great-great grandma was a slave. I just found that out but that's part of my story. I start there, slave. I don't even have to go back to Africa. Fuck Africa. Africa is like Wall, where we at, you shitty neighborhood, but worse. Rig got a great grandma from Mississippi who work her ass off in the cotton fields. Think about that. This pain we got is nothing. Even if you look unsuccessful as fuck, with this ratty-ass apartment, compared to what my grandma went through, this is nothing. She work as a slave, all but the last eight years of her life. Then she was free but she still work. Work constantly. I ended up a millionaire. Then brokeass. Then on my way back up. Way up. Would you pay to hear Rig tell that?"

"I would," I say, knowing I am partner to this, that I handed Rig the possibility of speaking truth for money, and I am happy to be here with him because to not be happy would be useless.

And his story sounds better than whatever version of his story I would have conceived.

Rig says, "I see you thinking."

"Nothing to think about."

"I ain't gonna use you up."

"I know that."

I sit here, shirtless on a chair I bought at Goodwill for thirteen bucks, the only other furniture in my ratty-ass apartment. I lean forward, my skinny arms on my knees.

Rig says, "I know it's a lot to ask but can I count on you?"

"Whatever you need," I say.

"I lost forty pounds."

"You look good."

"I could use me some of them abs you got."

"Mountain Dew."

"Bullshit," Rig says. "That shit'll give you the sugar."

I finish the last of my soda and toss it in the trash. I pull on the shirt I'd planned to wear to the track. I open the fridge and grab a couple waters. I pass one to Rig and he rolls it over his head like a lawnmower on a grassy hill.

I sit down and say, "But why MMA? You really want to get hit in the head?"

He says, "Hell no, I don't want hit in the head," like the question is preposterous, like I'd just suggested he learn ballet and take it to the stage, an elephant in a tutu. He pulls the water bottle to his cheek, enjoys the cold, then opens and chugs.

I say, "Then why MMA?"

He says, "Them MMA dudes, the loudmouths, they can do a lot of different shit, and one thing they do is professional wrestle."

"Professional wrestling? Like the fake kind?"

"Fuck yeah, the fake kind. The big stars make millions. The shit stars make a good living. That's all I'm asking. I want to make a living. I pinned Kurt Angle. That dude runs the show now. He's a big host or a manager or something. Wears a suit. Talks in a microphone. He on TV every Monday night, faking it up, bald head just like Rig. He a white boy but whatever. I beat that dude's ass in the real world. I'll bring it just like it needs brung."

I lean back on my Goodwill chair, befuddled.

I say, "I thought you were going to be a public speaker."

Rig says, "Am I not being clear?"

"Sort of," I say, "but not really."

He sighs and says, "How you be so slow-witted and teach college?"

"I do a lot of prep. I really read up on stuff before my classes."

"Allow me to start again. This time I speak slowly."

I miss the success of men who started poor, their frustrations and drive.

It's unfortunate that the gun shooters get all the attention.

Rig says, "I'm gonna public speak right now, starting soon. I got an agent. I got a whole bunch of agents. I'm officially represented by the Lavin Agency. You know who they are? The Lavin Agency?"

I shake my head, no idea.

"Right," he says. "You do not. But they represent big time sports stars. Football players. Basketball players. Women's basketball players. Olympic folk. And has-beens like me."

"I'm impressed," I say. "How'd you pull that off?"

"I texted Bryant Gumbel," he says, chest puffed, proud.

"The guys who hosts the sports show on HBO?"

"That guy. He been around forever."

"He's big time," I say.

"I know. That's why I text him."

"How'd you get his number?"

"He wanted to interview me when I was fucking up all the time. Used to call me three, four, five times a day. Have his assistant call, all that. Call Rig in the morning. Call Rig in the night. Was gonna get my side of the story out, that was his pitch. He was gonna let me tell my side to the world. Only my side was I was drinking and drugging and about going to jail. I didn't want that out there. That's downlow shit. You keep your lowdown lowdown. That's sense. They was already telling my story themselves, local news, ESPN, the shitty little sports magazines, all them assholes was blathering about Rig. I wanted to hide my fucking story, not get it out."

"I'm so impressed, I don't know what to say."

"You say: good job, Rig. Then you say: I'm proud of you, man."

"Public speaking, MMA, then pro wrestling."

"That's the plan. You gonna help Rig write this out?"

"I'd be honored to."

Rig says, "Pro wrestling."

I say, "Pro wrestling."

He takes a deep breath and, in a ring announcer's voice, says, "Hailing from Flood City, USA and weighing two hundred and seventy-five pounds." He flutters his hands like confetti falling. He says, "You dig me? I'm behind the scene then: boom! My music gonna come on and the crowd gonna go crazy."

"What's your name going to be?"

He stands and says, "Rig gonna be called Thunder. When the fans hear that clap, they gonna know I bring the motherfucking lightning."

BERRYMAN

Rig says, "Where's Berryman?"

"I don't know."

"Let's go find him. Rig got an AA meeting to attend."

AA, NO AA

I say, "No offense, I really don't want to go to your AA meeting."
Rig says, "Yes, you do."
"You're pushing me around."
"I know I said I wouldn't but I have to today."
I sit there, wanting to run.
I say, "Find Berryman. He'll go to your AA meeting."
Rig says, "Stop the obvious, cracker."

BERRYMAN, SURPRISED

Rig steps into Berryman's office, alone, while I wait in the hall, listening. It's Friday, a skip day for lots of the students, so the halls barely crackle, the best students moving slowly from class to class or the library, wondering why they care so much more than their classmates. A boy drops a textbook then kicks it down the hall like a soccer ball before finally picking it up.

Rig says, "Berryman, who you texting?"
Berryman, surprised, his voice glowing, says, "Rig!"
Rig says, "You texting a lady?"
Berryman says, "I was playing Gods of War."
"D'Hell is that?"
"It's a game for your phone."
"You know the god of war?"
"Ares."
Rig says, "Ares, that's right. Ares was the son of Zeus."
Berryman says, "It's good to see you. You had us worried."
"Rig was a god of war. He gonna be one again."
I step into the classroom before Berryman collapses under the weight of Rig's arrival and war talk and say, "We need a driver, Berryman."
Berryman says, "That's what I'm here for," and stands up and turns off his phone.
Rig says, "Berryman, putting away his phone, acting all grown up."
Berryman says, "How do you know about Ares?"
Rig says, "Rig won six national championships and have a college

degree. How you know about fucking Ares, Berryman?"

Berryman says, "I took two years of Greek in high school."

Rig laughs and says, "Berryman, you a full-fledged elitist."

THE CHURCH

I'm starting to care for Berryman too much to make him my driver, even for fun, so we take my truck and I handle the road. Traffic is nil as we come through the Squirrel Hill Tunnel. We circle into Greenfield and down the hill and roll along the Mon until we're almost downtown.

I hang a left and cross the river.

The church sits on the other side of the 10th Street Bridge across from CoGos, a crappy convenience store with three gas pumps and delicious pizza rolls spinning in a glass case on the counter by the register.

Turn around and drive back over the bridge. Skip the tunnel and hang a left. Then you'll see he Allegheny County Jail, where I picked Rig up months ago, sitting along the river, a hook and swerve from downtown Pittsburgh. It's the most legal and illegal patch of cement in the city, lawyers and bondsman and criminals and people desperately trying to convince other people they are upstanding citizens, one baseball mural with Willie Stargell leaning on a bat in a row with a bunch of other old timey ball players, and one Chinese restaurant buried down a side street with a chef who barely speaks English and makes the best egg foo yung in town.

I park near the old South Side High School, which will probably be condos soon.

At the BP gas station, under the pump awning, a man and woman in church clothes bicker over something, the woman backing the man up with her oversized hat, bumping his face with the brim. He is thin, nice beard, short afro. She is large, decked out in a white dress. When we get closer, I hear her say, "I'm not pumping my own gas, Stanley."

Rig whispers, "Stanley about to get his ass beat by that woman."

The church sits on the corner of Carson and 10th Street. Tenth Street consists of a strip of half-abandoned shops and row houses and a new Holiday Inn. The other way, down Carson Street, you pass a gay nightclub and the Onyx Bar and a sidewalk that leads to the South Side proper and more shops and another hundred bars—dives and music venues and fancy joints and places that used to be fancy but now look like sorority houses with their drink specials and sloppy drunk cliental and a few small plate restaurants for doctors and engineering professors to eat at. The church hosting the AA meeting must have been a diner because an old wooden Pepsi awning extends above both sides of the building, the red white and blue faded and peeling. It looks like a place where some kids might squat. We find the crosswalk and shuffle across the street, Rig leading us.

Berryman whispers, "Does Rig know what you did?"

"What?"

"The shooting and everything?"

"No," I say, "and don't mention it."

IN THE PRESENCE

Folding chairs form a circle in the center of the room. Booths remaining from the old diner line one wall. A busted-up counter of metal and plywood lines the other. A floor refrigerator sits tipped-over in the corner by the kitchen. The smell is dust and mold and the burnt-over smell of old wires and fuses. Nothing appears workable.

Rig says, "Hello?" but as quiet as his huge voice allows.

Berryman sneezes and I give him a look.

Then I instantly sneeze.

"See," Berryman says. Then, "How is this a church?"

Rig says, "People come here to worship and get healthy, that's how."

Nothing of a church, save the spirit, fills this place, not even a cross or a dimestore painting of Jesus. Part of the ceiling fell and has not been replaced so wires and tubes dangle down like snakes and demons. We three stand alone, waiting. I look for a pastor or a minister or an old alcoholic who will lead the group if anyone shows up. We take seats in the circle, unsure if we should speak. I try to feel whatever there is to feel.

Rig stands and looks at me.

I shrug.

"Anyone here?" Rig finally says, asking around, aiming his voice for the corners.

The whole room stands still.

Rig tries again.

The old walls eat his words without even an echo.

I imagine us driving all around the city, seeking a sober meeting.

Rig says, "Berryman, you a Catholic?"

Berryman says, "Not practicing."

Rig walks around and says, "We're here for the don't-drink meeting. Hello? Pastor Rob? Anyone? Hello? Yinz all hiding?"

We spin our necks looking for appearances.

Rig says, "Anyone? Alcoholics?"

Berryman says, "Christians?"

Rig says, "Don't be disrespectful, Berryman."

Berryman says, "It's a church," but sheepish.

We go back to staring at the floor, cracked linoleum and dust.

I say, "I wish I had a Mountain Dew."

Rig says, "I bet you do." He sits down and says, "CoGo's across the street."

I say, "You thirsty, Berryman?"

He says, "Sort of."

I say, "I buy, you fly."

Rig says, "Not yet," and kiboshes our plans to make a drink run.

We sit and wait.

Our size on the metal chairs makes the sounds of a machine dying.

No one shows up.

We sit and wait.

I say, "Maybe the meeting was earlier."

Rig stands and says, "I'm gonna talk."

Berryman says, "We support you."

Rig says, "Not drunk talk. I mean speaker talk." He looks at me and says, "I sketched out the ideas in my head. I don't have all the words right yet but I got the beginning, I think. You and me, we do the rest of that later, together. Tell me how I do."

Rig walks to counter and steps behind the wreckage. He pauses so we know the show is about to begin. A speaker has arrived, one who demands attention. He bends at the neck so his head goes down, prayer, fake prayer, meditation, a moment of silence. He breathes deep so his chest rises and falls. He does it again. He does it a third time. I wait for the nervousness to pass then realize Rig is not nervous. Rig is being dramatic. Breath for effect. Head bowed for humility. He gathers himself in a way that shows he is gathering, that what he reaches for and pulls back matters and holds weight. He looks up but not directly at me or Berryman. His brown eyes stare out the front glass doors and into the streets, finding people there, practicing finding people at least, and hooking them like the whole city wants and needs to hear him so they come and wait on the sidewalk for his story. I think he sees success the way I saw Brandon haunting. Rig knows he must speak to survive, to build the life he imagines. Brandon knew death answered all his questions about pain and anger.

Rig says, "I know I look big, bigger than anyone in this room, maybe bigger than anyone you ever seen in your life. And I is big, maybe bigger than anyone in your life. I look mean too, maybe the meanest you ever seen, but I ain't. Just big. And sometimes act crazy, crazy for fun and sometimes so crazy I could have ended up dead. I drove a motorcycle off a building and into a fountain. I lost thirty-six thousand dollars on one spin of roulette. I been a millionaire. I been a millionaire twice. I played professional football. I been shot at. I been hit by two bullets. I been straightjacketed by four cops, kicked in the head by a cop boot, and I won six national championships as a wrestler. No one else ever done that. Are you with me? You see my size?"

He raises a hand large enough to palm my head.

He says, "Big."

Berryman and I both nod, hooked on the theatrics, the story.

Rig pushes his hands on the counter and leans forward then pushes himself back up so he stands taller than he is, floating inches above the ground, and he opens up and flexes his back so he is as wide as a man with wings spreading under his shirt.

He says, louder, more passionate, "Are you with me?"

He looks at Berryman and me so we know he means us, we are the audience.

We nod again that we are with him.

He says, "You're with me?"

Berryman says, "We're with you."

Rig raises his hand and shows us his palm again.

He says, "My great-great grandma was small. My great-great grandma was a tiny woman. I feel like I fit her in my hand, though I know she weren't that small. My great-great grandma was a slave in Mississippi. She owned by white people. Picked their cotton. Pulled their water. Did their laundry, I bet. Cook they meals. She a slave all but the last eight years of her life. My great-great grandma. I think of her and I wanna reach back there with my big hand and pull her right outta slavery and put her right here, nice and safe. Pull her out of Mississippi in them olden times and put her right here in Pittsburgh with all yinz. You know what I tell her, my great-great grandma? You know what I say to that woman who probably come on some boat from Africa or maybe born here in a barn or in a field or in a stable like the baby Jesus, you know what I say to that woman? I say to her: thank you. I say thank you for staying alive. Thank you, great-great grandma, for staying alive. I know how hard that it is, and ain't no one own me but me. My grandma, she didn't have no choice. You a slave, you a slave. But me, I made myself a slave. I my own master and I still a slave, every day back then, even when I was a millionaire. Maybe you one too. Some of us don't have to do nothing but be free, when we already free, and still we fuck it up. I took that freedom my great grandma never had for most of her life and I dropped it on its head."

Rig stops and looks down and all the theatrics have turned sincere and the tears are so many they could be water painted on his face. I try not to cry. Then I cry but just with my eyes, focusing on controlling the rest. Breathe, I tell myself, and I breathe slow and deep as a mine shaft. I refuse to look toward Berryman who I'm sure drenches his own face. I hear him sob. Then sob again. Then apologize. Rig's breathing starts and stops, a couple gasps then deeper so his lungs fill then air out. Then another jagged gasp. He cannot stop crying.

His voice is as torn apart as this crumbling church on the South Side of Pittsburgh and he says, "I say thank you to my great-great grandma." He stops and breathes and says, "I say thank you for staying alive." He says, "I know how hard that is, staying alive." He says, "I'm gonna sit down now," and he steps from behind the counter.

Berryman, fully fucking bawling now, says, "That was amazing," and starts to clap.

I start to clap, faster than Berryman, louder.

We clap until Rig takes his seat.

Then he says, "I do it like that when I do it for real, except for all the crying. The crying caught me by surprise." He stops and wipes his cheeks with his thumb, a tool the size of a baby hammer, bone hard and delicate. He says, "I cussed some too." He presses his palms to his eyes and rubs. He says, "What you think? I fuck it up?"

I say, "Amazing," and start to choke, and say, "Better than amazing."

Rig says, "You think?"

He sits in the chair and I put my arm around him and he is so large I cannot reach his shoulder, though it doesn't matter, he leans and puts his head to mine.

Berryman says, "I'll tell you what, honestly, that was the best speech I've ever heard. Like in my whole life. I'm a mess from hearing it. Jesus, Rig, your story, I mean…" and he pauses before saying, "I'm going to start bawling again."

"Of course you are," Rig says, "you a pussy," and we all start to laugh.

PART TWENTY-SEVEN

Time and Time

As times passes I begin to understand that my clock will not move like my clock moved before and will maybe never move like I want it to again so I focus on having a clock, that time still exists.

I try to go to bed.

I try to wake up.

Daydreams and Awakeness

I don't see Megan for a few days, except for once in class. One of her bartenders keeps calling off so Megan covers shifts and studies and takes care of her grandmother. I write nonstop, on computers and on paper and in my head and once on a dirty car window, and I keep up with school and run eight miles a day and know that death in its ugliness is not enough to push me to some place that most people believe I should be. Dreams show up in the day like nightmares but not nightmares so I ride them to whatever time I want to call morning or first light. I see bullet holes in in the sun, in the moon, in a bowl of fucking macaroni. Bullet holes in cabinets. Bullet holes in windshields. Bullet holes in drapes. I dream about Brad Pitt but wake up and can't remember anything but

Brad Pitt, shirtless, lecturing. I think Brad Pitt supports me because he says encouraging things but he may be disappointed. He may be disgusted. I tell him he's the greatest actor of his generation. He says, "Lili Taylor was the greatest before she sold out."

I sleep for minutes, sometimes seconds.

I wake up from being awake, not as complex as it sounds.

I talk to Rig every night on the phone like we are teenagers and best friends. He reads his speech and wants suggestions but I mostly listen because it is great and sincere already. He mails me notecards. I mail notecards back. I drink a lot of Mountain Dew. Gallons. I go light on booze and stay clear of drugs. I query a couple agents. One agent says she liked my writing. I message her back: I like your agenting.

I write nonstop.

I write as much as I breathe.

Please don't argue that.

I set out to write this book about books and how difficult they are to make from a small corner in East Pittsburgh and it became something else and so I am an unpublished writer but maybe less unpublished because I feel larger up against death and closer to the truth of being alive and what a difficult and beautiful task that is.

Rig calls and says, "I got three talking gigs in September at colleges in California and Vermont and some shit school down south, maybe Louisiana. Not Nawleans. One of them lynching areas. I got another gig at a church in Atlanta. We need to clean up my mouth for that one. I know you teaching so I see you early summer, like June. These phone calls been great, Sellick, thanks. No shit. We like a couple teenage girls, gabbing and giggling. You remember *Fame,* that show? We like Coco and Leroy. You be Coco." He clears his enormous throat and laughs and says, "I'ma work on this myself now, just finish it. Then you call me, I call you, don't matter. You have to look at my notecards another time, maybe two. Then I'll finish it. You a good man, Sellick. Rig owes you. I owe you. When I turn pro wrestler and get big time, I bring you on as a manager. You be my hype man," and he belly laughs so it rattles the phone, like the satellites can't handle his voice, his re-found joy. He says, "We dress you like a welder and get you a fancy name, Sparksalot or something snappy like that."

I wish pro wrestling on Rig.

I'd like to be his manager.

Only I'd wear a tux and carry a cane.

Teenage Pop-Off

Tonight, Megan and I are lazy and movie-bound. We missed the earlier show, the 7:15, to hang at my apartment and make out and fool around. I know I am supposed to fuck her, that this is what adults do who care for each other, but we touch and I don't know how to make the final move. Megan took my clothes off while we kissed on the couch then she took her clothes off and I touched her and she touched me and she said, "This feels unbelievable," and I thought we would. I was sure we would. Then, in a mad shiver, I came all over her hand and belly and she said, "That was sweet," but I heard, "That was sad," because I wanted to hear, "That was sad," because that's how I sometimes hear the world.

If you can fix your mind about bullets, you can fix your mind about getting laid.

I want to believe it so I say it in my skull.

Fix your mind, I thought, getting dressed, you are not just a man with mat herpes that has not flared up in years, you are in love. Then I answered myself: no, you are the man who never went to the prom and never kissed a girl until the summer before college and she'd already slept with one dude at a party and he'd lost interest in her and I was standing by the keg, available. If I could turn my mind off, down even, something below eleven, I know I'd be a good lover, a good boyfriend, partner, husband, whatever. Things I do well in the world, I do well in the world—why is romance not part of my successes?

After I popped off like a teenager, as we walked to my truck, Megan held my hand like it was the only hand that ever mattered and she holds it like that now as we drive around, wasting time, being in love, being in love.

Megan Hates Dog Books, I Hate Marley

The next movie doesn't start until 9:25.

It's a shoot'em up.

She says, "You okay with a shoot'em up after everything?"

I say, "I love shoot'em ups," which is untrue but needs to be said.

She says, "I know, sorry for asking," and kisses my hand, an apology.

We go to a bookstore to build a little brainpower before we are consumed by guns and flames and fast cars, which are not guns and students and brain holes. I am seeing this film as some kind of test though I know not what that test is.

I park on Main Street, near the White Rabbit coffee shop, a great place to get a cookie and an iced tea or a fancy soda, and we walk to the window of the local bookshop in downtown Greensburg. The lights are dim. We press our faces to the glass. We are not sure if the store is closed for the night or has closed for good. The inside looks on the verge of being demolished. Books are randomly stacked on tables and the shelves show more wood than product. This is what cities look like before the wrecking ball swings down. Books are the new ghetto.

Megan says, "I hope it's not closing."

"It doesn't look good," I say.

We drive to Barnes and Noble, a huge brick building stuffed in a plaza by Chick Fil A. It shares space with an I-Hop, the world's worst pancake place, where people go to contract diabetes. We step into the parking lot and can smell the canned berries I-Hop dumps on everything. Their dumpster must be a bee's nest, swarming. Barnes and Noble is lit like a Walmart, like any other chain, but I don't know if there's a difference anymore between most local bookstores and the chains. Barnes and Noble stinks and sells more kids toys than literature but the local place in Greensburg, where we just visited and if it still exists, carries crafty gift items and fancy ink pens and leather notebooks and dark chocolate bars in displays where they should be stocking great books.

Megan loves Caliban, a used bookstore in Pittsburgh. She crushes on the counter guy with the blue glasses and the dreamy brown hair. He plays in a band and bangs drums like he's Bonzo, sticks blazing, those blue intellectual glasses going dark and intense. I love Caliban too, even the cute drummer, but they keep odd hours and aren't open most nights. It's the kind of bookstore you'd see in an indie film, meaning weird and perfect. The owner stands five feet tall, tops, and sometimes wears tennis clothes while he prices rare nautical books and old Vonnegut first editions but he's bearded and oddly gritty, speaking in a bark-laugh and sometimes motherfucking about something in the back office behind the cash register like he might be a bit mad. Once, as I waited at the counter, I heard him mutter, "Motherfucking second edition of *Ulysses* in leather but now the spine has a water crack, fuck me." Then he stepped from the back office and touched his beard and smiled. He always has these great recommendations. You just have to know to ask, to step into the bark-laugh. Years ago he turned me on to *Bleak House* and sent me on a Dickens bender. He turned me on to Jorbel. He once gave me a bilingual copy of Akhmatova's selected poems when I'd bought a couple Russian novels, only the bilingual languages were Russian and Spanish. "See what you make of this one," he said, and slipped it in my bag for free, smiling.

Now I turn to Megan and say, "Do you want to drive to The Manor?"

The Manor is the art theater in Squirrel Hill.

Megan says, "It's the weekend," and glimmer frowns.

She's right.

The city will be crowded with weekend maniacs searching out beer that can be drunk from fishbowls and other people talking about small plates and farm-to-table restaurants and theater people muddying up downtown with their theater clothes. Megan needs to be close to Harry's Bar in case the part-time bartender needs back-up or decides to bail for illness or other reasons, including laziness, so we make choices.

We park and climb from the car.

The crowd at Barnes and Noble is sparse. A few customers read magazines in the coffee house. The coffee house smells like ash. I wish sometimes I drank coffee but not at Barnes and Noble, near so many books written by conservative TV pundits. We walk around the front tables, browsing. Megan leans in and kisses my ear.

"I used to love bookstores," I say.

"I still do," Megan says.

"Caliban," I say.

"Caliban is fucking great," she says.

She puts her arm around me. Next weekend we are supposed to have dinner with Joanie and her veterinarian. Megan and Joanie have become fast pals. They text, they talk on the phone, they've been to lunch, they've gone for coffee. Joanie wants Megan to approve of her dog doctor. Or to not approve. To be present for. Involved.

I am still worried about Fat Bill. He called and left a message the day after his beatdown and thanked me profusely but I have not heard from him since. He could be in Iraq or Afghanistan by now. He could be in Syria. Where else are terrible things happening in the world? He could be there, on a tightrope. He could be shooting a machine gun or digging his hole to hide in or washing sand from his eyes with well water.

I worry about my students constantly. They are like stars that populate my brain and I dread the moment when they will supernova because I want them to keep burning, to stay bright but not burn out, to have money, lots of money, but still not be gross. I want them to have more success than I have but for their success to arrive faster so no one has to weld bridges and eat sparks in faraway towns.

Shay, the waitress with the kid, came to class yesterday and said, "I don't want to be a nurse," and started to cry. I told her, "Be whatever you want to be," but I think I meant, "Be whatever you can be," which was too realistic to speak.

It's how I've built my life, being whatever I could be.

I saw Berryman after class and he said, "Why is that girl crying?" and I said, "Money." He said, "These kids break my heart," and I believed him and maybe he's earned the right to have his heart broken by a kid like Shay. I hope Berryman stays with it, letting his heart break. Maybe he doesn't walk off to the private school with the rich wife and kid who plays hockey on the travel team and wears the most expensive equipment. Or maybe he does. Or maybe he doesn't. Berryman headed back to his shitty office. I stepped into mine

Now Megan says, "Let's go make fun of the bestsellers."

That sounds better than it should.

Megan pulls me along.

The few people who work here smile politely.

Megan brushed out her hair after we fooled around so it falls past her shoulders, one side behind her ear because it never stays. Her clothes are less tight, not loose, but her tits are packed away, her style more than her sex. I should wear tighter clothes. I have abs. I should talk about them more, my rippling stomach. Only I couldn't. Only gross. Megan says I make her happy. I know she makes me happy. She says she has decided to keep the bar, to never sell it. She has decided to turn it into a money-making machine so I can quit teaching to bartend and write. We will be famous writers, if only to each other. We will rent an apartment, a huge one, near the bar because of Harriet. We will thrive as writers and caretakers. Or caretakers and writers. And bar owners, of course. I often wonder if Harriet will ever give me a mug, if she'll ever remember my name, if she'll ever know the truth I feel when I am with her granddaughter.

Does it matter?

Everything does, I hope.

I feel it more each day, each hour sometimes.

Love, mostly. And money.

And pain.

Meaning how to avoid pain.

Megan thinks I would be an excellent bartender but I only know how to make two drinks: a beer and a shot. I ask Megan to pay me to drink. She doesn't think that would be possible.

And besides, I love teaching and I don't think I could ever let anyone support me, and besides, I love teaching. I love teaching.

Megan stops at a table of paperbacks stacked a foot high.

"*Marley and Me*," she says. "Doesn't that just make you want to puke."

"It really does," I say, "but that's old."

The cover is from the movie that was out a few years back, Owen Wilson and Jennifer Aniston looking airbrushed and shiny. And Marley, the dog, his snout airbrushed into a smile. They are all so beautiful, they are hideous. I don't know that I hate anything more than I hate dog books, the entire genre of dog books, and I say that as a man who occasionally dips into the prefab world of sobriety memoirs, the don't-drink books that the don't-drinkers love, even though they all end the same way, with people not drinking.

Alcoholics Anonymous and puppies are attacking literature.

I say, "There are more recent dog books," and I hold up another.

I look around and find two more on tables.

I hold up one.

Megan, still clutching *Marley and Me*, looks and says, "*My Dog Skip*. Harriet read that. It was just so fucking bad."

I snag another one and frame it in my hands.

"*A Dog's Purpose,*" Megan says. "Gross."

"It's the subtitle," I say, and read it out. "A Novel for Humans. That makes it exceptionally gross. He also wrote *8 Simple Rules for Dating My Teenage Daughter.*"

"The dog?"

"No, the author."

Megan says, "He should be shot." Then, "By his teenage daughter." She looks at me, mortified, catching herself. She says, "No one should be shot. I need to speak better."

"Dog book writers should be shot," I say. "I'm okay with it."

I put my dog book back on the pile.

Megan turns the pages on her dog book.

She reads the back cover.

The back cover says, "John and Jenny were just beginning life together. They were young and in love, with a perfect little house and not a care in the world."

Megan hands me the book.

I've read the cover before.

I'm oddly obsessed with *Marley and Me.* It's just another terrible book in a country of terrible books but I haven't been able to stop thinking about it, not since the teen novelization, not since the picture book, not since the movie tie-in and the slow motion preview of Jennifer Aniston and Owen Wilson running on the beach, mouthing, "Marley," while some sappy-ass piano music plays. The back of the book says, "Then they brought home Marley, a wiggly yellow furball of a puppy. Life would never be the same."

I do not know why this makes me want to choke Owen Wilson out.

Owen Wilson did not write *Marley and Me.*

John Grogan wrote *Marley and Me.*

I heard John Grogan on the radio one day. He writes for a newspaper, has a column. I hate this word: columnist. The radio person wanted to know why John Grogan started to write about Marley, his loveable pup. He wanted to know where the memoir came from. John said he wrote a column about Marley and he was flooded with emails. People ate it up. Usually he got three or four letters per column, tops. The Marley column brought in hundreds of letters and emails. "That's when," he said, "I knew I'd found my book." I pulled my car off the road. I punched myself in the chest twice. Bam, bam. Good solid heart punches. John Grogan, you motherfucker, I thought. Then I went home and opened my email and there was another agent saying, "Sorry, not for us," but by then I was too sad to heart-punch myself again. What kind of adult lets someone tell them what book to write, let alone a mob? It's high school. The most popular kid gets the book. Even if the most popular kid happens to be a dog.

Megan holds the *Marley and Me* over her head like she's trying to signal a plane flying too low, like she's trying to deflect the sun.

She says, "Has anyone ever read this?"

She says, "Will anyone here admit to liking *Marley and Me?*"

Customers stop to look.

A couple people laugh.

Most smile and move on.

One guy stops, sets his coffee down, and takes off the lid. He stirs the drink with his finger. To himself he says, "Hot." The coffee splashes on a stack of books. The guy doesn't worry about the splash, doesn't wipe it up or go for napkins. The coffee puddles, beige with cream. The guy licks his finger. He puts the lid back on, makes sure it fits, and heads toward the front doors, drinking hot coffee, slurping.

Megan says, *"Marley and Me?* Anyone?"

A teenage girl in a knit hat says, "My mom's read it."

Megan says, "And?"

The girl smiles and says, "Sugar tit."

Megan says, "Thank you, thank you, your honesty is much appreciated."

The girl says, "Cool," and walks off.

I look beyond Megan and see a giant Winnie the Pooh, six feet tall, the world's most popular bear, jaundiced yellow and dressed in his red shirt but always bottomless.

I love Winnie the Pooh, Winnie the Pooh from my childhood, Joanie reading Winnie the Pooh stories before my bedtime and saying, "That's one screwed-up bear." Joanie loved Winnie the Pooh. She related. We all do. Pooh was a fat, messed-up bear. He was lost and hungry. He barely knew what day it was. He wanted to do right but there was always something to eat that sounded better. He loved honey like junkies love dope. Pooh was sick, yes, but happy in his honey love sickness.

Who here is not Pooh?

In Barnes and Noble Winnie the Pooh stands as a huge wooden cutout in the kids section. He clutches an overflowing honey pot. He smiles his lost smile and steps with his stuffed legs. Pooh holds no answers and generates no philosophy but, possibly, be kind while you're being greedy. Find a best friend to make adventures with. Add to those friends and adventures.

I glance at the books on the table in front of me, on the shelves. I glance at Pooh. Back to the tables and shelves. Adults have started writing kids' books for other adults. We have become as sensitive and good-hearted as children never were. Tigger could write a better book than John Grogan. Roo and Rabbit and Owl have more personality than Jennifer Aniston and Owen Wilson. Eeyore, with his cynicism and negative outlook, looks like fucking Nietzsche compared to John Grogan and John Grogan as played by Owen Wilson.

I need to get away from this and into a bar.

Megan says, *"Marley and Me.* Anyone? Final takers?"

"I read it," an old woman says. She's maybe seventy, skinny, with a light blue scarf tied around her neck. We wait for her to say something else but she doesn't. Instead, she turns up her nose and makes a stinky sound.

"Exactly," Megan says, "thank you," then she suggests we skip the movie.

My Place vs. The Bar

I think I've had eight light beers. I don't know why this seems important, maybe because I didn't plan to drink or maybe because Megan believes so much in drinking. I believe in drinking too, unapologetically, except on the nights when I find a beer bottle in my mouth when I planned to see a film and would rather be sitting in a movie theater. None of this will matter in a couple more drinks. None of it matters now with my buzz.

Drinking cures any concerns related to drinking.

Harriet is upstairs, sound asleep. I put her to bed and she said, "You're with Megan?" and I said, "I am," and she said, "Make her be good to you," and I said, "I will."

The kid with the mustache, who bartends when Megan needs a night off, pours me a shot of some dark red liquor I did not order.

Megan drinks vodka and orange juice.

I don't know how many she's had.

A lot.

I wish John Grisham were here.

I haven't seen him in days.

For a man I barely know, I miss him a great deal.

People of composure are rare finds.

Megan says, "Do you want to go back to your place and fuck me?"

I finish my ninth beer and say, "Yes," and hope I mean it.

Dick don't fail me now.

WAA-WAA

Friday approaches. I look at the clock from my bed, waiting for the numbers to change. I have been in bed with Megan since Wednesday night, except to teach and once to buy milk and Mountain Dew. We have been fucking and eating cereal for twenty-six or so hours, sometimes with the TV on, fuzzy lines across the screen because I don't have cable and still watch movies on DVD. You can eat a lot of cereal in twenty-six hours. My dick is half-hard and numb. I have fucked well. I have enjoyed fucking well. I don't mean to brag but I see that I have fucked well in Megan's face and in the way her body moves, the little dance steps she does on the way to the bathroom or the refrigerator. I could do it again but I would be doing it to impress Megan, which is fine, but I would be happy to get some toast or maybe a sandwich or a large pizza with extra cheese, a pizza with so much cheese the slice cannot be lifted with one hand. I could drink a thousand Mountain Dews, put my mouth to the fountain and swallow.

Megan says, "My waa-waa hurts."

She is naked, standing inside my bedroom, the door closed. She spreads her pussy lips and looks into the mirror hanging crooked on the back of the door. It's a hairy pussy and her finger has disappeared into her bush.

"Your what-what hurts?" I say.

"My waa-waa," she says.

"Please never call it a waa-waa again," I say.

"Why?"

"Because it makes your pussy sound like a screaming infant."

"Harriet calls hers a waa-waa."

"I don't care what Harriet calls her pussy."

Megan strains her neck to better see her pussy. She's in front of the mirror but she's not using the mirror anymore. Her chin is pressed to the tops of her tits.

I say, "What are you looking for in there?"

"Your wacker," she says, and laughs her way back to the bed.

WRITING ABOUT SEX

I am always disappointed at how little Americans write about sex and how poorly the Americans who write about sex do—I'm looking at you, Henry Miller—but I am even more disappointed in the people who criticize the writers of sex, including Henry Miller, when they so seldom write about sex themselves. Look at you, sex writer, using the wrong language and taking the wrong approach, while I keep all of my sexual adventures private so you can't attack me.

You can't critique unless you reveal.

Make that a rule.

The rest is bullshit.

I apologize for only writing a few pages about my sexual adventures in this book but I haven't been laid in years and I'm just learning, the language and the act, all of it.

Maybe now is the time for you to start to criticize.

BUYING THE BAR

We decide not to fuck anymore and to get a sandwich instead. Megan's waa-waa needs a rest. My nuts are sore from slapping and swaying. I sit on the living room couch. I'm fully dressed. Megan hangs back in the bedroom, primping. It is almost three in the morning. No primping is necessary. I'm thinking Wayne's Diner in Homestead. Megan would like a burrito from Taco Bell. I could get a veggie hoagie with extra cheese from Sheetz.

Megan says, "Two minutes."

I say, "My stomach's rumbling."

She sticks her head into the hall. Her hands twist some sort of tailbraid into her hair and adds gumbands to hold it in place. It's a lot of hair.

She says, "I don't want to go to Pittsburgh. It's too far. It's too late."

"Taco Bell hurts my belly," I say.

"Sheetz," she says. "Chili-cheese dogs."

She finishes her hair and goes back to the bedroom. I said before that I do not have cable TV but being in love makes me desire it. I want to read but I cannot read with Megan in the apartment so we sit on the couch and pet each other and watch whatever comes with the bunny ears or watch my DVDs, which are mostly rock concerts and documentaries on writers, quite a few produced by PBS so they're scrubbed clean.

Right now I stare at static with the volume off.

I stand up to get a Mountain Dew from the fridge.

Outside, footsteps lightly move across my porch, which is also the other upstairs tenant's porch. The other tenant, in the apartment to the right if you're facing the building, drinks. I'm not sure what his job is but he usually carries a lunch pail and always wears steel-toed boots. We smile. We wave. We sometimes pull into the gravel parking lot at the same moment and politely stumble up the stairs like ducklings, waddling together but not quacking. Both our apartments are tiny and we try to respect the thin wall between us.

Is it strange that two grown men are not even remotely in contention to buy our own houses and that neither of us could scrape together a down payment?

I pretend it's not.

Maybe that's why he drinks.

Megan says, "Almost ready."

I close the fridge.

Someone knocks.

My neighbor has never knocked before, ever.

I think the knock is Fat Bill, just Bill, my student, and he will want me to hide him because he is AWOL from the wars in the desert.

Megan comes from the bedroom. She has on my sweatshirt and her pants, a lovely outfit. The only make-up she wears is lipstick which makes me feel the pull of her lips.

She says, "Was that someone at the door?"

"Someone's at the door," I say.

"Answer it?" she says.

I pop the top on the Mountain Dew.

I drink until my throat isn't dry.

I am not opposed to all wars, just the ones that take my students and the ones that my students create in their own heads and end with bullets to their brains.

I answer the door.

It's neither my neighbor nor Fat Bill.

John Grisham, dressed like the real John Grisham in a fancy JC Penney's suit and a paisley tie, stands there, grinning. He holds an open bottle of whiskey. It dangles at his side so I can't see how full it is. His suit is crinkle-cut from sitting in a booth in some bar.

"John Grisham," I say. "How did you find me?"

"The kid at Megan's bar with the mustache told me," he says. Then he says, "Is it late? If it's too late, I can come back. Or not come back. I invited myself."

"It's three in the morning, John Grisham," I say.

Megan says, "We were just going to Sheetz to get hot dogs."

"Megan!" John Grisham says.

He turns on like a lightbulb, one hundred watts.

"Oh John Grisham," Megan says.

He says, "I was hoping you'd be here. The kid with the mustache said you would be here but I hardly ever trust anyone with a mustache."

"Why don't you come and get some hotdogs with us?" Megan says.

John Grisham says, "Could I come in? This is really weird, standing in your doorway at three in the morning. It feels stalkerish."

"Of course," I say, and I mean it, but I am hungry too, hungry enough to fall out of love and dissolve any number of friendships to make a Sheetz run.

John Grisham says, "Want a drink?"

"I'm good," I say. "I want to get some chicken fingers or an Italian sub."

"I can do better than that," John Grisham says.

He walks from my doorway to my kitchen. John Grisham has the best energy of anyone I've ever met who looks like a terrible writer of legal thrillers. If I don't get away from him soon, I will never eat and my stomach will turn and I will drink his whiskey and I will lose another day to something else that I immensely enjoy but don't need when love and a hoagie with extra cheese and friendship would be more than enough to sustain me until morning.

John Grisham says, "You have a lot of pictures of people glued to your kitchen cabinets. Did you pay someone to do that or did you do that yourself?"

"I'm crafty," I say, "and a big fan of the arts."

John Grisham says, "I'll say," and points with his whiskey bottle.

Megan says, "Why don't you get a hotdog with us, John Grisham?"

John Grisham moves around my cabinets like an art exhibit at the Carnegie Museum. He looks at Townes Van Zandt with his acoustic guitar and Gerry Locklin with his Coors beer in the bathtub. He looks at a little sketch of Rimbaud in his dapper suit and tie, looking stunned, and he looks at Mohamed Choukri smoking a cigarette in a café in Morocco, acting very serious next to a woman in a burka and another woman in a string dress. John Grisham puts his finger on Howling Wolf's face and holds it there. He points and presses. Howling Wolf shouts into a microphone and sweats.

He says, "That's a man I would not want to fight in a back alley."

"That's Howling Wolf," I say. "He sang the blues."

"Are these people famous?" John Grisham says. "Because I don't know a single fucking one. Christ, sometimes I feel so stupid. Maybe you could play me some Howling Wolf or something like that. Did you say jazz?"

"Blues," I say.

He says, "My mom listened to Judy Garland records. I like KISS, even though they were supposed to be devil's music. I liked that rocker guys wore make-up and looked sort of kung-fooey. I dressed up like the spaceman for Halloween when I was like ten. Was that Gene Simmons or was he the devil?"

I say, "Gene Simmons was the demon. Ace Frehley was the spaceman."

Megan touches John Grisham's shoulder and says, "Maybe we could play you a hotdog or a hot cup of coffee."

John Grisham says, "Can I have a glass?"

"That cabinet, right there," I say, pointing. "How drunk are you?"

He says, "Moderate. Drunk enough to find out that you live out here in this very respectable yet opioid-infested community from a mustachioed twenty-something. Sober enough to drive here and be safe."

"Fair enough," I say.

He says, "This whole neighborhood smells like heroin."

"Thanks," I say.

He says, "I hate to drink from the bottle. It's classless."

He takes down three juice glasses. I did not know I had three juice glasses but there they are, lined up like cousins at a family reunion. John Grisham closes Howling Wolf and Townes Van Zandt and looks at their faces. He pours three whiskeys. He opens another cabinet, my cereal cabinet, and puts the bottle of whiskey next to the Lucky Charms.

"Unless that's iced tea," I say, "I'm out."

John Grisham says, "First, a question. Then, a toast."

He pauses and raises his whiskey glass. He drinks the shot in a gulp. He picks up the next glass. These shots, all three, all two now, belong to John Grisham. I hadn't realized that before but I am grateful it is so. He stands in a good place.

John Grisham says, "The question is: Megan, I would like to buy your bar. That's not a question. That's a statement. Now, before you answer, consider this: I'm a lawyer. I still plan on being a lawyer. I am an excellent lawyer. I apologize for the hubris. You would run the bar. We could work out a salary, whatever you want, and you could show me what an owner does. I would be as fair as fair can be."

Megan says, "You sound fair."

I say, "You do."

He picks up another shot. He downs it. He does not make the whiskey face that I make when I down whiskey. He smiles and raises the glass in a happy gesture like he's just discovered a vaccine for boredom or bad debt or the lonelies.

"What's the toast?" I say.

"What toast?" John Grisham says, and slugs the last shot of whiskey.

"There were questions and toasts," I say. "You promised."

John Grisham says, "Who said anything about a toast? We're talking business."

Megan laughs and says, "You are really drunk, John Grisham."

"I know," John Grisham says. "It's what I do on Thursdays."

Megan says, "It's Friday now."

John Grisham says, "Don't be mad."

Megan says, "You're smart."

He says, "It's why I want to buy your bar."

Hero Talk

Outside my apartment John Grisham opens Megan's door, the passenger side of his boat-sized fancy Chevy, and gestures like a chauffeur. Please, enter. Please, make yourself comfortable. If he wore a hat, it would tip itself, such is his chivalry. Megan slides into the backseat. She thanks him while he politely waits until she buckles her seatbelt. Then he closes the door.

He turns to me and says, "So, yeah."

I say, "You okay?"

He says, "Yep."

I wait for him to direct me or to open my door or for him to climb inside his Chevy so I can follow in my truck. Instead, he gently takes me by the shoulders, looks me in the eye, then hugs me. The hug is deep and firm. I try to match his sincerity. This goes on. Then he releases me. Then he hugs me again. The hug grows tighter. I squeeze back. Over his shoulder I see the hump in his backseat, that middle section, and it looks very comfortable.

I give him some pats, three taps in succession.

"Okay, big guy," I say.

He says, "You. You're the big guy," and clutches me again.

I appreciate the gesture but I am too sober and hungry for all this.

John Grisham says, "Can we talk? Two seconds?"

I say, "Can we talk in the car while we drive for food?"

"Two seconds," he says.

I think he is going to ask me to talk to Megan about buying her bar, to use my influence, or to ask about student papers, or to ask about cocaine, how he can score some, but instead he wants to talk about Brandon's suicide. Or he doesn't want to talk about Brandon's suicide. He wants to congratulate me or praise me or just hug me into being okay.

He says, "You're a hero, the way you acted. I've been thinking about it every day. Hero is the only word for it. Thank you, from me, from all of us."

"I appreciate that," I say. "But I also appreciate a good hotdog when I'm hungry as hell. What's your stance on a good hotdog?"

John Grisham steps back and says, "I see I'm making a fool of myself."

"You're not," I say. "I'm just tired and hungry."

He adjusts himself—tie, collar, jacket.

"If you want a good hotdog," John Grisham says, "why are you going to Sheetz? Their hotdogs are made of chicken beaks and cow anus. Everyone knows that GetGo has the best hotdogs. You drive, I'll treat."

"That's a deal," I say, and pour him into his own backseat.

PART TWENTY-EIGHT

Nona, Along for the Ride

It's noon. Dinner tonight with Joanie is at six. Or drinks are at six and dinner is at seven. I can't remember. Megan made the official plans and passed me the details. The veterinarian will come by at 5:30 to help with the cooking. He gets props for being a gentleman, even if he is younger than me. Megan has a late morning meeting with an advisor to schedule for next semester then she works at the bar. She'll arrive for dinner around seven. This whole thing has the making of a clusterfuck. I would have scheduled an event like this—a dinner, a meet-and-greet, a whatever—for Saturday or even Sunday but no one asked me. I serve more as an emergency hotline than a consultant but maybe if I were occasionally consulted there would be fewer emergencies.

Maybe I flatter myself.

I have this idea to invite Nona to dinner featuring Joanie and her veterinarian and Megan and anyone else who shows up.

I should call Joanie first.

I don't.

I put on my running clothes and drive to Nona's place.

Nona sits out back, in a rocking chair, reading her book. I remember my great-great uncle's novel, which I haven't read, which I'll probably never read, which has not crossed my mind since the last time I talked with Nona about it. The sun comes in under the awning but the light doesn't reach the rocking chairs. Nona looks up and smiles. The place looks like a Cracker Barrel. I never noticed that before. You can almost smell the chicken fried steak, the white gravy, the heart attacks, the racist waitresses.

"Where's my flowers?" Nona says, and laughs.

"It's not that kind of visit," I say. "I'm on my way to run."

"I can't run anywhere," she says. "That's a ridiculous idea."

She folds her book into her lap and thinks about this. It must not be an unpleasant thought, her inability to run, because her thin lips curl up into a smile.

"Not you," I say. "Me. I'm running. But I'm also supposed to have dinner with Joanie and her new boyfriend later on tonight and I was thinking you might come along. Eat some dinner. Make some small talk. It could be fun, getting everyone together."

"Well," she says. "That's a terrible idea if I ever heard one."

She wears her overalls again. Her hair is braided in pigtails. I look at her knuckles, the knots that hold her fingers to her hands, and I wonder how many more times she will be able to make her hair so precise.

I say, "You could wear your blue dress, like the one you wore to DeNunzios."

"Did you talk to your mother?" she says.

"I did not," I say. "I wanted to consult with you first."

She closes her eyes and rocks back the chair and stays there. I think she will look like this when she dies but I hope it is not here and I hope it is not for many years. She opens her eyes and rocks forwards. She leans and pushes and stretches and stands up.

"I'll do it," she says. "And I won't embarrass anyone at all."

"It'll be fun," I say.

"Oh, it will not," she says.

RUNNING

By now I should probably refer to it as therapy or what it is: escape. I burn the track with my feet.

DINNER

Joanie can't cook for shit, never could, but it's still weird that I can't smell anything when I'm standing outside her front door with Nona. Joanie's kitchen window is wide-open. Scents should be wafting, as they say on cooking shows. Garlic and ginger and all that. The time is five minutes past six o'clock, as late as Nona would allow us to arrive. Joanie lives on the top floor of a two-story house, a very fancy place with brown bricks and stucco. The awning is wavy and orange. I think this is all supposed to be Spanish or Mexican or something that was practical for poor people but is now fashionable for people who watch remodeling shows on cable TV. I ring the bell. Nona hangs on my arm, date-like, blue dress on, fancy shoes in a bag, tube socks pulled to her knees. I ring again.

Nona says, "I should have put my good shoes on at the home. I look ridiculous."

"You look great," I say. "You can change in the bedroom if you feel compelled."

I knock on the door. I look at my watch. The window is orange like the awning. The drapes are beige, some sort of canvas. I try to see inside. Maybe Joanie is in there, not cooking, peeking out, hiding from her mother like always.

Nona says, "I want to be at my best when I meet your mother's new boyfriend. You said he was a doctor. We are a doctor-worthy family."

"An animal doctor," I say.

She says, "Really?"

I say, "You are at your best."

She says, "I wish tennis shoes weren't so comfortable."

Below us is a small parking area for people who live here and who live across the street in another house turned apartment or condo or whatever these are called. I look down and spot Joanie's car. I see her neighbor's new Volkswagen. I look for a Mercedes or a Beamer or whatever car an animal doctor would drive but the lot is mostly filled with Fords and Chevys and a Honda minivan, nothing a man making six figures would drive.

I ring the bell.

Nona says, "Maybe we're early."

I say, "You know we're late."

"Just fashionably," she says.

The door opens slowly and Joanie peeks out. She sees us and opens wider but still not completely. She looks beautiful, wearing a white dress, tight but not as tight as usual, cleavage showing but not as full as usual. Her make-up appears less, her eyes not as smoky, so more real.

She steps onto the porch and says, "Mom, I'm so glad you came," and she says it with enough sincerity that she could be sincere.

Nona says, "I like your earrings."

Joanie says, "I like your blue dress."

OILS AND SPICES

Time passes painfully. It's almost seven and our number still stands at three. Joanie, politely but emphatically, has refused to start to cook. Nona sips from a glass of white wine. Joanie started drinking wine before we arrived but now she drinks gin and tonics, stirring with her finger, gulping. I drink Mountain Dew from a two-liter bottle I pour into a frosted mug. I should probably switch to something stronger to brace for whatever the night brings but I feel like someone should stay sober. My nerves will be frayed like wires cut during a burglary but I'll be great behind the wheel of my truck.

Joanie stands between the kitchen and the dining room, pacing, leaning. She does not sit. She has not sat. The dining room table is covered with new plates and cloth napkins and all kinds of silverware like each bite might need its own utensil. Nona sits at the head of the table. I lean against a wall, too busy thinking of things to keep the conversation going to hear what anyone actually says after I ask a question. And still the quiet sometimes wins. I sip my Mountain Dew then set the glass on the table. Nona takes my hand. I give her a squeeze. Nona and I do not make eye contact so we can avoid acknowledging how sad this is. She releases my hand. I look at her from behind and she is so tiny her chair looks like a throne. I could hold her on my lap like she was my young daughter. Joanie swishes the booze in her glass like she may need another drink. She would fit in my lap too. I could hold her with my other arm.

I have the strength and families need held and why not me?

Joanie says, "We could turn the TV on."

Nona says, "I should probably put my good shoes on."

"You're fine," Joanie says. "Let's all go in the living room."

The living room looks like a Pier 1 display. All the colors blend perfectly. The orange pillows brighten the brown suede couch. I sit in the beige chair with the fine yellow stripes. I put my feet up on the fuzzy hassock.

Joanie says, "That's not a real hassock."

"It looks like a real hassock," I say.

"Don't ruin it with your feet," she says.

I hear something that could be an animal doctor's car out in the street but the sound revs up and moves on.

Nona touches a picture of flowers.

Nona says, "I like real flowers."

"Real flowers are too much trouble," Joanie says.

Nona says, "I guess."

She slides back on the couch, feet dangling.

She says, "I could cook that food."

Joanie says, "We're fine."

Nona says, "I'm actually sort of hungry. Old people get that way."

"Maybe I could cut some cheese?" I say.

No one responds.

Joanie sits on the couch, at the opposite end. Her face is perfect with make-up and fitness and diet, yet so sad. She is like Nona in that she can get younger when she needs to get younger but unlike Nona in that she courts her own emotional destruction. Her hair is blonde but natural looking, her nails painted and polished. On her collar, a tiny smear of concealer. Her earrings are white gold with real diamonds. I know these things cost a lot of money. Joanie once said, "I'd rather live poor and look rich."

I think about that—live poor, look rich.

If I know what she means, and I'm not sure I do, I'm the opposite.

I hear something else outside.

Or I think I do.

Mostly I hear nothing.

Even the commuters are home from work and fed.

I put my feet down and adjust the hassock.

I put my feet up.

No one will say anything about the veterinarian, that he's late, that he exists, that he is my mother's boyfriend or was or will be again, that love is at stake here, or romance, or shame.

Joanie says, "Maybe let's go back to the dining room."

Nona says, "I like your cloth napkins."

Joanie says, "I thought you liked paper napkins."

I say, "All napkins are created equally."

Nona and I move back to the dining room while Joanie steps into the kitchen. Nona takes another seat, not at the head of the table. She unfolds the cloth napkin and puts it across her lap then she folds it back up, a trial run. Joanie slams a kitchen cabinet so hard it rattles glass.

Nona startles and says, "That was loud."

"I think I'll get a beer," I say.

I peek in the kitchen before I hit the refrigerator.

Joanie holds the phone in her hand.

I know she wants to call.

I know she wants it to ring.

I step inside and take the phone.

I have been taking the phone from my mother for most of my life. I do not mind. Maybe I did when I was younger but never enough to stop taking the phone. Now I consider it a gift, the lifting of other people's pain from their hands. My life is the life that Joanie allowed me to build. I am proud to be grateful. I know that she could have turned me over to Nona, that Nona would have raised me, that I would have been fine with Nona, great with Nona, but not in the place I am now, holding my mother. I know that Joanie could have run after my father or any number of men who would have loved her, single and ready to chase and be chased. She could have flown but instead she walked beside me and allowed me to keep up.

I am blessed to be here tonight, not eating dinner, with my mom.

COOKING

Nona says, "I really could cook us something. I'm good at it."

Joanie says, "Mom, that's enough."

Pretty and its Downfall

The veterinarian is still not here. He has not called or texted to say he is not coming but we know, all of us, even Joanie. The light and air and even the toilet running in the bathroom all do their jobs in accordance with the non-arrival of my mom's boyfriend.

Joanie says, "What a lousy fuck," like a joke, sarcasm, anger, then she says, "What a lousy fuck," in a voice so filled with disappointment it could be a leaky balloon falling from her hand to the floor or a flower wilting in lapsed time.

She knocks back the rest of her gin like her neck is on a hinge.

Nona says, "It's not a crime to be single."

I say, "Nona, say better things."

She says, "Well, it's not."

Joanie says, "You wouldn't know it by the world. People look at women my age, and they see you without a man, and they judge. You become invisible."

Nona says, "People judge everything."

Joanie says, "Just let me wallow, okay Mom?"

Chicken sits in the sink, thawed out, waiting. Potatoes are piled on the counter. Various oils and spices line the edge of the stove. None of these things are of any use to a woman who hates to cook and who will not let anyone else try. I wonder if Joanie knew what to buy. I picture her with her veterinarian, who I've never seen, who I've never imagined until now, in the grocery store. They walk the aisles. The veterinarian wears a white coat and sports a great head of thick hair and he directs Joanie by pointing to the shelves. She smiles and fills the cart. Then she doesn't. She stops. She turns. Then she points and the veterinarian bends and reaches and fills the cart. Joanie's entire romantic life has been a steady cluster of men she refuses to conform to or even get along with while begging each one to love her for her looks and body and fashion and nothing else, no depth, just surface. It's submission by confrontation. Pay attention to me, you fucker. Tell me I'm pretty or I swear I'll punch you in the teeth. Please don't leave.

The Other

Nona puts down her wine.

She says, "Well, the other girl is still coming, right?"

"Megan?" I say. "She'll be here," and even that makes me feel bad.

Dinner

Megan cooks the food. I did not know she could cook like this. I thought she made sandwiches and opened bags of chips. But now she fries the chicken and mashes the potatoes. She puts the oils and the spices back in the cabinets. The cabinets are almost empty. I am a little drunk. Joanie is very drunk but she does not show it, not in a way that Megan or Nona would notice, but I see the fake happiness in every gesture, the way she follows Megan around the kitchen like she would really like to know how to cook. Megan politely and sincerely talks to Joanie, showing her various tricks with flour and breadcrumbs and how to use a knife. She drinks from a glass of wine, not her usual beer-liquor combo. Nona sits on the couch, sleeping. All the smells are wonderful. I know this cannot be saved because it is not ours to save but I love Megan for trying.

"I should probably take your grandmother home," Joanie says.

"I'll take her," I say.

"You're both drunk," Megan says and laughs. "I'll take her after dinner. Maybe she'll wake up and be hungry."

"It was supposed to be chicken cacciatore," Joanie says. "I drank all the wine when I realized he wasn't coming."

"That's a gross wine to drink," I say.

Megan says, "I think you mean Marsala for chicken marsala. Cacciatore just uses regular white wine, nothing too sweet."

Joanie says, "Thank you, honey. Sometimes men don't understand."

"Did you just lump me in with men then dismiss the category?" I say.

Joanie says, "Yes."

"You should get on social media," I say. "You'd really fit in."

Megan says, "He could still come."

"I'm so stupid," Joanie says. "How can I be so old and still be so stupid? It seems impossible that someone could be both." She turns to Megan and says, "You're a great cook, honey. Everything smells so good."

"Thank you," Megan says. "Let's plate this and eat."

Joanie says, "I couldn't eat a thing."

Megan says, "It'll keep."

Joanie so seldom cries but she looks like she could. She looks like she could take her own head off and pour tears in a glass, a cry that has been building inside for years.

I open another beer.

I get out a spoon and try the mashed potatoes.

LATER

I wake Nona and she startles and says, "Never came, did he?" She closes her eyes and says, "I think I smell rosemary."

I say, "Megan is going to take you home."

"Good," Nona says, "I can chat her up about you," but her eyes stay closed.

We gather Nona's things and pack leftovers for everyone.

Everyone hugs like we're at the hospital or a funeral.

I pull Joanie aside and say, "Do you want me to stay?"

"Of course not," she says. "I'm going to binge eat everything Megan cooked. You barely put anything in your doggie bag. No one should have to see me gorging," and she laughs.

Megan and I walk Nona to the car.

We try to buckle her in and she says, "I can do it myself," but she lets us finish then immediately falls back to sleep.

We quietly click the front car door shut.

Megan says, "You have a lovely family."

"Thank you," I say, and we kiss.

A warm breeze blows across our faces so Megan needs to push the hair from her lips. The moon shines down but like a lightbulb without enough wattage. Up in her apartment Joanie cranks the kitchen window shut, we hear it, the cranking sound, probably so she can scream and not be heard. I set my leftovers on the roof and open Megan's door and she climbs inside without waking Nona and starts the engine. Her car is small enough to look like a ride at Kennywood, a bubble you could drive underwater or take to the Potato Patch to eat cheese fries with bacon. I close Megan's door and grab my leftovers. She kisses her fingers and presses them to the glass. She pulls out and drives off with Nona.

I drive to the bar.

Later, at the Bar

Megan is supposed to meet me here after she drops off Nona and changes clothes. The bar is packed with college students, mostly guys and a couple Seton Hill volleyball girls. The old men keep to themselves, hoping the night brings gifts. Vinnie has been to the dentist. All his teeth are gone so his smile is gums. No new teeth are on order because new teeth are considered cosmetic and Vinnie's insurance won't pay for cosmetic.

"When did teeth become cosmetic?" I say.

He shrugs.

I ask him how he chews.

He bounces his jaw up and down and says, "Num num num."

"That can't be pleasant," I say.

He says, "I mostly drink," and goes back to his beer.

I order another from the kid bartender with the mustache.

He says, "You want to run a tab?"

I say, "You want to shave that stupid fucking mustache?"

He fake-smiles, not sure if I'm joking.

I nod, not sure if I'm joking.

He brings my beer.

One of the Seton Hill girls sits down next to me at the bar. I remember her face. I think she is not the one who showed me her tits. I could be wrong. She has long hair, styled high and not very practical for athletics, almost a beehive. Without her uniform on, she looks eighteen, like a model for teen clothing. Her blouse sparkles.

She says, "Hey professor, you remember me?"

"Of course I remember you," I say.

"You want to see my boobs?" she says, and laughs.

I did not want to see her boobs on the first night, let alone tonight when she is dressed up like a CEO for a Fortune 500 Company selling teen clothing, but I appreciate the humor and her boldness and her memory and lack of regret.

She touches my arm and starts to walk off.

I say, "You're a funny lady."

She says, "Yes, I am."

I like people who can laugh, who cover their bloopers with a smile, even the rape-y types. They are, generally speaking, better than the people who don't show up for dinner.

I sip my beer and feel my mother dying.

Sleep

Outside the bar I sit for a minute inside my truck, remembering the times when I worked out of state on bridges and slept nights laid across the front seat because I didn't feel like paying for a motel or because I wanted to save money or because I worked a double and needed to be back to work in four hours to work another double.

It was a comfortable seat, considering.

I was raised to sleep anywhere under any circumstance.

But I don't have to sleep like that anymore.

Hold on, Joanie, I think, then sit up and drive.

Suicide Talk

I knock on Joanie's door and wait. I knock again. The window is still closed but I can smell the chicken and the mashed potatoes and the spices still lingering from dinner. I try to see through the glass but the kitchen is dim. I knock again and push the bell but quickly so it barely rings. When Joanie doesn't answer, I open the door and go inside. I hear her voice like she is talking to someone else, maybe her veterinarian. I let the door slowly close behind me. I listen and Joanie keeps talking but I do not hear another voice. Joanie's voice is loud, a happy slur.

I hope she is not talking to herself.

There are rules to heartbreak.

That's one.

I say, "Hello." I say, "It's me."

I walk like I do not want the floor to creak and wake someone up.

Joanie keeps talking.

I listen for the animal doctor. Of course he does not make a sound. Or he makes his sounds at his own apartment or house or mansion, away from my mom.

I step into the living room.

Joanie sits on the floor, her legs under the coffee table. She holds her phone to her ear. Her phone is the size of a toaster pastry, an off-brand rectangle that covers her ear and cheek. She is drunk and animated. A bottle of gin rests on the table, next to a bowl of crushed ice, the ice swimming in melted water. Joanie cannot cook but she can crush ice. I step closer and think about making a drink, of joining the misery so maybe I can change it to something else, joy, optimism, hope, but twenty pills, maybe thirty, are lined up so that they circle around the bowl of ice and the bottle of gin. I think they are xanax or maybe oxycotin or maybe oxycodone or hydrocodone or whatever Joanie milks from her doctors when she feels sadness and physical pain. I'm not good with pills. I'm glad I'm not good with pills.

Pills erase gravity without promise of flight.

Joanie smiles and waves to me, friendly, come closer, sweetie.

I think of my own swerving lines of cocaine.

This is not that.

"Is that the vet on the phone?" I whisper.

She puts her hand over the receiver and says, "It's the suicide hotline," but she says it more like, "We're having meatloaf for dinner."

"Are you thinking about killing yourself?" I ask.

"No," Joanie says. "I don't think I could."

"That's a lot of pills," I say.

"I know," she says. "That's why I called the suicide hotline."

It only sounds nonsensical because it makes so much sense.

She says, "Are you going to stay?"

"Of course I'm going to stay."

"Then go get yourself a beer," she says. "Is Megan coming back?"

"I don't know."

Joanie tells the suicide hotline to hold and says, "Well, did you invite her?"

I say, "Who?"

"Megan."

"Did I invite her where?"

"Here, to my place," Joanie says.

"She was here," I say. "I was worried about you."

"You always do," she says. "It's sweet but you don't have to worry anymore."

"Why's that?"

"It just is."

I nod and walk back to the kitchen and get myself a beer.

I know that the world is not like this for other people but it is for me and for my family and for the people I love and for the people I teach and it is more so right here and right now so I find a bottle opener and walk back to the living room.

Joanie's phone sits on the coffee table near her pills and booze and ice. The speaker is on so I hear the woman, the girl probably, on the other end of the line, the suicide prevention person, and she says, "We don't have to hang up. I have all night."

Joanie says, "My son is here now and my elbow is tired of holding my phone to my ear. I have you on speaker now. Don't say anything too self-helpie. My son will laugh at your best intentions. He doesn't like hippie-dippie."

"That's not true," I say.

The girl laughs and says, "It's nice to meet you."

I say, "Thank you for everything. I think we can take it from here."

The girl says, "You have a lovely mother."

"I know," I say.

GOODNIGHT

Joanie's hair is a shagged-out mess, pushed and pulled and nervously played with, but it looks better than when it was styled. She scrubbed the make-up from her face so she looks older but no less beautiful, the lines around her eyes giving her the illusion of wisdom, though I've never met a less wise person, despite her smarts and endless triumphs over a life that could have trampled her under. Her dress, perfectly pressed at the start of the evening, is crushed like a wad of tissue.

"You okay?" I say.

She gives me a look: obviously not.

She shifts her butt and turns and frees her legs and extends her arms to push up and moves from the floor to the couch in an awkward, ungraceful effort. She pulls her legs up underneath her and piles a couple orange pillows over her feet. Joanie's feet are always cold. She believes in socks and slippers and to see her toes not stuffed inside something, not even tights or pantyhose, means the sadness extends to all parts of her body, not just the usual ones she uses for drinking and talking and staring holes.

"Tell me what I can do," I say.

"You're here," she says. "Thank you."

I stand closer so I can better see the coffee table.

I start to count the pills and stop at twenty-seven.

"I thought he'd show," she says.

"He should have," I say.

"I just wanted to count the pills," she says. "I felt like I needed to do something dramatic. I love Nona but it's so boring when she's around. I know you love her so I shouldn't say that but your grandmother is just so blah." She drinks her gin. She fishes out an ice cube and crunches it up. "Boring," she says. "That's the truth."

"You love Nona," I say.

"Of course I love Nona," she says. "Just because your grandmother is boring doesn't mean I don't love her. You always get confused by that."

"You want me to make you another gin and tonic?" I say.

"How did you turn out so good?" she says.

"You raised me," I say. "You're the best."

PART TWENTY-NINE

Bill

Bill calls from Amsterdam. It's seven in the morning here in America, in my small town outside of Pittsburgh. I assumed the ringing meant a Joanie call, that she would finally have time to talk, but she is back to work, firing people, too busy to take my calls, leaving the occasional message when she knows I can't pick up.

Bill, though, needs to talk.

He has been drunk for three days. He's smoked a lot of hash. He's smoked other things, less hashy, sort of hashy, he's not completely sure. He babbles. Then he's coherent. He babbles again. He drinks beer so I can hear it gurgle down his throat. He's seen two women fuck each other with huge purple dildos up on a stage.

He says, "I thought it would be sexier."

"Yeah," I say, half asleep. "That doesn't sound too sexy."

"I think I really fucked up," he says.

"You're not going to Afghanistan?" I say, being obvious but also hopeful that I am wrong, that Bill will meet his contract with the Marines, however terrible and unfair, that Amsterdam is a side trip and not a way out. AWOL seems like a very bad choice.

"I couldn't do it," he says, and I think I hear crying.

"Come home," I say.

"I can't come home," he says, and hugely sniffles. He says, "They'll arrest me if I come into the country." He says, "Is that how it works? I think that's how it works."

"Are they looking for you? Does it work like that?"

"I don't know. I guess. I'm AWOL. They won't let Muslims into the country. Or Mexicans. Or anyone, I think. A fucking scaredy cat Marine who bails has to be worse than all those people. Those TSA people at airports are the worst with their little clubs and cans of mace. I saw a video where they made a new mother drink breastmilk just to prove it wasn't a liquid bomb or something. I'm so fucked," and he sniffles back a cry.

"Okay," I say, "let's think about things we can do."

He says, "I'm sorry I called."

"Don't be," I say.

He says, "You're the best professor I ever had."

I say, "Are you in a bar?"

I hear chatter and maybe dishes or glasses.

He says, "I'm in a hostel. It was the cheapest thing I could find. I never stayed in a hostel before. I'm in the room downstairs where everyone eats. They have bagels. I have a six-pack. You can drink anywhere over here."

"A Dutch bagel sounds good," I say.

"It pretty much tastes like Panera," he says.

I know less all the time but I'm sure that Bill can't stay in Amsterdam, getting high and watching sex shows for the rest of his life, working at a coffee shop and getting paid under the table or however he plans to live, even if Holland is a sane and decent country and our American wars have become increasingly bogus and detrimental to the lives of young soldiers.

I say, "Are you sure you can't come back to America?"

Bill says, "They'll arrest me," and he inhales a gob of snot then clears his throat and spits. He says, "I would fight if I knew what we were fighting for, you know, I would, I really would. What the fuck is this war even about? I'm not a total coward. I would fight."

"I know you would," I say. "We'll get you a good lawyer."

He says, "I can't afford a lawyer. I can barely afford a hostel."

I say, "You have to come home."

He says, "My dad is going to be so pissed."

"He won't be," I say. "Let me call you back."

"I love you," Bill says.

"I love you too," I say, not even considering what that means, like Bill is my girlfriend or boyfriend or mother or grandmother or son, and I hang up the phone.

LAWYER IMPERSONATING BAD NOVELIST TO THE RESCUE

I sit in bed with my phone, trying to rack up some options. I dial Megan and leave a message, saying to call me. I worry that she'll think I'm being cryptic and she'll assume I'm talking about Joanie, that Joanie has fallen over again. I call back.

I say, "It's about Fat Bill. He bailed on the Marines and he's hiding out in Amsterdam. I don't know what to do. Call me back."

I hold the phone before hanging up.

I say, "I love you."

I say, "Call me back."

I drop the phone on my chest and close my eyes.

Maybe the nurse at the community college will know what to do. I could feel how much she cared when I talked to her about my crazy student. She listened. She fumed. She wanted to help. When Brandon killed himself, she waited until the shitshow cleared then showed up at my office and hugged me, nothing else. She took me in her arms and said, "Anything at all, call me." Maybe the president of the university knows what to do. She loves students, especially the poorest ones. The president is the Statue of Liberty of college presidents. Bring her your tired. Bring her your huddled masses. She holds the torch. She loves the torch. She waved it in the faces of the Harvard-ities back when she was a student. She learned to row to be better than the rich at something the rich do. Bill is tired and poor. I bet, in Amsterdam, he is huddled with the masses. The president needs to talk to the school nurse. Then they can pull together their resources and have Bill declared temporarily insane. Let's be clear. Bill did not desert, he cracked. The fear of war twisted his instincts to anxiety and fear. The sounds of gunshot in boot camp broke brainwaves that now need to be repaired. Give Bill a bed, not a cell. Save Bill.

Everyone say it, please, and agree.

But Bill is not even a student anymore.

Why would the community college care?

We only take care of our own.

We barely take care of our own.

Sometimes we do not even take care of our own.

Bill needs a doctor. Doctors are required to do no harm. They take an oath. The oath says, first and foremost, above all else, they will do no harm. But doctors want money, above all else. It's the unspoken oath. Accept all payment. No payment, no service.

Bill needs a lawyer.

He said that.

He said he couldn't afford one.

Which is more expensive, doctor or lawyer?

I have insurance for my doctor bills.

Bill doesn't have insurance, not now.

I have never in my life needed a lawyer.

I have escaped so much trouble because my first priority has been to avoid trouble, always, since I was a teenager. I never tried sex in high school because I did not want a kid, did not want to be the father equivalent of Joanie, single and working and desperately trying to climb. In college, before I stole, I considered stealing, I considered stealing for a long time, then I stole and I held stealing close and I did not brag about my theft and made sure I had an alibi for stealing should I have gotten caught. Most of my actions are meant to better my life and the rest of my actions are to make sure my life does not get worse.

Other people are not like that, I know.

I pick up my phone and call John Grisham.

What we need now is some legal advice.

Foot Shooters

I babble to John Grisham and he listens thoughtfully, as thoughtfully as I hoped he would, then he says he'll meet me at the bar after lunch.

He says, "I have to be in court first thing this morning then I have to meet a client. Is after lunch okay? I can probably cancel with the client."

"That's great," I say. "I owe you, John Grisham."

He says, "I'm glad you called."

I say, "Are you really going to buy Megan's bar?"

"I'd love to," he says. "Let's see if we can keep your student out of jail. AWOL is serious. It's about the worst thing you can do in this country right now, save being a Muslim. Or just being a human being. Or Mexican. Or poor. It's tough all over."

"Let's focus on the positive," I say.

"Right," John Grisham says.

The phone is quiet.

I realize I am the one to bring the positivity because I was the one who presented positivity as an option.

John Grisham says, "Well?"

I say, "I'm blanking."

He says, "I wish Bill would have shot himself in the foot or something."

THE OPENING OF MY SKULL

I go for a long jog, running down through Wall and its houses on hills and old churches and into Wilmerding and up the hill to the Walmart in North Versailles and back down the other hill to Turtle Creek. Cars pass. I ignore them. Sun hits my back and neck. I pull my t-shirt off and toss it over the fence and into the dirt near the railroad tracks. Sweat pours from my body. I run fast and breathe perfect and open the top of my head as wide as it will open to receive whatever goodness motion brings. It helps but not as much as I want. I feel in control but like control could take itself and use me for darkness, though I refuse that. I make the turn back to Wall and start to walk then turn around and open my head again and keep running but faster. I sweat and somehow have to piss so I dip and move and slice into an alley and I piss behind an old abandoned church and walk back to my apartment. I shower and I dress and I pace and I go to the bar early to start drinking.

I check my phone while I drive.

I check my email while I park, not an easy thing on a crap phone.

I wish Megan would call.

She usually calls.

I can never remember her morning schedule.

I pull up a stool and pull out my wallet.

The kid with the mustache stands behind the bar, messing with his iPhone. The mustache is gone. His upper lip is a desert of white sand. He asks if I want a beer. I do. I'd like to order five or nine or a million. My skull is still open, still hoping. Most of the neon is dark. The chairs in the back sit on top of the tables. The jukebox is unplugged.

I say, "I'm sorry about your mustache."

"It's okay," he says. "I was thinking about shaving it anyway."

I finish my first beer before he finishes his next sentence.

MUSTACHE

Harriet comes downstairs in her bathrobe. The bathrobe is yellow and furry, chicks hatching from eggs all over the fabric. She wears slippers. Her hair is dented from sleep. I never noticed her make-up before but without it her face is blotchy and deeper with lines. I raise my beer. She smiles. She digs out a pen and paper from under the bar.

Harriet looks at the bartender and says, "What happened to your mustache?"

"I shaved it," he says, and rubs his chin, which has always been bald.

"It's different," Harriet says.

Then, making a note, she says, "We're out of pretzels."

She writes down a few more items and walks to the backroom.

The bartender says, "She never liked my mustache."

I say, "No one did. You were trying too hard."

He says, "That's why I shaved it off."

My cell is in my truck so I ask to use the phone. The kid bartender looks at me like I'm insane. I tell him it's a local call. He doesn't appear to know what a local call is.

He says, "Don't you have a cell phone?"

"I have a cell phone," I say.

He says, "You'd have to come behind the bar to use our phone."

"I liked you better when you had your mustache," I say.

"You'll probably need a phonebook too," he says.

I step behind the bar and pick up the phone, which feels like a brick in my hand. I dial Joanie's number. She doesn't answer. I have been calling her every morning. She is never there. She always calls back. I leave a short happy message. Maybe she is at breakfast with a new man. Maybe she is at the track. She is no longer worried about the veterinarian. She has decided to stick with the running. She will win at whatever she wants even if she doesn't always get to choose the race or the prize. Her knees hurt but that's okay.

Being old is great.

I can't wait to get there.

MEGAN ON BILL

Megan comes back from her early class. She is dressed in her bar clothes. The tits are out. The jeans are tight. Her hair is pulled back in a ponytail.

She says, "Titties on display, I'm ready to work."

"Good choice," I say.

She says, "You can't be drunk already."

"I could be," I say. "But I'm not."

"How's Bill?" she says.

I say, "No word since I left you a message."

"That poor kid," she says, and kisses me as she ties on an apron.

WAITING

We wait for John Grisham. Megan fills ketchup bottles. I fill salt shakers. The bartender messes with his phone, three steps away from our work. Megan wants me to eat a sandwich. I can't eat, something rare for me. Harriet is at the grocery store, two doors down, buying bar snacks. She walked out wearing her slippers.

Megan says, "What time is it in Amsterdam?"

The bartender says, "The middle of the night, and who cares."

Megan says, "Do better, Mr. Mustache."

SO LONG, MR. MUSTACHE

The kid bartender has been relieved. He is off to wherever young people without mustaches go in the early afternoon, probably to a friend's apartment to play video games. Megan and I take down the chairs from the tabletops. She plugs in the jukebox. I get a broom and look for places to spot-sweep. It's too early to pop the popcorn. Popcorn is a nighttime thing at Harry's Bar. I go back to the jukebox and spray the glass with water and vinegar then polish it to a shine.

Megan says, "My stomach hurts, I'm so nervous."

"Why is the world so hard?" I say.

"It just is," she says. "I think it's always been. Even for people who the world is not hard on, it's hard." She steps behind the bar and opens a case and puts bottles into the refrigerator. She says, "I'm so glad I'm a woman." She says. "No one expects us to do anything with guns. We don't have to pay for our own meals if we don't want to." She says, "The world is so unfair." She says, "I bet even rich people have it hard. They probably worry about being rich. They probably worry people are taking their money. They probably worry that they're not doing enough, that they're lazy and spoiled and that other people will notice they don't do anything except be rich. I'm telling you: rich people probably have it hard too."

"Let's not dwell on rich people," I say.

"No, of course not," she says. "I hate rich people. We should hate rich people, it should be required, I think that's the point."

"It's not the only point," I say.

"No, but it's worth noting," she says.

"What about the ACLU?" I say. "Maybe they have free lawyers for this."

"Let's wait on John Grisham," she says. "He'll know about the ACLU."

"I'm hoping John Grisham is like his own mini-ACLU."

"A one-man ACLU," Megan says.

The door opens.

Two men in paint-splattered jeans step inside the bar.

Megan says, "Where the hell is that John Grisham?"

JOHN GRISHAM TO THE RESCUE

John Grisham shows up late, apologizing profusely. He walks through the door, loaded down with his briefcase and an armful of papers, wearing a rumpled suit the color of dirty concrete. Dude is always rumpled. He must sit like a gorilla in court. The light outside is brilliant, the way it always is when peeking through a crack in a door to a dimly-lit bar. I stand to greet John Grisham, to be polite. He sweats less when he is sober but he still sweats plenty. His hair looks combed with a fingerless hand. His paisley tie hangs loose around his neck.

Megan says, "Finally," but not angry, more like: thank you.

John Grisham says, "I know, I know," and he drops the papers on a nearby table and heaves his briefcase onto the bar. He says, "That Bill is a nice kid. There was no reason for him to sign up for the Marines. He's not a fighter. The military is fine for fighters, if that's what they want. I'm not judging warriors but Bill is not that. Sensitive souls should not be handed guns and told to kill strangers. The world is bullshit. We need to correct this."

"Money," Megan says. "That's why Bill signed up."

"It always is," John Grisham says.

I say, "He wanted the Marines to pay for his tuition."

John Grisham says, "What kind of logic is that. College should be free."

I say, "You're a little wrinkled for this early in the day."

He says, "Try as I may, I have never learned to wear a suit."

Megan says, "Do you know anything about this?"

"This?" he says. "Young men going AWOL during times of war?"

"Yes," Megan says.

"Nothing," John Grisham says. "But I've been doing some research."

He taps on his briefcase.

Megan says, "What do you know about the ACLU?"

"We're not there yet," he says.

John Grisham pushes his palms into his eyes to clear his vision. He is wired for kindness and problem-solving. The heat of his imperfection and desire to be better warms us. He pops his briefcase. He puts on his reading glasses. The man is as serious as a salt wound. He digs out a pamphlet and a folder. He opens both and politely orders his first beer, a whiskey on the side. He pulls out a wad of money.

"No money today," Megan says.

"You're too kind," John Grisham says, and he tells me to get a pen and paper.

Megan says, "I really believe in you, John Grisham."

"Don't believe anything yet," he says. Then he says, "I wish Bill would have snuck into Canada. Canada would have been a hell of a lot easier."

I say, "We really appreciate this."

Megan says, "John Grisham, you were born for this."

He says, "I want to be."

It's two o'clock in the afternoon. The bar is empty except for the three of us and Harriet taking a nap upstairs. Megan hands me a pen and paper. I see Harriet's list, the one that starts with pretzels and ends with napkins. I see Harriet, dancing in my open skull, how lovely. I see Rig telling his life story, getting rich. I see Berryman, trying to help the poor, leaving poetry and his dreams of success behind. I see Nona, still Nona, my beautiful grandmother, not growing old, or growing so old death refuses her. I see Joanie. I will always see Joanie.

John Grisham says, "Are you ready?"

We are never ready, I want to tell John Grisham, which is why we are here, in a bar near East Pittsburgh, in Southwestern Pennsylvania, in America, on a planet burning up from its sun.

This is why we have to work.

CPSIA information can be obtained
at www.ICGtesting.com
Printed in the USA
LVHW030210120720
660355LV00003B/317